PETRICHOR BLOOMS

MINDI BRIAR

CITY OWL
PRESS

PETRICHOR BLOOMS
The Halcyon Universe, Book 2

CITY OWL PRESS
www.cityowlpress.com

Cover Design by MiblArt. All stock photos licensed appropriately.

Edited by Lisa Green.

For information on subsidiary rights, please contact the publisher at info@cityowlpress.com.

Print Edition ISBN: 978-1-64898-256-9

Digital Edition ISBN: 978-1-64898-257-6

Printed in the United States of America

To the leavers, the quitters, and the forgers of their own path forward.
It takes courage and hard work, but it's worth it.

AUTHOR'S NOTE

I deliberately write diverse characters into my books because I'm surrounded by a wonderful rainbow of people IRL and online. In my ideal future, there is space for everyone to find their happy ending. As part of my commitment to promoting diversity, I want to take the opportunity to uplift diverse voices when I can. Please check out my recommendations list in the acknowledgements section for some of the amazing sapphic books by authors of color that I've enjoyed reading recently.

Additionally, I want you to feel secure when reading my book, so please note the content information below.

- Strong language
- Bullying
- Genetic modification performed on children
- Past child/baby death
- Open-door sex scene

PART ONE

Year 3729, Week 50,

Daysix

CHAPTER ONE

Danya

SHERWOOD BASE

I dig my hands deep into the vat of fertilizer. The squelchy texture is satisfying, even through my gloves. My mask protects me from the worst of the smell, but I still catch a whiff: a pungent mix of composted food and human waste, fermented and processed to a perfect nutrient blend.

I draw out my hands and scrape a bit of the brown mixture into a test tube. Stripping off one glove, I tap a sequence of commands into the machine on the wall.

"Xiang!" My supervisor, Lowell, sticks his head through the door. I feel a wash of warm, humid air roll in from the greenhouse on the other side; it's always so chilly in the fertilizer room. "You finished testing those samples?"

A little tray shoots out from the machine, and I place the test tube into it. "It'll be a few minutes, sir."

Lowell shivers at the change in temperature. He's only wearing a jumpsuit—no protective coverall and no mask. I spare him a skeptical glance. "Can I help you with something, sir?" The food production managers never touch fertilizer if they can avoid it. That's why junior assistants, like me, get slapped with the chore.

He winces, covering his nose at the stench. "Marks just called off. He's in the infirmary getting antiviral treatment. Vijay got him sick too."

There's been a nasty cold going around. Close to four hundred and fifty thousand people call Sherwood Base their home, but half of them are deployed on planetside missions and crewing carrier ships for the Greenjackets—our rebel organization dedicated to fighting the oppressive Empire. Those of us who keep the home fires burning, so to speak, live in fairly close quarters. If someone brings in a virus, everybody gets it.

I take pity on Lowell and shuck off my other glove so that I can remove my mask and hand it to him. The fertilizer smells pretty rank, but I've worked with it enough to get used to it. "Marks is sick? Does that mean you need someone to cover his shift overseeing the harvest?" Little flowers of excitement bloom in my chest. I haven't been assigned anywhere near the growth pods in weeks. It's been fertilizer mixing, or cleaning the aquaponics tank, or repairing the irrigation pipes.

Lowell shakes his head. "I already got Hung to cover it. I was going to ask you if you could finish up here really quick, then take over Hung's job?"

"Yes, sir. What's he assigned to?"

"Delivery."

I sigh. Not the worst job—better than squishing my hands around in excrement—but hauling crates of vegetables and dead fish to the various dining halls across the base is time-consuming and boring.

"Give me ten minutes to finish and wash up," I tell Lowell.

His eyes crinkle above the mask. "Thanks, Xiang. At least *you* never complain."

Maybe I should complain more. Is that how my colleagues keep getting out of fertilizer duty?

I rush through the rest of the testing, though I do take the time to double-check the nutrient levels. This fertilizer is meant for a particularly finicky crop of crunchberry trees, and they'll shrivel if I get the balance wrong. The berries are delicious wrapped in a pancake for breakfast, so I have a vested interest in doing my job well.

When I'm finished, I undo my coverall and step out of it, holding it at arm's length so it won't befoul the all-purpose olive-green jumpsuit I wear underneath. The door swishes shut behind me as I step into the muggy heat of the greenhouse.

The air is heavy with the funk of growth and decay. Bots whirr along their tracks, monitoring each growth pod and its individualized weather pattern. I tilt my head back, taking in the ceiling-high carousels, each carrying dozens of pods filled with dirt or water, nurturing the plant life inside. Through the huge corrugated-metal door, I can see the other half of the greenhouse: the orchard, where rows of trees are cultivated both for their fruits and for the oxygen they help produce.

It's been weeks since I was assigned harvest duty, but the days when I get to climb inside the pods, brush my fingers along rows of soft leaves, feel the weight of ripe fruit in my hands...those days make my countless hours analyzing compost worthwhile.

This is the only place on Sherwood Base that doesn't feel sterile and bland. Most people hate the food production sector. They think it's filthy and smells awful, which is absolutely true. But to me, it's the only place that feels *alive*. The rest of the base is oppressively spartan: long, gunmetal-gray corridors, white-walled dormitories, training facilities with floor-to-ceiling holo-projector screens. I've lived my whole life inside this space station, this artificial environment carved into the side of a jagged moon that orbits a toxic planet. I've only ever seen the surfaces of other planets in fleeting images during approved educational programming. I'd stick my right arm in a blender for a chance to live planetside. *Any* planet. A desert! A poisonous bog! Perpetual winter! As long as it has breathable air, organic life forms, and maybe some interesting weather patterns.

I follow a harvester bot, its many attachments folded into its sides, trundling toward the refrigeration unit with a crate full of carrots. When it enters the chilly storage space—even colder than the fertilizer room— it detaches the crate from its front side, places it in the stack to be sorted, and picks up an empty one on its way out.

I reach for Hung's thermal jacket, hanging from a hook next to the door, and shrug it on, shivering.

A young trainee, barely fourteen—the same age I was when I started apprenticing in food production eight years ago—is running back and forth. A tablet in his hand displays the supply orders from each dining hall. He's already packed two large hoverbarrows and marked them with their destinations. "Oh good, are you here for Hung?" he calls. "I thought I was going to have to drive the rounds myself."

"Nope." I wrinkle my nose at him. "Anyway, you're not allowed to operate machinery yet."

He glares at me. "You can not be allowed to do something and still be capable of it."

"Oh, trust me, I know." *My sister Nox is living proof of that.*

I steer the first hoverbarrow toward the zip-lift, eager to escape the cold. *I wonder what Nox is doing right now?*

And just like that, without meaning to, I connect with her mind.

Petra Rochester grins down at Nox, brown eyes glinting with mischief. "We did it! I told you they wouldn't catch us!"

"I believe I told you that, Petra," my sister retorts. "You were the one who tried to talk me out of it this morning." She holds up a memory chip between her finger and thumb, and the two women examine it. There's nothing remarkable about it as far as I can see, but I can feel the excitement fizzing in Nox's blood. This is something they stole. Something important, something that has answers to—

::Dawn!::

Oops. She noticed.

::Stop spying on me, you—::

I anchor the hoverbarrow securely in the zip-lift and wedge myself between the vertical handrails jutting out from the wall. I wrap my hands around them tightly and brace my feet as the lift jolts, accelerating to a high speed.

I shouldn't have spied. I promised I wouldn't. But Nox and I spent most of our childhood in each other's heads. "How cute," the creche attendants used to say when we finished each other's sentences or knew about each other's cuts and bruises before anyone else. "It's almost like they have twin telepathy..."

We figured out pretty early that it would be a bad idea to tell anyone the full extent of our mind-reading abilities, but that didn't stop us from testing it. We shared everything. When one of us got punished, the other felt it. When Nox stole sweets from the dining hall, I tasted them.

But once we finished our education, things changed. We were evenly matched in academic pursuits, but Nox easily outshone me when it came to battle training. Eventually, she got pulled into a special training program for future Greenjacket officers, while I was assigned to work in food production full-time.

We didn't *intend* to grow apart. Nox may have been disappointed that I didn't make officer training alongside her, but she doesn't shun me for being a lowly laborer like all of our childhood friends do. Still, I know there are things she doesn't tell me. She and Petra, another elite trainee, are always sneaking around, whispering with their heads together. And the more I worry about Nox, the more she shuts me out.

The zip-lift jolts to a stop. Sighing, I put Nox out of my mind and focus on the hoverbarrow. The kitchbots are ready and waiting to help me unpack. Time to get back to work.

WHEN I STRAGGLE BACK TO THE DORMITORY THAT NIGHT, UTTERLY exhausted, I find Nox leaning against my sleep-pod with her arms folded. It's always jarring when my sister is angry with me; it's like catching sight of your face in the washroom mirror when you've gotten up to pee in the middle of the night, and for a moment you don't recognize the expression on your own face.

We're identical, Nox and I. With both of us dressed in standard-issue green jumpsuits, it's tough to spot the differences. We both have the same round, pale face with thin lips and dark eyes. We have the same haircut: shorn close on the sides, the top no longer than my middle finger. We're tied for shortest in our age group—all our peers tower over us.

A close observer might note that Nox wears her hair gelled back, as most of the soldiers do. My hair frizzes, unbrushed, because no one yells at food production workers for having messy hair—not when we spend half the day with our heads encased in a protective hood. Nox's arms bulge with muscle from the constant combat drills; I'm nowhere near as ripped, despite daily swim workouts and pushing heavy machinery around.

To me, what truly sets us at odds is our ambition. Her overabundance of it and my lack. I didn't flunk out of soldier training because I'm unskilled—I failed because I don't like hitting things and I throw up at the sight of blood. Weak, the officers called me. Coward.

Nox never had a problem with breaking a few heads to get things done. That's what gets you medals around here.

"Nox, I'm really not in the mood to fight," I say, bending to unsnap my boots. "Can we do this in the morning?"

"No. I need to talk to you now."

My jaw cracks with a yawn. "Can I sit down while you yell?"

Nox slips her hand into the crook of my arm and begins steering me toward the door, leading me back out into the corridor. My unsnapped boot flaps awkwardly as I struggle to keep up with her pace. "Nox, really, can I just..."

She notices a cambot patrolling the hallway ahead of us and wrenches open the nearest door, yanking me in. It's a supply closet. She makes me stand there in the chilly, mint-cleaner-scented darkness for what feels like ten minutes but is probably only two.

"I have to pee," I whisper. She slaps my shoulder and shushes me.

Nox must be counting the seconds, because she has an uncanny sense for how long it takes the cambot to whirr past and disappear around the corner. She sticks her head out of the closet to ensure the coast is clear, then resumes dragging me along. She's been obsessed with avoiding cambots lately. I wouldn't mind hiding in supply closets if it meant she'd actually *tell* me something about what she's up to, but she never does.

This time, our destination turns out to be a defunct residential sector that's been sealed off. Except Nox has a passcode, because of course she does.

The darkness ahead makes me pause, my throat closing with apprehension. Nox tugs my arm impatiently. She doesn't hesitate until we reach Suite 781, which still has a nameplate attached. *Hakim.* Who were they? Did they move to another sector when this one closed down? Or maybe they were sent off to fight, lost as casualties in some decades-ago battle.

The sector is on low power, so the door doesn't swish open automatically. Nox has to fit her fingers into the crack and roll it aside. I startle when I see that the room isn't empty. Petra is already inside, waiting cross-legged on the floor next to an emergency lantern.

My breath catches, like it always does when I see her. Did it just get hot in this freezing-cold sector?

Petra wears her long black hair slicked back into a high ponytail. When not sitting on the floor, she's a head taller than Nox and me. Aquiline nose, cheekbones to die for, brown eyes ringed with long, soft lashes. If she stepped on my face, I'd probably thank her.

She looks up as I enter, grinning and waving. My heart skips a beat, and I begin to smile back. Then her smile fades as Nox follows me in.

"You brought the twin?" Her voice is accusatory. I realize her initial smile was because she mistook me for Nox, and humiliation washes through me.

"Yeah, I did." Nox steps forward into the ring of light cast by the lantern, leaving me in shadow. "I think it's time for us to tell her what we've been working on."

"And you didn't think to run it by me first? This is a horrible idea, Nox. What if she can't keep her mouth shut?"

My cheeks burn. Has Nox been telling her that I'm not to be trusted? I back toward the door, ready to escape. But Nox is beckoning me to join her—and besides, I don't remember how to get back to the dorm on my own.

"Danya," Nox says gravely, "you have to promise, before I say another word, that you'll never tell anyone else about what we tell you."

I fold my arms, refusing to sit. "That depends on what you're going to tell me. Is it illegal? Are people going to get hurt?"

"See?" Petra whispers loudly. "No loyalty."

But Nox holds my gaze. "Does it really matter?" she asks. "Danya, please. You know you can trust me."

But I *don't* know that. I *used* to trust her. These days, she's a stranger who happens to wear an identical face.

"I won't tell," I promise warily. She relaxes, grinning, but I hurry to add, "I won't tell *unless* there's a good reason. If what you're doing is hurting people, I can't promise not to try to stop you."

Petra rolls her eyes and groans. But Nox nods, and I hear her voice in my head. *::You know I wouldn't ask you this if it weren't important. Please hear us out.::*

::All right.:: I can promise that much. I stoop to sit, wincing as the cold of the floor seeps through my jumpsuit. The room is bare of furniture; it must have been emptied when the entire sector was abandoned.

"Let's start with this," she says. "What do you think the Greenjackets' mission is? No propaganda lines. In your own words."

When I hesitate, her mental voice prompts me. *::There aren't any cambots listening. You can say what you think.::*

The problem is, I *don't* think about it. As soon as it became clear I wasn't cut out for combat, the Greenjackets' self-proclaimed "noble cause" became none of my business. What do I care if they succeed in overthrowing the Imperial regime on this or that random planet? I'll still be here, up to my elbows in fertilizer. Unless the Imperial Authorities decide to lay siege to Sherwood Base, I'll never raise a blaster in defense of the Greenjackets' lofty ideals.

And frankly, I don't have any desire to. Call it cowardice—all of Nox's friends do. But being demoted to food production was a relief. Battle simulations are scary and painful. I'd prefer to avoid the real thing.

"I guess..." I smooth the wrinkles on my jumpsuit, wondering what Nox wants me to say. "All I really know is what they tell us. They want to bring down the Authorities' control of the galaxy. Kill the Emperor, probably?" I sneak a peek at their faces. Petra's glaring at me. Was that not the right thing to say? "I know they talk a lot about planets reclaiming their sovereignty," I add. "That sounds like a good goal to me. I think the people who live on a planet deserve to control what happens to its resources."

"Well, she's certainly a product of our upbringing," Petra mutters. My face burns.

Nox's eyes are fixed on me, her expression solemn. "What if I told you we're not the good guys in this battle?"

I blink. "You're not suggesting the Empire is *good?*" Our educational program spent hours explaining otherwise, with plenty of vid evidence to back it up. I'll never be able to unsee the penal mining colonies where miners slowly waste away from illness and overexertion. Planets stripped of their resources and left in ruins, made uninhabitable for the native life forms. Lavish parties, glittering gowns, and mouthwatering feasts for the governors and the Monroe System elites, while the people they govern live a breath away from starvation. Imperial Authorities, their red uniforms like drops of blood scattered across the battlefield, ruthlessly gunning down any attempt at resistance.

We, the Greenjackets, are supposed to be the saviors of the poor. I may not have ever taken an interest in fighting the war, but it's news to me that I might be on the wrong side of it.

Nox laughs. "The Empire, good? No. Not at all. But that doesn't mean we're automatically good just by opposing them." She unrolls her scroll tablet, placing it flat on the floor in front of me. Tapping a sequence on her keycuff, she unlocks a passcoded file and brings up a vid for me to watch.

At first, it looks just like those vids they showed us as children. An aerial view captured by a drone, or maybe a starship slowly circling the city. I can't tell what I'm supposed to be looking at. It looks like a typical big-city spaceport surrounded by skyscrapers and hazed over with the smog of industry. Sunlight glints off the myriad small starships swooping in for a landing, replacing the ones that dart into the sky and vanish.

"I don't—"

The explosion blooms like a morning glory. For a split second, I think it was a single ship's engine melting down—but not even the most catastrophic accident could take out the whole spaceport. I watch in horror as the blast levels the entire block of buildings. Dust and smoke plume, obscuring the vid-capture.

"What happened?" I demand, breathless with horror.

"That's Gila Spaceport on the planet Esperanza, five years ago," Nox says. "The Greenjackets used the excuse of punishing a deserter to plant a bomb. They leveled the whole spaceport, then took advantage of the mayhem to take control of the local government. The Authorities fought back, and the whole city turned into a war zone. None of the civilians were able to escape because the spaceport was a crater and the surrounding terrain is toxic. Nearly a hundred thousand innocent people died. And we didn't even hold the city—the Authorities took back control after a month. It was the worst-managed shitshow I've ever seen, and yet the orders came directly from the General." Disgust drips from her tone. I've heard her allude to dissatisfaction with the Greenjackets, but this is utter contempt, long-simmering hatred.

The officers would call it treason.

"Esperanza..." The planet's name rings a bell. I remember learning about it during Galactic Social Studies. It's a manufacturing hub, one of the Empire's greatest assets, yet most of its citizens are indentured factory workers. Centuries of industry have wrecked the planet's ecosystem, turning its oceans to sludge and rendering its air barely breathable. The Greenjackets have long been fighting for a foothold there.

I'm not sure that playing devil's advocate is a wise move here, but I can't help it. "Esperanza's not exactly doing great under Imperial rule, is it? Maybe the General just wanted to try to help people. The explosion could have been an accident."

"It wasn't," Petra breaks in. *Stars, I need to stop blushing every time she speaks.* "That video was included in an entire file of reports on the Gila City incident. The commanding officers specifically mentioned that the civilian casualties were a 'necessary evil' to sow confusion and allow Greenjackets the opportunity to overthrow the Authorities."

"That's horrible," I say, "if it's true."

Nox starts bringing up more files on her scroll. Fear floods through me as I realize she has enough classified information on her personal device to incriminate herself as a spy. She could be executed for this.

"It's not an isolated incident," she says. "The Greenjackets didn't start out as a terror organization, but we've been trending in that direction for the past twenty years. Ever since General Bruna took power, she's been pushing for more and more violent attacks. It's all aimed at the Authorities, of course, with the goal to undermine and destabilize their rule. But the reality is that civilians keep getting caught in the crossfire."

She flicks through the files, trying to show me, but I don't have the stomach to look.

"Is it making a difference?" I ask, swallowing against my sudden nausea. "Do—do all those deaths make things better on those planets?"

But I know the answer before she says it.

"Better?" Nox's laugh is humorless. "When the Authorities eventually take back their territory—causing heavy losses on our side, mind you— the new governors tighten their grip and make life even harder for the poor citizens who happen to live there. So no, the attacks don't make things better. They make things *worse*."

"Look at her," Petra mutters. "She doesn't believe us."

I don't know what to believe. Who knows what my expression looks like right now? I'm so boggled, I can't tell which way's up.

::*What I saw earlier. You and Petra stealing a memory chip. Is that where you got all this information?*::

::*No,*:: Nox says. ::*We've known about the Gila siege for a while. What you saw was...never mind. New intel, that's all.*::

::*So what's the goal here? Are you two trying to...I don't know, stage a mutiny or something?*:: Dread coils in my gut. Rebellion could end in execution for both of them.

::*Something like that.*:: Nox's eyes find mine in the semi-dark. ::*Now you see why I'm trusting you with this, Dawn. I need you to understand how important it is that you can't tell any of the officers what you saw.*::

::*I was never going to,*:: I protest. ::*I know better than to report my own sister for espionage.*::

Nox reaches over and squeezes my hand. I can't muster the will to squeeze back. My hand lies limp and cold against her hot, moist palm.

"I...I need some time to process this," I say. "Maybe you can tell me more another time?" I stand up, my knees cracking. My butt is nearly numb from the cold, hard floor. I start edging toward the door, eager to be far away from Petra's judging gaze.

I can feel Nox's disappointment at my reaction. I think, deep down, she was hoping I'd get all fired up the way she does. That I'd finally be ready to grab a gun in each hand and go fight for The Cause...albeit a *different* cause than the one we grew up with.

She calls after me, "Be careful no one sees you. Check for cambots."

"Right, right."

It takes me nearly half an hour to find my way back. I wind through the corridors, dodging into blind corners and empty rooms whenever I hear the faint whirr of a cambot approaching. My body feels heavy, like Nox has dropped a backpack full of rocks on my shoulders.

If this is true, if the Greenjackets are hurting people in their fight against the Empire, I don't blame Nox for trying to stop it. But stealing intel from the General? Surely there's a better way. One that doesn't risk treason charges.

And what does she expect *me* to do with this knowledge? Carry it in secret, pretending it doesn't exist? It's obvious she wasn't planning to tell me—and wouldn't have, if I hadn't accidentally snooped this morning. Did she really think I'd report her and Petra if they didn't explain themselves? How far apart have we grown if that's what she thinks of me?

To be fair, she might've been right to hide it from me. There's no point in me knowing. I'm no help to them, skill-wise. Their training group has access to officer-level files and surveillance. All I have is access to vegetables.

And even if I could help...do I want to? It would mean getting involved in the very war I turned my back on years ago. Protecting civilians is a more immediate and achievable goal than taking down a galaxy-wide Empire, but it would still mean wielding a blaster. Potentially even turning on my fellow Greenjackets.

Call it cowardice, but I don't know if I can do that, no matter what the stakes are.

CHAPTER TWO

Amy

HALCYON UNIVERSITY

The spires of Halcyon University reach like glittering claws toward a cloudless violet sky. The university's roots sink deep into the volcanic bedrock of Daedalus Island in the Fifth Province archipelago, a tropical paradise that's home to thousands of students and Scholars from across the galaxy—bright young things, hungry for knowledge.

And then there's me. Sitting at a study cubicle in the library halfway up the tallest spire, drinking in the glorious view of the sun sinking toward the ocean, holding back the urge to stress-cry.

I drag my gaze away from the window and back to my screen. My latest research paper sits front and center on the messy collage of open tabs. Four paragraphs, painfully forced out over the last three months. I'm supposed to write at least ten thousand words by next Dayseven, and I've barely hit one thousand. I hate every single one of those words, even ones like "an" and "the." I'd fire the whole blazing thing into the sun if I had a good enough cannon.

Groaning, I let my head fall into my hands. I already know I'm not going to get any work done tonight. It's not that I don't have things to write about. Today's experiments had some interesting potential. I identified a gene in a waterweed sample that's similar to the expensively and unethically harvested glowworm gene that cosmetic companies use to give people luminescent eyes. It should be easy to sit down and write a couple thousand words about the potential benefits of using waterweed instead of killing off rare glowworms. Then a few more thousand words, outlining my proposal for a future experiment to be done to prove its viability as a substitute.

But my brain. Just. Won't.

I'm fully capable of doing this. I don't know why my brain won't concentrate. It's like I've built up a wall between myself and the task. I'm so frustrated I could scream.

I slump against the wall of the cubicle, feeling tears prick. I pull up the collar of my tunic, pressing the fabric into my eyes.

Honestly, I should never have enrolled. I don't know why I thought I could make this work—I've always hated academic pursuits. My caretakers were worried I wouldn't graduate my Galactic Standard education program because I couldn't stand still for more than an hour. They told me I should join our province's track team. Maybe I should've.

Except Mum's dying wish was for me to become a scientist like her. So here I am.

The university is free to attend for anyone with a curious, seeking mind. By Imperial standards, it's a chaotic mess. Many offworld organizations refuse to acknowledge a Halcyon University degree, preferring graduates from more "serious" academic backgrounds. There's no time limit on how long you can stay, nor are there requirements to meet for passing levels. A student's learning is guided by their own interest, and the Scholars determine when mastery has been achieved.

My mother attained the level of Scholar here before she died—she was a true genius, and she loved her work. I know I'm as smart as she is... I'm just not as good at concentrating.

Sometimes I wonder if this side of me comes from my dad. But I wouldn't know, would I? Mum never told me his name, and she took her secrets with her when she passed.

"Pardon me, are you Amethyst Ediya?"

I jump. The collar drops, and I see a woman peering around the corner of my cubicle. She's thirty-ish, super tall, with brown skin several shades lighter than mine, and a mane of black curls pulled into a low ponytail. Her no-nonsense expression immediately makes me feel like I'm in trouble. She's wearing a Scholar's black robe with ochre stripes down her sleeves to indicate her subject of expertise: history.

"Um." I sniff, hoping my eyes haven't gone all red yet. "I go by *Amy*, but yeah."

"Excellent," says the woman briskly. "Do you have a minute to talk?"

"Sure." I shut down the screen, hoping the Scholar hasn't noticed my tragic lack of progress. Not that she would care; I'm not even taking any history classes.

She leads me to one of the library's private study rooms and holds the door open. Her rigid posture and grumpy resting face would be more intimidating if I couldn't see what she's wearing under her Scholar robe: comfortable shoes (the kind worn mainly by people's grandmothers), casual black leggings, and a handknitted blue wool sweater. My fingers accidentally brush her sleeve as I pass, and I have to steady myself against the doorframe as I'm treated to a flash of insight into the old lady who knitted the sweater for her. *Creaky joints, laughing at a friend's joke, a baduk board in front of her. Her hands ache, but the pull of yarn between them soothes her...*

I shake off the vision, forcing myself to focus on the present.

The Scholar sits down at the study table, gesturing at the chair across from her. I slide into it and wait for her to speak first.

"My name is Dr. Athena Valik," the Scholar says, folding her hands on the table in front of her. "I am a xenoarchaeologist and historian. I spoke to a Scholar of biology and genetics earlier—Dr. Joaquin, I believe—about borrowing one of her brightest students to consult on an offplanet xenoarch dig. She gave me your name as someone who might be interested."

"Xenoarchaeology?" I lean forward. "What would you need a biology student for?"

"It's a bit need-to-know at this point," says Dr. Valik, which only intensifies my curiosity. "Suffice it to say, a consultant who has a background in genetics research is vital for the success of our project there. But none of the Scholars are interested in taking three months off of their duties here at the university. I do have to inform you, Miz Ediya, that this expedition will be rather...difficult. We will be living like settlers for awhile. Foraging our own food, setting up tents, fighting off local predators...it will not be for the faint of heart. Unfortunately, most of the biology department values the ability to bathe regularly over the scientific breakthroughs that such an expedition could..."

My heart starts to beat faster. Danger! Foraging! Fieldwork for *three whole months*. I'd probably have to write some boring article upon returning, but I'd have a nice long time to put it off.

"Would I have to put the rest of my studies on hold?" I ask. Hopefully, I don't sound too eager.

"Unfortunately, yes. Eureka is not on the uniweb grid. You won't be able to communicate with your Scholars or keep up with your assignments. If that poses a difficulty, then—"

"I'm in."

Dr. Valik raises her eyebrows. "You're welcome to take a day or two to think about—"

"I'm in," I repeat.

I *know* this is a cowardly thing to do. I'm running away from my research rather than complete the odious paperwork. It's exactly what Mum always used to chastise me for. "You never finish anything," she'd say. "You just chase whatever's interesting and leave a mess behind. You need to learn to *focus*, Amy."

But Mum's been dead since I was fourteen. Six years now. And despite what the Devotes like to tell me on the rare occasion I go to a prayer meeting, I doubt she's watching me from the aether.

I'm on my own now. I get to say where I go.

And there's no way I'm letting this opportunity slip away.

AT DR. VALIK'S SUGGESTION, I SPEND THE REST OF MY AFTERNOON study session composing messages to my Scholars, informing them that I will be taking time away from my studies. Part of me is tempted to add that I'm never coming back, but Mum's disapproving face swims through my mind. I can't bring myself to burn the bridge. Not when Mum cared so much about her legacy.

After I think about it for a minute, I decide to send a message to Phoenix Refuge as well. The Devotes there used to take care of me after Mum died. Technically, they stopped being my legal guardians when I moved to Halcyon University, but I know Sister Liv worries about me. I should let her know where I'm going before I disappear for months.

On the way back to my dorm, I pause on the boardwalk to watch the sunset darken from pink to red as dusk settles over the beach. Out on the water, two dragons dance above the waves, circling each other midair and ducking below the surface. Their snakelike forms, iridescent and transparent as soap bubbles, don't so much as ripple the water as they dive. They're not made of the same substance humans are. They're spirits, more or less. The ghosts of this planet's past.

Halcyonite children learn about this stuff when we're toddlers. Old Earth was a dying planet. Human civilizations fought over resources, desperate to survive. When the dragons found them, the world was on the brink of collapse.

The dragons were curious about humans and wanted to help them. So they chose to share their peculiar talent: the ability to teleport incomprehensible distances in the blink of an eye.

With their help, humans could finally travel far enough across space to settle new planets. Some they terraformed to their needs. Some they mined for resources and left for dead. On some planets they built sprawling cities, surpassing even the peak of Old Earth's technology. Those planets became what is now the Empire, a close-knit union of planets where the majority of the galaxy's economy is centered.

Halcyon was different.

It was more or less perfect for human habitation, without any need for terraforming. Its air was breathable, its sun was a similar size and distance. There were few dangerous plants and creatures.

But it could never belong to humans, because it first belonged to the dragons.

They may not have corporeal bodies anymore—they're made up of aether, the life energy that flows through all of us—but long ago, they were embodied like humans. No one knows what they looked like. Maybe they were humanoid. Maybe they were huge monsters with tentacles and a hundred teeth...the dragons won't tell us, either way.

Once they became spirit-creatures, teleporting across the universe at will, they didn't need to use their planet. But they still loved their homeland, and so they made a deal with Persia Ester, the first Halcyon settler, selected to be caretaker of their planet.

The dragons allow us free rein of their planet, but only so long as we follow their rules. We keep our cities underground and our farmlands under domes so as not to contaminate the rich biodiversity that already exists here. And we keep our society equal and fair, actively working together to make sure the system benefits all citizens, not just a handful of nobles.

Lots of colonists chose other planets because the rules were too restrictive for them. Even now, with every generation, many children born here choose to leave.

But an equal number seek our planet out. In a galaxy where the rich get richer and the poor end up indentured to factories, the idea of a society built on equality is an irresistible siren call. One that pulled my mum here when I was just a few months old.

The dragons, bored of their dance, wriggle upward toward the sky and vanish into the atmosphere. I turn to head back to my dormitory, then jump as a message pings in my ear. I take out my scroll-tablet to read it.

<*Dr. Valik: Hello, Miz Ediya. Now that you're signed on to our expedition, the xenoarchaeology team would love to meet you. Are you free to join us for dinner this evening?*>

<*Amy Ediya: Sure! That sounds fun!*>

<*Dr. Valik: Great. Meet us at Seaside Siri's.*>

The seafood kitch is crammed with students when I get there. It's little more than a roof with open walls decorated with fish carvings and aquatic-themed windchimes. Glow lamps begin to flicker brighter as the sun disappears beyond the horizon, taking the worst of the day's heat with it.

I weave between the crowded tables, scanning for Dr. Valik. But I manage to walk right past her, only stopping when she reaches out and taps my arm. She's changed out of her Scholar robe and embraced the ugly-sweater look. She blends right in with the students at her table. A gorgeous blonde is cozying up to her, one arm curving around her waist. Dr. Valik doesn't look nearly as fearsome now.

I find a free space on the bench across from her and wave at the group to introduce myself. "Hi, my name is Amy. I'll be the team's biology and genetics consultant."

A chorus of "Welcome" buoys my mood. The other students start introducing themselves, and I scramble to attach faces to names in my brain.

"I'm Prince," says the guy to my left. Oooh, he's *cute*. A bit shorter than me, with his hair styled into a maroon ridge and brown eyes full of humor. Studs glint in his lower lip, rings in each eyebrow, and several in his ear. His sleeves are rolled to the elbow, revealing neon-bright tattoos of fantastical creatures and abstract designs. He looks enough like a pirate to pique my interest.

"Hi, Prince," I say, quirking my eyebrows at him. "What's your role on this field trip?"

"Bush pilot and hired gun."

"He wishes!" one of the students calls. "He's a Knight."

"A not-quite Knight," Prince corrects. "Been contracting with 'em for a few years, and now I'm in training to become one. But *hired gun* sounds more badass, don't you think?"

Oh, I like this one.

"What made you want to become a Knight?" I ask. I've always thought the job sounded cool, but this is my first chance to speak to one of Halcyon's defenders in person. They work directly with the dragons, acting as enforcers for the dragons' law—restraining people who become violent and deporting those who can't safely rejoin society. But most of their time is taken up with charitable missions. They rescue refugees from war zones, drop supplies to planets in need, and provide medical care in the wake of disasters.

I even toyed with the idea of becoming a Knight when I was a teen. I thought it sounded like nonstop adventure and fun. But then I found out how much training I'd have to go through. Combat, first aid, sensitivity training for dealing with traumatized individuals. And of course, I'd have to be stellar at communicating with dragons, because they'd effectively be my bosses. In the end, going with my mum's prescribed career path seemed easier. If only I'd known.

"Dunno if it was any one thing that drew me to the Knights," Prince answers. "Guess I sorta fell into it by accident." Then he snorts. "Crash-landed, if you wanna get literal. My ship got fried, and Fairy here saved my life, though we took out half an orchard in the crash. Rest is history."

At first I think Fairy is the name of the woman next to him, a petite cutie with a green pixie cut. But then the air between us shimmers, and I realize he's talking about a *dragon*. Ze's barely visible, draping one end of zir transparent form across Prince's shoulder. Zir other end is pointed toward me. Hard to tell when dragons don't have faces, but I think ze's giving me an inquisitive once-over.

Taken aback, I blurt, "Do dragons usually have names?"

Prince shrugs. "This one does. I gave it to zem, and I guess ze doesn't mind answering to it."

Someone at the table passes me the menu tablet, but my mind's too busy exploding. I pick a food item at random and pass it on, returning my attention to Prince. I lower my voice, narrowing the conversation to just the two of us as the rest of the table loses interest. "But...if you can tell zem apart from other dragons...does that mean ze's bonded with you?"

Prince glances at the dragon's head-end with an affectionate smile. "Yep. Five years now, we've been together."

Stars a-blazing. I've never met someone with a bonded dragon companion. I'm awestruck. A thousand questions collide on my tongue and tie it up like a spaceport at rush hour.

The dragon is still eyelessly staring at me. I can feel the ghost of zir touch on my mind, sifting through my thoughts and emotions. Ze's testing me. Getting to know me.

"Hi," I say awkwardly.

Ze dips zir head-end in reply.

I turn my attention back to zir maroon-haired companion. "Where's the wildest place ze's ever taken you? Another galaxy?"

Prince laughs. "Oh, Fairy disapproves of me going on adventures. Ze seems to think I'll get myself killed. Pssh." He shakes his head. "It's only once or twice I've nearly died."

::More like six times, or seven,:: interjects Fairy. It's the first time I've heard a dragon speak, and it's jarring. Dragons don't have verbal language like humans do, so they sort of insert their meaning into your brain using images and emotions. In this case, I get six or seven flashes of Prince in mortal peril: his ship on fire, spiraling toward a planet. A bomb detonating right where his ship was meant to be anchored. A war zone, laser blasts narrowly missing him as he runs...

"Whoa!" I protest, blinking. I grip the table to ground myself. "Warn me before you do that, huh?" You'd think I'd be used to getting flashes of people's lives by now, but it never gets easier.

"Yeah, hearing dragons talk is weird the first time," Prince says easily. "It gets less..."

He trails off, cocking his head to cast a quizzical look at Fairy. "What're you talkin' about?" His eyes flick to me. "Uh, sorry if this is odd, but Fairy says you should be used to talking like that. Ze says that *objects* talk to you like that. What the blazes is that s'posed to mean?"

Trust a dragon to blab all my private thoughts. Not that my psychometry is a secret, precisely. I just don't...you know...tell anybody about it. Ever.

Sighing, I hold out my hands and flex my fingers. "I can touch things and know where they've been. I don't know why. I've always been able to do it." To demonstrate, I reach out to touch the decorative candle in the middle of the table. "The man who made this has a young son who's sick in the hospital. He worried about the kid while pouring the wax."

Prince's eyes go wide, but he tries to play nonchalant. "You could've made that up on the spot."

"Well, give me something of yours then. Something with a story I couldn't possibly know."

Slowly, he reaches up to unhook the hoop that pierces his left earlobe. It's gold with a tiny emerald pendant. As he drops it into my palm, I see that the pendant is in the shape of an eye, with the emerald forming the iris. I close my fingers over the earring and wait for the flash.

"You look like a proper pirate," a blue-haired man teases. No, a boy; the two of them are young, sixteen at most.

"It's too expensive," Prince complains.

"I've got friends in high places," his friend banters back.

"Your best friend gave this to you," I say, returning to the present moment. "He had blue hair. Teal-blue, styled in exactly the same way you style yours now."

Prince's hand flies to his carefully spiked hair.

"And something else..." I open my hand and run a fingertip over the eye shape. "He betrayed you. You were angry. But you wear this anyway, because you miss him."

Prince snatches the earring back. "Enough," he says roughly. "I believe you." His hand trembles as he fastens it into his lobe.

"I'm sorry. That got too personal." I busy my hands with pouring a glass of water from the pitcher in the middle of the table. "The visions kind of suck me in...I'm usually more careful." I raise the water cup, a plain ceramic one. "It's better if I only touch things like this, with a long, dull history of being washed and drunk from."

"It's fine," Prince assures me. "It was a long time ago. J—my friend—thought he was doing the right thing. He didn't know it would end with me almost getting killed."

He runs an absentminded finger along the curve of the earring. I'm torn between asking more questions and changing the subject, but I'm distracted when one of Dr. Valik's friends arrives. There's a swell of excited conversation as the Scholars jump up to hug her, and our private bubble bursts.

PART TWO

Year 3729, Week 50,

Dayseven

CHAPTER THREE

Danya

The stolen memory chip is a gold mine of information. Nox and Petra are working their daily shift as interns in the comm center, monitoring Imperial media and intercepting coded transmissions. But every time their supervisor turns away, they huddle together over Nox's tablet, eagerly scanning the messages contained on the chip.

<**Name Redacted** to **Andromeda Bruna**: Source states Phoenix to leave the Refuge on 3729/30/2.>

<**Andromeda Bruna** to **Tan Varion**: See attached intel. Now is our chance. Mobilize a team and wait for my go. This is the closest we've ever been to obtaining the asset.>

"*This is recent. Sent yesterday morning. That date is today,*" *Petra whispers.* "*General Bruna is up to something.*"

"*We've gotta get on that strike team,*" *Nox says.* "*Can you hack Captain Varion's wallscreen?*"

Petra swivels in her chair to face the monitor and begins to type.

I blink, and I'm back in my own head, sitting on the wastehole in the washroom. I fumble for the bidet button, my mind still reeling from what I saw in Nox's mind.

Why is she acting so reckless? Stealing messages out of General Bruna's personal account, for stars' sake—she's *asking* to get caught. Although after yesterday, I sort of understand *why* she feels the need to take these risks. But I still think it's stupid. If she gets herself executed, her all-important crusade will die with her. Has she considered that?

::*Mind your own business, Dawn.*::

Ah shit, she heard me. ::*Make your business more boring then.*::

Instead of replying in words, she focuses really hard on the mental image of an obscene hand gesture. That's sisterly love for you.

I flush the waster and pull up my jumpsuit halfway, tying the sleeves around my hips. My breastband is good enough coverage for the privacy of the washroom, even though as soon as I step out of the cubicle, said privacy is gone. The line of sinks is crowded with other laborers getting ready for their shifts: washing faces, combing hair, sucking on tooth-cleansing tablets. The whole bathroom is abuzz with conversation, groans of "I need coffee" as they jokingly shove each other out of the way for a spot at the mirror. There's some camaraderie between us, the mechanics and shit-shovelers who failed out of soldier training. Some are veterans with missing limbs that make them unfit for further service. Some have chronic illnesses that disqualify them. Some, like me, just don't have the stomach for combat.

They're warm, if gruff, and always willing to support a friend. They'll cover each other's asses the morning after they drink too much, and they'll shit-talk the officers (real quiet) when one of them gets disciplined for something stupid.

The memory of Petra sneering at me last night flashes through my mind, a stark juxtaposition to this scene of amity and acceptance. For a moment, I'm tempted to go turn her in for sheer spite. How dare she look down on people like me, just because war and killing aren't our life's purpose? We grow and cook the food she eats, maintain the life support systems that keep her alive, and repair the bots that clean the floor she walks on.

Then I realize I'm falling into the exact same clannish mindset. Making a "them" and "us" out of people who're all on the same side. I wonder if people who live planetside do this too. Do wheat farmers and sheep farmers call each other names? Do winemakers look down on beekeepers?

I can't picture it. Maybe I just don't want to. I'd love to believe there's a world out there where people support each other regardless of their occupation or abilities. Where everyone is truly equal.

Sighing, I splash cold water on my face, bite down on a tooth-cleanser, and stick my arms into my jumpsuit sleeves. Time for another day of shit-shoveling.

And I plan to *enjoy* it—so Petra can go fuck herself.

MORE OF THE FOOD PRODUCTION TEAM IS OUT SICK TODAY, INCLUDING Lowell himself. Through a little luck, a little begging, and offering to enter Hung's stats for him so he can go home early, I manage to get assigned harvesting work. Not the orchard—we have to go through special training to be allowed in there. But even spending all day on my knees in the dirt, disentangling protein-root and carrot tops from the harvest-bot's tines, is fun for me. Some might call it smelly, dirty work, but it's lightyears better than testing fertilizer.

As I work, I imagine I'm somewhere else. Somewhere with a real atmosphere—not artificial—and genuine, chaotic weather patterns. I imagine I'm wearing handspun fabric instead of the mass-produced synthetic weave of a Greenjacket jumpsuit. The fiber came from plants I grew on my own farm. Maybe my pretty wife, who wears her dark hair in a high ponytail, wove the cloth herself...

I'm not greedy. I don't fantasize I'm brave, or powerful, or well-known, or a genius. No, my wildest dream is to be *free*: to have a small farm to call my own, a few acres of crops, livestock grazing, honest work to get my hands dirty, a good meal cooked by a beautiful woman, and a warm bed to crawl into at the end of the day.

It's as unattainable as a dream of being a princess. But I cling to it anyway, because what other choice do I have?

On my lunch break, I gobble synthmeat, potatoes, and green salad, barely tasting the individual flavors. With fifteen minutes to spare, I climb the stairs to the atmo-control balcony and sit on the edge, dangling my legs over the edge with a safety rail between my knees. Below, neat circles of trees flourish under transparent bubble domes. In addition to catering to each plant's optimal climate, separating the species is supposed to prevent cross-contamination of diseases. But to me, it looks like the trees are lonely, forced to mingle only with their own kind, their branches reaching out toward the edges of the domes as if to pierce it, to bridge the distance.

Pain lances through my arm, and I scream out loud, clutching my head. It's not *my* pain. It's...

::NOX! Talk to me! Are you all right?::

I connect to her mind, but she's not coherent enough for words.

She's screaming, too, curled in a ball on the spongy mat of the practice arena, clutching her right arm.

She doesn't have to look down at its odd angle to know that it's broken. Curse that glitch Cortez, tripping her when she wasn't expecting it! She knows how to fall safely, she KNOWS, how the blazes did this—

I leap to my feet. I have to go help her. Be with her in the hospital. I—

"Xiang? Everything all right?" Logan, one of the atmo techs, has abandoned their workstation. "I heard you scream. Did you get too close to the edge over there?"

"Y-yeah." I scrape a hand through my messy hair. "I lost my balance for a sec. Won't happen again. Please don't report it."

"Gives me the heebies though. You're skinny enough to slip through the rails, and if you fell..." Logan shudders. "Be more careful, kiddo. I don't want to see you get hurt."

"Me neither. I'll be careful, I promise."

As they head back to their monitor screen, I exhale shakily. *::Nox?::*

Nox's brain is a litany of *::shitshitshitshitshit.::* I begin to pull away, figuring I can't be much help, but she latches onto my mind, keeping me close.

::Dawn. You need to have an accident too.::

"What?" I blurt out loud, then check over my shoulder to make sure no one heard me talking to the air. *::You want me to hurt myself? Why?::*

::Not really hurt yourself! Just pretend to break your arm. The right one, not the left one. And make sure they send you to the med center near the training gym.::

I frown. *::What are you up to?::*

::Just do it. PLEASE.::

The desperation in her mind is strong enough to overpower my misgivings. Without thinking too much about what I'm doing, I catch my foot on the edge of the top stair and allow myself to fall.

I hear Logan shout a warning. Pounding footsteps rush toward me. My head cracks hard against the metal lip of a stair. I scrabble to catch myself before I really *do* break my arm. It's not hard to lie there holding my wrist, moaning; I hurt everywhere, and I can feel a trickle of blood running down my face from where my forehead struck the stairs.

"Are you all right? Stars, Xiang, after I *just* told you to be careful!" Logan kneels on the stair below me, hissing when they see the blood. "Can you walk?"

"I think so." I hug my right arm against my body, pretending to cry out in pain.

"Your wrist. Ah, blazes. Let's get you to the infirmary." Logan takes me by the shoulders to help me up. "At least it wasn't your ankle, or I'd have to carry you. Er...do you need me to carry you?"

"No, no." I limp down the stairs. "I can go to the infirmary by myself. Can you just let the supervisor know what happened? I'll be back as soon as I can."

"Don't rush," Logan says. "I know they'll want you to work the rest of your shift, but screw that. After a head-bonk that hard, you need some rest. I'll tell 'em the doctor ordered you to take the day off."

I smile weakly. Logan's pretty all right. I feel bad lying to them.

"Thank you," I manage, before limping as fast as I can in the direction of the zip-lift.

Her arm doesn't hurt anymore; they gave her enough pain medication to see to that. But it still hangs useless, strapped across her chest in a sling. Dragging me down like a cinderblock, *she's thinking, incandescent with anger.*

"Nikola Xiang?" the healer asks, consulting her tablet.

Nox pastes on a smile. "Actually, it's Danya," she says. "Nikola is my twin sister. They mix us up all the time! Same DNA, you know..."

My mouth drops open in shock as the zip-lift jolts to a stop. ::*Nox! What are you doing?*::

::*Dawn! Get in here. But don't act injured anymore. And tell them you're me.*::

::*I'm going to need you to explain before I do that.*::

I can feel her sighing and rolling her eyes. ::*You saw that message from this morning?*::

::*The one you stole from General Bruna? Yeah....*::

::*Well, we need to investigate,*:: she says matter-of-factly, like it's all part of the job. ::*So Petra hacked in and got us assigned to the strike team that's leaving tomorrow to capture the target. I was supposed to be on it—but I can't if my arm's still healing. So I'm sending you.*::

I snort. ::*That better be a joke, Nox. You want me to pretend to be you on a combat mission? I'd get caught in five seconds.*::

::*Not if I'm in your head telling you what to do.*::

Stars help me, she's serious. ::*Nox. NO. I can't.*::

::*And I can't miss this mission, Dawn. I need you to be my eyes and ears. And legs and hands and face.*::

::*Nox...come on. We'll get caught. You know we will.*::

::*Remember when we used to swap places as kids? Nobody caught us then,*:: Nox counters. ::*If anyone could do it, it's us. C'mon, Dawn. If you do this for me, I swear Petra will never doubt you again. She'll kiss your boots until they're shiny.*:: A sly giggle lurks in her mind. ::*She might even give you a kiss somewhere else.*::

::*STOP!*:: My face has gone scarlet, I'm sure.

::Oh, so you don't *want an excuse to spend extra time staring at her?::*

I burst into the infirmary, looking around for Nox. My face must look wild, because a healer rushes over. "Can I help you? Are you all right? Oh! Your face!"

I nearly forgot the blood. "I'm fine. Just need to find my sister..." I hesitate. *::Nox, you owe me big.::* "Her name is Danya. Danya Xiang."

"Oh, of course. This way."

::Thank you, thank you, thank you,:: Nox says fervently.

::You have to guide me through everything. And I mean EVERYTHING. No shutting me out anymore, Nox. It's open communication from here on in.::

I sense her hesitation, and I double down, sure she's about to tell me to never mind. *::That means no more secrets. Anything you're doing, I get to know about. Period.::*

::Deal,:: she says. *::But the same goes for you too. I get to know everything that happens.::*

Shit. I really thought she'd back down. Does this mean I'm stuck helping her with this bizarre plan?

The healer points me to the cot where my twin sits, nursing her arm. I stride over to her, wordlessly examining the cast, unable to say anything out loud. I feel like I might vomit.

::I love you, sis.:: It's the first time she's said those words in...forever. Years, maybe. I hate that she's decided to pull them out now, when using them feels like a manipulation, a soft comfort to placate me and make me feel beholden.

I throw my arms around her, burying my face in her shoulder, but I don't say the words back.

Nox and I stand in the washroom, elbow-to-elbow, staring into the mirror. It's eerie how alike we look under dim light, reflected in smeared glass.

I'm clutching my spare uniform to my chest like a comfort blanket: soft and well-worn, patched knees, sleeves fraying a little. I unfold my arms deliberately, handing the uniform over. "Here," I whisper, even though we're alone in the washroom.

Nox offers me a bundle of cloth in return: her official Greenjacket soldier's uniform. It's darker and newer than my faded olive-green jumpsuit. The jacket feels crisp and heavy under my fingers. The metal buttons are rough-textured and cold. It smells clean, but slightly stale, the way clothes smell when they've been stored a long time without being worn.

We go into separate stalls, and I strip down. The skintight undershirt and trousers are easy to put on; they're similar to the underlayer everybody wears. But my hands begin to tremble again when I pick up the jacket.

These coats are a symbol of our rebellion, well-known across the galaxy. Wearing one is a coveted honor among the young trainees—earning your coat means you've won the right to represent the Greenjackets and all they stand for. It means you've proved your worth.

I've never worn one before.

"Nox," I say softly.

"Shh!" She sends me a mental poke. *::Talk like this. I don't want anyone to overhear us.::*

::No one's in here.::

::We can't be sure nobody's listening. No cambots doesn't mean no audio recorders.::

::Fine. Nox...are you sure you want to do this? Really sure? If we get caught....::

::We won't get caught.::

::But if we do...me wearing this uniform...do you know how seriously I could be punished?::

::Just say it's a prank. It's clothes, for stars' sake.::

::It's not just that, and you know it.:: I close my eyes. *::What if you get caught spying?::*

::I won't, Dawn.::

::But what if you do? What's your clever plan to get out of that? It's treason. They'd kill you.:: The mere thought of it chokes me. Losing my sister is the only thing I can imagine that's worse than death.

::You think I haven't thought of that? Some things are worth the risk.:: Nox sounds almost angry. *::You should try it sometime.::*

::Taking a risk? What do you think I'm doing right now?::

::No.:: Her mindvoice is hard, accusatory. *::I meant you should try caring about something. Enough to die for it.::*

We step out of the washroom stalls at the same time and turn to inspect each other. Nox has just washed her hair, and it's beginning to dry into the shape mine usually takes: tousled and fluffy, flopping over her forehead like a fringe.

I glance at the mirror, half-afraid to see myself. My heart skips a beat to see the uniform. I square my shoulders; a twinge in my muscles reminds me how poor my posture has become lately.

"You need hair gel," Nox says, keeping her voice low. She points at one of the dispensers that line the washroom's prep station. "I use that one. It'll be on the drop ship too, if you need to freshen up. Just one pump should be enough…yeah, that's it, rub your palms together. Now comb your hair back with your fingers. Like this." She demonstrates with a clean hand on her own hair, and I imitate her. The sticky sensation of the hair gel is revolting, but at least it smells kind of good. Minty.

Nox surveys my attempt with a critical eye. "Flatten the back."

I pat my hair into submission, and she nods her approval. *::Perfect. You look just like me now. May not fool Petra, but you'll fool the officers.::*

My stomach twinges with nerves. *::What time am I supposed to go to the briefing?::*

::Tenth hour. And make sure your—my—stuff is packed before then. The message I got this morning made it sound like they want to be cruising by eleventh hour.::

She finally notices how sick I look and pats my shoulder. "You'll do amazing," she says, softening her voice into what she must imagine I sound like. "Your first deployment! It's going to be great! Just follow orders and keep your head down, and you'll be fine." She wraps her unhurt arm around me—the first hug she's initiated in years. "And stay alive," she whispers in my ear.

"You too," I whisper back. And then, in my best Nox imitation, I step back and clear my throat. "I have to go pack. And you have to be at the greenhouse by ninth hour." I force a cocky grin onto my face. "Hope Sherwood isn't too boring without me...Dawn."

She laughs—though I'm not sure if it's at my halfhearted joke or at my awkward impersonation of her. "See you, Nox."

And then she runs off to the greenhouse. My job. My *life*.

While I'm left wondering how the blazes I'm going to fake being a Greenjacket soldier when I couldn't even fake my way through training.

CHAPTER FOUR

Amy

THE SKIES OVER EUREKA

"Hold on tight." Prince's voice sounds crackly over the com. He's left the flight deck door wide open, so he could've shouted instead, but I'm guessing he thinks he sounds cooler this way.

The entire field team is crammed into the twenty-seat passenger bay of Prince's ship. Some of the archaeologists look a bit motion-sick, but all I feel in my stomach is fluttering, like a tiny, swirling shoal of fish. My first space jump—well, first one I remember. I've dreamed about going offworld but never had the guts to do it.

I clench my fingers around the armrest at the slight jolt of the ship taking off. Gravity presses us back in our seats as we rise smoothly into the sky.

"Aaand 'porting in three...two..."

I close my eyes and brace. Dragon-aided teleporting is common on Halcyon as a means of transportation, but I've never really bothered with it all that much. Easier to walk, swim, or hovercycle to the place you want to go.

With dragon-'porting, you have to clear your mind as much as you can. Dragons are finicky about negative energy; sometimes, they'll refuse to teleport someone if that person is injured, ill, or even too upset.

Here on the ship, Prince is taking the lead. He's calming his mind for the dragon—Fairy—to latch onto so we don't have to focus as much as he does.

But we're not immune from the effects of 'porting.

Scientifically speaking, the prevailing theory is that teleporting is accomplished when a dragon takes a ship (or person, or object) into itself, temporarily transmuting its matter into aether—the intangible spirit-stuff that dragons are made of.

Knowing the science doesn't make the sensation any less weird. It's a bit like floating on a cloud, except I'm blind and deaf and my body has disappeared. In place of my deadened senses, there's a heightened awareness of anyone 'porting alongside me—if I focus, I can feel their emotions, even sometimes hear a flash of their thoughts. Most people politely pretend that this doesn't happen, but it's *highly* awkward. I like to keep my brain to myself, so I focus on bland, calm memories. *Watching my wetsuit dry out in the sun. Sand grains dripping through my fingers. The whoosh of waves against the shore.*

When Fairy drops us back into the material world, and I'm safely back in my own body with my mind firmly enclosed in my skull, I breathe a sigh of relief.

"Coming in for a nice, smooth landing," Prince says into the com. "Chilly day today, but the suns are poking through the clouds. Might warm up to be a balmy evening. Welcome, friends, to Eureka."

I crane my neck to look toward the walls of the passenger bay, even though there aren't any windows. The shoal of fish in my stomach starts thrashing, making it hard to sit still.

Dr. Valik didn't tell us anything about what this planet looks like. She sent me a briefing document, but my brain put up a roadblock whenever I tried to read it, so I'm basically going in blind. Not the smartest thing I've ever done, I'll admit.

As soon as we feel the *ba-bump* of the ship's landing gear hitting solid ground, Dr. Valik unstraps her safety belt and faces us. "I want you all to remember, before we exit, that this is an undeveloped world," she says. "This is not a safe environment. There are predators on this planet, so we'll need to have an armed watch at all times. Yes, I said *armed*. We aren't on Halcyon anymore, folks. Mas DeSanto has kindly agreed to let us use his personal blaster guns for self-defense."

I glance at Prince through the open flight deck door. He's busy shutting down the ship and isn't paying attention. But...yes, I do see a holster belted around his hips now. It wasn't there when we took off.

"And no wandering off by yourself," Dr. Valik continues. "Buddy system. Two or three people together at all times. Yes, even when you go off to pee. I'm not having anyone get chomped because they didn't have a buddy watching their back while they squat in the bushes. So you'd best pair up with someone you're comfortable with."

Groans and snickers from the students. Looking around, I see them making silent eye contact with their friends, nodding and pointing. They all know each other already. I'll be the odd one out.

But then I glance back to the flight deck and see Prince cocking an eyebrow at me. He points at me, then at himself. *Buddies?* he mouths.

I grin and nod, relieved that he still wants to hang out with me after that awkward stunt I pulled, doing a read on his earring. I was sure he'd ice me out after that. People always did back when I was still reckless enough to show off my psychic ability now and then. It's like farting the Imperial anthem—a cool talent, but it doesn't make people want to stand real close.

At that point, Prince wanders in and stands, slouchily casual, next to Dr. Valik and her knifeblade posture. "If anyone wants a gun, see me," he says. Then, forestalling all the hands shooting up, "You gotta prove to me that you can use it before I hand it over."

More groans. I bet half the students haven't even *seen* a gun before. Halcyon law doesn't allow anyone to carry weapons. Not even Knights.

I sidle up to Prince as the students begin lining up to exit the ship. "If you're my buddy now, does that mean I get a free shooting lesson?"

"Play your cards right," Prince says, tipping me a wink. "Now, everyone, let me through please! Man with the gun gets to be first out the door."

The cluster parts to let him through but closes before I can use my proximity to cut in line. I bounce on tiptoes, trying to see over everyone's heads to the world waiting outside the ship. It's an agonizing wait as Prince takes a few minutes to secure the area, but then Dr. Valik gives the all clear, and we file out into…

Wow.

I thought I was used to stunning views. I spent the last several years living on a tropical island, gazing wistfully out of the library windows at vivid sunsets and the deep-violet expanse of ocean stretching across the horizon. But this is unlike anything I've ever seen before.

The forest looks like it's aflame. Images of Old Earth's autumn, of deciduous trees shedding gold-orange-red leaves, spring to mind. But then I look closer and realize that the color comes from flower buds, not from leaves. And the trees aren't like the ones I'm used to, with a single trunk rising up and splitting into branches. They're more like vines, climbing over each other and reaching toward the sky in a race to drink down the most sunlight.

Mountains loom over us on all sides, but we seem to have landed in the lush valley between them. The bare patch where we've landed is quartzy rock, with bits and pieces that glint in the spare light that filters through the cast of clouds across the sky. At first, I can't tell if I'm really seeing shiny bits or if the rock is wet from a recent rain. As I look closer, I realize it's both.

One of the students sneezes into her sleeve. "Ugh," she complains. "Even on other planets, I still get allergies? Unfair!"

"All right, all right, you've gawked long enough," Dr. Valik calls briskly. "I need all hands to set up camp. I want to have our shield bubble raised and functional by nightfall. And if you don't want to sleep on cold, hard rock, I suggest you get the tents up too."

Prince taps my shoulder. "C'mon, buddy. I saw a river when I was flying us in for a landing. Come help me haul a few jugs of fresh water?"

It sounds more fun than pitching a tent. "Lead the way."

The water jugs are the size of my torso. Even empty, they're hard to carry. Lightweight, but my arms won't go all the way around them. "We can't haul these ourselves," I protest. "Is Fairy going to teleport them or what?"

Prince holds up a finger. "Just wait. I have my own magical power…I can lift things *with my mind*." He wiggles his fingers at me.

Then he crawls into the cargo hold and yanks out an old hoverbarrow, flicking its On switch so that it purrs gently down the ramp instead of scraping and clanking.

I roll my eyes. "Hover tech. That's cheating."

"What? Naw. I used my mind to think of bringing a hoverbarrow. That counts."

I snort, helping him load the barrow's bed with the empty jugs.

Once we're out of earshot of the other students, though, Prince turns serious. "D'you mind if I ask about...you know...the thing you did with my earring? Couldn't stop thinkin' about it afterward. I've got a hundred questions. But if you don't wanna talk about it, just tell me to shut my facehole."

It takes me a moment to decide whether I actually do want him to shut his facehole. His dragon spoiled my secret for me, and I don't really owe him an explanation. On the other hand...he knows about it, and he's not acting like I'm some freak. As far as I can tell, he genuinely wants to be my friend. I'm used to potential friends distancing themselves when my weirdness comes out. The fact that Prince is still here, asking questions, is...nice. I guess.

"You can ask," I say.

He grins. "Right then, first question: How'd you learn to do that?"

I shrug. "Didn't learn. I've been able to do it my whole life."

"Then you're a real psychic? Blazin' stars. I thought psychics were supposed to be fake. Y'know, they research people beforehand and then they make shit up until the person is like 'Granny, is that you?' or whatever."

"I'd never use it to trick people," I say indignantly. Though the existence of psychics has always made me wonder whether I'm the only one with weird powers they can't explain. "It's just a useless talent I have. Like being able to down three glasses of fizzy water in a row without retching."

"You can do that too?" Prince is looking at me like I'm his hero.

"Ew. No. One of the kids in my social group could. The way he burped afterward almost made *me* cast up."

"Awww." He grins. "Shame, that. I'd've liked to see it."

"No. Trust me. You wouldn't."

He snickers, then goes right back to questioning me. "You say reading objects is like talking to a dragon then?"

I nod. "Images and feelings, mostly."

Prince snaps his fingers. "Stars, no wonder Dr. Valik wanted you on her archaeology team! You can just touch things and know what they were used for!"

I grimace. "Dr. Valik doesn't know. Please don't tell her. They'll have me touching every dirty scrap of metal they dig up."

"But you could wipe out *years* of research and guesswork for them!"

"And ruin their fun?" I force a laugh, trying to play it off as a joke. "They'd have nothing to do. No academic papers to write. They'd never forgive me."

But really, I just don't want them to see me as more of a freak than I already am. They'll already despise me in a few weeks when I'm consistently late to work, when I keep getting distracted from the tasks at hand, when I can't finish anything I start. Me telling them I can psychically read their artifacts? Ha! They'd think I was making it up for attention.

"All right," Prince says dubiously, "I won't tell them if you don't want me to. But it's just so ace!"

"It's annoying, that's what it is." I lift a vine out of our way as we both duck under it. "I can't do something as simple as this—touching a tree— without knowing what animal rubbed its butt on the trunk this morning." It was something that had tentacles for a face. But I don't tell Prince that. The creature might still be nearby, and I don't want him freaking out.

"Hey!" Prince's eyebrows shoot up as he thinks of another question. "What happens if you touch a person? Can you read their thoughts?"

I shake my head. "I sometimes pick up feelings, I guess. But I don't get clear visions like I do for inanimate objects. People are constantly on the move, so their history is too muddled to read." Or something. It's not like this comes with a manual.

"Hmmm." Prince looks a tad disappointed, but with a dash of relief. I can't blame him. Who would want to hang around with someone who could see into their brain?

"Hey, can you hear that? It's the river!" I rush forward, hoping that the water source will distract Prince from the topic at hand.

"Hold up," he calls after me. "Slow down. We don't know if there's any predators—"

The tentacle-faced thing is on me before I can blink.

Reacting on pure instinct, I punch out at its face, swinging my fist like a hammer. The tentacles squish disgustingly, but they aren't slimy as I expected. They're more like feelers, maybe. Fleshy whiskers. *Yuck.*

There's a mouth somewhere under them and a dozen pairs of short, claw-footed legs behind that. As I attempt to kick the creature off me, the back of my brain is busy cataloging its features: *Warm-blooded. Sightless. Attacks based on sound? Looks like a centipede crossed with a star-nosed mole...*

Prince yells at me to get down so he can shoot it, but there's no way I'm going to hit the floor while wrestling with something that has about twenty arms. Instead, I brace myself, and when the centimole—molipede?—goes for my throat again, I throw all my energy into flinging it into the air.

Zzzt.

The laser blast doesn't make much noise, but it severs the molipede's body just below its voracious double line of teeth. Its claws spasm, its tentacles waving wildly. Then it goes still.

Prince lowers the blaster. "Sorry, friend," he says to the molipede's body.

I double over, bracing my hands on my knees, and gasp for breath.

"You hurt, Amy?"

I shake my head. Kinda feel like I might cast up, but... "It didn't bite me."

"And its feelers didn't have any toxins on 'em?"

I scrub my hands against my jumpsuit. "Ugh, I hope not."

Prince looks me over, inspecting my hands and neck. When he's satisfied I'm not poisoned or bleeding to death, he sighs, the relief visible in the loosening of his shoulders. "You did good, buddy." He pats me on the shoulder. "Those things were the creepiest critter on the debrief file Dr. Valik sent us. Wasn't looking forward to my first run-in with 'em. But you flipped it off you like no big deal."

"I still haven't read it," I confess. "I might've stayed home if I saw a pic of that thing."

Prince's eyebrows go up. "You better read it soon. There's some super-relevant info in there."

"Like?"

"Uh, like why they were so eager to have you on this trip?"

He resumes pushing the hoverbarrow toward the stream.

"Are you gonna elaborate?" I yell after him.

"Nope. You're just gonna have to read for yourself. C'mon, keep up. I don't want another of those things jumping on you."

He has a point. I jog to catch up, keeping a wary eye on the forest around us.

THE CAMPFIRE CASTS AN EERIE, ORANGE GLOW ON THE INSIDE OF THE shield dome, rain pattering against the outside. I tilt my head back, watching sparks fly up to fizzle out against the barrier's low ceiling. The energy barrier lets smoke pass through, so that we don't suffocate inside, but it'll keep those molipede creatures at bay while we sleep.

Even so, Dr. Valik doesn't trust the shield dome enough to go without a night watch. She's already patrolling the perimeter of the dome, holding one of Prince's blaster guns loosely at her side.

The students are exhausted. Setting up camp took until sundown, which was later than I expected. This planet turns more slowly than I'm used to, its day-night cycle just enough longer than Halcyon's to confuse my brain. But the important thing was that they got the dome up fast, saving everyone else from surprise molipede attacks.

I can hear the excitement in their chatter, despite their exhaustion. They're debating what time the suns are supposed to rise, allowing them to hike out to the dig site to secure it with another dome.

Prince nudges me with his shoulder, still shoveling campfire-heated bean stew into his mouth. "You read the debrief file yet?"

"No, I haven't. But I did open the message from Dr. Valik, so... progress!" I shake my head. "She spelled my name wrong on the message. A-M-Y-T-H-E-S-T. Everybody does that. Their brain thinks *Amy*, and they forget how to spell the word *Amethyst*."

"Ugh." Prince rolls his eyes. "Welcome to the unusual name club. I always get asked what I'm prince of."

"Well? What *are* you prince of?"

He wrinkles his nose at me. "All I survey. So are you never going to read it or what?"

"No. Ugh. I don't know." I want to, and I know I should. But as soon as I opened it and saw the long wall of text, my brain noped out. *You'll read it after dinner,* it lied. Now it's after dinner, and my brain is frantically groping for some other excuse.

To his credit, Prince sees the look on my face and drops the subject. Instead, he starts asking me about my mum...which is almost worse.

"You're related to Dr. Gaela Ediya, right? The geneticist who worked on the HTP?"

Reluctantly, I nod. The Human Teleportation Project got way more press than it should have for a failed endeavor, but everyone was wild about the idea. Basically, my mum and her team were trying to discover a tangible, studyable dragon genome so that they could isolate the part of a dragon's makeup that allows it to transition between aether and the material world. If they had succeeded—if humans had gotten the ability to teleport—it would have changed our entire galaxy. We wouldn't have needed to rely on dragons for so much, for starters.

Personally, I'm kind of glad they failed. There's already some grumbling among anti-alien fringe groups that we need to sever our ties with the dragons lest they "influence" humankind too much.

Bit late for that, three thousand-plus years after dragons first discovered Earth. But people always find reasons to complain.

"So I'm thinking that's why Dr. Valik invited you on this trip," Prince says.

"Hmm? Because of my mum?"

"Yeah." Sounds like he thinks it should be obvious. "Because of what they're studying. You'd know if you read the file. They think they've found an ancient civilization of dragons—their ancestors anyway—buried in volcanic ash."

I stare at him, my mouth hanging open. "You can't be serious." The dragons have always been cagey about their physical appearance before they evolved into spirit-beings. *We are as we are,* they always say and then change the subject.

That hasn't stopped countless generations of xenoarchaeologists from trying to discover their secrets. All we know for sure is that dragons originated on the planet Halcyon, but no trace has been found of their civilizations there, and there's some argument about what that signifies. One side insists that dragons lived as animals—sentient, but uninterested in building cities, developing technology, or shaping their environment. Another side holds that dragons must have been spacefaring and built their cities elsewhere, maintaining their home planet as an unspoiled utopia. Still others think that dragon civilizations exist, on Halcyon and maybe elsewhere, but that the creatures are masters of misdirection and camouflage, managing to hide their history from human eyes for all these centuries.

I don't know which theory to believe. Unlike all these students, I haven't read the numerous research papers and books on the topic. I haven't even read my own mother's research notes, though no one believes me when I say so. Journalists hunt me down at least twice a year to ask me about her. I've gotten really good at saying "No comment."

"I guess I do need to read that file," I say weakly. "Stars. Do they really think—? They have evidence it's really dragons?" No wonder Dr. Valik didn't tell me anything before we left Halcyon. She's going to have to keep this research as secret as possible until they have results to share. Otherwise, this whole planet will be shoulder-to-shoulder newsies, begging for a glimpse of the archaeologists' work.

"It's just guesswork right now. We're here to find the truth," Prince says. "I bet you got dragged along so you can carry on Gaela Ediya's research. If you can find some genetic material, construct a dragon genome, maybe you'll be the one to unlock human teleportation."

"I hope not!" I blurt.

Prince raises an eyebrow. "You don't want to be the one to discover it?"

"No. Stars, no. I'm two semesters into figuring out that I hate academia. If I complete Mum's research, no one will ever let me do anything else."

I can't look at Prince's face, terrified I'll see him judging me. But when he speaks, his voice is sympathetic. "University's that bad, huh?"

"I can't focus on anything." I let my face drop into my hands. "I faked my way through Galactic Standard education by half-assing every assignment at the last minute. I guess I was smart enough to fool everyone, and they wanted to be fooled because Mum's research was so important. Everyone wanted me to step into her shoes. I wanted that too. But I just can't make her shoes fit me."

He pats my shoulder. "Look, I dunno if anyone else has ever told you this, but you can quit if you want to."

"No!" I mutter. "I'm not a quitter."

"There's no shame in admitting that something isn't working out for you. Trust me. I've quit loads of things. Almost got recruited by Greenjackets, and they didn't give me an option to quit, but I escaped 'em anyways. Then I quit being a taxi pilot to go work for the Knights." A tinge of humor creeps into his voice. "I even tried dating a couple of folks before quitting that too. Terrible idea. Not for me. I'm very, very aromantic."

That admission shocks me out of my self-pity spiral. I raise my head to stare at him. "You are? Oh stars, I'm sorry. I was trying to flirt with you before."

"Nah, don't apologize. Dating ain't for me, but that doesn't mean I don't enjoy a little banter." He winks to prove it.

My mind quickly collapses back into its whirling mess of guilt and shame. "I don't think you understand though. Gaela Ediya's daughter can't just drop out of university."

"Gaela Ediya's daughter has her own name, and Amy gets to do whatever she wants," Prince counters. "That's how lives work. Everybody gets their own. You aren't obligated to finish your mother's work just because she didn't get to. Anyway, didn't she have a whole team helping her? Shouldn't *they* be responsible for that?"

I shrug. "Most of the team disbanded after Mum left. The only ones who still work on the HTP stuff, as far as I know, are Mum's triplets. My aunt and uncle."

"Oh yeah, I remember reading their names in the articles." Prince snaps his fingers. "Oberon and...Melissa?"

"Melanie."

"That's the one. What are they up to these days?"

"Who knows? I haven't heard from them since Mum died. They cleared out her lab right after the funeral. Didn't even say goodbye." Not that I'd wanted them to. Auntie Mel and Uncle O always struck me as a little bit weird. Auntie Mel talked to me in this weird, sugary, high-pitched voice, even though I was fourteen, not four. Uncle O barely talked at all, and he wouldn't meet my eyes.

"Well, for all you know, they're about to make a breakthrough, and your ma's legacy will carry on without your help." Prince's optimistic grin makes it hard to stay down. Lowering his voice conspiratorially, he says, "If you could do anything in the universe, what would you do?"

Stars. I genuinely don't know. "This? Exploring? I like seeing new things. I like swimming and hiking. I don't know if I loved fighting that creature before, but it felt good to do physical work for a change."

"You should be a Knight," Prince says triumphantly, as if I've proved him right. "I mean, I'm biased in thinking it's the best job, but it is. I get to go on exciting adventures and help people in the process. And no one's asked me to do any boring paperwork in five years. It's awesome."

My brain is still off-kilter, buzzing with the startling realization that I could just stop if I wanted to. Somehow, it genuinely never occurred to me before. I mean, I knew *logically* that quitting was an option, but I never imagined doing it. Sort of like how I know I *could* climb to the roof of the university and use its spire as a dancing pole, but why would I ever?

Except, now that Prince has put the idea into my head, it's eating me alive.

I could quit.

I think I'm *going* to quit.

But not yet. I've got to finish out this fieldwork first. The next three months will give me some time to plan my exit.

I turn to Prince and throw my arms around him. He jerks, startled, but then enfolds me in a warm, tight hug. Too bad he's not interested in dating—the guy gives *amazing* hugs.

"Thanks," I mumble into his shoulder.

"Aw, hey, what are friends for?" he says, and the thought warms me inside out.

I have a friend.

PART THREE

Year 3729, Week 51,

Dayone

CHAPTER FIVE

Danya

THE SKIES OVER EUREKA

"Xiang. You're sweating through your uniform."

I had been hoping no one would notice. But Ari Borisov, who's strapped into the shuttle seat across from me, has the keen eyes of someone constantly on the lookout for an excuse to tease or bully. I've seen that glint of mischief before, and it always signals misery.

My instinct, after all these years, is to curl in on myself and ignore him. But that's not what Nox would do. So, feeling a fresh wave of cold-sweat nausea wash over me, I look him straight in the eyes and curl my lip in a sneer.

"Yeah, so what? I get airsick. What's it to you?"

"Airsick?" he scoffs. "Since when? You flew circles around us all in pilot training."

"Yeah, and I cast my guts up afterward." I shrug. "Badasses still blow chunks sometimes, Arthur."

"It's Ari and you know it." He glares and mutters, "Glitch."

The power rush of being mean is intoxicating, though it leaves an aftertaste of guilt. I'm starting to understand why Nox wears this tough persona like armor. It's not comfortable, and I don't even really feel safe

—cruelty can be turned on its wielder in seconds—but I do feel like I could punch a hole in solid metal.

I also feel *moist*. Fear-sweat soaks my armpits and trickles down my sides. My stomach is a swamp bubbling with toxic gas.

The pilot announces over the com that we'll be landing shortly, and I brace my feet against the seat so my knees won't bounce with nervous energy.

I am Nox. Nox, who's never afraid of anything. Nox, who's probably never even considered *being airsick.*

I have to keep chanting it like a prayer in my head. *I am Nox. I am Nox.* Because if I forget, even for one second, I'm dead.

I'm lucky I've even made it this far. During this morning's briefing, there were a few moments when I thought I would pass out. Turns out when I'm not used to standing rigidly in the same posture for an entire hour, it really gets to me. That and the crippling anxiety that I might be discovered for a fraud.

The mission seems pretty straightforward though. All we're supposed to do is swoop in on this Halcyonite scientist group and capture one of the students. "Taking candy from a baby," is how our commanding officer, Captain Varion, put it. "Halcyonites are pacifists, so they won't be armed or combat-trained. We might not even have to kill anyone. Let's make this an in-and-out job, soldiers. We land, we secure the target, we're airborne and home by nighttime."

Good. The sooner Nox and I can swap back and be done with this farce, the better.

They haven't told us *why* we're snatching this woman, of course. Nox, watching the briefing through my eyes, was powerfully curious. ::*Ask them,*:: she urged me. But I didn't want to bring attention to myself, so I kept my mouth shut.

::*It might be important, Dawn!*::

::*Then get Petra to ask. Not me.*::

::*Coward.*:: She didn't push me though. I think she knows I'm right—the fewer eyes on me, the better.

The ship judders and clunks suddenly. I tug to tighten my safety belt, my heart (and stomach) in my throat. It's a rougher landing than I expected.

"Uh, my apologies." The pilot sounds stressed. "I've brought us down a little early to avoid the enemy ship detecting us. Good news: They don't know we're here yet." He chuckles nervously. "Bad news: We're gonna have to hike through some jungle to get to 'em."

Everyone groans, until Varion glares us into submission. But my heart leaps like a grasshopper taking flight.

Jungle.

For the first time in my life, I'm about to set foot on a *planet*.

The CO mutters into his wrist-com, "Can we confirm that Phoenix is with the enemy camp?"

The pilot replies after a second. "Negative, sir. We don't have any trackers on her. Gonna have to go by the intel we've got."

Phoenix. I search my brain's junk drawer, trying to remember where I heard it last. That encrypted message, seen through Nox's eyes: *Phoenix to leave the Refuge.*

This is it. This is why Nox insisted I come. The student we're picking up, she's the Phoenix.

I lock eyes with Petra, willing myself not to stare. She lifts her eyebrows ever so slightly. I wish I could mindspeak with her like I do with Nox, to find out what she's thinking.

Argh—scratch that. If I connected with her mind, she'd know all my dirty thoughts about her.

The pilot has anchored, and Varion gives us the all-clear to disembark. And then, with Nox's pistol an unfamiliar weight in my hands, I'm marching down the extended ramp...

The breeze hits my face, and I gasp at the cool moisture of it. The sky above us is gunmetal gray, and little pricks of cold hit my face and trickle down like tears.

Rain.

The smell of it is incredible. Sharp and earthy and leafy. It's a cleaner, wilder version of the scent that fills the greenhouse when the irrigation pipes are turned on. I breathe it hungrily, even as my feet follow Varion's orders to fan out and check the area for hostile life forms.

We've landed in a tangle of wild vines festooned with crimson buds. Some of the vines have already flowered, their petals littering the soil under our feet. Under the pretense of taking cover next to one of the vines, I bend close to one of the nubs, one stubborn petal still clinging to its edge. I can see the beginning of a fruit in the center of it.

Ideally, I ought to wait until the vines are fully fruited, the seeds mature. But I doubt I'll have a chance to come back. I pass the gun to my other hand and quickly break the nub off the vine, stuffing it into a pocket of my weapons belt before anyone sees.

Now all I need is to get this mission over with quickly so I can return to the greenhouse with the specimen fresh enough to study.

"Area secure, sir," Borisov shouts. Varion calls us to stay close together, and I jog to catch up, falling in at the rear of the group. Good. No eyes on me back here.

The rain begins to fall harder, soaking through our uniforms. I hear grumbles and complaints from everyone else, but I savor the drip of rainwater through my hair and down my cheeks. My temp-reg underlayer keeps me warm under the soaked jacket.

The front ranks decide to take turns hacking through the thick vines with laser cutters, which means I can't hide at the rear forever. Soon enough, someone presses the cutter handle into my palm and pushes me to the front of the group. I don't really know where we're supposed to be going, so I follow the lead of the other guy cutting vines beside me. His wrist cuff has a compass attachment, which he checks frequently, keeping us on a straight course.

But the compass doesn't warn us about the pond.

I'm so deep in the routine—cut, clear, step—that I'm knee-deep in scummy water before I've even noticed that there's a pond in my way.

My partner laughs at me, and the rest of the soldiers join in, albeit halfheartedly in their exhaustion. "Someone come give Xiang a break," Borisov calls. "She can't even look where she's going."

My face burns hot, but I'm so muddy I doubt anyone will notice. Lifting my chest and shoulders, I make as if to stride out of the water...

Only to be yanked off my feet, pond scum shooting up my nostrils as my face hits the water.

As my head goes under, I hear peals of laughter from the other soldiers and shouts of reprimand from the captain. They think I've slipped and fallen in the mud, embarrassing myself further.

They haven't noticed the claw that's gripping my ankle.

Pure terror shoots through me as my fingernails scrabble for purchase in the slimy-soft mud. The creature isn't dragging me down; it's just grabbed me to examine me, I think. To check if I'm food.

I kick out with my other foot, trying to break its hold on me, and push up with my hands against the bottom of the pond to hold my head above water. My nose and mouth break the surface, and I try to scream for help, but all I can manage is a gagging cough as my lungs reject the pond water. I manage to get one knee under myself, coming to all fours, but the other leg is still caught in a tug-of-war with whatever pond creature has got me.

The others are still laughing, curse them. See if I help if *they're* ever in danger.

"Help," I manage to croak. "Caught."

Finally, Captain Varion sees fit to act. He wades into the water, unsheathing the knife he carries at the back of his belt. He stabs at the water beside my foot and holds up what looks like a gnarled hand.

"Brave soldier," he says sarcastically. "Laid low by a waterweed root."

I get my feet under me, the aftereffects of the adrenaline rush making me shaky. I'm soaked to my underlayer now, water and mud cascading off me.

"I thought it was a pond creature," I choke, spitting scummy water. I've never been so thoroughly humiliated—not even when Petra called me a shit-shoveler that one time.

"Well, it wasn't." Varion tosses the clump of roots over his shoulder. "Fun's over. Let's keep moving. Burnell, you take over for Xiang."

Another woman steps forward to take the laser cutter from me, and I mutely hand it over. Part of me wants to sink back under the surface of the pond and settle into the mud until the shame drowns with me. But the other part—the one that's determined to make Nox proud—keeps propelling me forward.

"WE'LL REACH THE ENEMY CAMPSITE TOMORROW MORNING," VARION finally announces, as Eureka's suns dip below the horizon. "Terrain's too tangled up with these vines. No sense in fighting through them at night —the enemy'd see our lights long before we'd see them."

We haven't brought camping gear with us. Didn't think we needed it on this "in and out" mission. We huddle under shelter of the thicker vine growths, miserably wet, while the comrades who drew the short straws stand watch with pitifully dim emergency torches. At one point, I hear one of them yelp, curse, and fire his gun about twenty times. I curl my knees tighter to my chest, wishing that planets were more like greenhouses—all of the flora, none of the fauna. Maybe I was naïve to think planet life would be so wonderful.

The exhaustion should have dragged me down into sleep the moment I lay down after eating a dry, tasteless nutrient bar. But my brain keeps me awake, replaying the pond incident with the masochistic precision of a close-up holo-capture.

"Hey, Nox. You awake?"

At Petra's whisper, I jerk half-upright, propped on my elbows. "Yeah. What's up?"

"Still haven't managed to get any more info out of the captain." She sounds annoyed. "This Phoenix—the student—it makes no sense they would want her. I checked her social page, and she's just some random glitch. Did you have time to do more digging on that memory chip?"

"Uh...no?" ::*Nox, help,*:: I beg silently. ::*I thought you were going to tell Petra it's me.*:: But my sister is fast asleep already, useless to help me pretend to be her.

"I guess it's been a busy day," Petra concedes. *Whew.* "But we need to know more. Let me know tomorrow if you need me to cover for you. We can pretend you're having the shits and fall back—"

Things that were not high on my list of anticipated life experiences: hearing the most beautiful woman I've ever met talk about diarrhea. I let my head fall onto my forearms with a groan. Petra's giggling; dimly, I hear Burnell telling her to shush.

I don't know why I thought I could do this—play Nox's part. I don't know why *Nox* thought I could. The longer this mission drags out, the more likely it becomes that someone will catch me. And it won't just be me in trouble. They'll investigate Nox, find out she's been playing traitor-spy, and they'll probably execute both of us.

A quiet little voice in the back of my mind whispers, *Why not run?*

I can't, I tell myself firmly. *They'd catch me for sure.*

But what if they didn't? This is the best chance I'm ever going to get. I'm on a planet now. Could stay here forever if I wanted to.

That's assuming I could find food and water here. Without a lab to test, I can't verify if these vine-fruits are poisonous. And what about predators? The pond monster might not have been real, but whatever Jeune just shot—

And what about Nox? Am I just going to leave her to pretend to be me forever, while her name gets dragged through the mud as a deserter? She'd never forgive me. Might come hunt me down herself.

No. I can't stay.

This won't be for much longer anyway. We'll capture the target tomorrow, then be on our way back to Sherwood. I'll be me again before bed tomorrow.

Ah. Bed. I miss my sleep-pod...

My thoughts begin to blur as I drift off. I half-dream that I'm lying in one of the growth pods in the greenhouse, facedown in the dirt with plants sprouting out of my spine. A fine mist sprays from the irrigation pipes, and the roots dig deeper into my bones, the leaves reaching upward for the UV lamp.

The weirdest thing about the dream is how peaceful it feels. And when I'm jolted awake to a bright and early march, my clothing damp and musty, I cling hard to the lingering calm of that dream.

CHAPTER SIX

Amy

EUREKA DIG SITE

Dr. Valik angles the floodlight to give her students a better view of the cave wall. The carvings there look like nonsense symbols to me, but one of the students traces an outline of what could be a lizard-creature, if I turn my head to the side and close one eye.

However interesting it might be, the ancient alien art is not why we're here. I duck my head to make my way deeper into the cave, past the floodlight's beam to the dark recesses where my headlamp is the only light source.

The dry, cold air is stale down here. Dr. Valik made us all carry a map of the cave in our jumpsuit pockets, just in case we take a wrong turn and get lost in the neverending maze of lava tubes. But I don't need the map right now. I can see the flickering of other headlamps just ahead, the whispers of my student colleagues echoing in this close space. The weird shapes and curves make sound reverberate oddly in here—sometimes you can hear a voice that seems to be murmuring in your ear, only to realize its owner is standing far across the cavern.

Dr. Valik's voice says, "This way," and a chill spiders down my back. It sounds like she's standing right behind me.

Wait—she *is*. Stars. I nearly jump out of my skin as she brushes past me, picking her way across the uneven ground with her toolkit slung over her shoulder.

"Keep up," she says. "We've been waiting for you all morning."

I spent a few hours this morning setting up the testing equipment that Dr. Valik brought for me. My job here seems to be "run genetic tests on any organic matter the dig uncovers, and try to isolate the aliens' genome." I guess all other hypotheses and tests are going to have to wait until we pass that first hurdle: finding viable genetic matter. Which, given that this find is estimated to be at least six thousand years old, won't be easy. I'm expecting old bones at best.

I turn the corner into a dead-end alcove and gasp.

The alien bodies aren't bones or fossils. They're whole, undecomposed, encased in what appears to be some kind of hardened organic material that was once liquid. They hang from the ceiling in blobs, like weird stalactites, curled up as though asleep. I've seen animals that laid eggs in just this way. The blobs look like they should be squishy, but when I climb one of the students' ladders to touch one, it's rock-solid.

"It's like they're sleeping," I muse out loud.

"Isn't it?" Dr. Valik says. "For all we know, this is an extended hibernation. But when the expedition who found this site cracked one of them open, the creature inside had rotted away. Our current hypothesis is that this is some kind of burial ritual, like mummification. I just hope you'll get a good enough sample to use in your tests."

"Me too." If I don't, things will get pretty boring for me, stuck here for the next three months. "I'll need to open one of these bubbles to get at the creature inside. And I'll need to test a piece of this blob-stuff as well, just to be thorough."

"Already ahead of you." Dr. Valik gestures to a cluster of students on the ground, chipping away at a dislodged blob. It's almost as tall as I am, and judging by the cracked rock beneath it, they chiseled it out of the ceiling and let it drop unceremoniously to the floor. The occupant, still suspended in the hardened material, doesn't seem to be any worse for wear.

Though the cloudy substance encasing the creature distorts its appearance, I can tell it's a saurian-type creature, with a scaly, textured hide and a long tail coiled protectively around its body. I count six angular limbs, curled inward, four vestigial wing protrusions along its back, and a horselike head bearing at least eight faceted eyes.

"It looks like a dragon," I say in shock. When the others chuckle, I amend my outburst. "I mean, one of the Old Earth dragons, the lizard monsters. Not..."

"We know what you mean," says a student, whose name I think is Vi. "That's why they sent our team to study this site. The explorers who found this cave were *convinced* they'd found the dragons' ancestral form."

"Has anyone asked the dragons?"

"Sure, but you know how they are. They love being mysterious and unhelpful."

I place my hand on the outside of the blob, hesitant, bracing myself for the flash. It's faint and distant—nothing's touched it in thousands of years, so the memories are faded echoes. But I get a distinct image of a living creature just like this one, bundling its deceased comrade into a wad of sticky goo and smoothing the edges. Its emotions feel foreign, aching in parts of a body that I don't have, but I can guess they translate to sorrow. I get a sense of looming cold, like the onset of winter. I remember feeling something similar when Mum died—like nothing would ever be bright and good again.

The flash tells me nothing about whether the creatures were pre-dragons or not. Nothing that will shortcut anyone's research. So I ignore it and pick up a chisel to help chip away at the hardened casing. The sooner I get my hands on a cell sample, the sooner I can begin my tests.

"ANYTHING INTERESTING?" PRINCE ASKS, LEANING OVER MY SHOULDER to squint at the screen, where my microscope is projecting a magnified cell.

"Shh." I hold up a finger. "Don't distract me." The second I look up, my train of thought will jump its track, and I'll come back to these notes hours later to find it full of mystifying half-finished sentences.

"Oop. Sorry." I sense him backing away.

When I finally let myself look up from my work, Prince is several meters away, idly pacing the perimeter of our shield dome. He's been trekking back and forth between the camp and the dig site all day, guarding each group of students against potential predator attacks. So far, no more molipedes have shown up, to everyone's collective relief.

"Want to see what I've been working on?" I call out to him.

He immediately abandons his post and comes over. "What have you found out?"

"Well, my machine analysis dated this body more recently than we thought," I say. "It's only about two thousand years old. So unless our dragons split off as an old evolutionary branch of this species—"

"They're probably not dragons," Prince finishes my conclusion for me. "Blast. Can't say I'm surprised though. Fairy seems pretty disinterested in our cocooned friends in the cave. I'd expect more emotional turmoil from zem if they were zir ancestors."

"Doesn't mean this is a waste of a trip though," I say quickly. I definitely don't want to go home yet. "I'm checking for genetic evidence that they might have had abilities similar to dragons—teleportation or mind-reading. Any xeno we come across has the potential to have evolved in a way that we previously thought was impossible."

"Do you think you'll find anything?"

"Well, maybe—"

Whatever I was about to say flees my brain as Prince suddenly reaches for his gun. My head jerks up from my screen, and I flinch back as I see what he's just seen.

There are about twenty soldiers staring at us from the other side of the shield dome. All of them wear thigh-length, forest-green coats and carry lethal-looking guns.

And they're all looking directly at us with murder in their eyes.

"Get to the ship, Amy," Prince says, his voice flattening into a scary monotone. "Go!"

I abandon my workstation, already anticipating the tongue-lashing I'll get for not bothering to save thousands of credits' worth of machinery, plus those priceless DNA samples. The force-shield is programmed to respond to passcodes in our keycuffs, so the strange soldiers won't be able to breach it easily. That should give me and Prince just enough time to jump in his ship and escape before they overload the generator with prolonged laser fire. Will we be able to swing by the dig site and rescue Dr. Valik and the students, or will we have to go get help and hope they survive until then?

Prince shouts a warning, and I look over my shoulder to see a soldier stepping through the shield. Then another.

Then I see the keycuffs they're wearing, slipped over top of their coat sleeves. I recognize one—rose gold with dangly charms—as belonging to Vi, the student I worked with just this morning.

Shit.

Looks like rescuing the dig crew isn't going to work. Either they've already killed the students or they incapacitated them long enough to steal their keycuffs.

Why though? a tiny part of my mind wonders. Behind the litany of swears that's fueling my limbs to sprint for the ship, my brain is running a background analysis on the utter weirdness of this situation. We expected earthquakes, rain, predators, at worst a volcanic eruption. Nobody said anything about human soldiers. Halcyon is a pacifist planet, never at war with anyone. Not the Imperial Authorities, and certainly not the rebel Greenjackets.

These soldiers certainly look like the blurry vids of Greenjackets the newsies play. But they're supposed to be fighting the red-uniformed Imperial Authorities, hoping to tip the balance of galactic power and overthrow the Emperor. Why the blazes would they attack a bunch of student scientists?

And then it clicks.

Almost got recruited by Greenjackets, Prince said last night. *They didn't give me an option to quit, but I escaped 'em anyways.*

I skid to a halt and turn around. No *way* are they taking my buddy prisoner.

Prince is crouching behind a crate of supplies, trying to hold off the soldiers. But there are too many of them, and they have personal shield generators, deflecting every one of his shots. They're just about on top of him, and any second now they'll—

"HEY QUARKBRAINS!" I yell.

That gets their attention.

"It's her," I hear one of them saying. "Xiang, go, I'll handle this glitcher with the gun—"

It's her? As in me? Wait...what?

Getting the feeling that I might have just made a huge mistake, I back away toward the ship, glancing around for a crate or tent that I can use for cover.

A Greenjacket soldier advances toward me. Short. Severe haircut. Round face and dark eyes. With a stab of shock, I realize she's not much older than me.

She raises her gun, and I flinch, bracing myself for pain.

DANYA

The stunner trembles in my hand.

::Take the shot,:: Nox urges in my head. *::It won't even kill her. Honestly, why are you such a petal? She's going to get away.::*

My sister's been in my head all morning, breathing down my proverbial neck. She made sure to berate me when I cast up after my team stunned all those students by the cave. I managed to stumble behind a rock before my rations made a dramatic reappearance, so I don't think anyone noticed my moment of weakness—though I did notice Petra giving me a strange look afterward.

::Come on,:: Nox is yelling. Her frustration bleeds through into my mind, making my finger twitch on the trigger.

They showed us a holo of our target's face during our briefing, but the Phoenix looks different in person. Sweatier. Frizzier. Her stance is halfway between fight and flight, suggesting she hasn't quite decided which one to go for.

::She doesn't look like our enemy.::

::They never do.:: Nox is trying to make this sound easy, like she's stunned a thousand people before. Has she been forced to kill yet? I'm sure it'll only be a matter of time.

::Listen, if you just capture her, we can figure out why the General wants her. All right? You can't find out if she's innocent if she runs away.::

::FINE.:: I brace myself, screw my eyes shut, and pull the trigger.

The stun blast knocks my target off her feet, slamming her into the ground hard. I wince at the *thump* of her head hitting hard rock.

"Nice shot, Xiang," Varion calls. "Get her cuffed and let's get moving. I want to be back at the ship by nightfall." He's already on the ground cuffing the other guy, the one with the gun. I guess we're taking both of them.

I fumble for the magcuffs he tosses in my direction, fighting the dull burn of nausea in my gut. It isn't like I killed anybody. She's still breathing. I bend to check her pulse; her heartbeat's erratic but strong.

Even so, I know how much a stun blast hurts, and she only turned around because she wanted to help her friend. She might've gotten away otherwise—she's a fast runner. And I hesitated too long taking that shot.

As I secure the cuffs around her wrists, I study her face: eyes closed, lips parted, dark skin dewed with a sheen of sweat. Her curly hair is damp too—with blood, I realize.

I gently tilt her head to the side, feeling for the wound. It's not serious, but she's going to need a bandage.

There's an absorbent pocket square tucked into Nox's uniform. I've been using it to wipe my sweat as we march, so I doubt it's sanitary. But it's all I've got. I fold it into a thin strip, then tie it firmly around the prisoner's head like a headband, hoping the pressure will help slow the bleeding.

"You need help carrying her?" Petra approaches, hissing when she sees the blood on my fingers. "Captain's not gonna be happy. We need her in one piece for interrogation."

"She'll live," I say gruffly. That's what Nox keeps saying in my head. "Come on. Let's get her up."

We drape one of her arms over each of our shoulders, allowing us to drag her along. She's quite a bit taller than me, which makes it tricky—

but when Petra offers to replace me with someone taller, I shake my head. I sort of feel responsible for the prisoner now.

For *Amethyst Ediya*. That's her name; Varion let it slip when he was questioning those poor terrified students about where their colleague was. Her gun-toting friend called her *Amy*.

Maybe it's a selfish instinct that keeps me close to her. I'm the one who stunned her, and if she doesn't regain consciousness, I'll be a murderer. Or maybe it's loyalty to my sister—my behavior reflects on her, and I want everyone to see her as a hardworking, dependable soldier.

Or maybe it's because Amy's hair is soft under my fingers, and her sweat smells just like the rain.

CHAPTER SEVEN

Danya

THE JUNGLE OF EUREKA

The captain calls a halt once we're a few hours away from the scientists' camp. I'm ready to flop down and sleep on the nearest flat surface, but predictably, I get put on cooking duty. It's raining again, and the fires the other Greenjackets coax to life out of wet vine fragments are smoldery and weak. Just boiling water for a measly pot of reconstituted stew takes almost an hour.

Captain Varion and a couple of the other soldiers are huddled together, arguing in undertones about whether we should dump Amy's guard, the maroon-haired one they're calling DeSanto. Apparently, he's an old enemy of the Greenjackets, and bringing him in will look good on Varion's record...but the others argue that carrying two prisoners instead of one is slowing us down.

The prisoners in question are still lying where the soldiers tossed them, hands cuffed, limbs curled in to keep themselves warm. They're pretending to be unconscious, but I don't think they are. I saw DeSanto's leg twitch when a little lizard-bug-thing crawled over him.

Ringed by soldiers on guard, playing dead is a smart maneuver. It's what I would do. It's what I *have* done. Nox wasn't always around to protect me, back when I was still a cadet in combat training with the other teens. Sometimes they'd catch me alone in the locker room and mess with me because they knew I wasn't a fighter. They knew they could make me cry if they pitched my underlayer on top of the lockers, too high for me to reach. I waited for them to start pushing me around, because that made it easy to stumble against the bench, pretend to hit my head, and collapse unmoving onto the floor.

Predators get bored quick if their prey is already dead.

But Nox would always hear my mental cries, no matter where she was. She'd hustle back to the changing rooms, and she'd pick me up off the floor, shivering naked. She got really good at scaling the side of the lockers so she could retrieve my unders and toss them down to me. And she was always blazing furious on my behalf. "Whose ass do I beat?" she'd say. "Tell me, Dawn. Who?"

Sometimes I'd lie that I didn't know who it was. Sometimes I told her, because I was angry enough to want them to pay. Either way, it didn't stop until I failed out of training and got assigned to the greenhouse permanently.

After that I was untouchable—the same way you don't beat up on a pile of waste you step in by accident. There's no point. It's already shit.

Out of habit, I reach out to check on Nox, searching for a connection with her mind. She's been distracted most of the day. I keep feeling her tune in, then decide nothing interesting has happened yet and disappear. So much for being there for me every step of the way.

I snoop around for a moment to find out what she's doing. A smile tugs the corner of my mouth. She's been given light duty in the greenhouse because of her injured arm, but that just means they have her checking water samples for contaminants. It's a boring job, easy to do one-handed—but Nox hasn't done this kind of work before, and she has to focus intensely or miss a step that I could do in my sleep.

::How goes it?:: I ask.

I feel her jump at the intrusion. *::Stars, I about pissed myself, Dawn.::* A yawn, a back-cracking stretch. I yawn in sympathy. *::Your job hurts my brain,::* she complains.

::Well, yours hurts my...everything else.::

She snickers, flashing a memory of the pond incident. *::Your pride?::*

::And my feet, and my back, and muscles I didn't even know I had.::

::It's good for you,:: she says ruthlessly. *::Did you find out anything yet? Like why they want this Phoenix woman?::*

::Nope. Dunno if Petra heard anything either. Nox, she totally knows it's me. She's not stupid.::

::Well, even if she knows, she won't turn you in. You can count on her.::

::Only because she likes you. She thinks I'm basically garbage.::

::That's not true.:: But her denial is halfhearted. *::Listen, Dawn, I gotta get back to work. Let me know if anything interesting happens.::*

I stir the stew mechanically, thinking about Sherwood Base. About going back there after this fun little vacation I've had on Eureka. Hacking my way through trees instead of tending to their roots. Mistaking pondweed for a hungry swamp monster. Stunning a bunch of helpless student researchers who weren't even armed, just because they were in the way. I lost control of my nervous stomach after I saw them sprawled on the ground, their teacher in front. She'd tried to protect them with her body, but that just meant we stunned her first and hardest. I keep telling myself she's fine, but stunners can kill if the electrical charge is strong enough, and I don't...

No. I need to stop thinking about that or I'll cry.

The funny thing is, despite how uniformly awful this trip has been, I'm dreading going home. Of course I want a shower and clean bedding and good food. After this is over, I'll probably sleep for two days straight. But it hurts to think that this two-day trip—three if we don't make it back to the ship by nightfall—might be the only time I witness plants growing in their natural state, not cultivated by humans. It might be my last chance to ever experience *weather*, to smell the earthy scent of rain as it hits the soil.

Once again, I weigh the dangers and rewards of deserting the Greenjackets. Maybe if I tell them I have to pee, I can disappear into the forest and be gone before they know I'm missing. I could run back to the students' campsite and beg them to—

To what? Take me with them? I huff a silent laugh at my own stupidity. I'd be lucky if they didn't kill me on sight. I just helped kidnap two of their people. In this green coat, I'm indistinguishable from an enemy. Besides, I heard the commander ordering one of the soldiers to disable the students' ship. They'll be stranded here for days, maybe months, if no one comes to rescue them.

I pound my fist into my thigh, fighting the burn of angry tears at the back of my throat. For all the Greenjackets swear they're fighting for galactic freedom, they have me trapped as surely as if they put me in a cage. My own actions in their service make me a criminal by the Empire's standards, and my love for my sister keeps me from turning traitor. My entire being strains at this chance to leave—the best chance I'll ever get—and yet I hold back.

It's for the best, I tell myself, forlornly stirring the pot as it starts to bubble. *I'm tired. Wouldn't get far. And there's creatures out there. They aren't attacking us as a group, but if I set out alone...*

It's not the creatures that keep me here though. Deep inside, I know it's nothing but cowardice.

AMY

I force my limbs to relax, though I'm cramped from being sprawled on my side for so many hours. Through slitted eyes, I can see the soldiers getting ready to move again.

Prince's cuffed hands are centimeters from mine. Ever so slowly, I shift my wrist until my pinkie finger brushes the back of his hand. I see his eyelids flutter in response—just as I was hoping, he, too, is faking unconsciousness.

"All right, get them up!" the Greenjackets' commander yells. "Time to march again. I want us to find that blasted ship before nightfall."

Find? Are we lost?

Rough hands hoist me by the armpits, and I finally decide to "wake." Groaning, I flail my arms and mumble, "Let me go!"

"Aha! She's coming around." The red-haired soldier sets me upright. "Can you walk?"

My staggering first few steps are not feigned—my legs are cramping and numb. I catch myself against a branch and take a few deep breaths. "I can walk."

"Good. Hey, Xiang! Good news! The prisoner doesn't need to be carried anymore. You want babysitting duty?"

"Not really." It's the soldier who shot me, the one with short black hair. She marches up and grabs my elbow, holding me steady. "But I'll do it if you ask me nicely, Borisov."

Borisov flips her a rude gesture. She seems a little taken aback, but recovers quickly and blows him a kiss. He cackles and goes over to check on Prince, who seems to have decided now is a good time for him to miraculously recover consciousness as well.

I've been listening carefully ever since I woke up, hoping they'll be careless with their words if they think I'm unconscious. But I still haven't figured out why they were after me and Prince specifically. From their callous jokes about shooting fish in an aquaponics tank, I've gathered that they didn't take Dr. Valik or any of the students. Stunned them, it sounds like, and scuppered the ship—which means the whole xenoarchaeology team might be stuck here until someone notices they haven't checked in. That could be weeks. *Months*. And who knows how badly these Greenjacket scum injured them.

But *why?* That's the thing I can't wrap my head around. Prince mentioned he got in hot water with the Greenjackets a few years back— that's probably why they took him. But they weren't here *for* him. All current evidence points to me being their primary prisoner.

I don't know what I've done to merit capture. Procrastinated on too many term papers? I think back to all of my student research and draw an absolute blank. Nothing I've worked on has been groundbreaking enough to make me a target. This project—the one where I was supposed to find evidence of the dragons' ancestors—is the most potentially sensational thing I've ever worked on. And even then, if they wanted an expert in the subject, they should have kidnapped Dr. Valik, not me. I'd barely even started running tests when they turned up.

Is...is it possible they've mistaken me for Dr. Valik? We both have curly black hair and brown skin...but Dr. Valik is about ten years my senior. Besides, our faces couldn't be more dissimilar. Dr. Valik is obviously Earth Classic, wearing her natural flaws and curves with pride, while I have the symmetrical features and slim, muscular form that scream genetic modification. They'd have to be quarkbrained to not notice the difference.

The woman who shot me—Xiang, they called her?—tugs my arm roughly and says, "Let's move, Ediya."

Scratch that theory then. If they know my name, they're not mixing me up with Dr. Valik. That puts me back to square one.

I try another tack and focus my attention on my captor. "Why are you doing this?" I ask Xiang, looking down at the top of her head. Stars, she's tiny. I'm no giant, but it's a little galling to be dragged around by a one-and-a-half-meter pixie. Even if she *does* have muscles and a gun.

"Orders," she grunts.

"No, I mean, why'd they order you to take me? I'm no use. I'm just a student."

Xiang shrugs. I realize that maybe she genuinely doesn't know. What the fucking blazes do I do with that? Do I wait until they take me to their leader, who hopefully *does* have a reason?

There's no point in pleading for my freedom with a random soldier who doesn't have the power to grant it. My hope that I could appeal to Xiang's humanity dies a silent death, like a candle flame under a snuffer.

"You shouldn't talk," Xiang says shortly. "Save your energy for walking."

I know she's just trying to shut me up, but it's wise advice. I stow the rest of my questions for later and focus on not tripping over vines as we hike onward.

DANYA

Captain Varion calls a halt at dusk. He keeps his expression neutral when he says, "We'll make the rest of the journey tomorrow morning." But we all know he's extra flared off. Despite being in radio contact with the shuttle all day, we've managed to get lost in this endless vine forest. The trails we cut through the vines seem to grow back almost as soon as we pass. The others mutter how claustrophobic they feel, trapped in the dense tangle with no exit in sight.

My body feels like a carrot that's been left to rot in the dirt for a couple weeks. I'm running through my last reserves of energy, and I know the rest of the soldiers have to be getting there too. But as we make camp, I cram down a nutrient bar and force myself to stay awake and alert.

The captain isn't putting Amy and DeSanto at the center of our camp as I expected. He says it's so the soldiers have closer access to the heat of our pathetic, rain-damp campfire, but I'm not a fool. If he's separating them out, there's got to be a reason.

Though I'm desperate for the meager warmth of the fire, I shift my resting place as close to the fringe of camp as I dare, within earshot of the shelter where Varion is guarding our prisoners. I nibble my second nutrient bar, already sick of the fake chocolate taste. And once again, I reach out to Nox, only to find her sleeping.

Or maybe my constant checking in has annoyed her, and she's purposely icing me out. I'm hoping it's the former, because she promised she would help me through this, and blast it, I *need* her right now.

Darkness closes in. I lean against my pack, my eyelids heavy, my head starting to loll as I drift off despite my best intentions. I really should get some rest, or tomorrow will be rough...

But then I hear the low growl of Captain Varion's voice and Amy Ediya answering him.

I jerk awake. Folding my body into a crouch, I shuffle closer, straining to hear what they're talking about.

"You have to at least tell me why you captured me," Amy insists. "C'mon. I don't even know what I did. Give me something."

Varion grumbles, finally saying, "The General sent us to capture you because you know something about Gaela Ediya's research."

"Mum's research?" As I creep closer, I can hear the strain in Amy's tone. "My mum died six years ago. I was *fourteen*. Still in Gen Ed. The most scientific I got was dissecting a batmoth for a biology project. Mum's research was far above my head."

Varion's response is an uninterested grunt.

"You have to let me go. Tell them you got the wrong person."

The bushes rustle and crunch as Captain Varion gets up and stalks into the night, mumbling about discussing this later.

Now I'm even more confused. If all they want is her mother's research, why go to all this trouble to kidnap her? Why not just send her a vid-call like a normal person and *ask?* She's not some Imperial spy. In fact, I'm starting to suspect she isn't an enemy at all.

Nox's treasonous ideas about General Bruna's cruelty are starting to sound plausible. Stars help me.

"I'm sorry, Prince," Amy murmurs. "I meant to ask if he would free you. You haven't done anything."

"He wouldn't," DeSanto replies. "They've wanted me dead for five years. Knew they'd catch up to me eventually."

I wait until the captain is out of earshot, straining to hear Amy and DeSanto—Prince?—whispering. I choose my steps with care so that my creeping footsteps are all but silent. I come up behind Amy and Prince in their shelter, which consists of a few vines bound together and covered with a spare jacket to deflect the rain. It's not a green coat—no Greenjacket would dare to treat their uniform so cavalierly. Through the vines, I see flashes of Prince's bare arms, his neon tattoos glowing faintly in the dark. He must have sacrificed his own coat to keep them dry.

"But the molipedes," Amy's whispering to Prince. "Do you think..."

"Hey!" I rustle the vine a little to get their attention. "Hey! Amy! That's your name, right?"

She squints through the brambles. To my surprise, her gold eyes reflect light like a cat's. "Xiang?"

"I heard what Varion said. You really don't have what they're after, do you? You were telling the truth."

"Of course I was!" Amy snaps. "They want my mum's research, but I never had her files. Everything went to my aunt and uncle."

"Could you give them your aunt and uncle's location? Would that make the captain release you?"

"First of all, I'm not gonna throw my mum's siblings out the airlock," Amy says. "Second, even if I *wanted* to sell them out, I actually have no idea where they are. Third, I don't think anything will get Captain Asshole to let me go. He got ordered to bring me back, and he'd follow his orders even if it meant jumping off a cliff. Twice."

She's not wrong. But I can't stand to give up. "Could you...tell him he got the wrong person? Like, you're not actually Amy Ediya or...? There's got to be some way you can get out of this. I don't want to see you get hurt."

"Maybe you should have thought about that before you stunned her," Prince interjects sharply.

It stings because it's true. "Just following orders" is a poor excuse. I didn't have much of a choice, but I still could have stood back and let someone else fire the shot and capture her. Or I could have missed her on purpose. Would that have given her enough time to get to the ship and call for help?

Probably not. But maybe. What-ifs are hard to prove, but they're enough to keep a girl up at night.

As are the rustling sounds coming from the dense jungle of vines around us.

Prince hears them too, and I see his cuffed hands grope toward his side where an empty gun holster hangs from his belt. "Amy, hold onto my arm," he says, lips barely moving.

"Why?"

"Just do it."

He's staring intently into the dark, shifting to face those rustles head-on. And Amy's got this look on her face, this wide-eyed terror...she was all defiance when she faced me down just before I shot her. She didn't tremble at the commander's threats. But whatever's out there, she's scared now.

"A molipede?" she breathes, clutching Prince's wrist.

"Can't tell," he mutters back. "Hold tight. I'm calling Fairy. Ze'll get us out of here."

"Who's Fairy?" I hiss. "I thought we took all your coms. This planet isn't even connected to the uniweb. How are you planning to—"

"Well, well." I freeze at Varion's voice, terror raking down my spine like a clawed hand. "Mind telling me what's going on here, Xiang?"

I jump to my feet. "I-interrogating the prisoners, sir."

Varion narrows his eyes. "And? What are you interrogating them about, exactly? That intel is need-to-know only."

Shit. Shitshitshit. I forgot that I'm not supposed to know anything about the mission. *::Nox, I told you I couldn't do this!::*

My sister wakes, her mind groggy. *::What's goin' on?::*

"I've had my eye on you for awhile, Nikola Xiang," Varion says. "General Bruna knows there's a leak somewhere. She told me to keep a close watch on you and your little friend Petra. She'll be very interested to hear about—AAARGH!"

The attack comes from the side, a blur of motion that I hear more than see. Varion falls, sticky hot wetness bursting from him onto me. I reel back, and something rams into my side. It tears into my skin, pain slicing through my arm. I tumble backward through the vines, landing sprawled across Amy, who's yelling, "Go, go!"

Prince cries, "Fairy!"

And then...we disappear.

CHAPTER EIGHT

Amy

EUREKA BASE CAMP

It's so sudden. One minute, the Greenjacket captain is looming over us. The next, there's a molipede's mouth-tentacles where his head used to be. Prince yells for Fairy at the same moment Xiang falls on top of us.

Then we're floating in aetherspace, our minds jumbled together like vegetables in a soup pot. I can't tell which way's up or down, which thoughts are mine or Prince's. But I can tell one thing: by accident or intent, Fairy took Xiang with us.

Fairy drops us back into reality. I rematerialize without the magcuffs on—ze must've teleported us right out of them. I land hard on my butt, cursing and shoving at the weight sprawled across me. My fingers land on Xiang's weapons belt, and I take advantage of her disorientation to swipe the stunner holstered there. I tuck it under my ass as she fights for balance, elbowing me hard.

"Get off!" I squawk.

"*You* get off." Bracing her hand on my collarbone—and shoving me down in the process—Xiang rolls to her knees, clutching her left arm with a hiss of pain. "What just...where's Captain Varion? Where'd all the trees go? Ow, *shit,* my arm."

"We're well away from that glitcher," Prince says. "Fairy put us down by my ship. It'll take them hours to get back here. With any luck, that'll give me time to fix whatever they broke and get us airborne."

"Who the blazes is Fairy?" Xiang demands. "What are you talking about?"

"Fairy is a dragon," I say, feeling like I'm stating the obvious. "Ze teleported us."

"Dragon?" Xiang's eyes are as round as ancient coins. Eureka's moonslight glows just bright enough for me to see how pale she looks. And notice the dark splotches staining her green coat.

"Shit, you're injured."

"It scratched my arm. The—thing that—killed—the captain." She sounds nauseated just saying it out loud, and boy, do I relate. That molipede attack was the grossest thing I've ever seen in my life, and I'm a biology major.

"We've been calling them molipedes," Prince tells her. "I shot one when we landed. Who knows how many of 'em are out there?" He curses. "Speaking of which, we've gotta make sure the students and Dr. Valik are all right. I sent Fairy on rescue duty while we were captured, but I don't see any lights on at the camp, and it looks like the shield dome is powered down. Stars help 'em if they don't have shelter right now."

"One thing at a time," I say. "Let's get to the ship. We're gonna need torchlights and—" I almost say "a gun," but then I remember that I'm already sitting on Xiang's. Quickly, I shove it into my jumpsuit pocket, thanking the stars she hasn't noticed its absence.

I glance at Xiang, then lower my voice. "What do we do with the Greenjacket?"

"We gotta get her some bandages. I have a first aid kit in the cockpit."

"Prince, she might call her people and try to sell us out again!" I whisper. "Are you sure it's a good idea to bring her back to the ship?"

"That's easy to fix." Prince seizes Xiang's injured arm and, ignoring her yelp of pain, divests her of her keycuff. He plucks her earpiece out too, then tosses both to the ground and grinds them into the rock with his boot heel. "Now she can't contact anyone. I'm not gonna leave her out here bleeding, Amy. End of discussion."

He's right. Leaving her in the dark, smelling of blood, is as good as throwing her to the local predators with an apple in her mouth. She may be a kidnapper, but we'd be worse than that if we didn't help her.

"C'mon, then." I bend to help her up.

She shakes me off. "I can walk on my own."

"Fine." I hold up my hands in surrender. "It's not like you're *our* prisoner."

She winces. Is it pain from her arm or did my sarcastic comment hit the mark?

We only have to walk a few dozen meters before the hulking shadow of Prince's ship looms over us. Prince breathes an audible sigh of relief as he keys in his passcode and the passenger bay slides open. We dart inside as fast as we can...

Only to trip over the students in sleeping bags, snorting awake as we stumble into their midst. Several of them start screaming, and it's pandemonium for a moment until someone thinks to turn on a torchlight.

"It's us!" Prince yells. "Calm down, it's us!"

"Prince?" It's Dr. Valik, wading through the mass of writhing sleeping bags. She looks exhausted, her curly hair straggling out of its usual ponytail, but she's alive. *Thank stars.* "How the blazes did you escape them?"

"Fairy helped," Prince says. "And, uh, we had some local wildlife provide a convenient diversion."

"Is everybody all right?" I butt in, scanning the cramped passenger bay. "The Greenjackets didn't—um—hurt anybody?" *Kill* anybody is what I really mean. But I can't bring myself to say it.

"Well, getting stunned didn't feel *great*," one of the students mutters. "And then, as soon as it got dark, your blasted dragon yanked us out of the caves and into your ship, like we're cargo to put away for safekeeping..."

"We thought you two were the only casualties," Dr. Valik puts in, shushing the other guy. "I'm relieved to see you were—"

That's when everybody collectively notices the Greenjacket soldier lurking behind us, dripping blood on the floor. There's an awkward hush as everyone tenses up, staring at her.

"Um." I glance at her, wondering how to explain the situation. She has a look on her face like she'd have rather been thrown to the molipedes. "So...Xiang accidentally came with us when we 'ported..."

"Tie her up!" one of the students yells. There's a rumble of agreement. Several students stand up, apparently ready to attack. Xiang shrinks back, one foot out the door like she's about to run for it.

Then Dr. Valik muscles her way to the front. She takes Xiang's arm, examines the wound, and clicks her tongue. "Bleeding all over the place. Come here, girl, sit down, you look like you're about to pass out. Who has the first aid kit?"

A student reluctantly shuffles forward to hand the red case over.

"Everyone can go back to sleep," Dr. Valik adds sharply. "Show's over."

Prince jumps in. "Not quite. I need to assess the damage the Greenjackets did when they scuppered the ship. We still need to get out of here as fast as we can. Anyone with mechanic skills, I'd appreciate the help."

"Right, then." Dr. Valik waves her hand at him. "Get on with it. The rest of you—sleep. Now."

I don't have a sleeping bag, and there's still enough adrenaline zinging through my system to power a hovercycle. I take one of the passenger seats next to Xiang, drawing my feet up to rest on the chair cushion so I don't kick any of the sleepers on the floor.

"What's your name?" the Scholar asks gently, as she peels Xiang's shredded jacket sleeve away from her bleeding arm.

"Danya Xiang." The Greenjacket suddenly widens her eyes in a panic. "I mean Nikola! I mean—oh, you all don't care anyway." Her shoulders slump. "Nox is gonna kill me when she sees what I've done to her uniform."

Dr. Valik looks as confused as I feel. "Which do you prefer then? Danya or Nikola?"

"Danya," says the soldier firmly.

"All right then. Danya. It's nice to meet you. I'm Athena." Her mouth twists into a wry smile. "I had another name...once. So did my partner, for that matter. It's all right to give up the ones that don't suit you anymore. Amy, hand me that canteen, please?"

I pass it over, watching as Dr. Valik trickles the water over Danya's wounds. They're deep, still sluggishly oozing blood. Danya hisses at the light touch of a gauze pad against the wound.

"It's not like that," Danya says through gritted teeth. "My real name is Danya. Nikola is...my sister's name. This is her uniform too. I was supposed to pretend to be her." She sighs. "Never mind. It's a long story."

"Wait...what? *Never mind?*" She can't tease us with such an intriguing revelation and then leave us hanging. As Dr. Valik begins to bind Danya's wound, I lean forward and press for details. "Why would you pretend to be a Greenjacket? Are you a spy?"

Danya seems reluctant to say more. Her eyes dart between me, Dr. Valik, and the dozens of students "sleeping" on the floor around us (they're definitely eavesdropping).

"Oh my stars, you *are* a spy."

I'm mostly joking, but it flares her off. Dark color rushes into her cheeks, and her eyebrows furrow. "I'm not a spy," she spits back. "I'm a fucking shit-shoveler, all right?"

"A what?" Shoveling waste sounds like bot work, nothing that any civilized society would make a person do.

"A farmer. A gardener. Agricultural technician. I grow plants for food." She obviously expects to be mocked for this, though I'm at a loss as to why.

"A farmer gets stuck playacting as a Greenjacket? This story I've gotta hear." It's not a joke anymore. I'm genuinely fascinated. Either she's telling the truth, or she's made up the oddest cover story to keep us from turning her into the Authorities as a Greenjacket. Either way, I'm desperate to hear details.

She glances around the room again, and I get the message. She's afraid to talk in front of too many people she doesn't know. Oddly enough, that inclines me to believe her.

Casually, I shove my hand into my pocket, brushing my fingers along the stunner I stole. Somehow, Danya still hasn't noticed that it's missing.

I didn't pay any mind to the flashes of her life that I got when I touched it briefly to steal it. Now, I concentrate carefully.

The stunner gets carried, cleaned, and put away every night by someone who looks exactly like Danya. But that woman feels different: her touch is rougher, and the way she handles her weapon is confident, careless. Recent in its touch-memory is the feeling of being passed over into gentler hands, a woman who looks like its old owner but handles it gingerly, like it's a grenade with the pin pulled. She hesitates to use it, and nausea overcomes her when she does...

Well, that would seem to corroborate her story. I shift my hand, ready to squirm it back out of my pocket, when I brush something else. Something cold and waxy.

I yank my fingers out, grimacing at the thought that a bug might've crawled into my pocket. But it's not a bug; it's a *bud* from one of those vines that grow everywhere on Eureka.

Another flash overtakes me.

Awe. Excitement. Pure hedonistic joy. The simple scent of rain and growing things overwhelms her, fulfilling some deep vacancy in her soul. But there's guilt too, fear that she'll be caught. So it's with surreptitious speed that she snaps off this bud, concealing it in her weapons belt, dreaming of studying it later...

Wow. This woman's more of a biology nerd than I am. I let the subject drop though. She thinks we're enemies—of course she can't trust us.

But if my touch-readings are accurate, then I think we can trust her.

DANYA

::WHAT ARE YOU DOING?:: NOX YELLS IN MY HEAD. *::YOU CAN'T TRUST them. They're the enemy. You need to run! Get back to the team as quick as you can!::*

But I physically *can't* do that. Prince broke my keycuff, cutting me off from any possible contact with my team or Sherwood Base. Running alone into the dark would be suicide. And Nox is the only one who knows what I'm doing here. As long as there aren't any Greenjacket spies among Amy's crew—my last worry—then I am finally free to do whatever I want. Trust whomever I want.

Right now, I think I've decided—no, I *have decided*—to trust Amy.

And not just because she's pretty. Because she had a chance to treat me the way I treated her—like a prisoner—and instead, she and her friends helped me. Listened to me. Her teacher cleaned my cuts, even though I shot her with a stunner mere hours ago.

There's something different about these people. Especially Amy. She has a dozen reasons to hate me for stunning and kidnapping her, but she doesn't look at me the way someone looks at an enemy soldier.

She looks at me like I'm someone she rescued.

Honestly, I'm starting to think that's what I am.

PART FOUR

Year 3729, Week 30,

Dayfour

CHAPTER NINE

Amy

LEAVING EUREKA FOR HALCYON

Prince's ship repairs are finished not a moment too soon.

Early the next morning, after a long night of jerking awake at every sound, Prince rouses us all with a triumphant yell as the engine groans to a start. "Everybody strap in!" he shouts. "This is only a temporary fix! We're going airborne right now!"

Sleeping bags go flying as everybody scrambles for a seat. Danya gets left without one, so I offer her mine and take Prince's copilot seat.

"Don't touch anything," he warns me without looking up from the dash. The way he's frowning at his instruments tells me this ship isn't really fixed. It's more likely he's managed to tape a couple of things together so we can limp home.

But it gets worse. As Prince takes us into the sky, something impacts the side of the ship, rocking us to the side and making the students scream.

"HOLD ON!" Prince yells. He starts flying like a drunk pterosaur pretending it's a fighter pilot. The ship nearly does a barrel roll as he banks hard to the left. Then it twists abruptly the other way, engines whining. I dig my fingernails into the vinyl seat.

Through the viewport, I see a flash, a streak of light blazing toward us. Prince rolls and dodges it by a hair.

"That's the Greenjacket ship!" he yells. "Looks like they found their way back to it!"

"And decided to use their cannons on us." I grimace. "Are you going to teleport or what?"

"I will if you can get everyone back there to stop fuckin' screaming!"

"Hear that?" I yell. "Shut up and maybe we'll get outta here!"

I've never heard silence fall so fast.

Then we're in the weightless aetherspace, and a breath later we're out of it. I crane to see where Fairy's taken us, but all I see through the viewport is indigo water.

Wait...as Prince tilts the ship to circle around, a sandy peninsula comes into view. Its sheltered inlet holds dozens of floating gardens anchored in a stunning colorful reef. Between clusters of tropical trees, the peninsula is covered with thatched-roof huts.

I know this place. This is Phoenix Refuge.

Home.

Prince laughs at my dumbfounded expression. "Fairy saw it in your memories," he says. "I hope you don't mind."

Of course I don't mind. After what we've just been through, this might be the single safest place I can think of. The dragons won't let the Greenjackets come near Halcyon, not if their intent is violence and kidnapping. And they *definitely* won't allow anything to threaten a Refuge.

The Refuges are Halcyon's version of religious temples. Dotted all across the planet, they're safe spaces for citizens and newcomers alike to rest, meditate, and pray. The Devotes who live there year-round are somewhat like social workers or therapists, making sure that everyone who visits the Refuge can receive help if they need it. Citizens of Halcyon often make a habit of visiting once a year to refresh themselves and experience the tech-free, simplistic lifestyle of the Refuge.

But a Refuge is also perpetually open to immigrants, refugees, and offplanet visitors who need a place to stay. It's understood that anyone without a family or community can stay at a Refuge for as long as they need, no questions asked.

That's how I ended up at Phoenix as a rambunctious, hard-to-handle fourteen-year-old who'd just lost my mother. Mum promised me I wouldn't have to go to any other family if I didn't want to—in fact, she wrote it into her will. I grew up with the Devotes as my guardians, because I couldn't bear to have anyone try to replace Mum.

Prince brings us down for a graceless flop of a landing at the edge of the beach. Before we've even disembarked, we've drawn a crowd of curious Devotes. As I wobble down the ramp, still shaky from the scare of nearly being shot out of the sky, I spot a familiar face.

It's a wonder Sister Liv smiles to see me, given what a ridiculous brat I was back when I lived here. I took every chance to break rules. I skipped prayer meetings and sneaked out to the beach to swim in the dark after curfew, my golden cat-eyes needing no torchlight.

But though she was stern and often exasperated with my behavior, Sister Liv has a heart the size of a continent. Big enough even to fit a screwup like me in there somewhere.

"Oh, Amy, it's so good to see your face." Liv squeezes me tight, smacking kisses on both of my cheeks as she releases me. "We send you off to university and look what happens! You forget all about us!"

"I could never," I promise, patting the Devote's shoulder. "It's just, uh, schoolwork gets so—"

"You don't have to explain." She peers around me, taking in the tableau of Prince's ship disgorging its tired, traumatized passengers. "But I *would* like to hear the story that brought you here today. Stars! Is that man carrying a blaster? How did the dragons let him bring that onto Halcyon?"

I shoot Prince a warning glance and gesture for him to put away his gun. His eyes widen, embarrassed, and he shoves it down his trouser pocket to hide it. Bringing weapons onto Halcyon soil is strictly forbidden by the dragons' law, but Prince seems to get away with more than most people because Fairy likes him.

That reminds me. I still have to get rid of Danya's stunner.

"It's a long story," I tell Sister Liv. "But to tell it short: we were on an offworld dig and got attacked by Greenjackets."

Her eyebrows shoot up. "Greenjackets?"

"Mm-hmm. Prince and I got kidnapped. We were lucky to escape. Then Prince spent all night repairing the damage the Greenjackets did to his ship so we could fly home."

"My stars." She glances at the students again, sympathy written all over her face. One girl has just started crying, and Sister Liv can't resist the siren call of someone in need of help. She abandons me to run over and put an arm around the sobbing student.

"Everyone into the shade," another Devote calls—I think it's Brother Jude. He ushers the whole party down the Refuge's main path. He's leading us toward the dining pavilion, an open-walled shelter full of tables and benches. We pass the gathering pavilion, where they have prayer meetings three times a day, and the dormitories, where netted hammocks hang from sturdy roof beams. Only a few dozen Devotes live here full-time, but often there's up to a hundred people visiting. Our tiny little village never felt lonely—in fact, sometimes I wished there were more space so I could get five minutes to myself.

When we reach the dining pavilion, the Devotes are already rushing to bring water for everybody. I drink a full glass without taking a breath, suddenly realizing how starving and thirsty I am.

Danya hangs back, distancing herself from our group. At first I think it's shyness, and I open my mouth to call to her. But then I see the way her face is turned up to the sun, her eyes closed in bliss.

The flash I got from that little vine bud sticks in my memory. That lush, sensuous love for plants and weather is unlike anything I've ever picked up from anyone else. Even now, in what has to be the hottest weather she's ever experienced, she's stripping down to her underlayer and sweating waterfalls and *still grinning*. I mean, for stars' sake, I grew up at this Refuge, I'm *used* to this heat, but I'm not standing in full sunlight like a quarkbrain.

I take a moment to appreciate what she must be sensing: humid salt air, the distant crash of waves on the shore, and the calling of jungle creatures. I can complain about the heat all I want, but the smells, sounds, and textures of this place always feel like home to me.

I refill my water glass from the pitcher and go over to hand it to her. "Hot-weather lesson number one," I say, "you gotta drink as much as you're sweating off. Lesson two: if you stand in the sun for long, it'll burn you."

Her face is slowly going red, and I don't think it's the heat. She snatches the water and gulps from it. "Do I look that stupid?" she asks, a defensive snap that's also a genuine question.

"Nah. It's kinda cute how you get excited by ordinary stuff like sunlight." Oooh, I've *really* got her blushing now. "This is your first time planetside, huh? Other than Eureka, I mean."

"Yeah," she admits. "I grew up on Sh—um, a space station. Everything was underground temp-regulated hallways. We didn't ever have real weather."

"Well, then, welcome to it, in all its glory." I unzip my jumpsuit, pulling my arms out of the sleeves so I can tie them around my waist. I'm wearing a breastband underneath, so it's not like I'm getting naked in front of her, but she turns away and stares intently at the horizon.

"Ever been swimming?" I ask.

"Oh, all the time! My sister and I swim together every morning. Or... we used to." She frowns. "Lately, she's been too busy."

"Ever been swimming in an *ocean?*" I lift my eyebrows tauntingly. "Full of fish and coral and creatures with teeth?"

Her eyes go wide. "You can do that?"

"We can do it *right now* if you take your uniform the rest of the way off."

Stars, the way she blushes. What's up with Greenjacket modesty culture? Nobody better be shaming her for her body, 'cause she's cute as blazes.

Hold up. Am I *flirting* with her? A Greenjacket who literally kidnapped me? What is *wrong* with me? I mean, it's been, what, eight months since my last fling with that Phys Ed major...maybe I'm a little antsy in the pants. Might be time to find someone to hook up with and get it out of my system for another couple of months.

But not Danya. Even if she was just some random cute girl, she's obviously too innocent. I'm not about to mess with her feelings just because she kidnapped me. That would be rude.

I back off a little and beckon her toward the shelter. "C'mon. We can swim later. Right now, you look like you could use some shade." And some more water. And a big meal. If I'm starving, she has to be too.

"Thanks," Danya says. The look she gives me is somewhat bewildered. She seems surprised I'm being nice to her.

I don't know much about what Greenjackets are like...but based on the way Danya seems conditioned to expect cruelty from everybody around her, I'm starting to get the feeling that they suck.

"AND THEN THIS CAPTAIN GUY STARTED YELLING AT ME, ASKING IF I knew where Mum's research ended up..."

Sister Liv and her fellow Devotes are rapt as I recount the tale of my harrowing escape from the Greenjackets. Most of the students have 'ported home to recover. Even Scholar Valik left, though she told me to check in with her tomorrow to plan their return to the dig site. That leaves just me, Prince, and Danya lingering here at the Refuge, holding court in the dining pavilion.

As I wrap up my story, Sister Liv pats my arm. "Thank the Creator you're all right," she says. "It was hard enough to lose your mum. She had such a heart for helping people. It'd kill me to lose you too."

My nose gets all stuffy, like I'm about to cry. "Why do you think they wanted Mum's research so bad?" I ask in a small voice. "I know the Human Teleportation Project was important to a lot of people, but they could've talked to Auntie Mel and Uncle O any time in the last eight years. Why are they coming after *me?* And why *now?*"

Sister Liv turns her hands palms up. "Who knows? Your aunt and uncle do seem to value their privacy. Maybe the Greenjackets couldn't find them so they had to go through you. Have you talked to Melanie and Oberon lately?"

I laugh. "I didn't even talk to them when they came for Mum's funeral. I don't think they like kids. They just stood in the corner like weirdos, ignoring everybody. And then they cleaned out Mum's lab and left."

"Well, you're not a child now," Sister Liv points out.

"Oh, you don't say?"

She boops me on the nose. "Don't be sassy. I mean that if you contact your aunt and uncle now, they might actually speak to you."

"Why would I want to do that?" I was perfectly happy *not* talking to my mum's weird siblings for the first twenty years of my life. I don't see any point in starting now.

"Well," says Sister Liv, like it should be obvious, "you might want to let them know that the Greenjackets are after your mother's research. Which is now *theirs*."

I shrug. "That's their problem."

Sister Liv's disapproving look stings, even after all these years. It's that "I'm not mad, just disappointed" face that guilted me into repenting for every rule broken as a child.

"They're your mother's family, Amy," she says solemnly. "*Your* family, whether you like it or not. Would you be so careless if the Greenjackets kidnapped them, as they planned to do to you, and tortured them for information?"

Well, when she puts it that way, I *do* feel a little uncomfy about the whole thing. "That won't happen," I argue.

"Don't be so sure." I glance over in surprise at Danya's soft voice breaking in. She's been listening intently this whole time, and I suppose I should have been more careful guarding my words in case she's spying on me...

But she seems to want to help me now, because she goes on, "The Greenjackets have eyes everywhere. Spies that report back to them from every town on every planet. That's probably how they found out about you in the first place. Someone was watching you. I saw—my sister saw a coded message about you. They called you 'the Phoenix' leaving 'the Refuge.' I'm guessing they were talking about this place, which means you're not safe, even here."

A chill runs down my arms, making me shiver. "So you think they *will* find my aunt and uncle? Maybe hurt them?"

"I don't know all their plans," Danya admits, looking down to examine her blunt fingernails. "I'm just a food production worker. But I do know if your mum's research is something they really want, then they're not going to give up just because you got away once. They're going to keep trying. If they can't get to you while you're here on Halcyon, they'll find another way to get to your aunt and uncle."

All right, together they've succeeded in making me feel bad. "But even if I wanted to warn them, I can't," I protest. "I don't know their call codes. I don't even have a clue where they are. They disappeared into the void after Mum's funeral. I figured I'd never see them again."

"Where was the last place they lived?" Prince asks. "Do you know the planet name? Maybe they left a forwarding address?"

I sigh. "All I know is, before I was born, Mum did some research on a planet called Atlantis. I think Uncle O and Auntie Mel were with her there. But that's been more than twenty years. There's no way they're still there."

"Well," Prince says, lifting his eyebrows, "I got a dragon, a starship, and nothin' to do all evening. Anyone interested in going to check it out?"

I shake my head. "You can't be serious."

"Hey, I love a good mystery as much as the next guy." Prince smirks. "Also, I'm intimately aware of how much of a pain in the ass it is to have the Greenjackets hunting you everywhere you go. I wanna help you sort this out so you can move on with your life."

"I appreciate it, I really do," I say, "but isn't your ship broken? Maybe we should wait for repairs before we..."

"I think she can hold out for one more trip." Prince jumps to his feet. "C'mon, what d'you say? Let's go!"

I sigh. "Fine." Then my eyes land on Danya, who looks slightly panicked, probably at the prospect of being left behind while the only two people she knows on this planet jet off without her. "Danya, you can come too."

Prince lifts an eyebrow at me. "You sure?"

"Danya," I say, "are you spying on us and reporting everything you see back to the Greenjackets?"

She gives me a confused look. "No. Even if I wanted to, you broke my keycuff."

"There ya go." I hold out a hand to her. "She started this whole thing. Might as well help us investigate."

She stands slowly, ignoring my hand. "I won't be much help," she warns.

I grin. "Neither will I. I plan to be totally useless the entire time."

"All right then."

And my stomach does a little flip when I see an answering smile lift the corners of her mouth.

CHAPTER TEN

Danya

THE SKIES OVER ATLANTIS

I didn't exactly lie when I told Amy I wasn't spying on them.

But I didn't tell her the truth either.

Nox is wide awake and paying attention to everything I do. I'm fairly certain she's not reporting any of this back to the officers—how would she explain it? "I have a secret telepathic link with my twin, who, by the way, I swapped places with"?—but I can feel the gears in her mind turning faster and faster. Amy's conversation with that Devote lady was a gold mine of information, apparently. The knowledge that it's Gaela Ediya's teleportation research the Greenjackets are after, and that Oberon and Melanie Ediya likely possess said asset, was exactly the info Nox has been looking for.

.::What're you planning to do?:: I ask. ::Your arm's broken, and Petra is gone.::

::The healer says my arm will be usable by next week. And Petra got back a few hours ago. She messaged me—you—as soon as she arrived. She knows, Danya. Somehow she figured out it was you.::

::I TOLD you she would.::

::The General's absolutely furious. Between you going missing and Captain Varion getting eaten, heads are about to roll around here. You're lucky Petra was *quick on her feet and told everybody that you got kidnapped by the escaped prisoners. If they thought you—I—deserted on purpose...::*

::*But I didn't desert on purpose!::* I just thought about it. A lot. ::*Prince and Amy didn't mean to teleport me with them. It was an accident. What was I supposed to do? Just casually teleport back?::*

::*I'm starting to think we should all learn how to use dragon-teleporting like Halcyonites do,::* Nox muses. ::*It seems very useful..::*

::*Nox, focus. You still didn't answer my question. Why can I still feel you scheming? Your arm's broken, and your identity is missing in action. Even if everyone knew you're the real Nikola Xiang, you wouldn't be able to sneak onto the mission to go after Amy's aunt and uncle. No way will the General send the same team that lost Amy. With how flared off she is, she'll probably demote them all to cleaning bot parts for the next six weeks.::*

::*Who says we're gonna wait for the General to send us?::* Nox says coyly. ::*Petra thinks it's time we officially declare our independence from* all *tyrannical government structures. Including the General's.::*

::*Nox! That's treason!::*

::*If we get to this Oberon and Melanie Ediya before the General does, and secure the asset before they do, then they'll have to negotiate with us,::* Nox says, as though that's obvious. Which, in my opinion, it certainly is not. ::*And if they don't...well...they want this research so badly for a reason. Maybe it's to create some kind of powerful tool or weapon to help them win the war. Maybe if Petra and I build it first....::*

::*Nox, please, I'm begging you. Be careful. You're going to get killed!::*

::*It's sweet that you're worried..::* I can feel her pulling back, ending the conversation. ::*I think your pilot is about to land. Talk later, Dawn.::*

::*Nox——::*

But she's gone silent, and as I tune back into real life, I realize she's right. Prince is circling for a landing.

It's been about half an hour of relentless scanning, back and forth across the endless waves below. Amy swears there used to be a research base somewhere, but Prince hasn't found any human life signs to lead him there.

"We finally found it!" Amy calls from the flight deck—she called dibs on the copilot seat, relegating me to the passenger bay. "It's uninhabited, but still afloat after all these years. Prince thinks we'll be able to land."

"It'll be delicate," Prince adds. "Whole place is takin' on water. It'll be on the bottom of the ocean in another month. Here we go...slow and easy does it..."

"What happens if we sink?" I ask nervously.

"Nothin' much. The ship can handle it. I'll just get Fairy to teleport us back into the sky, and we'll try again."

Nox has a point—the casual ease with which Halcyonites utilize dragon-aided teleportation is fascinating. On Sherwood Base, it's pretty much just pilots who learn to call a dragon, and even then, they don't do it very often. Most pilots only fly short-range fighters that don't stray far from their carrier ship. Interstellar flights are few and carefully monitored. Before I met Prince and Amy, I don't remember ever teleporting in my life.

Maybe we *should* teach everyone to 'port, like Halcyonites do. It does seem to come in handy. Someone's about to shoot you—just teleport out of the way!

On the other hand, it would make it a lot easier for people like me to desert. I wonder if that's *really* why they discourage it.

Prince manages to find a landing pad that's not underwater and sets us down with teeth-gritting, knuckle-whitening precision. He breathes a long sigh of relief. "I half-expected the whole place to tip over, but it's holding. Whose idea was it anyway to build a floating base?"

Amy's already unstrapped from her seat, bolting toward the exit. "Is it safe to go out?"

"Sure. I guess. Just, uh, take a breather mask with you, all right?"

That doesn't sound "safe" to me. I wait for Prince to rummage through his emergency kit and produce the masks, then hang one around my neck. Amy shoves hers into her back pocket and dashes out the door.

Prince and I follow, sloshing through pools of water collecting on the landing pad. One puddle comes almost to my knees. I think Prince's estimate of this base sinking by month's end is generous. I wouldn't put credits on it lasting a week.

The water soaking through my jumpsuit is cold, but the air above it is mild. It'd probably be warmer without the stiff wind that whistles around the corners of the base, making it rock under our feet. Gray clouds gather high in the sky. I hope we're not in for a storm.

Amy forces one of the doors open, which she's able to do because the base—including its security system—is completely powered down. The passcode-protected doors stand ajar. Inside, the air smells stale, and the corridor is void-black.

Prince splashes back to the ship to get some headlamps. As we strap them on, he murmurs, "Best wear those breathers now. I've seen the holo-dramas."

"What holo-dramas?" I haven't ever been allowed to watch any. Greenjacket leadership considers all Monroe-made entertainment—which is most of it—Imperialist propaganda and censors it heavily.

"You know. The horror ones. Where people go into abandoned research bases and they're full of evil mutated viruses that cause fungi to grow out of your eyeballs."

I pull the breather mask over my nose without further comment.

Amy seems not to notice how creepy the place is. She bounds ahead of us, headlamp flashing this way and that, breather working overtime as she pants in excitement.

"I always wanted to see what this place was like!" Her voice is muffled behind the mask, but it's hard to miss the enthusiasm. "Mum would never talk about it. She was always so cagey about her past."

Prince is more practical-minded. "There's usually a data storage area in the center of these facilities," he says, striding forward to guide Amy away from an errant left turn. "That seems like the best place to find information about your aunt and uncle, if they left anything behind."

We make our way deeper into the base. I hope Prince and Amy are paying attention to where we're going, because I'm already lost. This base is built on a much smaller scale than Sherwood, and I'm starting to feel claustrophobic as we pass these tiny living spaces. The feeling gets worse when I remember we're surrounded by water and only barely staying afloat.

"Aha!" Amy wrenches a door open, pushing her mask down to her chin. "Here's the control room. Let's get some lights on in here."

"Wait—"

She doesn't bother waiting for Prince to finish his sentence. She begins yanking on levers and blowing dust off screens and sensors. There's a groaning whirr, and slowly, the lights flicker from dim to bright.

"That was a terrible idea," Prince tells her severely. "That door we just came in was passcode-locked. If we can't get back out..."

Amy rolls her eyes. "Relax. You have a dragon. C'mon, I want to find the library."

I have to admit, finding our way around is much easier with the lights on. The corridors come alive with maintenance bots, sweeping away dust and hurrying to fix whatever's broken down during the base's long sleep.

"What *did* your mum tell you about this base?" I ask, the quiet question echoing loudly in the emptiness. "She had to mention it at least once, since you know it by name."

Amy shrugs. "She usually didn't talk about her old life to me. She didn't even want me to know I was born away from Halcyon. But she did once say, when I asked about my dad, that she worked with him here on Atlantis." She sighs. "That's all. She wouldn't even tell me his name. I was kinda hoping...maybe they'll have birth records here. Maybe I'll finally get to know the other half of me, you know?"

Prince pats her shoulder. "I feel that. Don't set yourself up for disappointment though. You could find a whole other family out there... but you could just as well find sadness." He drops his arm, looking down when he speaks again. "When I went looking for my pa, after working my way out of the factory he sold me to, my aunt told me he was probably patching mind-alts in an alley somewhere. Since then, I've decided it doesn't matter what my parents do. Only matters what *I* do."

A bitter laugh bursts out of me. "Isn't that the truth?"

They both look at me with identical raised-eyebrow curiosity. "What's growing up in a Greenjacket base like, then?" Amy asks.

I swallow hard. I've never talked about this to anyone—not even Nox. It was always unspoken between us, a pain that we shared but never examined. "Recruitment has fallen in the last few decades. That's why I was born: because the Greenjackets need young, strong bodies to fight for them. My parents were matched for genetic compatibility. They love the Cause...but they don't give a fuck about each other. And they only think about me and Nox when they want to congratulate themselves on birthing strong soldiers to fight the Empire. I've met them maybe five times in my life. Every time, they seem disappointed."

We walk in silence for a moment, and I bite my lip, fighting the horrible, squishy feeling of having been too vulnerable. I've learned not to say things like this out loud; it invites bullies.

But then Amy drops back to put a gentle arm around my shoulders. "Prince is right," she says. "Your parents only show their own lack of worth when they dismiss yours."

Warmth surges through my veins, like that wonderful moment when a cold shower turns hot. Amy's unlike anyone I've ever met.

And having met her, I'm afraid to go back.

AMY

Abandoned research base, Atlantis

My veins are on fire with anticipation. After all those years of Mum avoiding questions about her past and changing the subject... finally, I have a chance to get some answers. Why didn't I think of coming here sooner?

I hope no one wiped the data library when they abandoned the base. If I'm lucky, they'll have only taken the really important stuff—research backups, security vids, that kind of thing—and left some basic info about the inhabitants of the base.

When we find the data library, its wallscreen takes a while to power on. It hasn't been updated in over ten years, so it has to run all sorts of diagnostics on itself. I can barely contain myself, flitting around the room to look at the scrolls and log-screens. Those have to update too.

"Welcome to Marine Xenobiology Research Base I, Atlantis, Echo System," says a cool female voice.

I whirl around to find Prince and Danya admiring a holo projection of a bald woman wearing a plain white tunic.

"I am Lyric, your librarian," the projection informs us. "To access the uniweb, point here with your gauntlet. To access this library's saved files, point here. If you have any questions, speak aloud to ask me. Or, if you'd prefer, you can minimize me by pointing here."

"Ugh," Prince groans. "Why didn't they uninstall the annoying AI helper? No one uses her. She just stands there staring at you. It's unsettling."

But I haven't ever used a wallscreen with an AI helper before. *This is so cool!* "Lyric," I say loudly and clearly, "can you help me find files related to Oberon Ediya?"

"Searching," says Lyric. The projection just stands there, her eyes focused on the wall behind my head. Suddenly, she speaks again. "Results. Six hundred and thirty-two mentions of *Oberon Ediya*."

A list displays in the air next to Lyric. I scour the room for the control gauntlet. Danya finds it behind a pile of rubbish and offers it to me. I slip it over my dominant hand. After a moment of wiggling my fingers to calibrate its movements, I lift the gauntlet and begin to scroll through the list.

Most of the hits are entries in a research diary. My heart skips a beat, wondering if we could have found the fabled research everyone's after—but when I try to select one of the entries, it informs me that the information was stored on a separate drive that has been removed from the data library.

Behind me, Danya lets out a disappointed sigh.

A search on "Melanie Ediya" produces similar results. Her research has been removed from the computer's memory too.

"Lyric, which rooms did Oberon and Melanie last live in?" I ask.

Lyric thinks about it. "Gaela and Melanie Ediya were assigned to Room 103. Oberon Ediya and Emerson Black were assigned to Room 104," she responds. "This assignment ended in year 3709. Melanie Ediya requested a transfer to a new base after Gaela Ediya abandoned the project. Oberon Ediya requested a transfer at the same time, and Emerson Black was registered as deceased."

Prince raises his eyebrows. "Sounds like some drama went down twenty years ago."

The curiosity is going to kill me. "Lyric, do you have any surveillance footage or diary entries from that time? *Anything?*"

"That part of my storage has been removed," Lyric says.

I swallow hard. "All right then. Show me all Gaela Ediya's visits to the med center, in chronological order, from 3708 to 3709. I just want to confirm something."

"Confidential information. ID scan required."

I offer my keycuff. "Check me. I'm Gaela Ediya's daughter."

A flickering scanlight runs over my arm. Then the med records open before my eyes...and my suspicions are confirmed. In late 3708, the infirmary bot confirmed my mother's pregnancy. She had all the usual prenatal checkups, and nine months later, there's a record of a birth certificate.

Amethyst Ediya. Born to Gaela Ediya and Emerson Black.

I'm starting to cry, and I don't know why. No, I *do* know. For so many years, I've searched my face for any sign of his, any feature that differentiated me from a clone of Mum. Now I have his name.

And the knowledge that he's dead.

"Wh-what did Emerson Black look like?" I ask shakily. "Lyric. Search him."

"Searching."

"Amy," Prince murmurs. I almost forgot he was here. "If this is too much for you, we can..."

"Shut up. I'm fine." I'm wheezing, tears dripping down my face, but there's no way I'm leaving.

"Results," Lyric pipes up. "Three hundred thousand, four hundred and seven mentions of *him*."

"Blazing glitching useless piece of—!"

"I told you the AI helpers are awful." Prince's lip is twitching; he's doing a really bad job of keeping a straight face. "Lyric, search for Emerson Black. Something with an image."

"Searching."

Prince puts a hand on my shoulder, and I lean into it, needing the contact for comfort. Then I feel pressure on my other arm and glance over in astonishment. Danya's hand is on my bicep, a shy, barely-there touch that still fills me with warmth.

Lyric displays my father's face.

It's a still pic, larger than life. An unsmiling man staring straight at the camera. There's little in his face I can find to compare to mine; I've taken after Mum almost completely. His skin is lighter than mine. His eyes are plain brown, not gold. His face is more angular than mine, his lips thinner.

He looks serious. Smart. Was he really? Or did he just try to look professional for the camera? I'd hate to be judged on the student pic they took when I entered university. I was wearing the ugliest shirt, my hair was all frizzed, and I was grinning like I was so excited to be there. My eyes were half-closed, because *of course*. They always take five, then use the only one where I blinked.

What was Emerson Black like behind the photo?

"Wow." While I've been staring at my father's face, Prince has been scrolling through the text accompanying the photo: an official government employee's bio. "He was a xenobiologist and archaeologist. Head of this research base, looks like. Smart guy. He and your mum must've made a good pair."

"How did he die?" I ask quietly.

Prince scrolls further down. There's information on Emerson Black's research and publications, his professional accomplishments... *Personal life. Where's the details on his personal life?*

<Personal: No registered legal partnerships. Surviving family members: one child, born after death. Current information on EDIYA, AMETHYST unavailable.>

"Lyric! Is there any information on Emerson Black's death? How did he die?"

"Classified. ID scan required."

"Nnngah!" I claw at my hair, wanting to strangle the hologram. "You already scanned me. I'm his *daughter!*"

"This information requires security clearance from the Imperial Institute of Scientific Research."

At that point, I fully lose it—sobbing, snotting, howling. This is the kind of breakdown I usually save for when I'm locked tight in my sleep-pod at night. I hate that Prince and Danya are witnessing it.

"Right, that's it, we're going back to the ship," Prince says. He takes me by the shoulders and begins marching me down the hall. "You need a break. This type of thing is better to take in small doses."

"D-don't take us back to Halcyon yet," I blubber. "I still have questions!"

"Yes, yes." He's rubbing my back soothingly. Danya runs ahead of us to open the doors, through which, thankfully, we don't need the passcode to leave. We'll need one to go back in though.

"Don't let it shut!" I cry, flinging my body in front of the sensor. Stars, I'm *never* this dramatic. I've got to get ahold of myself before I embarrass myself even worse.

Danya finds a pile of sandbags in a storage closet and uses them to prop the door open so it can't lock us out.

"Thank you," I mumble.

She shrugs mutely. Obviously, she doesn't know what to say to a bawling, tear-streaked mess like me. But when I meet her eyes, I see sympathy there.

I'm glad she told me about her parents. Prince too. It helps to know I'm not alone, not the only fucked-up kid who lost too much, too early.

I let them usher me back onto the ship and cover me with blankets. It feels nice to not have to be strong for once.

PART FIVE

Year 3729, Week 51,

Daythree

CHAPTER ELEVEN

Amy

ATLANTIS

A sudden lurch and shift.

Consciousness comes back to me slowly. Reality feels heavy, like floating in a bathtub of warm honey. I meant to nap for just a few minutes, but clearly I've overshot my goal.

Prince and Danya are talking in low, strained voices somewhere nearby. I grasp for the thread of their conversation, fighting the syrupy muddle of sleep.

"...going down with it..."

"Should we try to rescue the data?"

"We should wake her. It's her call."

I moan. "'M awake. What's goin' on?"

"Uh...you might want to come see for yourself..."

I roll myself upright. Lying across four passenger seats to take a nap wasn't the most comfortable rest I've ever had; my neck already aches. When I try to stand, I stumble sharply to the right, holding my arms out for balance. "Wow," I mutter. "I'm really out of it."

"It's not you," Danya says. "The ship is tilted."

"The ship is—*what?*"

They beckon me over to the viewport. "Look."

At first, all I see is darkness. But Prince wouldn't have that wide-eyed, worried look if we were in space. He practically *lives* in the blackness between stars. Which means...

A cluster of fat bubbles drifts past the viewscreen, and it finally clicks. "Oh no."

"Mm-hmm." Prince points up at the faint glow of light far above us. "That's where we were ten minutes ago. And that," he says, pointing at the deeper dark below, "is where the entire base is headed. We're not sinking as fast, because we're not taking on water."

The news is a punch in my gut. "The library! The data—"

"Might still be fine," Prince says quickly. "Data backups tend to be waterproof. But it'll be hard to access them when they're on the bottom of the ocean."

"Are we...I mean, we can get out of here, right?"

"Yup. The ship's engine isn't made for underwater travel, but it'll stay airtight until Fairy can 'port us somewhere dry." The dragon in question is draped across Prince's dash like a long, opalescent feather boa, observing us with zir eyeless head-end. Ze seems strangely agitated, zir colors flickering from faded to bright pink-blue-orange. "The question is," Prince continues, "what do we do about getting that data? I'm assuming you still want it."

"Is that even a question?" I fumble in my back pocket. The breather mask is still in there. "Will this thing work at this depth?"

"Whoa now, hang on," Prince says. "First of all, no, you're gonna want a bubble suit. Second, I was thinking we should get some help and tow the base back to the surface—not dive for it. Have you ever gone diving this deep?"

I plant my hands on my hips. "Yes, actually. When I lived at Phoenix Refuge, I was constantly sneaking out to do night dives. Sometimes I didn't even use a breather mask—I just held my breath."

Prince grimaces. "Uh, well, for obvious reasons, let's not do that. I do have a bubble suit in cargo."

"Where is it?" I stride toward the cargo hold.

"Do you have two?"

Danya's question—quiet, but firmly resolved—stops me short.

"You don't need to risk yourself," I tell her. "This is my family history. My shit to deal with."

"It's dangerous to dive alone," Danya fires back. "And I'm a strong swimmer. I practiced every day back on Sh—back home."

"In a swimming pool that was how deep?"

She doesn't answer, but her mouth firms into a thin line. "You shouldn't go alone."

"She's right," Prince says, the traitor. "And I *do* have two suits. Four, actually, but someone has to stay aboard the ship."

Good. One fewer person I'm putting in danger. I'm happy to take my own risks all day, but the idea of Danya's life depending on my bad decisions is a bucket of cold water dumped over my head. I force myself to slow down and think this through.

"How do we get out of this ship? You don't have an airlock."

Prince nods. "This is a short-range shuttle. Built for teleporting, not for long-haul interstellar travel. I've never even needed to use the bubble suits. We do repairs when we're firmly anchored to the ground."

Danya says, "Could the dragon do it? Teleport us out of the ship into the water?"

We both look at Prince for confirmation. He shakes his head. "I still think this is quarkbrained. But yeah, ze could. You're gonna have to calm zem down first though. Ze doesn't like this planet. Ze's been getting really flickery since we sank."

I look over at Fairy once again. Ze's floated up to the ceiling, where ze circles, zir colors shimmering bright-pale-bright.

::*Fairy?*:: I ask tentatively. ::*Will you help us?*::

::*Danger,*:: Fairy flashes back. ::*Lost Ones here.*::

I can't quite parse what ze means. The images ze's sending are of dark shapes in the water and a complicated history of remembered emotions: pity, love, loss, fear, guilt.

"Fairy says there's some kind of local life form that you need to watch out for," Prince translates. "That must be what's freaking zem out. Amy, I really don't like this. I can see if the Knights will let me borrow some equipment to haul the base back to the surface. We don't have to—"

"No," I say firmly. I can deal with whatever local beastie lurks in the depths. "I don't want to bother the Knights. Even if they decide to help, it'll take, like, a week to get the base afloat, if we're lucky. If I just dive for it now, I'll save everybody the trouble."

"Fine." Prince reaches to trail his fingers along Fairy's underside. "But if Fairy even senses the faintest whiff of trouble, I'm sending zem to drop you back on the ship, no matter what."

DANYA

ATLANTIS, UNDERWATER

Bubble suits are weird to get used to. They're versatile, malleable personal shields made for spacewalks but able to withstand almost any type of environment. They look like a puddle of clear, shiny goo until they're put on. Once activated, the shield becomes a literal bubble around the wearer, allowing them to walk or float in a small protected environment.

Once Amy and I give the thumbs up that our oxygen tanks are working, Fairy drops us into the water outside the ship and promptly disappears. Ze's clearly uncomfortable with whatever's hiding in the dark around us.

I have a headlamp to light our way, but Amy claims she doesn't need one. Her reflective golden eyes apparently give her perfect night vision. I'm going to have to ask about that later...but I can't right now, because our suits block verbal communication. It's basic sign language or nothing.

Even though Amy kept talking about how this was her first time wearing a bubble suit, I'm envious at how quickly she learns to move with it on. My usual crawl stroke doesn't work with the bubble suit around me. Amy seems to instinctively know how to move through the water; she creates a wave motion by undulating her entire body, arms at her sides, propelling herself forward like a dolphin. She reminds me of the Old Earth depictions of mermaids, beautiful part-fish women who lure hapless humans into the depths.

I remember learning that myth as an innocent child, thinking to myself, *No matter how pretty the mermaid, how could anyone ever be so stupid as to jump in the water with one?*

I'm eating my words now.

Clumsily, I copy Amy's movements until my body makes sense of them. I follow in her wake like a love-drunk sailor, deeper and deeper into the cold, crushing dark.

Once we descend past a certain depth, winks of bioluminescence begin to appear around us. We're close to the bottom, and far below I see the glow of strange corals and shell-creatures, lighting their bodies to attract prey. And against that backdrop, the bulky outline of the research station, listing to one side as it settles onto the uneven, rocky ocean floor.

I wasn't that scared of those empty, silent corridors before. But now that the base is under shiplengths of water, I have to admit the prospect of going inside terrifies me. The base isn't made to withstand pressure the way Prince's starship is. I don't know if it's my imagination, but I think I can see the outer walls buckling. If it crumples while we're inside...

The quicker we get this over with, the better.

Amy barges ahead, and I steel myself to follow. The lights are out again, and my headlamp reflects the little cleaner bots drifting uselessly. They're not waterproof, poor little things.

The deeper we go, the worse my shakes get. I grit my teeth, hoping Amy won't notice the trembling of my headlamp's beam. We were *so* lucky we weren't in here when it sank. A shiver crawls over my skin as I imagine being trapped in that library, water creeping in...

The dragon flits in front of me. Underwater, ze looks more like a strange, shimmery ripple than a defined creature. I feel zem brush my consciousness, but I don't know how to speak to zem. Ze moves to Amy, who looks back at me and gestures, *Are you all right?*

I nod vigorously, hoping it'll cover my lie. Amy doesn't know what a coward I am—I want to be brave for her. She frowns, not totally convinced, but we carry on.

I half-expect to float into the library and discover Lyric standing in the exact spot we left her, offering unhelpfully to search drowning statistics. But the wallscreen is dead, probably ruined. A spare control gauntlet floats past my head, the fingers wiggling in the stirred-up current.

Amy yanks on the wallscreen, trying to pull it off the wall, but it's firmly mounted. I point to the retract button on the side, and she jabs at it. The screen demagnetizes from its stand but doesn't roll up on its own like it should. Amy pulls at it, but that only unbalances the whole structure, sending it toppling down over her.

I thrash in my bubble suit, going nowhere. I won't be able to push her out of the way. A wordless shout rises up in my throat, choked by my breather mask.

The water resistance slows the frame's fall just enough for her to dart out from under it. I exhale in relief—lucky she's better at swimming in these suits than I am. She catches my eye and grins through the breather mask, her chest rising and falling heavily.

Her eyes catch and reflect the light from my headlamp. Her expression is wild and alive, every bit as dangerous as a siren's song. I almost forget where I am.

But Amy doesn't. She turns to the newly bare wall and zeroes in on a blinking orange light indicating the location of the actual data storage. It's behind a thin panel, almost impossible to pry out without the proper tools. I could kick myself—why didn't we think to bring anything?

Amy starts looking around for something to use, gesturing for me to shine my headlamp to aid in her search. I sweep the beam slowly across the floor, working my way toward the back of the room.

I've just noticed a sharp edge of metal we might be able to use, and I'm reaching for it when Amy freezes in my peripheral. I shoot her a questioning look, and she points at the dark hallway beyond the still-open door.

I raise my palms. *What?*

She points again, gesturing for me to shine the headlamp in that direction. But there's nothing there. Just a dark, water-choked hallway.

She points to her eyes and then mimes a large shape. *I saw something big.*

I go to the door and peer out, but again, all I see is empty water. I tap my temple. *Maybe you imagined it?*

She shakes her head but resumes the search. The metal piece I saw before seems like it'll work; she picks it up and begins wedging it into the crack between the panel and the wall. With only a minute or two of prying, the panel pops out.

The data bank hidden inside the wall is stubbornly connected by fistfuls of wire. Amy rips right through it, so I guess the wiring must not be important. At least, I hope it's not. We're *definitely* not coming back here if we forget something.

Disconnected from all its peripheral tech, the data bank is about the size of Amy's two cupped hands. She has to hold onto it through the bubble suit, a slippery task when trying to swim at the same time. She kicks off from the wall, floating toward the open doorway...

Only to find it blocked by a monster.

I scream into my breather mask, recoiling. The gigantic shape barely fits in the doorframe. Wide, toothy mouth. A scattering of yellow eyes across the front and sides of its head. A long, smooth, gray body, eel-like, with wavy mottling on the side.

Amy tries to backpedal, but her kickoff from the wall has given her too much momentum. She sails right past me, straight into the sea monster's mouth.

CHAPTER TWELVE

Amy

ATLANTIS, CURRENTLY BEING EATEN

The weird giant eel-thing opens its mouth, engulfs my bubble suit, and swallows me whole.

The scientific part of my brain is fascinated as I slide, encased in my malleable protective shield, through wet gray tissue into a pouch under the creature's tongue. My class dissections didn't prepare me *at all* for the reality of seeing a living, pulsing digestive system from the inside.

The rest of my brain is going, *Ewwwwwww.*

The sea monster is moving, its muscles undulating and pressing against my bubble suit. I try to get a hand up to my face to hold my breather mask in place, but my elbow is pinned to my side. I feel the data core slipping and tighten my grip on it.

A little whimper escapes my throat. I clamp down on the urge to cry. *Suck it up, Ames. You may have been eaten by a giant fish, but you've gotten through worse than this. You will stay calm. You will—*

::*Who are you?*::

The voice is like Fairy's—an alien mind, communicating through images and emotions, but visceral in a way dragons' memories seldom are. This is the consciousness of someone who *feels* rather than watches how others feel.

::Um...hi?:: I respond carefully. *::Are you the thing that just ate me?::*

The response I get is a mental image of this creature swallowing its young to protect them from danger, holding them in the same pouch that I now occupy.

Ah, so I haven't been eaten. I've been joey'd.

::Interesting. I have a lot of questions.::

::We, also.:: It sends me an image of more creatures like it, hundreds of them, separated by distance but telepathically linked. The Shoal—which is what it wants me to call them—seem to be a collective, making decisions together and sharing each other's memories and experiences.

It repeats its first question. *::Who are you?::*

Explaining who I am and what I'm doing here, using only pictures and feelings, is surprisingly difficult. Sister Liv would be ashamed of me. Learning how to communicate with dragons is kid stuff, something they teach to the littles at the Refuge. But I never used the skill that often, so I never got very good at it.

It takes several tries before I feel a flicker of understanding from the giant fish.

::Emerson Black..:: It shows a mental picture of my father's face. This is no stiff, professional portrait—this is a man in diving gear waving excitedly as he descends, trailing bubbles, from the Above into the Shoal's domain.

::My father,:: I confirm. The notion of "male parent" should be easy to get across. Unless this species doesn't have a male and female binary...

::Emerson's calf?:: the creature tries, showing me an image of a tangle of tails and eyes. Its young, newly born.

::Yes. Yes!::

I feel the creature's muscles ripple around me, and then it spits me out into the open water, its myriad yellow eyes examining me closely.

It's trying to tell me something. Something involving a shoal of its kind swimming close together, their songs blending...

::Family?:: Is that what it means? *::Yes, I'm Emerson's family....::*

Its frustration sizzles through me. *::No. Family. You and Shoal.::*

I must be misunderstanding. *::I can't be part of your family. I'm human,* *you're a water-dweller. My kind evolved on Old Earth, your people evolved...here?::*

::*No,::* says the creature. And in its mind, I see an ocean that I recognize.

::*Halcyon! You evolved on Halcyon? How did you get here?::*

I barely understand the barrage of images and thoughts that come next.

::*There was a rift among the Shoal...some were using violence to take control of the best grazing places, the warmest waters. Others refused to fight and were driven away by the violent ones. Then something happened to them. The peaceful ones changed, and they went into the Above.::*

I raise my eyebrows. ::*Space travel? Your kind is capable of building ships?::*

::*Not the sky,::* the creature tries to explain. ::*The Above.::*

The two concepts sound the same to me, but the creature is already moving on. ::*After the nonviolent ones went into the Above, they came back and removed the violent ones from Halcyon by force. They took them here, to this distant planet—something like a penal colony. Those violent ones cried out to them, begging to go back, but the others never listened, even until this day.::*

::*How long ago?::* I ask. The answer is a long line of calves growing to maturity and calving...almost a hundred generations.

::*That's got to be around three or four thousand years! And your kind never came back for you in all that time?::*

::*Some have been found worthy and were taken to the Above. The rest of us still labor to be worthy.::*

While I'm still trying to digest that, there's a horrible, screeching rumble that vibrates through the water. I turn my head just in time to see the walls of the base collapse inward.

"DANYA!" I scream her name aloud, thrashing to get closer to the base. ::*My friend! She's still in there! Help me!::*

::*Worry not.::*

::*Are you fucking serious? She could be crushed!::*

::*She is safe,::* the great eel-fish says calmly.

To my astonishment, a second creature appears out of the murk. This one has the same yellow eyes as the one I've been speaking to, but its long flank and tail are dotted with luminescent blue-green instead of solid gray.

It swims right up to me and, with a horrible retching motion, disgorges Danya's bubble-suited body. She's limp, her eyes closed, but I can see her chest rising and falling, her breather mask fogging. She's alive.

I nearly pass out from relief. If I could hug her through this blasted suit, I would.

::*We are sorry for swallowing you,*:: says the second eel-fish, ::*but we saw the metal box buckling. You would have been trapped, little cousin.*::

::*Then thank you for rescuing us,*:: I say. ::*But why do you call me your cousin? You know I'm Emerson Black's child. I can't be part of your Shoal.*::

::*Emerson Black told us about his calf,*:: it says. ::*The woman took our blood and mixed it with her blood and his, and they made a calf.*::

"The woman" in its mind is unquestionably Mum. And the creature's mental image of blood-mixing looks an awful lot like genetic modification.

With a sick jolt, I realize that the eel-fish's reflective gold eyes are just like mine. Except, thankfully, I only have two of them.

::*Mum always told me I was gen-modded. But she didn't tell me I was part-fish.*::

As I'm trying to figure out what to say next, I feel another presence wrap around me. I have just enough time to register that it's Fairy before I'm plucked out of the ocean and dropped into the passenger bay of Prince's starship.

I flop around like a beached dolphin, searching for the disengage mechanism on the bubble suit.

"It's the button on top of your left wrist," says Prince. He's abandoned his pilot seat to see if I'm all right.

Fairy reappears, dropping Danya next to me. She's just coherent enough to disengage her own bubble suit, then peel herself out of it halfway, before being thoroughly sick on the floor.

I struggle my way partially out of my suit so that I can pat her back. Touching her feels oddly electric all of a sudden. The flash that I get from the fabric of her jumpsuit is an unusually strong impression of her personality: anxious, shy, but fiercely loyal to the few she loves.

That's odd. The last few times I've brushed against her clothes, I've gotten a stronger impression of her sister.

Prince is already running for towels and disinfectant. "What happened out there? Fairy was panicking, telling me something's wrong, and then all of a sudden this horrifying fish-monster swam right past my viewport and barfed you out!"

I finally crawl free of the bubble suit, leaving the transparent casing deflated in a large puddle of water. Danya's finished casting up and fallen sideways in a fetal position, moaning. I gently free her from her suit, then hang the gooey shields over the back of a seat to dry.

"Where to begin," I say slowly. "Uh...well, I got the data core." Somehow, I didn't let go of it when I was in the fish's throat-pouch. I pick it up and wave it triumphantly at Prince. "Also, we're going to have to go through Emerson's research data a lot more closely...because that eel-fish says I'm its cousin."

TWENTY MINUTES LATER, PRINCE STILL DOESN'T QUITE BELIEVE ANY of what I've just told him. He's agreed to wire the data core into his ship's computer, though, hoping that we can get to the bottom of what Mum and Emerson Black were doing at this research base, and why it resulted in...well...me.

"Did you hack this thing out of the wall with a spoon?" Prince mutters. "It's mangled to blazes."

"I thought you didn't need the wires. They're the nervous system, but this is the brain. Right?"

"Well, yeah, but it'd help if the box wasn't waterlogged with bits of broken wire still plugged into it."

I shrug. "I was under a little pressure at the time. What d'you want from me?"

"Eyy, *pressure*, good one," says Prince. "How about, you were in a time *crunch?*"

I can tell he's covering his terror with humor. I kinda feel bad for making him worry...but I'm alive and not in a fish's stomach, so it all worked out fine.

Danya, on the other hand, is a little less fine. Getting swallowed was apparently more than she could handle. It's her turn to nap on the passenger seats, bundled up in a ball of blankets.

Honestly, I could tell she was pissing herself about going into the base at all, so the fact that she did it anyway makes her a certified badass. I prop my chin on my hand, absentmindedly staring at the dark splay of her hair against the blankets. Something changed between us down there, and I'm still not quite sure what it was. I started *feeling* her, the way I can feel our fish friends. It's this low-key buzz in the back of my mind, the awareness that they're calling their Shoal to come meet us. And the awareness of *her*. Knowing she's shivering, even though I can't see the blankets tremble.

Suddenly, she sits bolt upright and shoves the blankets to the side. Prince dives for a bucket, but she's not going to be sick again. (How do I *know* that?) Her brown eyes open wide, and she whispers, "They're coming."

"Who? The fish?" I thought I was the only one who could hear them talking. I was starting to think I was special—that my fish DNA connected me to them or something. "Danya, can you hear them too?"

She shudders. "They're calling to me. So many memories."

"They don't mean any harm. I think..." I glance at Fairy. "I think being able to talk to a dragon helps you understand them. Greenjackets don't really teach you dragon-speak, do they?"

She shakes her head, fumbling to wrap one of the blankets around herself. I lift the edge for her, tucking it snugly across her shoulders.

"We should go," Danya whispers. "We need to..."

"I can move the ship," Prince offers. "I *should* move the ship. All this water is going to get her rusty."

"Wait. No. We can't go yet," I interrupt. "I'm not done talking to the Shoal. But first...we need to know what the blazes my mum was up to here. Fixing that data bank should be a priority."

"I guess it won't hurt to stick around for another hour or so." Prince shakes the cube, dislodging a lump of what might have been waterweed, or skin from the inside of the fish's throat. He uses the edge of a cleaning rag to dry as much of it as he can. "It should work now. I think."

He gingerly inserts the wires. There's a long, agonizing moment of nothing happening. Then the screen blips to life with a whirring noise from the computer's holo projector as it clicks on.

"Oh, good. Nothing's sparking," Prince quips.

I stride over to take the control gauntlet from him. With a few deft flicks of my fingers, I bring back the search on Emerson Black (minus Lyric, thank stars). I skip over the personal information, figuring I'll just get upset if I dig into his death again, and refine my query to info pertaining to my father's research.

It looks like I may be in luck. My mum, aunt, and uncle's research was all stored separately and those modules removed when they left the base. But since Emerson Black died before leaving the base, no one thought to wipe the archives of his research diaries. I dive into the oldest ones, scanning hungrily for clues.

His first few entries outline his hypotheses and the experiments he planned to run here. It's all encased in the heavy-duty armor of academic smart-speak. For once, I'm glad I have academic experience. If I didn't, this would look like a pile of incomprehensible jargon. As it is...

"Stars, no wonder I'm a weirdo," I mutter. "*Ascension of material life forms to nonmaterial states. Temporospatial manipulation in material and nonmaterial life forms.* Who even cares if aliens have souls?"

"Well, aliens, probably," Prince says. "Is that what all of those long words mean?"

"Well, yeah, kind of. The second one means, basically, the study of whether different life forms can do magic."

Prince's eyebrows shoot skyward. "Magic?"

"Well, close enough. Manipulating space-time. You know, like how dragons teleport. What I don't get is why he had to be out on this middle-of-nowhere planet to research stuff like this. It had to be these telepathic fish aliens, right? Something special about them?"

"Keep reading. He might explain it."

So I continue wading through the diary entries. *It would have been nice if Emerson kept vid diaries instead of text ones.* I have a hard time taking in information by reading. I can do it when I have a good enough incentive. But seriously—my kingdom for an audio recording, or a video lecture!

Thank stars it's finally starting to get interesting. According to Emerson, he brought a research team to this planet on the recommendation of an explorer friend, Hue Tran. Hue, like Prince, had a bonded dragon companion, and the two of them were planetary explorers. They surveyed uncharted worlds for potential settlement and sold the information to the Imperial Authorities.

There wasn't any serious interest in a planet completely covered in water, but the explorer found something else that made the place irresistible to Emerson. The native species of piscines were genetically almost identical to an extinct fossil species previously assumed to be native to Halcyon, a planet on the opposite end of the galaxy. The piscines were both sentient and highly intelligent.

So far, it all checks out.

I skip through weeks of entries as Emerson learns to communicate with the creatures. In the meantime, it seems like other scientists were reading his journal entries—some of which he posted on a public uniweb page—and interest was rising. Applications to join his team were overflowing in his inbox. Emerson was annoyed that they were encroaching on his territory, but they were offering to bring a better floating base—the old one was more or less a starship on pontoons—and he acquiesced, hiring a handful of new researchers.

The list includes three Ediyas: Gaela, Oberon, and Melanie.

Mum's name starts cropping up more and more in the research journals. She believed the eel-fish were her missing link in the search for dragons' ancestors. Emerson had gotten the same story out of them that I did: the violent members of the species were brought to Atlantis from Halcyon as a sort of penal colony. As Mum studied the eel-fish, she noticed that local dragons seemed fearful and avoided the giant creatures, though Emerson and Mum never personally observed any aggressive behavior from them.

After a particularly intense and confusing interview with one of the piscines, Mum offered the theory that "going to the Above" was the fishes' way of explaining ascension to a new form—a *spiritual* form. That the fish who "went to the Above" had shed their bodies and become dragons.

Emerson wanted to believe it too. He started counting the generations back, like I did. After questioning the piscines about their ancestral memories and timekeeping systems, he concluded that the date the piscines first "went to the Above" was on or near the same date that Old Earth made contact with dragons: August 14, 2100 CE. Also known as 0.0.0 DE—Dragon Era. Three thousand, seven hundred, and twenty-nine years ago.

Emerson went on to do several experiments to prove his theory, calling dragons and asking them to speak to the piscines or to teleport them somewhere. While the dragons would not admit kinship with the creatures, they also, for no apparent reason, flatly refused to have anything to do with them—which fit with the story of the rift between the shoals.

It also explains why Fairy's been acting strange since we landed.

Once Emerson accepted the theory that the piscines had attained spiritual enlightenment and become dragons, he and Mum became obsessed with the implications it might have for humanity. Emerson believed that this was evidence to prove another old theory, long-debated: that dragons are trying to groom humanity toward a certain evolutionary goal. When dragons brought a colony of humans to Halcyon, he argued, that was them accepting us as the next race to ascend to a spirit-state.

Mum was less interested in that half of the theory. She was more fascinated by the prospect of harvesting DNA from living, breathing dragon-ancestors. She urged Emerson to keep their theories and findings secret, and according to one particularly irate journal entry, she even posted to his public journal with misleading information calculated to make the interest in Atlantis die down.

At this point, Emerson was starting to get suspicious of her motives. He referenced some kind of scandal she and her siblings were involved in, and he started trying to decide how to extricate his work from her clutches. But apparently, he got over himself pretty fast, because by the next entry, they were working together on some kind of gen-modding project.

Oh no. I think I know where this is going.

And, yup, the entry after that references "the fetus." So much for any romantic ideas I ever had about being a love child. As far as I can tell, Emerson and my mum were never even in a relationship—they simply used their own DNA for ease of access, and Mum offered to carry their test-tube embryo in her womb because they didn't have good enough incubation tech out here in the middle of an endless ocean.

And, stars, the experiments they did to create me! It's a bit horrifying reading them listed out in meticulous detail. It's a wonder I'm even vaguely human-shaped. It seems like Emerson and Mum had different motives for splicing the fish genes with mine. Emerson was hoping to find the biological secret to spiritual ascension. Meanwhile, Mum was laser-focused on what had been her goal all along: gen-modding a human who could teleport the way dragons can.

But whatever their reasons, they were able to work together enough to create a viable embryo, which they implanted in Mum's uterus. They were proud of their work, excited to see what I would become...

And then the entries end, mid-experiment.

My father didn't live to see my birth.

I collapse into a chair, peeling off the control gauntlet and resting it on the seat. "Huh," is all I can think to say.

Prince hangs over the edge of the seat. He's been reading over my shoulder—and so has Danya, I realize. I've been so focused, I didn't even notice her perching on the chair arm next to me.

"You all right?" she asks quietly, her fingers brushing my shoulder. "That was...a lot."

I shrug, digging my thumb into a ragged hole in the chair's cushion. "I knew I was gen-modded. Mum never lied to me about that."

"Do you think your dad was right? That dragons are fish who ascended to a higher consciousness and they want us to be next?"

"I guess it's possible." Though I somehow have a feeling that's not the aspect of the research that the Greenjackets care so much about. "He and Mum screwed up though. I can't teleport by myself." I think back to all the times we visited Phoenix Refuge when I was little. Mum *was* oddly intense about me needing to learn how to 'port with a dragon. Maybe that was why I rebelled and rarely practiced it. "I wonder if she was disappointed when she figured out it didn't work."

"Didn't it?" Prince says quietly. "You can't teleport, but..."

His fingers are fiddling conspicuously with that eye earring. And it clicks. "You think *that* is because I share DNA with the fish?"

Danya's looking at us curiously, her brow furrowed. It's rude of us to be dancing around my ability, keeping her in the dark. But what if it makes her Greenjacket buddies want me more?

Well, they're not here, are they?

"I usually don't talk about it," I tell her, "but I get these...these flashes when I touch objects. They're like visions of the past, sort of. I'll be minding my own business, and brush up against a tree or whatever, and then I see the last bug that landed on the tree. Or I pick up a fork at supper and I know who washed it." I tilt my head back to meet her gaze. "You can't tell *anybody*. If the Greenjackets knew..."

She shakes her head, grimacing. She knows what they'd do better than I.

I jump up, reaching for the drying bubble suits. "Prince, I need to go talk to the Shoal again. I have to know if that's something they can do too."

"Wait, wait, wait. You don't have to go out there again, do you? They're telepathic. You can hear them from in here."

"Kind of...but not really." I'm already shimmying into the suit. "Through the ship's walls, it feels muted. I think if I'm in the water with them, it's easier to understand what they're saying."

"Amy, please, don't," Danya begs. "They admitted themselves, they're descended from their kind's version of violent criminals. Why do you trust them?"

I stop, bubble suit jellied around my shoulders, and look her straight in the eye. "The same way I trust you," I say. "And Prince too. When I touch you, the flashes I get...they tell me what kind of person you are. I knew as soon as I stole your stunner that you'd never hurt me."

Her eyebrows shoot up. "*You* stole my—I thought I lost it!"

"It's under the passenger seat, if you want it back," I tell her. "But you can't stop me from going out there again. I need to talk to the Shoal. I need to know—"

I need to know what I am.

CHAPTER THIRTEEN

Danya

ATLANTIS, UNDERWATER

I'm right on the edge of telling them everything.

I'm psychic too, in a different way. I have a telepathic connection with my sister. She's listening to everything we say, and I think the monster fish can tell—they're hijacking my connection with Nox, putting alien emotions and dark memories into my brain, and I can't...I can't focus...I think Nox is trying to tell me something and it won't come through...I need to get away from here. Away from the monsters.

It's all on the tip of my tongue, but I can't say it. It might be fear stopping me—the fear that kept me and Nox quiet since we were little kids. Or the fear that Amy will be furious that I've lied about being in contact with the Greenjackets. She just said she trusts me, but that'll only make it a worse betrayal when she finds out I don't deserve it.

Or is it the fish-creatures muddling my mind that makes my words jumble up? I can't tell. I hardly know which way is up anymore. I just want this feeling to stop.

But Amy is determined to go out and talk to them, so we can't leave until she's done.

I lie back down on the passenger seats, my head spinning.

AMY

THE PISCINES FROM EARLIER HAVE BEEN JOINED BY AT LEAST TWENTY other members of their Shoal. Fairy takes some convincing to teleport me into the water again—ze isn't exactly afraid of the creatures, but ze doesn't want to be near them. I eventually convince zem to drop me a little way apart from the Shoal. They immediately swim closer to circle me, humming and clicking in what I hope is friendly interest.

::Uh, hi. Do you guys have names or...distinguishing characteristics?:: I'm already having a hard time telling which eel-fish I talked to before. There seems to be a wide range of markings among them, from plain gray to luminescent shimmers in a rainbow spectrum.

They start to tell me their names, but they're all strings of growling, chittering sounds that would give me a sore throat to imitate, mixed with mental impressions that, blended together, make me dizzy.

::Right then. Forget the names.:: I get right down to business. *::Are dragons really your relatives?::*

They send me the same series of images of their cousins rising into "the Above." I figure that's as close as I'm gonna get to a yes.

::Then...do you have visions like I do? Do you touch objects and see their past?::

That confuses them for a moment. They seem to think I'm asking if they *talk* to each other, since the majority of their communication is through telepathically-shared memories and visions.

Eventually, I get them to understand that I'm seeing these things involuntarily—that no one is communicating them to me. That causes a stir of excitement, and several of them back off a little, like they think I might explode.

::What? What does it mean?::

The memory they send me is shockingly clear. When their ancestors ascended, they first became...*prophets*. That's the nearest word I can think of. They started seeing things that no one could have told them:

the future, the past, the faraway present. After a time, they started being able to travel there bodily.

And then, one day, their bodies simply vanished, and they became part of the Above.

::*You are worthy,*:: the Shoal tells me in excited awe. ::*You will ascend.*::

An irrational stab of fear shivers through me. *Am I going to just... disappear? With no warning? I'm too young to die. Or live forever?*

I close my eyes and take several deep breaths. Even if the piscines' superstitions prove correct, I'm still in the early stages. I haven't started teleporting on my own. Maybe I never will. The experiment Mum did on me is still ongoing. It's a shame neither she nor Emerson Black—*Dad* —are here to tell me their theory about what happens next.

But Oberon and Melanie are still alive.

Before, I only wanted to find them to warn them that the Greenjackets are after them. Now, I have some very specific questions I'd like answered. Mum's research can fill in some of the blanks, but Oberon and Melanie were there on the Atlantis research base when Mum and Dad made me. They were part of the team.

I need to ask them, if Mum's experiment succeeds, what's going to happen to me.

I wave goodbye to the piscines and begin swimming back toward the ship. I'm just about to call Fairy to bring me aboard when I feel something clamp onto my bubble suit from the back.

::*Hey,*:: I protest. ::*If you're trying to swallow me again, I really would rather you didn't....*::

But the eel-fish aren't listening. They're moaning a chorus of ::*Danger, danger, danger.*::

And the thing that has me caught...it's not a piscine's jaws.

It pulls tight around me, binding my arms to my sides. A cable, looped around me like a lasso. And at the other end of it, a dark shape in a dive suit and helmet, pulling me toward the surface like a master angler.

::*Fairy!*:: I call, panicking.

But either ze can't hear me, or ze's been driven off by my surging terror. I thrash, trying to free myself, but it's no use.

As I break the surface of the water, the underside of a shuttle opens above me. Hands reach down from the cargo bay to drag us in—first me and then my captor. They hoist me in with the cable, which tightens painfully around my midsection. Then they plop my bubble-suited body on the floor and start congratulating my captor on their catch.

This is a smallish ship, barely bigger than Prince's taxi-style vehicle, but with much less passenger space. It's cargo—military, I think—but it isn't made to travel on its own. A supply shuttle like this one has to belong to a carrier ship.

I struggle into a sitting position, and even though I know they won't be able to hear me through the suit, I yell, "HEY! Wanna take this cable off so I can breathe?"

One of them notices my writhing. She comes over and loosens the cable, then when I disengage the bubble suit, she helps me peel it away from my face.

"Who the blazes are you people?" I snap.

In answer, the diver who caught me takes her helmet off one-handed. She balances it on her hip with her splinted right hand while she runs her left one through her short, dark hair.

My jaw drops. *"Danya?"*

"Guess again," says the woman who looks exactly like Danya. My pulse starts to pound, because I recognize that confident, sardonic tone. It's the way Danya used to speak, back when she was pretending to be a soldier.

"Nikola. That's your name, isn't it?"

Her mouth twists into a smirk.

DANYA

THE DRAGON IS AGITATED. ZE'S FLYING CIRCLES AROUND PRINCE'S head, moving the way a fish moves when it's being hunted: weaving in quick, darting motions.

Dragons don't look anything like those giant fish-monsters. But I'll admit, when I watch them move, I can kind of see the resemblance.

"What are you saying?" Prince has his hands up like he's trying to catch Fairy, but I think he's just trying to calm zem down. "Someone's here? *Who's* here?"

Then his eyes find me, and his eyes go wide.

"Your sister," he says, voice low and horrified. "Does she look exactly like you? Scarily alike?"

I nod. "We're twins."

"Fairy's trying to tell me that Amy just got snatched out of the water by someone who looks like you. They're flying a Greenjacket supply shuttle."

I bolt to my feet. I *knew* Nox was trying to reach me. Blast these blazing fish, filling up my mind with their incessant noise! I can't connect with Nox, so I have no idea what she's thinking. Why wouldn't she just hail Prince's ship and *talk* to us, instead of snatching Amy? "We have to go after them!"

"Agreed." Prince is already in the pilot seat, fastening his safety straps. "Better sit down and hold on, kid."

I'm not sure I like being called "kid" by someone who's at most a couple years older than me, but I don't argue.

The second my safety belt is locked, Prince cracks his knuckles and braces his hands against the dash. "This might be a rough ride," he warns me. "Take us up, Fairy!"

I've 'ported more times in the last few days than I have in my entire life, but I'm still not used to it. The weird floaty feeling, combined with a terrifying lack of control, reminds me of the few times Sherwood Base experienced a grav-simulator malfunction. It's that sick, falling feeling as I realize I don't have anything to hold onto, not knowing when gravity will kick back on and send me crashing to the floor.

This time, when light, sound, and gravity return...we *are* falling.

My fingernails are going to leave permanent dents in the armrest. I clench my teeth, so the sound emitting involuntarily from my throat is a moan rather than a scream. Prince lets out a wild whoop, his hands flying across the dash as he attempts to start the ship's engine mid-fall.

"Glitchin' piece-a shit!" he yells. "Start, blast it, start!"

But the engine—which still hasn't been overhauled properly since Captain Varion scuppered it—has fully given out. Being submerged for hours probably didn't do it any good. So instead of zooming after Nox's ship, which is already jetting off into Atlantis's upper atmosphere, we can't do anything except plummet.

"No no no no—" Prince slams his fist on one last button, but nothing happens. "Fuck! Fairy, it's now or never. Take us somewhere dry!"

I brace myself just in time. We 'port again.

Fairy interprets "somewhere dry" as a completely different planet. (I guess that's fair enough. Atlantis doesn't seem to *do* dry.) With the precision of a dragon who's been working with zir pilot for a very long time, ze releases us only a few feet above the ground. Our landing is a solid, crushing jolt, but we don't die on impact, which I'd consider a success.

We sit there in stunned silence for a minute, and then I slowly unstrap my safety belt. "We lost them, didn't we?"

"Uh..." Prince sighs, rubbing his cricked neck. "Yeah. Yeah, we did."

"Are we marooned here?"

"No. At least, we should be fine, I think. I recognize this ass-ugly desert. This is Susannah. The Knights come here every few months to drop supplies, 'cause the Empire likes to forget these people exist. There's a farming town near here. Their mechanic can help me get this ship back in the air."

Well, that's a crumb of good news in the moldy bread that this day has turned out to be. "And Amy? Nox? How do we catch up with them?" I shoot a hard glare at him. "You're going to help me rescue her, right?"

Prince sighs. "The Chief Knight's gonna have my head for this. But yeah, I can't live with myself if I let her get kidnapped and don't try to save her." He levers himself upright, leaning heavily on the dash as he tests all his limbs. "As to how we're gonna do that...I'm out of ideas. Was hopin' you might have one."

"Well, actually..." Now that we're out of range of the fish-monsters, I can hear myself think again. More importantly, I can reach Nox...if she'll listen.

Slowly, I say, "There's something I need to tell you." Then, in an almost-whisper, like if I say it too loud the whole world might hear and judge, I tell Prince about my connection with Nox.

He doesn't respond for a long minute. I wait for the anger, the suspicion, the accusations...

"Fairy told me awhile back," he says finally. "Ze didn't think you were a threat to us. Didn't see this comin', with your sister taking Amy though. I guess that means we both fucked up. I appreciate you being honest with me."

Relief floods through me. "You're not angry?"

"Oh, I'm right flared off, but it's not at you. Your sister's got a lot of explainin' to do." Prince stretches his arms above his head, groaning as his back cracks. "You sit tight and get in touch with her as soon as you can. I'm headed to the town to talk to the mechanic."

He makes as if to walk off, then turns back around. "Oh, and if you're hungry, have a nutrient bar." He pulls a drawer filled with emergency rations out of the wall. "Don't eat the cheese-flavored ones though. I only keep those to hand out to passengers who complain. Coffee and chocolate flavor are all right."

Then he and Fairy teleport away.

I sit there for a minute, brain whirling as I process what just happened. He knew I was passing information to Nox all along? And he let me stay—even now, when my sister seems to be acting as our enemy?

I've never met anyone quite like these Halcyonites. The way they casually trust each other. The way they've treated me—an enemy—as a person worthy of respect. The way they assume everyone's motives are pure until proven otherwise. I've shown them my weakness, and instead of lunging for the kill, they open their arms to help me.

Part of me keeps waiting for the other shoe to drop. For there to be some catch, some price for their kindness.

But another part of me really wants to believe in them. I just pathetically, selfishly *want* there to be good people in the world.

And if Amy's really, truly a good person...then I want her far away from the Greenjackets. If I can't be good for anything else, at least I can try to protect her.

Closing my eyes, I reach out for my sister's mind.

PART SIX

Year 3729, Week 51,

Dayfour

CHAPTER FOURTEEN

Danya

SUSANNAH (A DRY FARMING PLANET)

Nox is reluctant to talk to me, but I'm not taking no for an answer. I worm my way into her brain, past her attempts to close me out, and start yelling.

::*All right, all right! You've got my attention. Stars, Dawn. I'm flying at the moment. You want me to crash into something?*::

::*Oh, right, because space is so full of things to crash into.*:: Then I register, through her eyes, where she is. ::*You're in an asteroid field? What the blazes are you doing there?*::

::*Following a lead.*::

::*How did you even get a ship? Did the officers find out you're not me?*::

::*Ha! As if I'd let them get that far.*:: A quick flash of memory flits through her mind: her and Petra sneaking into the hangar, setting a fire as a distraction—*stars above, Nox, what is wrong with you?*—and using the chaos to steal a small cargo shuttle.

I keep trying to mine her consciousness for information, but she doubles down on shutting me out. Her intent focus on the asteroids in her path blocks me from her other memories.

::*Nox. I'm serious. You have to talk to me. You swore you would.*::

::*That was when you were pretending to be me. Now I'm me again, and your part in this is done.::* She swerves sharply, breathing a curse. *::The Greenjackets think you're gone for good, Dawn. Let them keep thinking that. Go be a farmer on some colony planet, like you've always wanted. Get married and adopt a bunch of cute orphans. You're free.::*

The emotions that well up in my chest hearing her say that are indescribable. She's offering me the chance to reach out and take the life I've wanted ever since I was a child. She knows what that dream means to me...and she'll know how much it's costing me to refuse.

::I can't walk away now. You know I can't, Nox. Not when you took Amy and won't tell me why.:: Tears burn in my eyes. *::Besides, I never wanted that life if it meant I had to lose you.::*

::You can't have it both ways,:: Nox retorts. *::I'm a fighter, Dawn, and you're not. It's that simple. You can keep denying your true self to follow me around, or you can go live the life you want. But not both.::*

There's an element of truth to what she says, and I can't pretend it doesn't sting. *::If you give Amy back, I'll leave you alone to whatever scheme you're concocting. Just, please, let her go. She's innocent in all this. She doesn't know anything about her parents' research.::*

::She doesn't have to,:: Nox snaps back. *::When I saw that data through your eyes, I figured it out, Dawn. The Greenjackets didn't want her because they thought she knew something. She* is *her parents' research. And I'm taking her to the only people who can decode the information she carries in her genes.::*

She shoves me out of her mind, blocking me out—but not before I catch a glimpse of what she's up to. Dread settles cold in my gut.

Nox knows where to find Oberon and Melanie Ediya. They're on a Greenjacket outpost called Arrow Station. The only way to get there is to fly through the asteroid field I saw in her mind, relying on visual landmarks.

The good news: Nox is going by a map that's available to download for any Greenjacket with a keycuff. The bad news: I don't have my keycuff anymore.

I guess we're going to have to get creative.

THE MECHANIC, WHOSE NAME IS JOSEFA, TAKES ONE LOOK AT PRINCE'S
ship and tells us it's going to be at least a full day's job to fix. Both of us
offer to help—I'm not bad with machines myself, having spent a lot of
time tending them in the greenhouse—but even so, the planet's dusk
settles over us long before the ship is skyworthy.

The desert at night is a little more forgiving than the eye-stabbing,
dry-hot assault of the sun-up hours. Josefa invites us back to town to
have dinner with her family, and we gratefully follow her across the sands
to her family's homestead. There's a hot, earthy smell rising from the
ground as it cools off. Outside the beam of Josefa's torchlight, scuttling
shapes announce the presence of nocturnal beasties out on the prowl.
Their eerie chirps and screeches keep me close to Prince's side, even
though he keeps saying they're more scared of me than I of them.

Josefa lives with two partners, Whit and Laurie. A baby gurgles in its
rocking cradle next to the table, Laurie pushing it back and forth with an
idle motion of her foot.

Whit gets home just after we arrive. "You're our first off-planet
visitors in eight months," he says, brushing sandy soil from his trousers
as he removes his shoes by the door. "Pardon our dust. We didn't know
to expect company."

"Not at all, not at all," Prince says, waving his hands to put them at
ease. "We didn't expect the royal welcome when we crash-landed here. I
do appreciate your hospitality—the food smells delicious."

It's standard colony fare: dense bread, root vegetables, and a roasted
chunk of some cactus-like plant that, to my surprise, tastes like a juicy,
melt-in-your-mouth synthsteak.

"What's this called?" I ask.

"Rainsucker," Whit replies. "It's a native plant to Susannah, but we've
been working with a geneticist to make it more palatable for human
consumption. Lots of vitamins in it."

"It's the best thing I've eaten in years," I say. "Would it be rude to ask
for a sampling of the seeds? And perhaps you could tell me how much
rainfall you get in a year? I've got to start growing this when I get back."

Back to what though? my brain whispers. I push that thought deep
down where I don't have to look at it.

Josefa passes me the dish and urges me to take another helping. "I guess we're all so sick of the stuff, we don't rightly know whether it's good or not," she laughs. "Maybe we should try selling a few jars of canned rainsucker when the next merchant shuttle comes through."

They send me away with three rainsucker seeds folded in a clean kerchief and a promise that I can come back anytime to survey their weather patterns or get planting instructions.

We head back to the ship and tinker for a little longer, before Prince catches me yawning and tells me to take the sleep-pod.

I protest—even though I'm tired, my brain wants to get back in the air and go after Nox as soon as we can—but I know he's right. We both need to rest.

I hope Amy feels safe enough to sleep...wherever she is.

AMY

Aboard Nox's stolen shuttle

"Let me take over flying," Petra insists. "You're still blissed from 'porting us. I've been through pilot training too."

"I've got this," Nox snaps.

"No you don't. You've nearly crashed four times in twelve minutes."

After a minute, Nox concedes, but grumbles the whole time.

I've been aboard their ship for hours now. I figured out from listening to their banter that the woman with a bad case of resting glitch face is called Petra, and that Danya's sister Nikola goes by "Nox." I asked why, and she said it's her initials: Nikola Octavia Xiang.

She gets flared off if I call her Nikola, so obviously I've been calling her that every chance I get.

They seem to think they're some kind of secret spy duo. But all I see is a couple of girls more or less my age, half-assing their way through everything.

I can't quite figure out why we're flying through this asteroid field instead of teleporting through it. I mean, I know that offworlders aren't used to teleporting as much as Halcyonites. But they've still got to do it for interstellar flights, right? Even neighboring star systems are separated by decades' worth of space travel, and that's if your ship is outfitted with state-of-the-art engines.

Nox swings herself into the seat across from mine and fastens her safety belt. I glare her down, arms folded across my chest.

She finally bites. "Don't give me that look, Ediya. You were looking for your aunt and uncle anyway, weren't you? Well, I'm doing you a favor and taking you to them. Win-win."

"What I want to know," I say slowly, "aside from how you know all this stuff about me—we'll get to that—is how come you snatched me and left your own sister behind. If you knew where I was, you had to know she was there too."

Nox scoffs. "This doesn't concern her. She covered for me while I was injured, but now I'm fine, and she doesn't need to be a part of this. She never wanted it in the first place. I did her a favor by leaving her."

I wrinkle my nose. "Kinda sounds to me like you're making excuses."

"I didn't ask for your opinion." Nox's lip curls.

I get a tiny boost of satisfaction from flaring her off. I'm not about to make this easy for her—she doesn't get to sit here all smug, thinking she's the good guy. If she's actually taking me to Oberon and Melanie, then technically she *is* doing me a favor. But there's a huge difference between seeking them out and being taken to them by force. And therein lies my annoyance. I intended to crash-land in Uncle O's back field, march up to his door, and pound on it demanding answers. It feels...embarrassing, I suppose...to be deposited on his doorstep like a package from the Monroe Interplanetary Delivery Service.

"Almost there now," Petra says from the pilot seat.

I let my head fall back. Stars, I'm exhausted. What with all this planet-hopping, it must be a full twenty-five-hour cycle since I got any decent rest. Maybe longer.

I wish I trusted these glitches enough to sleep.

DANYA

STILL ON SUSANNAH

Even though my body is limp with exhaustion, sleep doesn't come easy. When I finally drift off, my dreams are full of half-formed plans for wild escapes.

After an amount of time—could be one hour, could be eight—my bladder wakes me with the urge to pee. I climb out of the sleep-pod and use the washroom in the back of the ship. On my way out, I hear the rustle of movement from the flight deck and notice a screen-lit glow. It's dark outside, which means we're still in the middle of Susannah's night. Has Prince not finished the repairs yet?

"Prince?" I call, stumbling my way through the passenger bay to peer through the door into his domain. "What's going on?"

He's slumped in the pilot seat, looking very much like he needs some sleep, scrolling through the information from that data core we stole from the Atlantis base. He grunts a hello at me, but doesn't look away from whatever he's reading.

"What time is it?" I ask.

He flicks a glance at his keycuff. "You want local time or Galactic Standard?"

"Never mind. Just wanted to know how long I was asleep for."

"Six hours, give or take. It'll be dawn soon."

"Then you should go lie down for a few hours too," I tell him severely. "You look half-dead."

"Tried. I can't blazin' sleep." Prince rubs his eyes and groans. "I keep thinkin' about what you told me. I just don't know how we're gonna get Amy out of this. I was going through the Atlantis stuff again—thought I might find something else on Amy's aunt and uncle."

"Well, did you?"

"I sure did," Prince says. From his tone, it's nothing good. "Wasn't on the data core though. One of the other researchers' diaries mentioned they weren't happy working with the Ediyas. Thought they were shady, and they mentioned some covered-up scandal they'd been in. Well...I chased that lead. Synced us with the uniweb...and look what I found."

He switches to another window.

<*Triplet Geneticist Team Expelled from Association for Inappropriate Experimentation,*> blares a newsie's headline. <*Ediya Triplets Disgraced After Murder Allegations.*>

"This was a couple of years before they got involved in the Atlantis research," he says as I scan the text in shock.

The article doesn't show Gaela Ediya or her two siblings in a flattering light. It alleges that the three of them, working together, conceived the idea to "raise humanity to the next level" by creating genetically superior superhumans. They secured Imperial funding by telling the Emperor they were going to strengthen his bloodline so that his rule would never be questioned. But their true intent was to *replace* the Emperor's bloodline with one they could control.

The writer of the article, a journalist named Adalia Browning, claims to have found a way to access the Ediyas' secret research records. She discovered that they'd tested their experimental gen-mods on lab-grown babies instead of willing adult volunteers. Some of the early results had gone horrifyingly wrong, resulting in several of their subjects "mysteriously disappearing." Browning's investigation turned up evidence that the triplets had euthanized the children whose outcomes had been less than desirable. As of the publication of the article, there were still standing arrest warrants on all three of them. An edit below the original text notes that when the Human Teleportation Project gained visibility a few years later, the Emperor granted them a conditional pardon, noting that any further law-breaking would result in the death penalty.

The article is a little too vicious in painting the Ediyas as evil monsters, which makes me wonder how much of it is hyperbole. I've been raised to be suspicious of Imperial propaganda, and I see the marks of it all over this. But the best propaganda is usually rooted in fact.

I lean against the armrest of Prince's pilot seat, feeling rather sick. "That's horrible," I say. "The killing babies part anyway. But this article is acting like it isn't normal to do human trials on infants before they do gene therapy on fully grown adults. At least, the Greenjackets do. Something about bodies responding better when they're still growing and changing." Gene editing was covered extensively in my Greenjacket education program. Nox and I weren't the only incubator babies; several of our classmates were too. Some of them even went on to apprentice as geneticists themselves.

I imagine the Greenjackets would've been extremely onboard with the goal of replacing the Emperor's bloodline with a better one. And given what I know of General Bruna, I'm thinking they'd have no qualms about killing a few babies to reach that goal. This article doesn't connect the Ediyas to the Greenjackets specifically, but it doesn't take a genius to add two and two. I wonder if that's the *real* reason the Emperor shut them down. Prince says, "They're supposed to run a ton of simulations before they ever do human trials at all. Browning accused the Ediyas of failing to test their proposed modifications thoroughly enough. They shouldn't've rushed into trials without eliminating all possible risk— doing that was the whole reason they had test subjects who didn't make it."

I skim the article again. My heart goes out to those poor incubator babies who never had a chance. "Whatever happened to the kids? Were there any that survived?"

"There was another newsie article that mentions a few test subjects who were still alive." Prince turns back to his screen and types a search query. "Oh, here! There were five or six seized by the Authorities. They were young though. All under the age of two."

I wince. "Five or six kids under the age of two! What were they planning to do with them if all those tests were successful? Raise them all? That's...*so many babies*."

"Anyway..." Prince seems eager to change the subject away from babies. "So the Ediyas dropped out of academic circles for awhile. Nobody heard from them. The next time they popped up is when they started making waves with their teleportation research. That's when Emerson Black hired them for the Atlantis project. Their involvement was kept really quiet, so hardly anyone knew they were there, until one of the assistants leaked it to the newsies. But by that time..."

He pulls up another article, this one describing Emerson Black's death by drowning.

<Respected xenobiologist Dr. Emerson Black drowned Dayone evening after

his oxygen mask malfunctioned on a routine dive at an undisclosed research base. Imperial Authorities have launched an investigation into whether foul play was involved.> That's basically all the article says. The rest of it is an obituary listing his published essays and several science awards.

"Foul play?" I raise my eyebrows. "Do they think the Ediyas *killed* Amy's father?"

"They never proved it," says Prince.

I shake my head. "The Empire always has an agenda. I bet they wanted to plant evidence so they had an excuse to arrest the Ediyas. Their research must have been making the Emperor nervous again." I let out a slow breath. "No wonder the Greenjackets want it so bad."

Prince nods, his eyes still fixed on the screen. "I'd love to hear their side of the story," he says absently.

"Me too," I say, "and thanks to Nox, we can go ask them." I explain about Arrow Station and the map to find it. "Is the ship fixed yet?"

"Oh, that. Yeah, I got it running hours ago."

"Can it navigate an asteroid field?"

Prince makes a casual flicking gesture. "I could do it in my sleep."

The bags under his eyes are dark enough that I want to say, *I guess we'll find out.* But I hold back the quip.

I stand up straight and roll out the soreness in my shoulders. My muscles are still cramped from the extremely unpleasant sensation of being swallowed by a fish. "Let's stop wasting time then." I belt myself into the copilot's chair. "We need to get to Arrow Station. Which means we have to get our hands on that map. Which means we need a Greenjacket keycuff."

I hesitate, knowing what I'm about to say is treason.

"I can give you the coordinates to Sherwood Base. It'll be tricky to sneak you in, but..."

"No need for that," Prince interrupts. He fingers the eye-shaped earring dangling from his left ear. "I've got someone in mind who can help us out. An old friend."

CHAPTER FIFTEEN

Danya

Gila City, Esperanza

When I was growing up on Sherwood Base, I imagined the glory of living on a planet with a real atmosphere and actual plants. In my mind, every planet was a farmland utopia bursting with life. It was true for Eureka, Halcyon, and even Susannah, where a seemingly barren desert hid plenty of growth. Esperanza though...the first time I see it, it's a blow to the chest.

Prince tells me he grew up in this city. Sold as an indenture to one of the factories when he was young. Paid off his debt in his teens, got into flight school, almost got recruited as a Greenjacket, and ended up on Halcyon hiding from their wrath. He speaks about his past with rueful, nostalgic fondness—the way I'd describe growing up in the creche with Nox maybe. Like looking back with that new adult knowledge that my childhood was terrible, but it was the only childhood I got, and I somehow weirdly miss it.

But I don't see how anyone could even feel remotely fond of time spent on this planet.

The air is choked with smoke and fumes, byproducts of the factories that swallow up most of the city, lined up in their militaristic ranks. Everything below us as Prince brings us in for a landing is gray and boxy, even the high-rise buildings where people live. There's no color to be seen, no life beyond the swarm of people rushing through the streets, eager to be back in filtered environments that protect them from the toxicity of the outside air.

The oceans are vast sludge pits. The mountains are dented and pocked from ruthless mining. Any crops that grow have to be coaxed to do so in greenhouses not unlike the one on Sherwood Base.

"Why would anyone settle here?" I wonder aloud, feeling somehow betrayed. "Why don't people go to other planets that aren't toxic? There's got to be lots of those."

Prince shrugs and says, "There're jobs here."

I still can't imagine any level of desperation for a job that would persuade me to live here. But I don't want to offend Prince, since this is his home planet. So I shut up.

We park and anchor at a public hangar in Gila Spaceport, where Prince casually mentions he has to register under a false name. "I just got away from the Greenjackets. Not giving them another chance to capture me," he says. "Er, no offense."

He straps a breather mask over his face before we leave the ship, claiming it's "common for folks who have asthma to wear these." But the way he flips up his jacket hood to hide his distinctive hair tells me this is a disguise. He's a lot more nervous than he's letting on about landing on this planet.

One lungful of Esperanza's air, and I run back to the ship for a breather mask of my own. The air has a *taste*, sour-smoky, that settles in the back of my throat and scrapes my nose dry. I hope we don't need to spend much time here, because I was ready to leave five minutes ago.

Prince leads me out of the spaceport and through several blocks of city streets, weaving through the crowd with the confidence of a guy who knows where he's going. He points up at the flashing lights of signs advertising the businesses inside this particular building. They're as neon-bright as the tattoos he wore a jacket to cover.

"Twelfth floor. Luz de las Estrellas," he murmurs to me, his voice muffled behind the mask. "If Joel X isn't there this time of day, I'll eat my boots."

As we wait for the zip-lift, he explains, "Luz is a public lounge where me and my pilot friends used to hang during training. Spent half our nights and most of our credits there. Joel is a compulsive gambler, and I doubt he's broken the habit since I last saw him."

I remove my breather mask as soon as we're indoors, but Prince keeps his in place. "Pretty sure they've got posters up advertising a reward for my capture," he mutters. "But then again, maybe not. I doubt they ever expected to see me again."

The zip-lift arrives with a faint *ding*, and Prince squares his shoulders, striding into the elevator pod like he owns the building.

It smells faintly of urine inside the lift. The loose straps, sudden lurches, and pervasive odors make my stomach hurt, but Prince has that wistful look in his eye like this is the height of nostalgia.

He and Joel X are laughing, holding each other up, both of them star-dancing on whatever they'd drunk or patched. Running from a fight Heather Jung had started, swearing at the top of their lungs to make her madder as they stumbled down the dank stairwell. Joel was there when Prince got his first tattoo: a fluorescent pink dragon on his left arm. Prince was there when Joel overdosed on a new mind-alt and spent four days recovering in an infirmary.

I startle, staring at Prince with wide eyes.

"What?" he asks. "You all right?"

"Uh...yeah...fine." Stars blazing above. I just read his mind. I felt what he was thinking—exactly the way I do with Nox.

It had to be those cursed fish, back on Atlantis. They hacked into my brain somehow. They've messed around with my connection to Nox, crossing wires somewhere.

It's always only been the two of us who share minds. Only me and my sister. No one else. The thought that I could read *anyone's* mind—and that anyone could read *mine*—sends me into a panic spiral. At least Prince didn't seem to notice anything. I throw up my strongest mental block, just to make sure.

The zip-lift clunks to a halt, disgorging us into a dim hallway lit by glowing signs advertising a myriad of alcohol brands and mind-alts.

Prince strides to the doorway at the end of the hall and, hesitating only briefly, steps in.

He walks slowly down the length of the lounge, scanning the booths, me trailing behind him. Having accidentally seen his memories, I know who he's looking for: a skinny white man with a turquoise fauxhawk and ragged facial hair, wearing an identical eye earring.

He sees Joel X before I do, and I don't have to be connected to Prince's mind to notice the way he freezes, his body tightening. Hurt deepens the faint lines in the corners of his eyes.

Joel sits at a card table with a handful of pirate-ish disreputables. He's wearing the Greenjacket uniform, but from the rumpled collar and the rolled-up sleeves, I'm guessing he's off duty. None of the other players at his table wear green; they're sporting an assortment of black leather, metal accessories, and uncomfortable-looking body mods like spikes in tongues.

"Joel," says Prince softly. "Can we talk?"

Between one blink and the next, Joel is on his feet, drawing a laser pistol from the holster at his side. I reach for my stunner, but Prince hasn't gone for his weapon at all. He's holding his hands palm out, eyes locked on Joel's.

"Don't move," Joel growls.

"I'm not here to hurt you." Prince is still using that quiet, calm voice. I wonder if that's a thing he learned working for the Halcyonites—some tactic meant to smooth ruffled feelings and de-escalate arguments.

Joel's friends have all gone still, their hands straying toward sheathed weapons. You could twang the tension in this room like a guitar string. One wrong move, and both me and Prince are going to be riddled with blast holes.

Nox would love this. She'd be mentally running the odds, planning which way to duck and roll, calculating how many of them she could shoot before getting hit.

"Hey, c'mon, let's not make a scene," Prince says. "It's been five years. Let me buy you a drink, and we'll catch up."

Joel laughs, displaying crooked, discolored teeth. "Do you have any idea how much trouble you got me in? I should shoot you right now and stick your head in cryo. Special delivery for the Greenjacket officers."

"That would be disgusting," I say before I can stop myself. "General Bruna wouldn't want that cluttering up her desk."

Joel's eyebrows shoot up, his eyes flicking to scan my face. I left Nox's uniform jacket on the ship, but my jumpsuit is standard Greenjacket issue. I can tell he recognizes it.

"Who's the girlfriend?" he demands.

I don't answer. For all I know, my name is on their wanted list too.

Prince rolls his eyes. "Joel, how many times do I gotta tell you I'm aroace? Listen, holster your gun and hear us out, will you? People are starin'."

"I got a poker game to finish," Joel says, but he lowers the gun.

"We'll wait at a booth over there." Prince drags me over to an empty one, where he orders three beers from the table's built-in screen.

A serv-bot rolls up to set our drinks on the table. I sip at mine, curious. Greenjackets frown upon using mind-alts of any kind; keeping your mind sharp could save your life in a dangerous situation. That's what they always told us.

Beer tastes different than I expected it to. There's a bitterness to it and a shocking tingle in the throat. I wince, sticking out my tongue. "People drink this for *fun?*"

Prince chuckles. "That's just the mild stuff, kid."

I frown. "Why do you keep calling me kid? I'm twenty-two. How old are you even?"

"Twenty-three," Prince admits. "I'll quit, if it makes you feel bad. It's just...you're a grown-ass woman, I know that, but you seem so much like a kid still. It's the way the Greenjackets treat you, I'm guessin'. Like, they keep you in thrall to authority all your life and punish anything you do they don't approve of. Yeah?"

I exhale. "Yeah." He's got a point. I've been an adult according to the laws of the Empire for four years...but only now, since escaping the constant scrutiny of the Greenjackets, am I starting to *feel* like one. Like someone who's in control of my own life.

"For what it's worth," says Prince softly, "you deserve better."

I can't do anything but nod. I'm afraid my voice will wobble if I say anything.

Just then, Joel X slides into the opposite bench, facing us inside the booth. He hits the privacy screen, a shield that flickers across the booth entrance to blur out our features and muffle our conversation. Downing half his beer in a long chug, he slams the glass on the table and glares at Prince.

"What the blazes do you want, DeSanto? You got some nerve, showing up here in front of all them folks. Any one of 'em could report me for not capturing you on the spot."

Prince meets Joel's gaze steadily. "We need your help with something. I couldn't think of anyone better to ask."

"Oh, you couldn't? Not one single other person in the galaxy you ain't screwed over worse than me?" Joel snorts. "I vouched for you. Told my boss you was a good prospective recruit. And then you run off and join up with Halcyonites? You ain't the man I thought you was."

"Man, you coulda *asked* first!" Prince erupts, his coolheaded shell cracking. "I woulda told you I ain't interested in any political movement that blows up innocent people!"

"Oh, you'd rather join some religious cult that brainwashes everybody?"

"It's not..." Prince groans and rubs his forehead. Then he goes for a subject change. "I saw they rebuilt the spaceport. You still doing taxi work or are you recruiting for the Greenjackets full-time?"

"They pay better," Joel mutters. "Don't sit there and judge me, DeSanto. You know the Empire's sucking Esperanza dry. I was tired of just being another flatliner living in debt all my life. This way I can do something to fight back."

"*Thousands* of civilians died in that explosion."

"Yeah, and so did a fuckload of Authorities! We held the city for four weeks before the Reds retook it."

Until now, I've only had a vague idea of what they're talking about. Now I realize why it sounds so familiar. I'd almost forgotten it, given everything that's happened since then. This was the Gila City incident Nox showed me, when she and Petra were trying to convince me we're not the good guys. The explosion that destroyed the spaceport. Nox said the Greenjackets were chasing a deserter when they planted that bomb.

The deserter...*Prince.*

And Joel's the man who betrayed him, who set off the whole chain of events.

Stars above. Nox would piss herself if she could hear this. Too bad she isn't listening.

"How 'bout you, DeSanto? The cultists pay you good?" Joel's taunting him now, trying to cut back through to that anger festering inside.

But Prince doesn't take the bait. "Enough to pay off my debt from flight school. And don't call 'em cultists."

"Aw, are you one of 'em now? You pray to the dragons? Got one following you around now, keepin' an eye on you."

"Listen, I'm not here to argue over ideals, all right? This is business. Straight up."

Joel chuckles, a mean sound, low in the throat. "Lay it on me then. This better be good."

Prince looks at me, so I jump in. "We need information. A friend of ours got captured by a rogue team. We think they're going to an old defunct Greenjacket base called Arrow Station. It's in the middle of an asteroid field, super hard to get to. There's a map to all current and former Greenjacket outposts easily accessible to anyone who has a keycuff issued by them. Problem is...I've lost my cuff."

"*Arrow Station?*" Joel shakes his head. "I heard it blew up. Ain't there no more."

"I have compelling evidence to the contrary." Namely, my sister's conviction that it's not only still running, but that Oberon and Melanie Ediya live there. If she's wrong, well, we'll figure out what to do about that later.

Joel eyes me, then Prince, like he's trying to figure out how serious we are. "Right," he says finally. "I'll get you a copy of the map. But you gotta do somethin' for me first."

"Fair's fair," Prince says. "What d'you have in mind?"

"Oh, not much." Joel grins. "Just a little package I need delivered. Quick and easy. Won't take you more than a couple of hours at most."

"So it's mind-alts, right?" I say, surveying the sealed cryo-storage box Joel had us pick up.

We've just gone through a ridiculous dance to get the blazing thing. Joel told us to teleport to a particular Gila City rooftop, find a man wearing a snake earring, and say the password "banana peel." That man turned out to be a security guard, and just before he threw us bodily into a zip-lift while yelling at us never to trespass again, he handed us the box.

It's about the size of a watermelon, rectangular, quite heavy. The whole thing is wrapped in black cloth, which I guess is supposed to make it more discreet. In my opinion, it just makes the package look more suspicious.

"I don't even want to know." Prince kicks the box under the pilot seat. "The less I know, the more convincingly innocent I'll look when the Authorities are questioning me."

It's definitely mind-alts. Something super-addictive and super-illegal, I'd bet money on it. Joel X is totally the kind of guy who smuggles drugs on the side.

I wish we had another Greenjacket contact who was less shady, but I don't know anyone who lives away from Sherwood Base. So it looks like we have to do the deed and take the risk. Our only other option is to pry into Nox's mind for exact coordinates, except I can barely even *feel* her anymore. She's determined not to let me in.

"What was Joel's next instruction, after we got this thing?" I ask.

"He gave me some coordinates. I guess we hand it off to whoever's there, then bring the receipt back to Luz?"

"You don't sound very confident."

Prince laughs. Or at least, that's how I interpret the high-pitched, strained noise he makes. "I don't get asked to smuggle contraband very often. Sorry if I'm a bit on edge."

"Fair." I belt myself into the copilot seat. "Let's get this over with."

Fairy doesn't seem terribly excited about this whole business either. Prince has to take a minute to convince zem to 'port us as ze flits around the flight deck in agitation.

"Please, Fairy," Prince murmurs. "You know you can trust me."

I hear zir reply, though I don't think I was supposed to. *::It's not you I don't trust. It's that creep Joel.::*

I quickly block out the rest of their mental conversation, not wanting to intrude. Prince and Joel clearly have some history, and it's none of my business why Prince trusts him or why Fairy clearly hates his guts (as much as a pacifist floaty bubble-snake is capable of hatred).

I focus very hard on staying inside my own head. It's so effective that I nearly don't notice when we teleport. A moment of floating, a stomach-jolting heaviness as we transition back into the physical world...

Rain lashes against the viewport. It's night on this world, and we've 'ported right into the middle of a storm. Prince mutters a curse under his breath, frantically tapping the scanner as he maneuvers the ship with his other hand. "Not a lot of good landing spots here. Thanks a bunch, Joel."

"Just throw the package out the cargo door and fly off," I suggest.

"Too dangerous. Besides, Joel said I gotta make the handoff or no deal." He chews his lip, eyes flicking back and forth across his instruments. "Right, I think I can take us down on that little ledge in front of the cave. It'll be tight, but that's the only spot I see that's clear for a landing. And—yep—I see life signs, way back inside the cave. Someone's home."

"Mind-alt dealers," I mutter.

"They'll be happy to see their package. Ain't gonna shoot us if they're gettin' what they want."

I'm starting to think Prince might be too much of an optimist for his own good. It's nail-bitingly tense watching him land on the narrow ledge. I have to give him credit; he's a blazing good pilot. He anticipates the ship's response, nudging the controls just the right amount to the left or right. He doesn't rush it, nor does he hesitate.

The moment our landing gear touches solid rock, he breathes out a massive sigh of relief and engages the anchor mechanism. "Let's hand off the package and then scram."

I'm none too eager to stick around. Prince hauls the package out from under his seat. I grab Nox's jacket and hold it above my head as a rain shield while we disembark. There's a faint, steady glow of lamplight emanating from deep inside the cave. A rumble of voices echoes off the walls, a mix of laughter and good-natured arguing.

Prince places the package conspicuously in the middle of the cave opening. "They'll find it eventually, right?" he whispers. "This is close enough..."

I nod vigorously. The echoes sound too close for comfort. Time to get gone.

We turn around...just in time to see two dark shapes step out of the shadows on either side of the cave's entrance. I stifle a scream, leaping back.

"What's this? That little rat Joel X sent someone else to do his dirty work?" The guard is a feline-humanoid man with scraggly ginger fur all across his face and arms. He and his friend, an Earth Classic guy with a bald head and beard, have guns pointed straight at our heads.

"Don't even think about touching your holster, bucko," Beard Guy tells Prince. "I've got murder charges on six worlds. This planet ain't even got a judicial system to make it seven."

Prince shows his empty palms. "Look, we delivered the package. Now let us go."

"I think not." Ginger Guy is inspecting me up and down, noticing my green jumpsuit. "Y'all are still Greenjackets."

"What? No! I mean, yeah, she is, but she's not involved with any of their business. In fact, we're trying to stop them from—"

"Take 'em to the boss," Ginger says. Before I have time to dodge him, he's got a firm grip on my upper arm, his large furry fingers circling all the way around. He's strong enough to flip me over his shoulder like a sack of potatoes, so I don't bother resisting. Beard Guy divests Prince of his blaster and then shoves Joel's package back into his hands. They march us down the tunnel, pushing us when we trip over the uneven lumpiness of the cave floor.

We round a curve and are faced with a group of about twenty people warming their hands around a portable space heater. Lit up by a dozen torchlights, their faces all turn toward us, and some jump to their feet.

What's funny is they don't look like what I thought mind-alt runners would look like—tattooed, leather-clad, like Joel's gang. No, these people are dressed in what I'd call business casual: plain robes in dark colors, well-tailored trousers, bold jewel-toned shirts. I see the glint of expensive jewelry in ears and noses, circling wrists, and nestling against collarbones. This crowd wouldn't be out of the ordinary on any middle-class Imperial world.

Oh stars.

Have we just been captured by Imperials?

"These two brought the last payment from that glitcher Joel X," Ginger says. "Looks like he got scared and sent a couple of his Greenjacket buddies to take the blast for him."

A chorus of boos.

I know Prince has to be pissing his pants right now—I sure am—but he sounds totally calm when he speaks. "Anyone wanna tell me what Joel did this time? Besides just...being himself."

"Cheated us, that's what he did!" a woman yells. "Told us he'd get us a nice fat bonus if we sold all our best weapons to his Greenjacket supply guy. Then that fucker had the nerve to say he'd added an extra zero when he quoted our payment. He was tryin' to pay us a tenth of what he owed!" She snorts. "Well, Royal turned him upside-down and shook 'im a bit, and what d'you know, a bunch more credits fell out. Serves us right for thinkin' we could trust him!"

"They're all the same," another man grumbles. "Every time we sell to Greenjackets, they try to swindle us. Or they try to recruit us so we'll work for free. Or they blow up another one of our safehouses. They do nothin' but make it harder for honest pirates to make a living in this blasted galaxy."

I can't imagine what my face looks like now. I'm reeling a bit from the dissonance of hearing what outsiders think of us. I spent so long complacent in the lies I was told, the assurances that everything we did was for the greater good. It should be easy to brush away the hatred of pirates as meaningless, as flaring off the right people...but these folks aren't Imperials. If anything, they operate on the same (bad) side of Imperial law as Greenjackets do.

But apparently, we've gotten a reputation for being dishonest cheats. Among *pirates*.

Yeah…that one hurts.

I look to Prince for backup, but he isn't paying attention to me. He's staring, wide-eyed and slack-jawed, into the crowd. "*Who* did you say beat up Joel?" he asks, his voice shaking.

"Our boss. Royal."

A new voice speaks up. "That'd be me."

He strides to the front of the pack: a burly, short man with a suntanned face, long, dark hair, and a beard trimmed to frame his mouth. His sweeping black robe has golden skulls and crowns embroidered all over it, and his boots jingle with gold chains. He's got a gun holster slung across his hips, and thick, bejeweled rings on all his fingers. He dresses like a wealthy merchant, but there's iron in his stance that says he'll punch our teeth out the back of our heads if we cross him.

Only, right now, he's staring at Prince like he's just seen a ghost.

Prince has gone pale. The package slips from his hands and falls to the cave floor with a heavy thud.

No amount of mental blocking could stop me from hearing the one word echoing over and over in his mind, resonant with confused emotion…

::Pa?::

CHAPTER SIXTEEN

Amy

ARROW STATION

Nox puts me in magcuffs before she lets me off the shuttle. "Not that you could get past us if you tried," she says, giving me a snide once-over. "Better safe than sorry though."

Is that her passive-aggressive way of calling me a weakling? I'm a head taller than her. I could totally take her.

My hands are pinned behind me, but I do a rude hand gesture where she can't see it.

They haven't fed me since they snatched me out of Atlantis's ocean. Though, to be fair, I'm not sure they thought to *bring* food, since I haven't seen her or Petra eat either. The wild swerving between asteroids has my empty stomach throbbing with a dull nausea, and I'd kill for a drink of water. I hope wherever they're taking me has some.

I imagine meeting Oberon and Melanie like they're a regular person's aunt and uncle. We show up at their door; they coo over their "beautiful niece, so grown up now," and then they offer me a huge slice of freshly baked pie. Or a bowl of chunky vegetable soup. Or a tall glass of lemonade, weeping condensation on the table as my aunt teases me about not having a partner yet. I imagine them sending me to their guest bedroom for a nice, refreshing nap on a soft mattress stacked with fluffy pillows.

As if Oberon and Melanie would ever be the type to own soft furniture, or bake, or give a shit about their niece.

They meet us in the hallway outside the shuttle dock. A little jolt sizzles through my body when I see them. They're wearing identical khaki trousers and white smocks. Uncle O has gloves on and a pair of goggles shoved up on his bald head. I can still see the red marks around his eyes. He seems annoyed at this distraction from his work.

Auntie Mel has a huge fake smile pasted on. Her sleeves are rolled up, revealing an old-fashioned, baby-pink leather keycuff strap and short nails coated with clear varnish. She's the one who comes at me first, holding out her arms like she means to hug me. I dodge back, putting Petra between me and her.

"Amethyst," she effuses. "At last! We thought you'd never make it."

I raise my eyebrows. "You were expecting me?"

"Of course! Who do you think tipped off the Greenjackets to come get you? When Sister Liv told us you were finally leaving Halcyon, we knew it might be our only chance to see our precious niece."

I peer around Petra's shoulder, gasping in outrage. "Sister *Liv* tipped you off? How long has she been sending you information about me?"

"Oh, a few years now," says Melanie, with a casual handwave. "We wanted to make sure you were being treated well, sweetie. We heard you're studying at university, by the way! Good for you!"

"Here's a thought," I say, my teeth grinding now, because I'm working up to a full nuclear meltdown. "How about instead of spying on me, you just *called once in awhile* like regular relatives? You could even have, I don't know, *asked* me to come visit you, instead of sending a bunch of rebel thugs to *fucking kidnap me!*"

"Hey!" Nox protests. I shoulder-check her and send her stumbling into Petra. She's lucky my hands are bound. If they were free...I'm angry enough to start throwing punches.

Oberon's wearing this stank-face expression, like my yelling, uncooperative little ass is exactly what he expected, and he'd like to shove me back on the shuttle as soon as possible. But Melanie keeps trying.

"We've got to keep a low profile, honey. I hope you understand. The Imperials want us dead. They kept your offworld calls monitored because they knew we'd be likely to contact you. We *had* to sneak around, talking to your Devote friend, just to try to stay off their scanner."

Interesting story, but I don't buy it. "You could've had Sister Liv relay messages to me. Except you wouldn't have asked me to come for a casual visit, would you? You two want to *study* me. Am I right? I'll bet it didn't even occur to you to extend a polite invitation, like a normal aunt and uncle, because I'm not even a niece to you, am I? I'm just another fucking test subject."

"Now, sweetie, that's just not true," says Melanie in a saccharine tone that means, *It's totally true.* "I'll bet you're just exhausted from your trip. Oberon, take her to her room, and we'll let her rest a little while. I'll arrange for some dinner too. Would you like that?"

"Kiss my ass," I choke, sucking in my abs to try to stop my stomach from growling.

DANYA

Pirate's Cave, Unknown Planet

"After all these years...is it really you?" The pirate boss steps forward, holding out a hand. "Prince...it's me. Royal. Your pa."

"I'm gonna kill Joel," Prince mutters.

Royal DeSanto chuckles. "That's my boy. Glad to see you grew up all right."

"No thanks to you," Prince bites out. "*Pa.*"

The resemblance between them is clear. Prince has dyed his hair and done a lot more body mods, but under the beard, his father has the same face shape. The same pale-brown skin, a little more weathered. The same brown eyes and smirky curl to his mouth when he smiles.

"How come you brought a Greenjacket into my hideout? You better not be runnin' with that scum."

Prince's eyes narrow. He kicks the package toward his pa. "My friends are none of your business," he snaps, stepping in front of me. "Take your contraband and have a nice life."

"Wait, wait, wait. Don't run off." Royal jumps right over the package and grabs Prince's arm. "Come. Sit with us a minute. I want to chat with my son. Man to man."

"Man who sold his kid to a factory to man who worked his ass off climbing back out of that debt?" Prince rips his arm out of Royal's grasp. "Forget it, Pa. You told me all I needed to know about you when I was ten."

He starts backing away from Royal, pulling me with him. Ginger and Beard Guy seem to be taking their cues from the boss, and they don't move to stop us.

But then Royal says, "Would it mean anything to you if I said I was sorry?"

Prince lets go of me and slowly turns around.

"I do regret it, son," his pa says. The torchlight illuminates the scuffs on his boots, twinkling on the chains, but it leaves his face in shadow. "Your ma had just died. I knew I was gonna have to take up some unsavory activities to put food on the table. It wasn't safe for a kid to be part of that world. What can I say? I panicked. Knew a guy whose kids worked at that factory, and he swore to me they were treated good. Three meals a day, health care, all that. So I let 'em have you. I swear, I didn't know that'd be the last time I saw you. They forgot to warn me they didn't allow visitation..."

I can feel Prince's rage and grief, rippling out from him in waves that threaten to bowl me over. He's remembering what it felt like to be that abandoned child.

Voice breaking, he says, "I appreciate your apology, but it can't fix what you did."

"Come on, stay awhile," Royal begs. "Let's talk."

I can see from Prince's face that he's having none of it. "I've got somewhere to be," he snarls. "A friend to save. You got your package. I'm done."

Royal fumbles in his pocket and holds out a credit chip. "Then at least take payment for your trouble with the delivery. That cheap bastard Joel won't pay you."

"I don't want your—"

I elbow Prince and hiss, "Take it."

So, grudgingly, Prince accepts the chip from his father's hand, shoving it deep into the pocket of his jumpsuit. Then he stalks back to the ship without a word.

I would try to say something to smooth things over with Royal, but I'm *persona non grata* here. I settle for an awkward wave before following Prince back onto the ship. As the stairs retract into the side of the ship, I look down and notice the credit chip glinting in a puddle. Prince must have pitched it before climbing aboard.

I secure the door and make my way to my seat. I've barely strapped myself in before we're already airborne. Prince hits the accelerator, pressing us back in our seats as the cave disappears in our wake.

"D'you wanna talk about—" I venture.

"No."

All right then. I brace myself for the teleport, but Prince speeds into the night, breathing heavily as the ship responds valiantly to his emotional outburst.

I pretend I don't notice the tears tracking glittering lines down his cheeks.

AMY

Arrow Station

I eat the fucking dinner that my fucking aunt sent to my fucking room.

It's delicious. Synthmeat loaf with a sweet, smoky sauce, buttery corn, and potato mash. I'm starving. Of course I'm gonna eat it. But I don't have to be happy about it.

The room, at least, is ugly, so I can be properly flared off about something. It looks like an interior decorator's idea of a prison cell. Metallic gray walls, hideous grainy tan carpet. One wall is dominated by a wallscreen that's been programmed to play a semi-realistic holo of a window looking out on a tropical beach. The bed is an alcove cut out of the wall, lined with an unyielding mattress pad and thin, scratchy blankets. The washroom folds out of another part of the wall—a seat connecting to a waste collection tube, with a cleansing unit just big enough to decontaminate my hands. Maybe my hair, if I got desperate enough to bend at a ninety-degree angle and shove my head through a hole in the wall.

Satisfying as it is to imagine my aunt as an evil sorceress imprisoning her hapless niece in a dungeon, I doubt the ugly decor is her fault. This whole station looks just as wretched, from what I saw as they dragged me through the halls. From eavesdropping on Nox and Petra, I've gathered that this place is supposed to be abandoned. It was a thriving Greenjacket base about fifty years ago, protected by the asteroid field. But apparently, the Emperor got wise to them and launched an all-out attack.

It's bold of Melanie and Oberon to hide out from the Authorities in a base that the Empire *still knows about*. They're apparently gambling on the Authorities being too busy to check the base for signs of life. Maybe it's a sign of the Imperials' overconfidence that, so far, they *haven't* checked.

After I eat, I take advantage of the time alone to freshen up and have a nap. I don't sleep for very long—it's hard to rest when I feel like I'm being watched—but it's enough to make me feel halfway alive again. Then I start trying to figure out how to escape.

They locked the room, of course. I expected that. Next trick: try to call a dragon. No go on that one either. Some prisons use a disruptor field to scare the dragons off so that they won't go anywhere near the prisoners, even if someone is calling for help. I don't know how to tell if that's what Oberon and Melanie are using, but it's either that or the dragons suddenly hate me. I even try calling Fairy specifically—I know ze's Prince's bonded companion, but I figure we're friendly enough that ze might bend the rules of zir species to help me. But no. Dragons can hear a call nearly anywhere in the known universe...but not here. I'm out of luck.

That gets me thinking though. The eel-fish said I was exhibiting the same signs their ancestors showed right before they began to learn teleportation and ascended into spirit-beings.

I'm not entirely sold on the idea of becoming a ghost-snake. It'd be awesome to teleport around the galaxy and be unkillable and all that... but like...dragons can't have sex. Or feel the giddy burn of anticipation right before a kiss. Or cry at the sight of a stupidly cute kitten. They can't *eat*, for stars' sake.

I'm a disaster at being a human in this universe, I know. But there's so much I love about it. The pleasures and the adrenaline rushes and the bittersweet nostalgia. Even heartbreak and grief. I could never give those up. Grieving for Mum was the only way I knew how to love her after she was gone.

So I don't want to "ascend"—at least, not yet. But on the other hand...teleporting would be an extremely useful skill to have.

I wish I'd asked the eel-fish so many more questions while I had the chance. Like, *How long can you balance on the line between becoming a "prophet" and full ascension? How does someone learn to teleport? Do I need to meditate like a Devote seeking enlightenment?*

Well, I could try. Meditation never did work that well for me—I have a hard time sitting still—but I'm stuck in a blazin' prison cell. It's not like I don't have the time on my hands.

Settling into a crisscross position on the hard mattress, I close my eyes and breathe slow and deep. My brain immediately resists. My foot twitches with the urge to fidget. This is normally where, if I was trying this in my dormitory back at Phoenix Refuge or Halcyon University, I'd give up and go down to the beach for a swim.

But I'm stuck here. So I push through the boredom and the twitchy muscles and focus hard on my breath. *In one-two-three. Out one-two-three. In one-two—*

The door slides open. I tense up, losing what little relaxation I managed to achieve.

"Amethyst." It's Uncle Oberon, wearing the annoyed expression that

I'm starting to think might be his normal resting face.

"I go by Amy," I correct him automatically.

"We're ready for you in the lab."

"Ready to do what? Vivisect me? Harvest my ovaries?"

"What? No." His confusion is genuine. Unlike Auntie Mel, he can't act for shit.

Right, so they're not trying to kill me. Bare minimum of avuncular courtesy achieved.

"We just want to ask you some questions," he says. "It's about the mods Gaela did on you when you were a baby. You know about those, don't you?"

Hesitantly, I nod.

"We would like to know about any of the effects from those gen-mods you might be experiencing now that you're grown to adulthood. That's all. No vivisection."

Was that an attempt at humor? I think the grimace he just made was supposed to be a smile. Someone needs to enroll Oberon in How To Be an Uncle for Beginners. Maybe teach him how to make puns (but not ones about vivisection).

I climb down from the bed alcove and come to meet him at the door. "I'll come," I say. "But I have some conditions."

"What are they?"

"Not yet. I want Auntie Mel to hear this too."

Oberon leads me through the corridor. I try to peek in every open door we pass, but most of the rooms are dark. Only one is lit up, and when I glance inside, I see a kitchbot serving something that smells buttery-sweet. Nox and Petra are in there, laughing and shoving each other.

"*They're* still here?"

"The asteroid field is difficult to navigate," Oberon says tonelessly. "They wanted to rest up before making the journey again."

"Ah." *So there's still a chance I can escape.*

The lab, when we reach it, is one of the largest rooms on the station. It might've been used as a med center before. The cots have been repurposed into long tables, piled with crates of samples. A high-powered microscope has the place of honor in the middle of the room. Directly across from it, a huge wallscreen projects a document full of scribbled notes in two distinct handwritings. They've struck an interesting balance between "immaculately clean" and "chaotic mess."

Melanie is in the process of adding to the wallscreen notes. When she hears us come in, she minimizes what she's working on and turns to face me, stripping off her control gauntlet. "Amethyst," she says, in what she probably imagines to be a warm, welcoming tone.

Nope. Not letting her treat me like a baby for one more second.

"I want you both to understand one thing, if we're going to work together," I say, hands on hips. "I'm not a child anymore. And I'm not an object to experiment on. I'm a person, and I expect you to treat me like one. You'll explain to me all the tests you're performing on me. I'm in a genetics course at university, so don't worry, I'll understand the tricky bits. Also, from now on, if you want me to do anything, you'll ask first, the way you'd ask a colleague."

Melanie blinks several times. "All right, sweetie..."

"Oh, also? Stop calling me cutesy nicknames. My name is Amy."

I catch a lightning flash of anger in Melanie's eyes, but she conceals it quickly. "Very well, Amy. I'm sorry if we've made you feel uncomfortable here. You have to understand, in our minds, you *are* still a baby."

I wait, thinking there's going to be more to that apology, but that's all she's got.

"Well, come have a seat," she redirects briskly. "Now, all we want to do today is conduct a little interview, just to find out what long-term effects you might be experiencing from Gaela's gen-mod experimentation. And if you'll allow it, I'd like to take a blood sample as well."

"We'll see how this goes," I say, settling onto the tall stool she offers me.

In the privacy of my mind, I vow not to tell them anything important. Nothing about my psychic ability—and definitely not what the eel-fish told me. They're going to have to earn that knowledge.

And if they prove untrustworthy, they'll have to use a scalpel to dig it out of my cold dead brain.

PART SEVEN

Year 3729, Week 30,

Dayseven

CHAPTER SEVENTEEN

Danya

LUZ DE LAS ESTRELLAS, GILA CITY, ESPERANZA

It's the next morning by the time we return to Luz de las Estrellas. I insisted on Prince taking at least eight hours in the sleep-pod, because he looked...not stellar last night. I don't know how much sleep he got, but I'm hoping he's cooled off a little. Seeing his dad really messed him up, and I'm afraid he's directing all of his frustration at the easier target: Joel.

Joel's waiting for us in a private room. He bought the drinks this time; tiny glasses of some hair-curlingly strong liquor sit blue and innocent on the table between us. He's got his feet up on the empty chair next to him and looks smug as a cat with a bird in its mouth.

The second we walk in, I experience the same surge of boiling fury that goes through Prince. I jump to close the door before the yelling starts.

"You knew my pa was a pirate! You *knew* and you didn't bother to warn me! Give me one good reason why I shouldn't punch your lights out."

"Hey, whoa—" I put a hand on his arm, but he shakes me off, caught up in the storm of his anger.

"Here's the good reason." Joel unrolls his scroll on the table. With a few flicks of his fingers, he brings up the map we need, an intricate simulation of each asteroid and its projected movements. In the middle, a glowing circle indicates Arrow Station.

"You glitcher—" Prince starts. I slap his shoulder repeatedly, trying to get him to stop before he gives Joel a reason to take the map back.

But Joel interrupts first. "Don't read too much into it, DeSanto. I owed the SkullKings a payment. They don't like Greenjackets, so I didn't wanna deliver it myself. The fact that your pa is a member of their gang... well, I admit, I thought it'd be funny to mess with you a little."

Prince lunges. I catch him by the back of his jumpsuit just in time. "Don't," I hiss.

Fairy swoops down and twines zir body around his neck. Whatever ze's saying to him finally gets through, because he takes a deep breath and backs down.

"Send the map to my keycuff," he says, voice shaking with the effort to keep calm. "Then you'll never see us again."

Joel taps on his scroll. "When you inevitably get caught sticking your nose in dangerous business, don't tell 'em it was me who gave you this."

"Fine," says Prince. "As long as you're not the one who tells 'em what business I'm sticking my nose into."

"Aw, c'mon, would I?" Joel goes all wide-eyed and innocent. The expression reminds me of Nox as a kid when she was about to blame a misdeed on someone else to get out of trouble.

But the sad eyes work on Prince. He softens, just a little, and says, "We were friends once, Joel. I haven't forgotten."

::I miss you,:: he doesn't say out loud. It reverberates through his brain, a vulnerable and squishy feeling that he no longer trusts Joel enough to voice.

He's leaking emotions into my mind again. I can see just how much his friendship with Joel meant. Physical attraction wasn't a factor, nor were his feelings precisely romantic...but it was love nonetheless. Ride-or-die, fight-an-army-to-save-him *love*.

And here Joel is, five years later, making mean jokes at Prince's expense. No wonder the man's hurting. I'd be furious too if someone treated me like this. I'd...

Stars, I know exactly how I'd act. I'd be a fucking doormat, meekly allowing the abuse, grateful they're bothering to notice me enough to be cruel.

This is how Petra treats me.

Wow.

That realization kicks me hard in the throat, almost making me tear up. I've been such a pathetic little punching bag, haven't I? I was so used to being bullied, I even allowed it—*expected* it—from the person I dreamed of kissing.

As Prince and I walk away, I can feel him working to reconcile the fond memories of Joel with the cold asshole he is now. *::Was he always like this, or has he changed?::*

My heart breaks along with his.

I *know* Petra has always been a bully. She could change, maybe, someday...but for the first time in my life, I'm not interested in waiting around to watch it happen. She's not the best option I've got. Not anymore.

I've met a woman who had every reason to hate me and showed mercy instead. A woman who comforted me when I was out of my depth, who rubbed my back when I was casting up...

Oh blazes. I've caught feelings for Amy. And if we don't hurry up and rescue her, I may never see her again.

AMY

ARROW STATION

I think Auntie Mel is getting fed up with me. We're in her lab, sitting across a table from each other, a cambot recording my every move. I can smell the fresh disinfectant from the surface of the table. In fact, the whole lab has been deep-cleaned top to bottom. I bet they were worried I'd start snooping into their research if they left anything lying around.

Honestly, they were right, and I'm annoyed they anticipated me.

This whole interview feels like a chess match. I'm not interested in letting them pump me for information, but they're equally disinterested in telling me what the fuck they're up to. We keep answering each other's questions with questions, going nowhere.

Melanie: "What did your mother tell you about your genetic history?"

Me: "If you take my blood, what are you going to be looking for?"

Melanie: "What did you find at that old Atlantis base?"

Me: "So are you working for the Greenjackets? Or are *they* working for *you?*"

Melanie: "Did Gaela manage to teach you to teleport without a dragon?"

Me: "What were you and my mum trying to accomplish with the Human Teleportation Project? Who benefits if we don't need dragons anymore?"

The funny thing is, I can tell Oberon desperately wants to answer me. He's one of those guys who can't resist monologuing about their research. It's Melanie who wears the glitch face now. Her replies to my questions are terse redirections, but I'm not giving her anything. She's doing that trick where she tries to pretend she knows more than she really does, to make me lower my guard and admit everything. But she's fixated on my gold eyes as the sole expression of my genetic weirdness, so she keeps telling me how "it must be strange, seeing things that aren't there sometimes."

She has no idea. I'm just not seeing them *with my eyes*.

In the end, I agree to give them a blood sample—but only on the condition that they tell me everything they discover. I think that's a reasonable demand—after all, it's *my* blood. They grumble about it a bit, but they want the sample badly enough that they finally agree.

Then they send for one of their lab assistants to get rid of me. Or, uh, "take me back to my room to rest." The guy they summon to babysit me looks younger than I am. Have they been poaching university students with promises of internships? The scrawny eighteen-year-old has the nerves of a bunny, with prominent front teeth to match.

He guides me down the hall the way an animal tamer might guide a half-feral predator. He really shouldn't act so skittish. It's making me want to act wild, since he obviously expects me to try to eat him or something.

I stop next to the open door where Nox and Petra still sit, chatting over the remains of their meal.

"Miz Ediya," the intern says nervously. "We should go..."

I square my shoulders and march in, facing the Greenjackets with arms akimbo. The intern squeaks in protest, but I ignore him.

"Why the blazes are you still here?" I demand. "You got what you came for. Dropped me off on my aunt and uncle's doorstep, special delivery. Now why don't you get the fuck out?"

"Can't yet," Nox says from where she slouches against the table, cheek propped up on her hand. "Gotta wait for the ship to finish fueling."

Well, that doesn't make sense. It's been *hours*. "How long does it take to fuel a shuttle?"

Nox shrugs. "They told me it wasn't done yet."

Ah. So Oberon and Melanie are keeping them here. Why? Who knows? Maybe they need more subjects to experiment on. Maybe they're tired of their weedy intern flinching at every sound and they're looking to replace him.

I'm trying to figure out how I can ask them to sneak me aboard the shuttle when they leave without the intern overhearing, but then Nox cuts me off. "So what's the deal with the Ediyas anyway? They tell you anything interesting?"

"Not much," I admit.

"Hey," she says, glancing at Petra with raised eyebrows. "You got a wallscreen in your room, Amy?"

"Yeah, why? You want to watch *Bikini Vampires of Black Sand Beach* or...?"

A slow smirk spreads across Nox's face. "Yeah. That's my show. You mind if I come over to watch an episode?"

There's no way *Bikini Vampires* is actually Nox's favorite show. But she's got something up her sleeve, and even though I don't like her much, I'm curious to know what she's up to. "Why not? C'mon over."

We march the rest of the way down the hall to my room. These long corridors are super creepy, full of missing ceiling panels, hanging wires, and the bland whirring of life-support systems. Is this the environment Danya grew up in? I can't blame her for being obsessed with sunlight, if these sad windowless metal tubes are all she ever knew.

The intern skitters away as soon as the door to my room swishes open, forgetting to lock me in. I hit the switch to shut the door behind us. "He's going to go tell Oberon and Melanie we're conspiring in here," I say. "Whatever you two are up to, do it fast."

Nox rolls her eyes. "If they come to check up, just pretend you're having sex with us and they'll leave. Works every time."

"No offense, but ew."

Petra shoots me the glitchiest sneer I've ever seen. "Full offense, but same."

"Now that we're all on the same page," Nox says, in a *shut the fuck up* tone, "can we focus, please?"

Petra's already hacking her way into the wallscreen. The screen is locked in window mode—I checked when I was trying to plot an escape —but Petra must be a tech wizard. She's got the thing in admin mode, and even though the control gauntlet is nowhere in sight, she's using bare hand-gestures to type an access code that, to my immense shock, *actually works*.

"I knew it!" she says under her breath, with a small fistpump of victory. "They're running on a Greenjacket system. The same one I've got all the passcodes for. Thanks for making this easy for me, quarkbrains." She taps for another few seconds, then curses. "No uniweb access. How do they stand it?"

"To be fair, it'd be hard to get a daily uniweb sync delivered to the middle of an asteroid field," I point out. The uniweb is a complicated process—because space is huge, it's impossible to broadcast between planets. So every day, each planet creates a copy of its local uniweb updates and sends a syncship to a central location somewhere in the Monroe system. Those are compiled into one, re-uploaded, and teleported back to the planets.

Some planets, usually the big ones full of rich Imperials, sync their uniweb multiple times a day. Like, once per hour, something wild like that. Poorer planets can barely afford to sync once a fortnight. Halcyon's pretty middle-of-the-road with a once-a-day sync. It happens at night usually. Any messages we send to our offplanet loved ones have a day or so of wait time before being answered. Our local uniweb coverage is great—vid-calls and messages go through instantaneously—but contacting anyone offworld is a time-consuming, agonizing wait.

Knowing all that, I can't imagine there's a single syncship pilot in the galaxy who would agree to fly that asteroid field even once a week. And if they're trying to keep this base secret from the Imperials, they probably wouldn't want a record of syncships coming in and out.

But Petra has already moved on. "At least we've got basic networking between this wallscreen and the rest of the base...I can work with that. Let's see. D'you think they encrypt their files if they're isolated out here with no one to spy on them?"

She answers herself in a moment: "Password-locked. Ohhh, they're not even trying. I could bypass this in my sleep."

I turn to Nox, eyebrows lifted. "So...she's trying to hack into Oberon and Melanie's personal research files?"

"Obviously." Nox folds her arms across her chest. "We're not just here to drop you off and be on our merry way. We came here because the Greenjackets are up to something involving you and your weird aunt and uncle. If your family knows something that could help us take down the corrupt Greenjacket leadership, then we're gonna find it and use it."

"Mmm. Gotcha." If Melanie figures out what they're doing, she'll space them without even feeling bad about it. But I have to admit, I'm curious what they're going to dig up.

Once Petra gets through to the files, though, she runs into the same problem that I did with my father's Atlantis research. It's just *so much reading.* And time is not on our side; any second now, that intern's gonna tell Melanie that Nox and I are up to something in this room, and Melanie will storm in, and then I'll have to pretend to kiss Nox or something...

I won't lie, I have somewhat uncomfy feelings about that. It's not that Nox isn't cute. It's that she looks *exactly* like Danya...but *isn't.* There's something hard and cynical about the way her face rests, where

Danya is all soft and open. She even speaks differently—more confident, more opinionated, and frankly, a lot ruder.

And yeah, fine, I'm attracted to Danya. She's cute as blazes. I'd be fibbing if I said I hadn't pictured her rising up on her tiptoes and pressing herself against my chest...the way her lips would feel against mine...

But here's what's weird: even though Nox looks *literally exactly the same*, the idea of kissing her grosses me out. Same goes for Petra, though I won't deny she's drop-dead gorgeous.

I've known for a long time that I like people of any gender. But this just confirms to me that it's not their bodies that interest me at all. It's the person inside who lights my fire—or throws sand on it and stomps on the ashes.

The stark difference between how I feel about Nox and how I feel for Danya is what's making me uncomfortable. Not the idea of kissing Nox for a ruse—that's whatever. I'll do what I need to survive. But thinking about it is making me realize how much I *do* want to kiss Danya. How, in just a day or two (I lost count, between all these time zones), her softness and vulnerability wormed their way into my affections.

Blast this. I'm not letting Oberon and Melanie keep me here. There's a woman out there in the universe just waiting for me to ask her out.

I open my mouth to suggest an escape to Nox, but she and Petra are engrossed in the screen. "Stars a-blazin'," Petra whispers. "Nox. Does this mean what I think?"

I lean over their shoulders to see what they're looking at. It's a list of names, some of them only given number designations, with research files attached to each of them. A list of Oberon and Melanie's test subjects? The paragraph above them dates this list twenty-two years ago, and the birth dates next to each name suggest that all of these test subjects were babies at the time.

Most of them are marked with an X: deceased. But there's a few at the bottom who are still alive, and those are the names Nox and Petra are staring at, fingers over mouths, whispering obscenities.

Because the two names at the very bottom are familiar...

<Nikola Octavia Xiang. 3707/4/2. Donors: Edwin Xiang, Alexis Orlov. Adopted by donors 3709/16/1. File attached.

Danya Augusta Xiang. 3707/4/2. Donors: Edwin Xiang, Alexis Orlov. Adopted by donors 3709/16/1. File attached.>

Holy shit.

CHAPTER EIGHTEEN

Danya

EN ROUTE TO ARROW STATION

"So what's our plan here?" Prince asks. He's making this flight look easy, even though the way we're twisting and weaving through the asteroid field is enough to churn my stomach. I focus on the blinking lights on the dash, keeping my eyes averted from the viewport.

"Plan? I thought *you* were coming up with one."

"Uh…well, all right then, guess it's seat-of-our-pants time. Pretty standard for me, or that's what Fairy'll tell you." Prince doesn't look away from the viewport for a second. His hands move in a confident, graceful dance across the instruments. "So here's what I'm thinking. We land. I send Fairy in to get Amy and—" He breaks off and overcorrects a turn as he glances at the dragon hovering just above his head. "What d'you *mean*, you can't go get her?"

Fairy broadcasts zir answer to both of us. ::*Arrow Station has a dragon-repulsing shield. I cannot go near it. Even now we draw too close. I will have to leave you soon.*::

"Hang on, *no*," Prince protests. "I don't wanna go anywhere you can't come with me."

::*You must. I will be waiting when you emerge. Take care, love.*::

I can't hear Prince's response, but when Fairy's incorporeal form fades into invisibility, I hear him grunt an angry curse.

I guess it's on me to take over planning. "What if...we land, you stay with the ship to make sure they don't capture it, and I go find Amy and break her out."

"Alone? What if you need backup?"

I take a deep breath. "I'm going to get my sister to help me."

"Uh, isn't your sister the one who kidnapped her in the first place? I thought you said she's, like, unhinged."

"I wouldn't go that far!" Maybe Nox can get a little...fanatical. But she isn't unreasonable. I believe, at her core, all she wants is to help people. "I can use what we learned from those files as leverage. I'll tell her we have more information that can help her cause. She only took Amy because she wanted to get to the bottom of this thing with the Ediyas. If I offer her a chance to do that..."

"I s'pose you know her best." But Prince sounds skeptical. "It's not like I have a better plan. Just...try not to get caught, yeah? I like you. Amy too. Kinda wanna keep you around." He chuckles wryly. "Also, I don't want to go home to Halcyon and tell my boss I let you *both* get kidnapped. Getting yelled at ain't fun."

"Thanks for everything, Prince," I say. "Seriously. You didn't have to do any of this. If you get in trouble with your officers, I'll take all the blame for you."

"Can't do that if you get captured, now, can you?" He flashes me a nose-wrinkling, impish smile. "So don't get caught."

"Yes, sir."

"We're just about through the field," he murmurs. "We'll be on-base in about five minutes. Better get ready."

My insides feel like they're fermenting. Nerves turn my stomach bubbly and sour. I drag my eyes away from the viewport, determined not to cast up in Prince's ship *again*.

::Nox. Can you hear me? I'm coming. Please talk to me.::

AMY

ARROW STATION

Nox and Petra are frantically scrolling through the file that documents the genetic experiments performed on Danya and Nox as babies. The room is pin-drop quiet as they read, flicking past irrelevant segments to get to the juicy stuff.

I'm still trying to wrap my head around it. Two years before I was even born, my aunt and uncle got genetic material samples from Greenjackets and made a whole batch of test-tube embryos. It's not entirely clear from their notes what they were trying to do, but it must have been something to do with the Human Teleportation Project, right? Only they didn't have ancestral dragon DNA to work with yet. So I guess they were just blindly tweaking the poor babies' genes to see what would work.

Stars, if that's true, no wonder so many of them died.

Nox gets to the end of the file, and I shuffle forward to read the addendum from my uncle:

<Though these subjects show promise, we have been forced to surrender custody. Fortunately, Greenjacket leadership had a close eye on our dealings with the Authorities, and they were able to step in and claim two—the twins—by right of biological parentage. It will be beneficial to see the subjects raised in a controlled environment away from the corrupting influence of the Empire. We look forward to observing developments as the children age. The other subjects may be lost to us now, but perhaps there will be a chance later to examine their progress.>

I think I understand Mum a little better now. I always wondered why she would leave her life's work behind to settle on Halcyon. It must have been because we were under the dragons' protection. When she died, she left explicit instructions that I was not to be adopted—I was to be raised as a ward of Phoenix Refuge. I wonder if Oberon and Melanie had already tried to convince Mum to bring me to their lab. She knew they'd turn me into a little pet for them to experiment on, and she chose to keep me safe.

And then, like a fool, I agreed to go on that offplanet field trip, taking me out of the dragons' realm of protection and right into the Greenjackets' clutches.

"Well?" says Petra softly. "Nox, have you noticed anything weird? Did their experiments do anything?"

Nox hesitates a few seconds too long. There *is* something, I can tell. But she lets out a breath and shakes her head. "I'm normal."

"Try telling that to Oberon and Melanie," I butt in. "If they know who you are—and I think they do, which is why they're stalling your ship —then they won't let you leave here without being tested. They may not let us leave here, period."

Nox moans. "This was a trap."

I don't think so. "*You* were the one who decided to kidnap me and bring me here. Nobody made you do that. You dug this hole and jumped in it with both feet. They're just two vultures who got lucky."

She glares at me, annoyed because I'm right. Then her expression changes, and she goes blank for a second, staring at the wall.

"Dawn," she whispers. And then she turns and sprints, almost running smack into the door in her haste to exit. The door slams shut behind her.

"What's that all about?" I ask Petra.

"Dunno." Petra keeps scrolling. "She gets weird sometimes. You know, I've always kinda got the feeling she and Danya are...mind-linked? Like sometimes one of them will get hurt, and then the other one turns up asking what happened. Stuff like that. D'you think that could be what the Ediyas were trying to gen-mod into them?"

"Maybe," I say. "Is there anything in Nox's file about the specific changes that were made to her genes?"

"Yeah, there were some notes, but it was all science jargon." Petra makes a face.

"Lucky for you," I say, "I happen to be fluent."

She's really good at that subtle eyebrow lift, the one that says, *I think you're full of shit, but whatever, I'll let you embarrass yourself.* "All right then." She scrolls back to the section in question. "Have at it."

DANYA

I WAS EXPECTING SOME DIFFICULTY WITH DOCKING—LIKE WE'D HAVE to lie to the traffic controller or fake a password—but Arrow Station's dock seems not to be monitored. The station itself is tiny compared to Sherwood, barely large enough to support a hundred people, so its traffic control seems to be automated. All Prince has to do is transmit a docking request, and the airlock whirrs open to admit us. He times his approach to match the rotation of the station's interconnected rings.

"That was too easy," I mutter.

"Yeah." Prince lets out a long breath, his shoulders loosening. He waits for the pressurization cycle to finish, then maneuvers into the dock and anchors the ship. When everything's powered down, he turns to me.

"I'll be back before you know it," I promise.

"Be back before the *Ediyas* know it. Yeah?"

"Yeah." I feel bad leaving him alone with no dragon to look out for him. He's really feeling zir absence; the man's been wound progressively tighter since ze vanished.

But suddenly I can hear Nox's voice in my head, responding at last—yelling, in fact. I disembark from the ship, hoping I'm not about to get my ass kicked.

I don't even make it halfway across the hangar before Nox bursts in. She must have run all the way here, because she's panting hard, striding toward me with eyes on fire. She grabs me in a fierce hug that may or may not also be a headlock. "You quarkbrained little fool. Why did you come? Why couldn't you just let me keep you safe?"

"Keep me safe? That's what you're calling it, when you stole my friend and left me with no explanation? I had to figure out how to find you all by myself."

She gives me a little shake. "You shouldn't have. Don't you get it? This place is dangerous for us." She shudders. "We only just figured out how dangerous."

A glimpse of her mind, and I see what she's talking about. *Our names on a list of the Ediya triplets' experiments.*

My breath shortens. "Oh stars." I might be about to have a panic attack. *We* were those babies? The lucky few they didn't euthanize?

"And I think Melanie knows who I am," Nox is babbling, her words tripping over each other in their feverish rush to get out. "You have to get back on that ship and go, before they realize they have the other twin here! If they catch you, if they figure out how our minds are linked—"

"I can't go!" I protest. "Not without Amy."

"Forget about it! The Ediyas will never let her go. She's their prize experiment, their own flesh and blood mixed with the dragons'."

Ah, so Nox was watching at least some of the time on Atlantis. "I don't care," I say. "We dragged her into this. She didn't ask for any of it. So we owe it to her to help her escape."

"What if she doesn't want to? She *is* their niece. Maybe she wants to help them."

"Well, then she can tell me so herself," I snap. "For someone who talks about how much you hate the Greenjackets, you sure are doing some mental gymnastics to justify kidnapping."

I can tell that blow lands hard. Her eyebrows come together, and her eyes flash with an electric current of anger. She opens her mouth to retort, then closes it again.

"Take me to her," I say, soft but firm. "And then we're getting out of here. You, too, if you want."

I can see in her eyes—can feel in her mind—that she's wavering. That she might actually listen to me.

That's when the stun blasts hit us full force.

PRINCE

Without Fairy nearby, I feel *less* somehow. This is the first time since I met zem that I've gone somewhere ze can't follow. It leaves an empty, hollow sensation in my gut.

I keep an eye on Danya through the viewport as she reunites with her twin. Stars, it's weird seeing the two of them together; they're mirror images of each other, but not so perfectly matched that I can't tell the difference. It's something in the way they hold themselves—how Nox lifts her chin imperiously and Danya is always ducking inward. I see her making an effort to stand straight, to meet her sister as an equal. She's growing in confidence by the minute, like an alien vine reaching toward the sky. It warms me to see. *Go, girl.*

My ship's anchor emits a few panicked *bleep*s, drawing my attention away. A quick scan of the readout tells me that someone's trying to anchor-lock my ship.

"Nuh-uh," I mutter. I jam my finger on the *disengage* button, retracting the anchor before the lock can pin it down. *Danya, better hurry, they're onto us...*

I look out the viewport again and double-take when I catch sight of a stranger standing in the hangar entrance She's dark, curly-haired, with perfect posture. Her face is exactly what Amy might look like in twenty years. She's older than the pictures in the article that called her a murderer...but it's unmistakably Melanie Ediya.

With a stunner in her hand.

I jump to my feet with a shout, but too late. Melanie's already firing, bringing down both Danya and Nox in quick succession. The two collapse in a heap, and Melanie strides forward, looking up toward my viewport. Even though I know she can't see me through the mirrored shield, I duck down.

I've gotta get out of here. I'm no good helping them escape if I get caught. Especially not without Fairy.

Without even bothering to fasten my safety belt, I reverse toward the airlock, praying Melanie didn't think to seal it. My last bit of luck holds. The airlock opens, closes, and spits me out into space.

I feel like an absolute bastard. Saving my own skin, leaving the others.

I'll come back for you. I will. I swear.

I just need to recruit some backup first.

AMY

ONCE PETRA GIVES OVER CONTROL OF THE FILES, I CAN'T STOP digging through them. There's so much fascinating information here. Research logs documenting their process day by day. Searching telepathic alien species for similar gene structures. Replicating a similar gene to fit into human DNA. Running simulations. Finding out that the simulations gave telepathic humans a seventy percent chance of going mad, unable to handle knowledge of everybody else's mind.

They went through with the project anyway.

Some of the children grew up with defects the simulation couldn't even predict. Brains too large to fit inside their skulls. Babies that cried and cried and cried without ceasing, refusing milk or comfort, because they couldn't handle the cacophony of thoughts ringing in their minds.

A few of them died naturally. Some, as Uncle Oberon dispassionately recorded, had to be "put out of their misery" like they were wild animals. The thought sickens me. If I followed down my mother's career path, would I, too, have found myself in the position of euthanizing a human child I had created, a baby unable to thrive in this world because of defects I caused?

I'd already made up my mind to leave the university, but now I know I won't regret it. I'm done playing with people's genes. Even the little stuff, the frivolous cosmetic changes and the editing-out of diseases...it's spoiled for me, knowing the truth of my mother's legacy. If I had come out wrong, what would Mum have done? Would she have kept me or...?

I'm still reeling from considering that question when Petra stops my scrolling and points. "What's that?"

I open the file to find another list. More names. Fewer exed, this time. And the birth dates...they're younger than me. Some not by a lot—seventeen, eighteen years old. Some are barely five years old.

"Fuck," I whisper.

"What? Who are these ones?"

"I think these are...these are a new batch. Kids the Ediyas made after Mum ran away to Halcyon with me." I press my fingers to my lips. "They must have figured out what she was up to with Emerson—my father.

They took the dragon-ancestors' genes and tried to make more like me."
I stare at the list of files. "Stars blazing. What if they did it?" What if all
these kids are like me—so-called *prophets* who can learn an item's history
with a single touch? What if they've progressed even further and they're
learning to teleport?

Is that why there's a dragon shield on this station—so the kids can't
cheat as they learn?

"If this is right, then these kids might still be here," I say. "We have
to find them."

Petra's eyes gleam. "You're right! This could be the scandal that ruins
the Greenjacket leaders."

I narrow my eyes. "I want to *help* these kids. Not use them to start a
revolution."

"Sure." Petra waves her hand dramatically. "Bring up a map of this
station. Let's figure out where they're keeping 'em."

CHAPTER NINETEEN

Amy

ARROW STATION

Arrow Station is circular, with three rings rotating around a central nucleus where the power generator is located. The inner ring contains a food production sector, water filtration, and power controls; the middle and outer rings contain dormitories, starship hangars, and living spaces like gyms, washrooms, and dining areas.

That's about all the helpful information we get from the map Petra finds in Uncle Oberon's files. Sadly, there's no X marking where a bunch of secret test-tube kids might be kept.

"I think we're here." Petra points to a spot on the middle ring. "I haven't seen anybody on this level except Oberon, Melanie, you, and that teenager who was trying to play bodyguard."

"Yeah." Now that she mentions it, it's a little bit weird that there's *literally* no one else aboard. I chalked it up to my aunt and uncle wanting to keep their research secret, but they used to have a whole team helping them out. One intern isn't enough.

"Do you think there's more people living in the big outer ring?"

Petra nods. "That's where I'd look first."

We creep out into the hall, looking both ways before we go. It's still creepy-quiet; Melanie and Oberon must be busy studying my blood or something.

Instead of taking the zip-pods, which might draw attention, Petra shows me where to find the connecting shafts that stretch between rings. They're supposed to be for emergency use, probably because crawling through them makes me very aware that only a skinny little tube separates me from the hungry cold of space. Fighting dizziness, I press forward, focusing on the next step, and the next.

When we stumble out of the shaft, we find ourselves in another narrow corridor. It looks identical to the inner ring, just with a somewhat more distant horizon.

"Looks just like Sherwood Base in here," Petra mutters. "Creativity isn't the Greenjackets' strong suit."

I shush her. "Let's get going." It's only a matter of time before Melanie decides to check on me and discovers I'm gone from my room. I wonder if the intern actually did rat us out, or if he decided to keep quiet for his own safety.

Most of the doors here are unlocked, the lights powered down. I peer into each room as we pass, wondering where the Ediyas would hide a creche full of children. One room appears to be a dining area, complete with a set of dormant kitchbots in their charging docks. Is it my imagination or do I smell a recent meal lingering over the artificial scent of cleaner?

We pass what looks like a fitness training gym, also spotless and recently cleaned, also empty. Washrooms. Laboratories...these are locked, to my disappointment, but there are windows I can peer into, enough to see that they don't look as messy as Oberon and Melanie's other lab in the inner ring.

Then Petra pushes open a door that leads to a dormitory. Sleep-pods line the walls in stacks of three, with ladders between. It, too, has been recently cleaned—but I'm beginning to suspect we've come in right after the bots' nightly clean cycle. That this is the middle of the night for the residents of this ring.

Because every single pod—all twenty of them—shows the steady blue light of a sleeping inhabitant. And against the far wall, powered down in their docks, I can make out the distinctive curvy shape of five nannybots.

"Petra," I whisper. "This is it."

"Maybe. Who knows who's in those pods? Could be a bunch of lab technicians or something." Petra strides over to the nearest sleep-pod, stabs the wake-up button, and waits for the lid to unlatch so she can lift it.

"Petra!" I whisper-yell. "You're just going to wake them up?"

"I'm sorry, I thought this was kind of *urgent,* Ediya."

"Well, what if they *are* lab techs and they try to call my aunt?"

She shrugs. "Knock them out, then close the lid?"

I wince. Violence isn't my go-to solution, but it's too late to argue now. Petra throws the lid of the sleep-pod open.

Inside lies a child in a soft pink sleepsuit. A girl, I think. I'm bad at judging kids' ages, but I'd guess she's between eight and ten. Her soft brown hair is coiled in a long braid against the pillow. She's curled on her side in fetal position, hugging her pillow like it's a snuggle toy. As the soft *bing-bing-bing* of the pod's wake-up tone begins to sound, she moans and squirms before opening her eyes.

Seeing us, she bolts up with a gasp. "Nanny!" she yells.

The five nannybots come awake at once, registering our presence. They disengage from their charging docks and roll toward us.

"Hey, hey," I cry, raising my hands in surrender. "We're not here to hurt you. We want to help."

The little girl's lip trembles. "I don't know you," she whimpers. "Where did you come from?"

"Look! Now we've scared her!" I hiss at Petra. "I told you not to rip the pod open with no warning."

"Boo-hoo." Petra's unimpressed. She's facing the nannybots now, hand on her blaster.

Clearly, it's up to me to defuse this situation. "My name is Amy," I say, trying to sound like a nonthreatening, friendly adult. Stars, I probably sound as condescending as Melanie does when she talks to me. "I'm from a planet far away. I know it's probably scary seeing someone new, but I promise I'm not going to hurt you."

The girl's eyes flick to Petra.

"Uh, yeah, she's not going to hurt you either." *I don't think.* "Petra, want to introduce yourself?"

"Sounds like you just did it for me."

I roll my eyes. "Well, that's Petra, and she's not as mean as she sounds." *She's worse.* "We found out about you from my aunt and uncle— that's Oberon and Melanie Ediya." Not technically a lie; I read the information in their files, which counts as them telling me, in a roundabout way. "I was once a kid they experimented on, just like you. Can I ask you some questions?"

The nannybots aren't trying to herd us out of the room anymore, so I guess my attempt at a comforting tone is working. Or maybe they registered that I'm related to the Ediyas.

The kid seems to take her cue from them and transfers her wide-eyed gaze back to me. "What questions?"

"What's your name?"

"Miri."

Thank stars they didn't name her something wild like *Amethyst.* "Do my aunt and uncle treat you good? You can tell me the truth. I won't be mad if you say they don't."

Miri shrugs.

"Do you get enough food?"

Nod.

"Do they do experiments on you?"

"Sometimes..."

"Does it hurt?"

Another shrug.

"Do they ever touch you in a way you don't—"

"Stars, Ediya, seriously?" Petra cuts in.

"I'm just trying to make sure they're not being abused here!"

Petra rolls her eyes. "None of this matters! All we need is evidence the Greenjackets knew about these secret experiments on children. That'll be enough to sink them."

"Excuse me if I give half a fuck about the actual child!" I snap. I probably shouldn't be swearing in front of them, but blast it, Petra's driving me mad. "I could have been one of them! Nox and Danya too!"

Petra blinks. "You could have been raised in a creche, in a space station, never seeing your parents or knowing what the outside world was like? Stars, that sounds like *such* a hard life." Her voice drips with sarcasm. "Every Greenjacket I know was raised like this. So adjust your big-girl unders. There's more at stake than some kids having less than your idyllic planetside childhood."

I'm about to shove her into the wall. So much for my nonviolent ideals. One of the nannybots rolls forward to protect Miri from the fists that are about to fly.

But then the door behind us whooshes open. I turn around, panicking that it's Oberon or Melanie, but to my surprise, it's the scrawny intern.

"Raoul!" Miri cries. She vaults out of the sleep-pod and runs to him, throwing her arms around his middle.

He puts her behind him, staring me down with the same look of mistrust that I see in her eyes.

Oh blazes. Their eyes.

With the light just right, both of them facing me, their eyes reflect gold. Just like mine...

That's when it clicks.

He's no intern. *He's one of the experiments.* Oberon and Melanie may have put him to work for them, but that doesn't mean they *hired* him. They *grew* him.

"Raoul," I say gently. "Is that your name? I'm sorry you've been kept prisoner here. It isn't right, what my aunt and uncle are doing to you. But we came to help—"

I'm still midsentence when I hear his voice in my head.

::Sleep,:: he's saying. *::Calm, calm, slowing heartbeat and even breath. Sink to the floor and rest. You've done enough to help. You can relax. Relax and sleep.::*

"Oh for stars' sake," Petra says. "This glitch is trying to hypnotize...us..."

She's out before she hits the ground. And I'm on my knees without intending to fall.

"I swear to you, we're here to help," I slur. "You don't need to do this. I..."

I forgot what I was saying. I'm so sleepy. The floor is cool and hard against my cheek. Sharp-smelling cleaner pricks my nostrils. I'm drifting.

PRINCE

Gila City, Esperanza

Coming back here, so soon after I swore I'd never darken this planet's doorstep again, is a galling mouthful of pride to swallow. But I can't see that I have any other choice.

I went to the Halcyon Knights first, of course. They're the only ones I really trust to handle a situation like this. I figured they'd be annoyed with me for creating the problem in the first place, but I never doubted they'd help me rescue Amy and Danya.

And then I met with Chief Knight Jostlin, who tore into me.

"Mas DeSanto, we hired you under the impression that you were no longer involved in anything with the Greenjackets."

"I'm not! Or, that is, I'd really like not to be! But they kidnapped my friends—or some scientists who work for them did—and I can't rescue them alone."

"Prince." Jostlin's voice mellowed a little. "I don't want to tell you no. Most of the time, I'd already be calling up the troops to rescue those women. But we have to be very cautious when it comes to the Greenjackets. They're somewhat trigger-happy lately. Getting on their bad side could be disastrous for Halcyon's interplanetary relations. Plus, the Imperial Authorities are watching us like hawks. One single hint that the Knights are breaking our neutrality agreement—even if it's to attack their rivals—and they'll be on us, forcing us to choose sides." He sighed. "I could maybe float the idea of a rescue with Parliament, but we'd have to wait while a vote goes through, and that'd be a week at least."

I had to sit quiet for a moment, letting that sink in. I don't really *get* politics. That's part of why joining the Greenjackets never appealed to me. I'm a straightforward guy. The tricky business of knowing whose toes I can and can't step on is for other folks to get tied up in knots about, not me.

"With your permission, sir, I'd like to take a week's leave," I said at last.

Jostlin granted it. "Let the record show that, while on leave, your actions don't represent the Halcyon Knights," he added as I got up to leave. "You can do whatever you want, start fights with whomever you want...just as long as it isn't under our banner."

"Thanks, sir," I said, "but I was going to do it with or without your permission."

Then I got back into my ship and had a good, long heart-to-heart with Fairy. That dragon knows me inside-out, upside-down. Ze knows the only two options I have left—and the reason why one of them is a last resort only.

With time ticking, I asked Fairy to set me down in Gila Spaceport for what I hope to be the last time.

I'm exhausted. Haven't gotten any sleep since whatever I snatched after the run-in with Pa. My body walks me to Luz de las Estrellas on autopilot.

The grimy, stinking zip-lift carries me up twelve floors. It burps me out into the neon-lit hallway. It feels like I'm walking to my death—and maybe I am. It all depends what mood Joel X is in since our last conversation.

Meeting him again, after all this time, felt like being horse-kicked in the ribcage. Despite that long-ago betrayal, I can't un-care for Joel. Even the cruel joke of sending me, unknowing, to meet my father's pirate gang...it makes me furious to even think about, but even now, I can't stop hoping Joel will apologize. Then we'll shake hands and forget, and things might go back to how they used to be.

Except they can't. We won't fit comfortably in shoes we've outgrown. Five years is a lot of time for two guys to be changing in two opposite directions.

I walk slowly down the aisles of Luz, checking each private booth for spiky teal-blue hair. But Joel, wonders never cease, is not here.

"DeSanto!" a rough feminine voice calls out.

I turn to see the tall, hulking frame of Heather Jung. Studded leather jacket, tight trousers, pale skin, thick dirty-blonde braid hanging to her mid-back and decorated with sharp spikes. She came up from the factory with us, went to pilot school with us too. My ass knows the exact outline of her foot, painted in bruise-purple.

I rub the spot reflexively, my skin remembering long-ago pain. "Hi, Heather."

"What the blazes are you doin' back here?" she growls. "Lookin' to get Joel in more trouble?"

My pulse thumps. "He got in trouble?"

"Them other Greenjackets got word you two were lookin' cozy in Luz yesterday. They were askin' too many questions. He had to bolt."

I squeeze my eyes shut. "Do you know where he might be?"

"I dunno. He didn't tell me so I couldn't rat him out. Fair enough too, I might've. I got debts to pay, same as all of us."

Shit. With Joel in the wind, that means there's only one more place I can go for help. I'd rather eat glass, but it looks like I'm out of options. I back toward the door. "Thanks, Heather, I'll see you—"

My shoulder bumps into something hard. When I turn around, I find myself staring at the chest of a man who's even taller than Heather, and that's saying something. The man breathes hot and menacing down my neck, a large callused hand resting tense on the butt of a holstered gun.

"The Greenjackets said they'd pay a fortune in credits if we caught you," Heather says. "Sorry, DeSanto. Girl's gotta eat."

::Fairy—::

Tall Muscley Man clamps a hand on my upper arm, but I'm already in motion. I duck, escaping the man's not-quite-grasp, and do a quick sideways roll toward the bar. Heather's thugs have the exit covered, and I'm only backing himself into a corner...but I don't plan to leave through the door.

Fairy wraps zirself around me, admonishing me for getting myself into yet another dangerous scrape.

::I can't help it if trouble finds me.::

::You can make yourself a little harder to find.::

In a blink, ze carries me from Luz to the pilot seat of my starship, depositing me just close enough to the edge of the chair that I almost fall off.

.::*Nice, Fairy, thanks for that.*:: I disengage the anchor and rush through the pre-flight checks, knowing Heather and the Greenjackets might be on my tail. .::*You remember the coordinates of that cave from last time?*::

.::*They may not still be there.*::

.::*It's a place to start.*::

I take the ship into the air, and Fairy takes it into the aether.

CHAPTER TWENTY

Danya

ARROW STATION

I jolt back into consciousness and discover a dozen bruises at once. I roll to my side with a groan. The floor under me is cold and gray, and the walls are close; I'm in a small, unfurnished room. There are voices behind me, so I lever myself into a sitting position and turn my aching neck to see who else is in here.

Oh great. It's Petra.

She's kneeling next to Nox, who's just woken up too. Nox is lying on the metal shelf that is this room's only furnishing. I think it's meant to be a bed, but it looks even less comfortable than sleeping on the ground.

She turns her head and notices that I'm awake. "Danya! Good, you're alive. We were just discussing our escape plan."

I take in the room again: four plain walls, a metal slab for a bed, and a door that I don't even have to test to know is locked. "We're in a holding cell," I point out. "What escape is there?"

"We're thinking that when they come in to get us for testing or whatever, Petra's going to wait by the door and jump them."

"You know, they're probably listening," I say wearily, pressing a hand to the throbbing lump on my head.

Nox shakes her head. "My keycuff ran a bug-scan. Didn't pick anything up."

I fall back onto the floor, achy and angry. I don't know if I'm more annoyed at myself for getting captured so easily, or at Nox for making this assheaded attempt at a rescue necessary in the first place.

And I *still* don't know where Amy is.

"Where are they keeping Amy?" I ask. "Is she in a holding cell like us?"

Nox shrugs. "Who knows? Petra was the last to see her. They were going through the Ediyas' files."

"Oh yeah! I meant to tell you," Petra exclaims. "We found a bunch of secret gen-mod kids the Ediyas are keeping hidden. One of them put me to sleep with his mind. When I woke up, I was here with you two, and Amy was gone. Maybe she escaped."

Petra and Amy working together...stars save me. I can't tell if that mental image makes me worried, jealous, or horny. All of the above?

Nox and Petra go back to debating the best way to fight their way out of this room, but I throw an arm over my eyes and try to go back to sleep. If I've judged the Ediyas correctly, I don't think we're getting out of here anytime soon.

I'm just grateful Amy might have escaped.

AMY

Elsewhere on Arrow Station

"Five more minutesssss," I mumble. I'm so warm and cozy. There's a soft surface under and around me. I turn my head away from the sharpness of the light stabbing through my eyelids and pulling me out of my cocoon.

"Ah. She's coming around." That's Uncle Oberon's voice. Why is he in my bedroom?

Then memory hits me in a rush, and adrenaline jolts me awake. Raoul hypnotized me, that little shit! Put me right to sleep like I was a baby and he was singing a fucking lullaby. I'm going to kick his scrawny little ass.

But first I have to figure out what's going on. What happened while I was out? Where am I? I blink against the brightness and manage to open my eyes in a squint.

The "comfy bed" I've been snuggling into is a cot in the med bay. There's a soft blanket draped over me, but underneath it I've been stripped to my unders. Auntie Mel is squinting into a microscope at a table across the room, and Uncle Oberon is...

...coming at me with a syringe.

Oh no you don't. I regain control of my muscles in time to roll off the cot away from him. I flop gracelessly to the floor, tangled in the blanket. Thrashing it off me, I stand up, the temp-controlled air chilling my exposed skin. "Stay away from me!"

Melanie looks up from her workstation. "Amy, sweetheart, it's all right," she says in what she probably imagines is a comforting tone.

"Like blazes it is! You were drugging me!"

"We have a few more tests to do, and we wanted you to be comfortable," Melanie says. "But it's all right if you want to do them awake. Actually, I have an interesting theory to test, but we'll need you in the brain-scanner. If you'll just lie back down—"

"No way." I snatch the nearest weapon-like object and brandish it at them. Unfortunately, this med bay is devoid of convenient scalpels and bonesaws. (Holo-dramas have lied to me!) My best option is a metal bedpan.

"We don't have time for this," Oberon mutters. I don't think he means me to hear it, but too bad, 'cause I do. "Mel, let's just put her under and get it done. The General's on her way, and we still need to process the twins."

I'm backed into a corner now, between two cots. Melanie blocks one exit and Oberon the other. I know I'm not the kind of person who can beat her aunt and uncle to death with a bedpan, so my "weapon" is useless. I'm screwed.

A kind of dreamlike calm steals over me as soon as I accept it. Oberon and Melanie are going to sedate me and scan my brain for who-knows-what. I can't fight them both, and honestly, I don't *want* to. They're Mum's siblings. That's still worth something.

But all I can think about is what Oberon just said about "the twins." With all their incubator babies, there could be a dozen sets of twins aboard this station...but there's only one set I care about.

Well. One-half of a set.

It's Danya's face I see in my mind's eye as I drop the bedpan, close my eyes, and raise my hands in surrender.

And then the gravity goes out.

The air, too, and the lights. I gasp and my lungs find nothing to pull in. It's dark and I'm floating and naked—

Then the lights come back, bright as ever. I throw my arm across my eyes to shield them. My feet are back on the floor. I'm breathing, although hyperventilating might be a better way to describe it.

"What the blazes?" a voice yelps. "How did she just—"

That's not Oberon or Melanie.

I lower my arm. I'm not in the med bay anymore. I'm in a tiny room —a cell—jammed in with three other people.

And, oh yeah. I'm in my skivs.

I'm still blinking, trying to process what just happened, when one of the figures lying on the floor rises to her feet. "Amy?" she says—just my name, in a tone of utter disbelief.

One word is all it takes. I know that voice, and I know it's *not* Nox. "Danya," I gasp. "How are you here?"

"I could ask you the same! You just appeared out of thin air! How'd you get around the dragon shield? Even Prince couldn't make his dragon teleport here!"

"Prince? Is Prince here?"

"No, he—" At that point I notice the other people in the room. "Petra! What the blazes happened with Raoul?"

The next few minutes are a chaotic babble as Danya, Nox, Petra, and I catch up on everything that's happened. I tell them about finding the gen-mod kids and getting hypnotized by Intern Raoul; Danya tells us how Prince brought her here and barely escaped after Melanie and Oberon caught her.

But the one thing none of us can answer is how the blazing fuck I ended up in this room.

"I don't know!" I protest, when Nox tries to grill me. "I woke up in the med bay, and the Ediyas were doing something to me. They were going to sedate me again. I had this bedpan, and I was gonna try to smash them with it, but then I...I dunno, I kind of gave up? No, that's not quite...I knew they were probably going to hurt me, but instead of fighting, I let go and thought about..." *I thought about Danya.* Heat surges to my cheeks. "I thought about, um, happy things. And then it felt like... stars, it felt like I teleported, but I didn't feel a dragon anywhere around."

Saying it all out loud makes it click in my mind. I see Nox and Danya figuring it out too.

"It worked," Danya says softly. "Whatever your mum tried to do to you. It worked. You're the first human who can teleport like a dragon."

Chills rush down my arms.

"They're going to want you even more now," Nox says. "You realize that, right? You teleported right in front of them, like a fucking quarkbrain. Could've at least done it when they weren't around."

"It's not like I had any choice, did I?" I fire back. My knees are going a little weak. I sit down abruptly, leaning against the wall. This is happening too fast. Back in my room, when I was trying to teleport out, it all felt hypothetical. Like a fable I was allowing myself to believe. Now it's real, and I'm legitimately terrified.

I don't want to become a dragon.

"Hey." Danya crouches next to me, hand on my shoulder. "You look like your soul went for a walk."

I want to tell her everything, but with Nox and Petra sitting a meter away, this doesn't feel private enough. "I'm just scaring myself a little," I say, forcing a smile. "Hi, by the way."

Her smile is like a rose blooming—a tight, cold bud opening all at once into a burst of surprising beauty. Warmth blooms in my chest to match it.

"It's good to see you," she murmurs. "Wish it wasn't in this cell."

I reach for her hand. "Maybe it doesn't have to be. I happen to know someone who teleports."

Her fingers brush mine, and another chill crawls across my skin. It's as if my senses are suddenly heightened. My heart beats in double time, almost like—*like I can feel two heartbeats?*

::Oh stars, I can read her.::

It's Danya's voice, but her lips haven't moved. Her eyes widen, staring into mine before flicking down to our linked hands.

::Can you hear me too?:: she asks.

Slowly, I nod.

Color rises to her cheeks, and she rips her hand back.

Ah. So that answers that question. The Ediyas' experiments on Danya worked just as well as the ones on me. I guess this is a new discovery for her—she's just as shocked as I am. Another thing we'll have to discuss when we're somewhere other than a tiny cell.

"Give me your hand again," I say.

She shakes her head. Can't say I blame her for not wanting intruders in her brain, but how am I supposed to get us out of here if she won't hold onto me? Dragon-teleporting two people together requires direct physical contact. I have to assume mine works the same way.

That's when we both hear it at the same time: the high-pitched *beep-beep-beep* of someone keying in a passcode on the other side of the door. Danya's eyes flash with fear, and her palm finds mine, lacing our fingers together. "Get us out of here!" she whispers.

I wish I had more time to practice. Closing my eyes, I reach for that calm, centered feeling of accepting danger. It reminds me of swimming in the ocean at Phoenix Refuge, allowing the currents to pull me along. Letting myself be driftwood.

Before, I focused on Danya, and found myself in the room with her. Now, she's holding my hand, and I need a new focus. Where can we be safe aboard this ship?

Everywhere I can think of—my room, the children's dormitory, the docks—are all places Melanie would think to look for us. My brain is losing its calm, becoming a panicked soup, and the door is sliding open.

"I know a place," says Danya, and my mind fills with leafy green: her memories, not mine. I cling to it like a lifeline, and it becomes a current pulling us away.

Just before the dark weightlessness takes us, I hear Melanie yell, "DON'T YOU DARE!"

But we're already gone.

DANYA

GREENHOUSE, ARROW STATION

Light and weight burst back in. And with them, *scent*—something I've been missing like a phantom limb since we left Susannah. No, since we left Eureka, if I'm being honest. Susannah only smelled like dust and horses. It was the growing, decaying, *living* perfume of the Eurekan vine forest that smelled of home to me.

I breathe slowly in, savoring the scent—and trying not to cast up. I honestly wasn't sure this would work. I was afraid sending Amy a memory of the Sherwood greenhouse would make her teleport us to Sherwood—a journey we surely wouldn't have survived. Teleporting that distance without a starship would have killed us.

But it *worked*. We're still on Arrow Station. This is a much smaller greenhouse than the Sherwood one. It seems to be entirely automated, with a fleet of bots doing the tasks I would have done back home. (Even mixing fertilizer—ha! I *knew* it was bot work.) They trundle around us, oblivious to our presence. As I suspected, there's no security cams. It'll take a long time for anyone to think of searching for us here.

"Where are we?" Amy's looking around in wonder. Has she ever seen a space station's greenhouse before? The artificial sunlight filtering through rows of air-cleansing trees; the growth pods, their clear windows dripping with condensation; the maze of tubes and pipes pumping specially mixed air, water, and fertilizer to each tiny biosphere. It's quite literally the heart of the station, whether or not the people who live here know it. If its delicate life-support balance fails, they'll be subsisting on stale air and nutrient bars, begging for the next starship home.

"It's the only place I feel safe on my home station," I tell her. "It was all I could think of in a panic."

"But we're not—this is still Arrow Station, yeah?"

I nod. "Pretty sure."

"Stars, if I'd accidentally traveled further…" She shudders, imagining the same fate I feared. "Well, good. I'm not done here yet. Oberon and Melanie still have all those children captive, and I want to get them out."

"And I have to get Nox," I add. "But for now, I think we should hide and wait. Oberon and Melanie are going to be looking for us."

She nods. "Good idea. I just have one question."

"Yes?"

"Is there a washroom in here? I have to go."

Both of us break down in giggles.

"There isn't a washroom," I tell her. "You might be able to, uh, deposit waste in the fertilizer vats. That's where waste goes in the end."

That only makes her laugh harder.

Eventually, though, she does use the fertilizer vats. I do too. (I wasn't about to use the waste receptacle in that tiny cell with other people watching.) It's a bit of a production to figure out how to squat over them without falling in, but we figure it out.

We're able to snatch some half-ripe apples from the orchard. As we crunch our way through them, we walk a slow circuit of the greenhouse, scoping out the best places to hide in case someone thinks to search here. Amy finds a slim space behind an aquaponic tank, just wide enough for the two of us to slide in, as long as we're careful not to bump any of the pipes and wires feeding into the tank.

"So," she murmurs. "Mind-reading, hmm?"

I swallow, my mouth going dry. "Yeah." Talking in undertones in this dark, confined space feels strangely intimate. It doesn't help that Amy's still in her underlayer: a skintight pair of shorts and breastband that leave little to the imagination. My heart begins to race.

"How long?" she asks. "I noticed, on Atlantis…you could hear the fish, couldn't you?"

"Nox and I have been able to hear each other since we were little," I confess. "But I do think those creepy fish on Atlantis did something to me. Ever since then, I've started hearing other people."

Amy nods, taking a thoughtful bite out of her apple. "Maybe touching another telepath's mind opened your perception? Can you hear everybody now?"

"No. I heard Prince a few times, but only when he was feeling really strong emotions." I blush. "And...when you touched my hand."

She smiles. "Yeah. I heard you then." She holds up her hand in front of her eyes, examining it as though checking for the mark of my fingers. Then, slowly, deliberately, she extends her hand to me.

"I...I'd rather not," I say, feeling hot all over. "It's...letting someone into my mind is..."

Amy nods, taking back her hand. "I get it." Another bite of apple. There's a drip of juice on her lower lip, and stars, I want to kiss it off her. Why didn't I just take her hand? Why am I like this?

"I have another question," she says. "And tell me to shut up if you don't want to keep talking about it, all right? But I was wondering if you can read Nox's mind right now. Can *she* read *you?* Will she tell Melanie where we are?"

I suck the inside of my lower lip. "I'm blocking her out right now." The same thought had occurred to me—that she might see our location and tell Melanie. It's not that I don't trust my sister. I genuinely don't think she wants us to get captured and experimented on. But I can't be sure that Oberon and Melanie won't make one of their gen-mod experiments read her mind.

"Mmm." Amy traces a line through the condensation on the outside of the aquaponic tank. Through the glass, I can see the blurry outlines of fish swimming sluggishly back and forth. "Here's an idea. Can you keep her from seeing *your* mind while you read hers?"

"Maaaybe?" It'd be a risk. But I *am* worried about her. The Ediyas seem to want to experiment on us next. What if they're messing with Nox right now?

I'm going to have to do this carefully. Blocking Nox is a skill I've built up over the years, until it's something I can do with minimal thought, like keeping my fingers crossed. But I've never tried to access *her* mind while keeping mine hidden. I'll have to keep my memories and emotions perfectly blank and focus entirely on her.

I press my back into the wall and close my eyes. *I am nowhere. I feel nothing.* It helps to envision a black hole, a sucking void in the dark of space that takes in light and sound but gives none back. I will be a black hole in Nox's mind.

When I make contact with her, she startles violently. I guess I disguised myself too well; she doesn't recognize me, and I've scared her.

"What is it now?" Melanie asks, annoyed.

"N-nothing."

Melanie is leading Nox along the hallway, one firm hand gripping her shoulder. The irony is that Nox, though shorter, is physically stronger; she could flip Melanie on her back if she wanted to. But she isn't doing that, and as she glances nervously behind her, I see why.

There's a team of five Greenjacket soldiers marching behind them. Nobody I recognize. I don't get much information from that quick glance, but I can feel the glimmer of fear in Nox's mind. Bruna's soldiers, she's thinking.

Melanie guides Nox into what passes for a bedroom on this station: small, with all its furniture slotted into the wall. One wall is dedicated to a huge wallscreen, which is currently displaying a solid blue error screen. Standing in front of that wall of blue, a woman with fox-red hair tied into a low ponytail faces away from Nox.

We both know who she is before she turns. General Andromeda Bruna is the scary bedtime story of Greenjacket creche kids. "Be good, or the General will get mad!" "Take only your fair share of dessert, or General Bruna will punish you!" She's only about twenty years older than us, but my earliest memories are overshadowed by her tight-ship rule of Sherwood Base. She must have been newly promoted then—early twenties, flame-haired, knockout gorgeous. Sharp teeth and brass knuckles. The senior officers didn't know what hit them. One minute she was a cadet, the next she was giving them orders.

Behind Nox's fear, I can sense that she grudgingly respects the woman. Bruna is the kind of powerful badass glitch Nox plans to grow up to be. But first, she has to live to grow up. And second, she has to figure out how to knock Bruna out of the top spot.

"Nikola Xiang, sir," one of the Greenjacket guards announces. Bruna turns around, her sharp brown eyes connecting with Nox's. I feel the shiver that goes down Nox's spine all the way back in my own body.

"Nikola Xiang. I keep hearing that name." Bruna takes a few steps forward, which has the effect of forcing Nox to tilt her head back to look up at her. Nox knows Bruna's doing it on purpose. Anger flares in her chest, but she makes an effort to keep it out of her expression.

Bruna's still talking. "First I hear you've gone AWOL and ruined a very important mission. Then I hear your twin sister, who's actually you, has stolen a shuttle. Then I get a call from Melanie Ediya, of all people, asking why I sent a couple of cadets to do an officer's job." She sneers. "At least you had the good fortune to be useful to their research. Otherwise, I'd be sending you on a one-way trip to the med bay."

My blood goes cold. "Going to the med bay and never coming back" is Greenjacket slang for execution. Surely they wouldn't...?

But Nox has done more than enough to deserve it, by their estimation. And so have I, while pretending to be her.

"Now," Bruna continues, "Miz Ediya has informed me of the situation. I think it's about time a senior officer takes charge of this station and its research. I've been informed of some ridiculous goings-on, and I'm not about to let them continue."

Nox follows Bruna's gaze to her left and gasps. Petra must have already had her audience with Bruna. The tall, black-haired beauty kneels with her hands magcuffed behind her, dripping blood from her nose. She's being held by a pair of Greenjacket soldiers, but behind them, I see a young blonde child standing wide-eyed and fearful.

"Clara," Bruna says sweetly, "you did well to tell me everything. Now, go get Raoul. We might need him again."

That has to be one of the gen-mod children. I was right to suspect there were more mind-readers than just Nox and me. How much does Bruna know?

When Nox looks back at Bruna, the woman has leaned in close. Her sharp, freckled nose almost touches Nox's forehead as she says softly, "I'm not going to ask you twice. Where's your sister hiding?"

I gasp and retreat in a rush, throwing up my mental block as hard as I can. Nox didn't see anything, did she? Nothing she could tell, even if a mind-reader dug deep?

But she knows me well. If they press her enough, she'll guess where I'm most likely to go.

I can't just hide here until they corner me like a cat with a mouse.

I have to fight back.

CHAPTER TWENTY-ONE

Prince

PIRATE'S CAVE, UNKNOWN PLANET

The pirates' cave is empty.

Figures.

I let out a heartfelt curse and kick an upturned packing crate that the pirates left behind. Burying my face in my hands, I lean against the damp cave wall. *::I fucked up, Fairy. I failed them.::*

::All is not lost,:: Fairy replies. The touch of zir consciousness smooths down the spiky edges of my frustration. *::We have to find out where else they hide. Pirates never stay in one place for very long.::*

::And how am I supposed to find them? My pa's made himself real scarce the last ten-odd years. Why's he gonna start leaving clues now?::

::Maybe,:: Fairy suggests, *::because he actually does care about you.::*

::Dog shit.::

Fairy doesn't argue, but ze does flit around the cave checking for signs of where the pirates might have gone long after I've given up.

I begin trudging back to the mouth of the cave. I have no idea where I'll go next, or if there's any hope left for rescuing Amy and Danya. Maybe I should go back to Halcyon. Maybe the women will rescue themselves. They're smart and resourceful...

Why not just admit you're abandoning your friends? whispers a cruel corner of my brain that speaks with Joel's voice.

Wait.

Joel.

If there's anyone who reliably knows where to find pirates, it's Joel X. True, I don't know where Joel is either...but I can make several educated guesses, based on our habits when we were young.

::*Fairy?*::

::*Way ahead of you.*:: Ze races me back to my ship, and I've barely got time to fire up the engine before ze teleports us.

Back when I used to come here often, Fairy and I weren't partnered yet. But Fairy's seen this place dozens of times in my memory. Grandma & Grandma's Waystation Café is a grungy, sticky hole-in-the-wall, located in a place of prominence right next to the docking bay on a moon orbiting a bustling mining planet. It's become a beloved pit stop for long-haul pilots—from syncships to taxis to heavy freighters. For some reason, it's never caught on with either the Imperials or the Greenjackets. My theory is that both armies are too squeamish for the café's rundown aesthetic and unwashed clientele.

But joke's on them, because the elderly couple of ladies who run this joint are the best cooks in the entire galaxy. I've been to a lot of kitches on a lot of planets, but no one makes a crunchberry pie like Grandma Rae. And Grandma Toni...well, a person ain't lived 'til they've had her potato chowder, served piping hot in a bread bowl with a sprinkle of dried seaweed.

The food's dirt cheap and makes my taste buds sing a mushy love song, which is why, when Joel and I discovered it as hotshot sixteen-year-olds, we made a point of hitching a ride here every chance we got. We'd always sit in the same booth, the far back one, sharing a basket of thick-cut fries and surreptitiously people-watching as pilots trooped in and out. It was our place to go when we needed to be invisible, to get away from the pressures of pilot school, shitty side jobs, and Heather Jung's fists.

It's been five years, but the minute I walk in the door, hearing the gentle chime of the Grandmas' lucky bell above my head, the mouthwatering smell of food wraps around me like a blanket. I could almost cry, I've missed this place that much. There've been days when all I wanted, more than anything in the galaxy, was a plate of Grandma's pie. Any flavor. I could've come back here anytime I wanted...but I always stopped short. Because this place was Joel's and mine, and I couldn't bear the possibility of running into my ex-friend here.

But today, I'm counting on it.

I stride to that back booth and slide in across from the hooded figure sitting there picking at a crispy synthmeat sandwich, confident I've guessed right.

And I look up into an alien's face, green-scaled and long-snouted.

"Oh my stars, I am so, so sorry," I babble, scooting back out of the booth. "I thought you were someone else—absolutely my mistake—I'll just—"

That's when I notice the alien isn't eating the sandwich with its mouth. It's halfway through the action of lifting a torn-off piece and tucking it *under its chin*.

That's not an alien's face. It's a blazing *mask*.

I snatch the mask's snout and flip it up before the owner can protest. Sure enough, underneath it, Joel's face stares back at me. Teal-haired, flared off, with mustard smeared all over his chin.

"You scared the shit out of me," I sigh, sitting back down.

"What d'you want me to say? Sorry?" Joel gives up on feeding himself under the mask and lifts the whole sandwich. Mustard spurts out from the sides as he bites down. "I'm stuck here because *your* quarkbrained ass got me in hot water with the Greenjackets. Don't have anywhere left to go. Them bastards own whatever part of this galaxy the Imperials don't."

"Joel," I start. I was intending to make a speech about saving Amy, but now that I'm looking into my old friend's face, hearing his words, remembering how things used to be...suddenly, there are other words rising up in my throat. "Aren't you sick of this? Walking the tightrope between two masters, Authorities and Greenjackets, both ready to skin you alive for the smallest oops?"

Joel gives me an eyebrow-lifted stare. "'Course I'm fuckin' tired of it. Done *been*. I joined the Jackets thinkin' they'd take care of me, y'know?

The Authorities never gave a fart about us, so I thought maybe them guys who wanna overthrow 'em will do better. But nah. I'm a lackey to them, a lowlife who does their recruiting work. They've as good as told me I'll never amount to enough to be *worthy* of soldier training. Someone like me, a guy who deals mind-alts and buys weapons from the SkullKings on the side, ain't got a place in anyone's ideal galactic order. Not the Empire, not whatever future the Greenjackets fight for."

"Then why do you still bother fighting for them?"

Joel shrugs. "'Cause they'd kill me if I don't?"

"That's a stupid reason," I say. Joel's already flared off at me—might as well be blunt. "Joel, you're a good guy, or you used to be anyhow. I know you ain't done anything to deserve getting hunted down by the Greenjackets, no more than I did five years ago. Any group that hangs onto power by killing or intimidating people who disagree with them... that group shouldn't be in charge."

Joel wipes his chin with the back of his hand. "Well, too bad. They are."

"Not everywhere," I say. "The Knights—"

"I swear, DeSanto, if you try to convert me to your weird religion, I'll—"

"It's not a religion," I argue. "It's a planetary democracy where some religious folks happen to live. Look at me. Do I look like the kinda guy who prays all day?"

Joel snorts.

"Exactly. I fuckin' ain't. I joined the Halcyon Knights because they actually do some good in this wretched galaxy, believe it or not. They genuinely help folks, and it ain't for some cause, or to get more power, or to try to religiosify people. It's because they give half a shit about making other people's lives better. So don't go thinkin' there's no good in this galaxy, Joel, because there *is*."

Joel puts down the gnawed remains of his sandwich and stares at me for a second. Then he says, tiredly, "What d'you want, DeSanto?"

I sigh. "I went to try to get my friend back. The Ediyas snatched my other friend instead, and I barely got away. I need an army to go at 'em again."

"Oh, that'll go well, I'm sure," Joel mutters. "Why didn't you ask your saintly Knight friends?"

"They won't help. Politics." I roll my eyes. "You're my only other friend in the galaxy. Before today, I'd've said you gotta have some pilot buddies you can pull out of somewhere to help me out. But I was just at Luz and talking to Heather Jung—"

"Oh, that glitch—"

"—and she made it clear you ain't got any friends who won't sell you for half a credit and a smoke," I finish. "So I came here to ask you if you know where to find the SkullKings."

A slow, humorless smile stretches Joel's mouth. "Oh, that's hilarious, DeSanto. You're actually so desperate you'd crawl back to Pa?"

"I want my friends alive and free," I say. "I'd do just about anything to make that happen. What, you ain't got anyone you'd do the same for?"

"I used to," Joel says. His blue eyes lock on mine, and there's a wringing sensation in my chest. It's a strange sort of heartbreak to be missing someone who's right in front of me.

Joel stands up in a rush, flipping the mask down over his face once again. "Well, let's go. You wanna see the SkullKings or what?"

I jump up. "Thank you, Joel. But, um...do you mind waiting fifteen more minutes?"

"What for?"

"I gotta order me some pie."

AMY

Arrow Station

Ever since Danya came out of her listening trance, or whatever it was, she's been running around the greenhouse like a cat with her tail on fire. She's focusing on control panels, but so far, she hasn't found what she's looking for.

"Uh...maybe I could help?" I suggest, trailing behind her. "If you tell me what to look for..."

"Right now, I'm taking stock of what we have to work with," Danya replies over her shoulder. "How are you with mechanical things?"

"Well...average." Every child has to take a mechanics class at some point during our Gen Ed years. I know how to take apart a wallscreen holo-projector and put it back together; I could probably fix a broken cleaner-bot if someone handed me the instructions.

Danya turns to me and puts her hands on her hips. "General Bruna has my sister, and now she's looking for me." I'm taken aback by the non sequitur, but mostly the way she says it. Like she's projecting a veneer of calm over a volcano of rage and terror.

"Wait, back up. Who's General Bruna?"

"The current leader of the Greenjackets. Nox has been investigating her for...well, I don't know how long. She believes Bruna's leadership is the reason the Greenjackets have started launching more violent attacks against the Authorities, hurting more civilians in the process. She's been looking for some way to discredit her and knock her out of her leadership position."

"Ah, yes, Petra said something to that effect."

"Bruna has Petra too," Danya says. "From something Bruna said, Nox thinks they made this little girl mind-read Petra. Unclear how much Bruna knows, but I bet it's enough for her to justify executing Nox."

I hiss between my teeth. "How long do we have?"

"Well, clearly Bruna wants to use Nox to find me, so...however long I can stay hidden." Her eyes close in a brief wince.

"Fuck that," I say, soft but intense.

When she opens her eyes, they lock on mine in an expression of fiery determination. "Exactly. I don't know what I can do from here, but it's got to be something. The life-support functions are usually controlled in the greenhouse, since all the air flow circulates through here."

"Well, we can't kill them. Not if Nox is in there too. And all those kids."

"All the waste drains into here too. And the—" She stops, blinking. "The water purifies here..."

"What? What are you thinking?"

"There's a sprinkler system in case of fire," she says. "If I turn those on, they'll know I'm down here and come running. Maybe leave Nox alone. If I divert them, you can teleport to where Nox is and free her."

"And get you thrown out the airlock in the process? No way!"

"I'm not going to hand myself to them on a platter," Danya argues. "I know how to get into the ventilation tubes. I'm small enough. I could run them around in circles for hours, long enough for you and Nox to get to the docks. Her shuttle should still be there. You can escape, and I'll... well, I'll figure something out..."

"No way," I repeat. "I can get Nox and Petra out of there, sure. But then I'm coming back for you."

She blinks, stopping mid-sentence to stare at me. "I know," she says softly. "I'm counting on it."

Then she steps closer, goes up on her tiptoes, and brushes a swift kiss against my lips.

If I thought it was electric just touching her hand, I wasn't at all prepared for this. The kiss itself is shy and chaste, but with it comes the strongest flash I've ever felt. This isn't a flash of knowledge about her uniform or any item she has in her pocket—this is *her*. The imprint of her soul.

And something else. Not a memory this time. In one blinding-fast snapshot, I see a vision of Danya as she *will* be. I see her wearing coveralls and a sun hat, knee-deep in muck, shouting good-natured curses at a harvester bot. Her hair is longer, braided loosely over her shoulder and tied off with a scrap of multicolored fabric. She's gained weight. Her skin glows.

I'm seeing the *future*. Danya's future.

She won't die here on this space station. Won't be captured and forced back into the service of a corrupt regime. She will live.

I pull her close and kiss her back, because I finally believe we have a chance to leave here in one piece. Together.

PRINCE

TORTUGA SPACE STATION

Joel keeps the scaly, green alien mask firmly attached to his face as the two of us venture out of the docking bay into the station's maze of shops, kitches, casinos, and courtesan houses. I worry the mask is going to draw attention, but the more people we pass, I begin to realize that *not* wearing one might draw more attention. Masks are everywhere, from black dominos to theater masks to opaque bubble helmets.

"Is this a cultural thing?" I mutter out of the side of my mouth.

Joel says flatly, "It's a survival thing. Half these people have bounties on their heads."

I'm afraid to ask my next question, but Joel answers it anyway. "This place ain't just for SkullKings, it's for *all* pirates. Anyone who operates south of the law gets safe berth here. Well, safe as can be, when you're rubbin' shoulders with a crowd of cutthroats."

I don't like to think of myself as a prude in any sense of the word. I'm happy to let folks do whatever they want, so long as it's not hurting anybody. I'll hang with rich and poor, virtuous and shady, and treat 'em all with equal amiability if they've got a vibe I like.

But I have to admit, this place gives me an uncomfortableness. It's the stark awareness that, in another life—another choice made in youth —this wouldn't just be a casual visit. These grimy, neon-lit shopfronts and dark alleys might have been my home.

Would Fairy have bonded with me if that's what I chose? Or would it have made me a different, harder, crueler man?

"Unclench, man," Joel mutters, elbowing me. "You look like you're gonna puke."

I might. "Where are the SkullKings?" I ask through gritted teeth.

"Who fuckin' knows? This is one of their hideouts though. Someone's bound to know." Joel veers down a side alley, aiming for an extra-grungy public lounge.

"Oh, yeah, and I s'pose the first person you're gonna ask is hiding at the bottom of a beer glass?"

Joel throws him a roguish smirk. "How'd you guess?"

"We don't have time for this," I hiss, but Joel ignores me and struts into the lounge.

He goes straight to the bar, leaning there and making a strange handsign to the bartender.

The blue-crested saurian flicks a glance at us. "That mask is uglier than your real face, human."

"Modeled it after your mom," Joel shoots back. Another twist of his fingers, the motion hidden from all but me and the bartender.

The saurian growls, their crest rising in aggression. They lean across the bar as if about to hiss a threat in Joel's face, but instead they whisper, "Madam Taryn's. Say you're there for a tea party."

"Thanks." Joel drops a credit chip on the bar, and the bartender swipes it up without blinking. "Nice seeing you again, Risk."

"That's what your mother said. You buying or what?"

"We're pressed for time," I interject, before Joel can say yes. "Maybe later."

The saurian turns away. "Quit stinkin' up my lounge then."

"Fuck you too," Joel says cheerfully as I pull him toward the door. As soon as it closes behind us, he grins. "Count on Risk to know where everyone is. See, I came through for you, didn't I, DeSanto?"

"We'll see. Where's this tea party we're supposed to go to?"

"It's in a brothel." And Joel's smirk widens as he watches the look of horror dawn on my face.

CHAPTER TWENTY-TWO

Prince

MADAM TARYN'S COURTESAN HOUSE, TORTUGA

Seems to me like Joel is enjoying this awkward turn of events way too much.

Joel never quite understood when I came out as aroace. Didn't really believe that a human man could have no interest in sex with any gender or species. He'd drag me to courtesan houses again and again, attempting to triangulate what kinks would finally make me realize that sex was fun. The pressure made those outings excruciating: long evenings sitting in the corner of some dark room hazy with perfume and incense, nursing a drink and waiting for Joel to get bored so I could fly his blissed-out ass home.

At least the courtesans usually respected my boundaries. As soon as I told them I wasn't interested, they'd either back off or hang around to joke and play cards with me. "People don't realize sex isn't the only pleasure you can find here," I remember a lady telling me once. "Flirty banter, strong whiskey, deep tissue massage, a good long clothes-on cuddle...everyone likes at least one of those, in my experience."

It always kinda flared me off that my best friend wouldn't respect my identity when strangers would. I grew to hate getting dragged to those places, even though the courtesans themselves were absolute gems.

Anyway, after an incident involving a bordello catering to wannabe vampires and bloodplay, I put my foot down and refused to go anymore. Joel must've realized that he went too far, because after that, we didn't talk about sexuality anymore. It was better than the alternative, so I was happy to let it rest.

But seeing Joel shoot me a meaningful sideways glance as we enter the fairy-light-strung archway leading to Madam Taryn's courtesan house, I wonder if there's still a conversation to be had between us. Was it too much to hope that Joel would do his own research in the last five years and realize he was being an ass?

"Well, well, good to see you, darlin'. Been some time."

The man greeting us has golden-brown skin, shoulder-length black hair, and the perfect cheekbones of a gen-mod. He doesn't need makeup to look fantastic, but the way he's outlined his dark eyes in rich purple is stunning. I might be ace, but I know when I'm looking at a gorgeous human being.

Joel stares at him the way I might drool over a cake. "K-Kris," he stammers, apparently taken off-guard by this man's presence. "I didn't know you were on Tortuga."

"Transferred here from Glittering Falls last year." The courtesan chucks him under the chin. "And who's this cutie you brought along? Got yourself a boyfriend since I last saw you?"

I've never seen Joel's face go that red. He looks like he might spontaneously combust. "N-no, he's—"

"I'm his super-platonic asexual friend," I break in. The sooner I drop the "ace" word with courtesans, the better. "We're here to ask about a tea party?"

Kris can't quite hide his surprise. "Are you?" He trails a hand across Joel's shoulder. "I thought you were banned from...drinking tea...these days, Joel X."

"Yeah..." Joel hunches his shoulders. "This is a special circumstance? They'll forgive me when they see my...friend. I think. Probably."

"Hmm." Kris glances over his shoulder. "One moment, sweetheart. I need to talk to Madam."

He swoops off in a cloud of light floral perfume. Joel and I hover in the doorway. I take care not to make eye contact with any of the courtesans lounging around the front room.

Joel's staring at a burn mark on the carpet, kicking at it with his toe. His shoulders are still tensed up, his hands shoved in his pockets. "So yeah," he mutters. "I'm gay. Surprise."

I gawk at him, experiencing one of those odd disorienting moments where the entire world shifts under my feet. Has Joel been anxious about *his* sexuality this whole time? Did he drag me to all of those courtesan houses, ostentatiously picking up ladies, to try to prove something?

"I never cared," I blurt, half in shock. "It wouldn't have mattered to me, Joel. You didn't need to hide it."

"Yeah, well, maybe I *wanted* you to care."

When Joel meets my eyes, my heart drops. *Is he saying that he—that he wanted us to—?* Conflicting emotions swamp me all at once. I'm examining my every word in a new light, realizing how my indifference must have tormented him...and yet, how could I have ever reacted differently, even if I knew the truth?

Skies above, this is awkward. I open my mouth, unsure what I'm about to say, but feeling compelled to say *something*.

But just then, Kris returns. He flashes us a smile that I can tell is a coverup for an internal nervous wreck. *I know the feeling.*

"Come with me," he says, taking Joel's hand to lead us both into the dark hallway beyond the front room.

I've rarely been this deep into a courtesan house before. My body's gone all gut-sick and shaky. I can't tell if I'm reacting to the memory of being forced into places like this for reasons that made me uncomfortable or if it's the reality that I'm here to find my father. On purpose this time.

Probably it's both.

It's definitely not because of the bomb Joel just dropped on me. I've decided to file that one away to process later.

Kris leads us to a room with double sliding doors. He opens one just a crack, then motions me and Joel inside. "I can't come in," he says, with a wry little smile. "Good luck, sweetie. I hope they don't eat you."

I bite the bullet and enter the room first. Probably best if I do. I'm the one the SkullKings are least likely to shoot on sight.

The pirate gang is sitting around an oblong gaming table, and oof, there are more of them than I realized. At least twenty-five, plus a smattering of half-naked courtesans serving them drinks and sitting on laps. Most of the pirates are Earth Classic humans, although I spot a woman with a bat nose and the same ginger feline-humanoid guard from before. Royal's at the head of the table, dealing a new virtual hand to everyone's screen. A courtesan stands behind him in little else but a set of fancy unders, running her silver-tipped fingers down his chest.

When Royal sees us, he pushes his chair back abruptly, almost knocking the courtesan over. "Prince!"

"Pa," I reply tightly.

"You came back to find me. I hoped you would."

"I need to ask a favor." The words taste sour. I spit them out as quickly as possible. "My friend...the Greenjacket you saw last time...she's been kidnapped by Oberon and Melanie Ediya."

Royal's face lights up with confused recognition. "Those scientists? I thought they've been in prison for years. Or dead."

I shake my head. "They've been working for the Greenjackets. Or... alongside them. They have two of my friends. I want them back. But I can't take on a whole space station as one guy in a taxi ship."

"Ahhh." Royal nods. "You need hired guns."

"I dunno how I can pay you," I admit. My brain screams, *No, shut up, that's how you talk them out of it!*

Royal's expression softens a little. "I've got plenty to make up for, son. I'm happy to pay my debt. But you need more than one old man."

The pirate crew isn't bothering to pretend they're not listening. They're leaning forward on elbows, tilting chairs back, to hear what Royal will declare next. I'm fairly sure my pa could order them all to fight for him without payment—they might even agree. But it'd be a risky move.

Royal's eyes flash to Joel, who's positioned himself directly behind me. If he was hoping no one would notice him back there, then he must've forgotten he's a head taller with bright blue hair. "You. Greenjacket. Why are you helpin'? Ain't they your people?"

Joel spits. "My people who want me dead 'cause I dared to help my old buddy." He puts a hand on my shoulder. "I licked their boots for too long. Now I'm fixin' to take 'em down a peg."

I don't look at Joel. But I can't help a small smile. It feels good to be on the same side again.

"I reckon that might be payment enough for us," Royal says. He looks back at the game table. "Whatchy'all think? Want to help my kid stick it to the Jackets? Break some of their toys for 'em?"

There's a breath-held moment of silence as the pirates look at each other. One of them pounds a fist on the table, and the others start joining in.

"Is...is that a yes?" I ask.

"Blazin' right," Royal says, grinning savagely. "You got yourself a backup squad, son. When do we leave?"

A euphoric sweep of relief washes through me. "As soon as possible."

DANYA

ARROW STATION

All those restless teenage fantasies, the nights I practiced tonguing the back of my hand as I drifted to sleep in my dormitory pod, all the built-up anticipation, didn't come close to preparing me for what it's like to kiss an actual, real, live woman.

Amy's lips are soft, like I expected, but *alive* and responsive in a way I somehow failed to imagine. She freezes up at first, and in my nervous terror I'm afraid I've read her wrong. But then she comes alive under my hands, reaching out and pulling me in until our bodies collide. Her mouth takes charge, crushing against mine, nibbling my lower lip, and stars, I might pass out. My kneecaps are jelly. My brain is pollen: horniness incarnate, floating weightless on air. I lock my hands behind her neck, because I'm too shy to explore her curves without asking first.

Honestly, I don't know where I even got the courage to initiate the kiss. But the way she grips my waist, the way she sucks my tongue into her mouth like she wants to devour me, tells me that permission is very, very granted.

For a long, hot minute, I don't care how much danger we're in. The station could vent atmo right now, and I wouldn't mind. I'd die kissing Amy. Literally the best way to go that I can think of.

But then she breaks away, panting a little, wild golden eyes opening into mine. "We should...this is a bit of a bad time..."

"Yeah." This must be what being drunk feels like. I can't think two words in succession without her scent overwhelming me—sweet, earthy sweat like the smell of rain. Am I transmitting all my thoughts to her? Stars, can she feel how much of a wreck I am? I'm surprised her thoughts aren't bleeding into mine yet. Or maybe that's why I feel double horny right now.

"Nox," she murmurs, releasing the handful of my uniform she gripped to pull me in. "I should...go. Save her."

"Mm-hmm." That does sound vaguely important, now that she mentions it.

"To be continued though," Amy adds. "I'm not done with you yet."

It's all I can do not to yank her back to me. Regretfully, I take a step back. "I have to activate the sprinkler system."

"Yeah. Do that." She clears her throat, bracing herself against the wall. I guess I'm not the only one with weak knees.

I have to hunt around for a minute longer to find the water system controls. They're ridiculously complex—a different switch for every single growth pod and aquaponic tank in the greenhouse, plus pipes leading to kitches and washrooms and labs. At last, I locate the emergency sprinkler system, only to find it can't be manually toggled on. It requires an actual emergency unless I have the override code.

"Shit!" I hiss.

"What is it?" Amy asks.

I explain about the code, and her eyes light up. "I think I can help. May I?"

I stand aside, and she rests her fingers gently across the sprinkler controls. She closes her eyes, breathing in sharply. Then she opens them and smiles. "I know the code."

"That quick?" My surprise evaporates as I remember what she told me back on Atlantis, not so long ago. *I get these "flashes"...they're like visions of the past.* "You saw the machine's history?"

She nods, a shiver going through her. "I've never asked the flashes to show me any specific information before. That was new." New and scary, judging by the look on her face. I can relate—both of us seem to be going through some kind of telepathic puberty.

Amy punches in the code. We don't have to wait very long before an artificial rain begins misting down from the ceiling, drenching us in seconds. It's accompanied by an alarm, a shrill *tweep-tweep-tweep* that stabs into my eardrums.

"No going back," Amy says. She squares her shoulders, hesitates, then grabs my cheeks and plants a firm, smacking kiss on my lips. Tingles wriggle down my body like fingerlings in an aquaponic tank.

"Please be safe," she whispers against my mouth. And then she's gone, running through the mist toward the exit.

I wipe a hand across my wet forehead and plaster my hair down. Time to play the deadliest game of hide and seek I've ever played.

CHAPTER TWENTY-THREE

Amy

I BARELY MAKE IT OUT INTO THE HALLWAY BEFORE I HEAR POUNDING footsteps. That was quick. The soldiers must've already been on their way to check the greenhouse.

There's nowhere to hide. I'm going to have to flex my new teleporting skill sooner rather than later, though the more I try it, the less I'm keen to. Closing my eyes, I picture the room where I was stashed when I first came aboard. I picture myself in the wall-inset bed, and I relax, letting all tension flow out of me.

I hate that this is becoming easy. That I can just decide to be somewhere, and *boom*. This time, I pay attention as my body goes through the motion of dematerializing, as I float in that sense-blind soup of the in-between world. How am I actually doing this? Teleportation has to be a scientific process like any other biological change. Just because human scientists can't understand it doesn't mean it defies logic.

When teleporting in a group, it's common for the boundaries between minds to become a little thin. People who aren't telepaths might gain a momentary insight into their companions' thoughts or emotions. It's happened to me before, so that's nothing new.

But now I'm teleporting alone—not even a dragon for company—and I notice something else. The flashes I'm seeing aren't anyone else's thoughts. I'm sensing *movement*. If I concentrate on my periphery, on the senses that don't require eyes or nose or ears...I can sense myself flowing like water through hallways and shafts. I blow past the soldiers rushing toward the greenhouse. Down a connector shaft linking this ring with the outer station rings.

I'm not disappearing and reappearing somewhere else. Not really.

I think I'm *slowing down time*.

There've been so many theories over the years trying to explain how dragons teleport. My own mother dedicated her life to trying to learn the mystery. Now I'm more certain than ever that she would have cracked it, if she had lived. Maybe she and I could have figured it out together. Hopefully, before I got kidnapped by her estranged siblings.

Time-slowing makes so much sense. That's why we still need to ride in spaceships to teleport out of atmo—because you can't travel through space in your bare skin, whether time is flowing at its normal rate or not.

Does this mean dragons could reverse time if they wanted to? Could they take people back in time with them?

Yikes, talk about a scary thought. I'll save that one for later.

I rematerialize exactly where I intended to: on the bed in "my" room, the one with the hacked wallscreen. Only now, it seems the room is being used as a prison cell for Nox and Petra. The door is locked, but the only guard inside the room is that glitch Raoul.

Good. I owe him an ass-kicking.

Nox notices me first. She's kneeling next to Petra, seemingly comforting her. But then she looks up and sees me. Her eyes widen. "Hey, Rafael!"

For a second I think she's going to rat me out. But instead she says, "I gotta pee. Can you face the door for a minute?"

"Nice try," Raoul grumbles, but I see the way his feet shift uncomfortably. "And it's Raoul, not—"

"I promise I'm not gonna try anything," she says. She's moving, shifting Raoul's position as he turns to face her, so that his back is to me now. "It's just awkward to try to piss with someone watching."

"I'm sorry, Miz Xiang, but you heard my orders," Raoul says. "Miz Ediya told me not to take my eyes off you."

Moving carefully so that I don't make a sound, I climb off the bed alcove and creep toward them.

"I know, I know...could you, like, I don't know, look the other way for a sec? Look at Petra instead of me?" Petra appears to be in some kind of waking coma; her eyes are open, and she's sitting upright, but she's not registering any of what's going on. *Stars. What did they do to her?* "C'mon, man, if you had to piss and I was your guard, would you want me watching?"

Approaching them on silent feet, I consider my options for where to strike. Knocking him out would be best, but I don't have a weapon to hit him that hard. I could kick his knees out from under him, but if I misjudge the maneuver, he could recover and tackle me. If I had a belt or a strap, I could loop it around his throat and strangle him, but I don't want him *dead*...

"Well, I...maybe we can put up a privacy screen..."

Shit! Shit! He's turning around! I fly into action and jump onto his back, wrapping my legs around him and locking my arm around his throat. He goes down hard, taking me with him. My ass hits the floor, pain shooting up my spine.

"If you even think about hypnotizing us, I'll gouge out your eyeballs," I whisper in his ear. Hopefully, he believes me, because I don't want to have to follow through on that threat. It sounds gross.

Nox joins the struggle, pinning Raoul's flailing legs and swiping his stunner. "Nice one, Ediya," she says. "Here, stand back, I'll stun him out."

"No! Please!" Raoul chokes. "I won't—I'll help you!"

"Oh yeah? You're not just going to turn us over to my aunt like last time? Sorry, I find that hard to believe, given that *last time* was a couple hours ago."

"I panicked!" he squeaks. "I walked in and saw you talking to Miri, and I thought she was in danger! But then she told me you had a friendly aura."

"A what?"

"She can kind of *see* feelings," Raoul explains with a helpless shrug.

"She always says the Ediyas have hungry auras. They scare her. But you didn't."

I loosen my hold, letting him breathe easier. "She can see auras? Stars, I have so much to talk to you kids about. Do you know if any of them can—" With some effort, I stop myself. I can't get wrapped up in discussing our powers. That's not important right now. "What happened to Petra? She looks like a zombie!"

"That was me. I can undo that," Raoul says hastily. "I made a mistake. Her mind was too angry and hateful. I tried to calm her down without knocking her out, but I guess I went too far..."

I release him from the headlock, and he crawls over to kneel in front of Petra, putting his fingertips at her temples. She blinks, inhaling sharply, and then winces. "My feet are numb. Where'd that glitch Bruna go?"

"You do realize," Nox says, arms folded across her chest, "being able to do things like that isn't normal?"

Raoul shrugs miserably. "Being able to do things is how we survive here. The ones who can't make anything happen...they disappear."

As if I needed more reasons to take down my aunt and uncle. "We need to get you away from here," I say. "You aren't safe, and neither are any of those children, whether or not they have powers. I need you to get them all to the docks without being seen. Can you do that?"

Raoul shakes his head. "There're a dozen guards outside this door. After I let you escape last time, Melanie isn't taking any chances. And the General will be back any minute with the other twin. When the sprinklers went off, they ran to capture her."

Danya, please be safe.

"Are all the children still in their dormitory?" I ask.

Raoul nods.

I offer him my hand. "I can take you there without being seen. Just hold on."

DANYA

I USED TO LOVE THIS GAME. WHENEVER NOX—IT WAS INEVITABLY Nox—did something bad, getting us both in trouble, we'd run giggling for the nearest storage cupboard to see how long it'd take the creche-minders to lose interest and forget about us. We had dozens of secret spots, from bots' service tunnels to abandoned residential suites. Eight times out of ten, we'd escape being caught.

In the last few years, Nox's schemes got more subtle, and her partner in crime was Petra, not me. But I never forgot what I learned by tagging along in her wake.

The ventilation shaft is near the ceiling, tricky to get to. Or it would be, if there didn't happen to be a mini-grove of trees right underneath it. I test the lower branches. They're not the sturdiest foothold, but they'll do.

But climbing the tree takes too long. I'm still prying at the edge of the vent, cursing my lack of tools, when I hear the door swish open behind me.

I've never climbed down a tree so fast in my life. (I've never climbed a tree at all, to be honest.) With scraped palms and a thundering heartbeat, I duck down behind the tree and pray they won't notice its leaves trembling more than the others.

"You're sure this is where the sprinkler system is controlled?" That's Bruna's voice.

"Yes, and it doesn't randomly go off like that," responds a female voice. "Somebody's been in here tampering with it." I'm guessing it belongs to Melanie Ediya, but I don't dare peek around the tree trunk to confirm.

"Think they're still here?" That's a man's voice. Oberon maybe, or one of Bruna's soldiers.

I'm pleased the plan worked, drawing them all away from Nox so that Amy can rescue her. But my end of the plan hasn't been as easy as I pictured. I'm kinda up shit creek here. If they decide to comb the entire greenhouse, they'll find me for sure.

I hold myself agonizingly still, afraid even the slightest motion might draw attention to me. But my eyes cast around desperately for a way out, or at least a safer hiding spot. How deep is the earth the trees are planted in? Could I dig myself under...?

And then I remember the aquaponic tank. Its long, rectangular shape hugs the wall off to my left. The tank is about a meter high, covered by a frame that holds plant roots in place. Leafy vegetables festoon the frame, thriving on the excretions from the fish in the tank below. If I could distract them long enough to move the lid aside a fraction—just enough to slide through the opening and into the tank without splashing—I'm sure they'd never look for me in there.

I pat the pocket of my jumpsuit and grin. The breather mask I wore on Atlantis and Esperanza is still there.

"Spread out and search!" Bruna yells. "If they're still here, I want them found. The ducts too. Search everywhere."

Well, shit. Good thing I didn't hide there.

My mind churns, trying to think of a way to distract them while I get into the tank. *If only I had gen-mod dragon powers like Amy's. I could just teleport into the tank. I could...*

Hang on a minute. I do have gen-mod powers. Just...different ones.

I'm not used to thinking of myself as a telepath. For most of my life, I figured that my link with Nox was a rare quirk of twinhood. A myth made real.

But I've felt Amy's mind and Prince's. My abilities aren't bound by shared blood. If anything, I'd guess my mind protected itself by limiting thought-sharing to people with whom I'm emotionally connected—people I trust. Until now, there hasn't been anybody but Nox.

But then, in a shocking turn of events, I started making friends.

Now I'm determined to push myself beyond that. Because if I want to use this gen-mod power to save my ass, I'm going to have to connect with minds I *don't* vibe with. Minds I'd like to stay far away from, given the choice.

I have enough practice breaking through Nox's mental barriers when she's trying to block me out. I focus carefully on one thought, one mental image: *I heard a sound over there.* I picture it from their perspective: a strange scraping, over by the fertilizer bins. *What's that? Better investigate.*

At first, I try to attack individual soldiers. But I don't know them well enough to make that initial connection. So instead I broadcast it as a suggestion, rather than an implanted thought. Something they might pick up on subconsciously.

"Did you hear that?" one guy says. "Over there."

"I heard it too."

They abandon their search—which was drawing dangerously close to my hiding spot—and rush over to the fertilizer bins to check. I take the opportunity to sprint the few meters from the orchard to the aquaponics tank.

Thank stars, the lid isn't bolted in place. I peek over the edge. Through the bushy leaves of a lettuce plant, I see them opening the fertilizer bins, checking inside them. I swallow a laugh as they groan at the smell. Then I throw out another suggestion of a sound, coming from behind the bins this time...but as I send it, I make the real sound: shifting the aquaponic frame slightly to the side.

It's not heavy. But it's not silent either, and I freeze, thinking for a terrifying second that my mental suggestion won't work, that they'll look this way.

But it does work. They're on their knees searching behind the bins by the time I work up the courage to strap on my breather and climb into the aquaponic tank, shifting the lid back into place behind me.

The tank is warm, choked with hanging roots and full of darting, tickling shapes that brush against every centimeter of my exposed skin. Panic builds in my throat, an echo of my fears from Atlantis. Amy might be comfortable exploring enclosed underwater spaces, but I'm used to swimming on the surface of a clean, filtered pool. I have to force myself to relax and ignore the fish. I sink to the bottom, where I'll be hardest to find, breathing slowly and evenly through the mask.

The phrase "sleeping with the fishes" drifts through my mind. A euphemism for death—and it's hard not to feel every ounce of my mortality right now. Only a breather mask between me and drowning. Only murky water and some lettuce leaves between me and torture.

Am I imagining shapes moving on the other side of the glass? I want to reach out to the searchers' minds to know what they're thinking, but I'm afraid I'll slip and they'll hear *my* thoughts.

I close my eyes against the sting of the water and the curious questing nibbles of the fish. Fearing each breath will be my last, I lie still and wait.

CHAPTER TWENTY-FOUR

Amy

ARROW STATION

After dropping Raoul off at the dormitory—and borrowing one of his spare jumpsuits so I don't have to run around in my unders anymore—I leave him to corral the children while I teleport back to the room to collect Petra and Nox. Petra's still recovering from whatever hypnosis-thing Raoul did to her, but she's awake and aware enough that she's asking questions about how I'm able to disappear at will.

I dodge the question. "It's a long story. No time. We gotta go."

She and Nox both take my hand, and I focus on my memory of the ship we flew in on. This teleporting thing is getting scarily easy. I try not to think about what that means.

We materialize right in front of the shuttle. Nox and Petra scramble to climb aboard, but I take a second to scan the hangar. There are three ships here: a zippy little black five-seater, probably Oberon and Melanie's, plus two Greenjacket shuttles. In addition to the ugly, boxy supply shuttle that Nox and Petra flew me in on, there's the large passenger vessel that must be Bruna's.

"Hey, Nikola!" I yell. "We need to go look at Bruna's shuttle."

"I refuse to respond to that name!" Nox calls back.

Petra adds, "Who cares about Bruna's ship? This one will get us gone just as fast."

"I'm thinking for the kids," I say. "There're dozens of them, and Raoul's bringing them here as we speak. If we get them aboard Bruna's ship, we can fly them all out of here in one trip...plus, some of Bruna's guards will be stranded. There's no way they can fit more than half of them on this little supply runner."

Petra and Nox look at each other, then back to me. "Not a bad plan, Ediya," says Nox grudgingly. "How long do we have to wait for the kids to get here? Or are you going to teleport them all too?"

I shake my head. "I've got one more rescue. Danya's still in the greenhouse."

Nox's eyes widen. "She didn't leave when the General came running down there?"

"She thought she'd be able to hide from them."

Nox curses softly. "I hope she's right."

BOOM.

I look up, startled. "That came from outside the station."

"Cannon blast, I think," Petra confirms. "But Bruna is here. Why would the Greenjackets be attacking their own General?"

"Unless it's not the Greenjackets," I say.

The way both of them go sick-pale in unison would be comical if it wasn't so frightening.

"Imperials," Petra breathes.

Nox shoots a hard look at me. "We don't have time to waste. Go get Danya now. Blast your way through the soldiers if you have to."

"With what gun—?"

She's already tossing me one that she just pulled from a lockbox under the pilot's seat. I catch it, weigh it in my hand, and swallow hard against a sudden dry mouth.

"Go," Nox insists. But it takes me a moment to reach that calm brainspace that I need to be in to teleport. The flash I got from the gun as I held it was nothing especially violent—just a memory of the Greenjacket weapons specialist testing and charging its battery before packing it away—but it's enough to remind me that this is a tool for killing.

I wish Prince was here so I could ask him how he deals with having a dragon companion and carrying a gun at the same time. The two seem diametrically opposed: a pacifist spirit being and an item made for physical destruction. Teleporting to the greenhouse, knowing I might have to kill people there, is the most difficult jump I've done so far.

In the end, I manage it by shoving the gun into my back pocket and pretending it doesn't exist. I picture the spot behind the aquaponics tank where Danya and I hid, figuring I have a better chance of going undetected if I materialize somewhere out of the way.

That was a good instinct. When reality settles back in around me, smelling of plant-rot and fish food, I hold still to take stock of my surroundings. Oberon and Melanie are still in here—I can hear them talking in undertones, their footsteps tapping this way and that.

They're still searching. So they haven't found her. That's good news, at least.

The other good news is that they seem to be alone. I hear Melanie complain that "this would be so much easier with those soldiers helping," and Oberon responds sarcastically that if she'd like to let the Imperials blow up the station unopposed, he can call them back here.

"Face it, Mel," he adds, after a moment of miffed silence between them, "the girl's just not here, is she? The two of them must have activated the sprinklers and run off. I bet this whole thing is a distraction."

Uncle O is a smart one. I wait for him to suggest searching other locations—hopefully, somewhere far away from here. But then Melanie jumps in, chilling me as she says, "The subjects. Amethyst saw them. Why would she want us distracted, if not..."

"To steal them?" Oberon groans. "We're fools."

"Get to the dormitory!" Melanie snaps. "I'll run to the docks to head them off."

"What if the Imperials are boarding?"

"Blast the Imperials! If they get ahold of our test subjects, we're dead anyway. Let Andromeda deal with the intruders. *Find those children.*"

I hold my breath as their footsteps recede. I wait a minute more, hardly daring to move in case they come springing back in to shout "aha!" But they're really gone.

Gone to catch us in the middle of our rescue.

Well, this is not good. Not good at all. I'm half-tempted to teleport straight back to the docks to warn Nox and Petra, but I swore to Danya I'd be back for her. I just...have to *find* her. The quicker the better. This would be much easier if I had her telepathic skill; I could connect to her mind and ask where she is. But all I've got is my useless touch-flashes and the new, scary teleporting.

Wait. The flashes could help me. I'd just have to find something she recently touched. Like the sprinkler controls!

I brace my hand on the lid of the aquaponics tank, preparing to hoist myself upright...

She slithers through the small opening into the tank, gasping into her mask as the warm and wriggling fish-water engulfs her—

The flash hits me upside the head, staggering me backward. I catch myself before I step on one of the pipes.

She went *into the tank?* Is she quarkbrained?

I shove the lid aside and peer in, but the green water is thick with fish and algae. "Danya!" I yell. "Come out!"

Nothing. She might not hear me, or the water's distorting my voice to make me sound like Melanie. Or...stars, is she even still conscious? What if she passed out under there and is slowly drowning?

Oh no. I'm going to have to get into this tank, aren't I?

Cursing, I strip off my borrowed jumpsuit. I've spent way too much time in my unders today, but I guess I'm not done. I plant my palms on the lip of the tank and use my arms to hoist myself up, flipping a knee over the side. More curses spill out as I struggle, caught on the edge. My leg slips in up to the thigh, and I shudder, feeling the soft lick of slippery fish bodies brushing against my bare skin.

A hand grabs my ankle. I stifle a shriek. "Danya! It's me!"

It's hard to see Danya through the murk and darting fish, but as soon as I catch her flailing hand, I can feel the outline of her mind, blurry as her body's shape through water. I tug on her hand, urging her to the surface.

"Are they gone?" is the first thing she says, once her breather mask comes off.

I nod. "But they figured out this is a distraction. Melanie went to the docks to stop us leaving with the children."

"The what?" Danya sighs. "Of course you tried to rescue the children."

I'm already dismounting from the rim of the tank. "Hurry! We have to go!"

It's a bit gross, pulling my clean jumpsuit back over my skin beslimed with algae and fish residue. But there's no time to go find a washroom or even to dry off. Danya, soaked through in her sister's uniform, has to make do with wringing handfuls of the fabric.

Is it wrong of me to think she looks cute all wet and bedraggled like this? It's definitely wrong of me to want to suggest she take everything off and run around in her skivs. Right?

I tighten the reins on those frisky thoughts. "Are you ready?"

This time, she's the one who holds out her hand, with a shy smile that warms me right through.

PRINCE

ASTEROID FIELD SURROUNDING ARROW STATION

Royal DeSanto doesn't half-ass things. I asked for backup to break into Arrow Station, but I thought I was just asking Royal's gang—twenty to thirty pirates max, flying maybe five or six ships between them.

I didn't plan on Royal having so many friends on Tortuga. Or those friends hating the Greenjackets quite so much.

A veritable armada of pirate ships follow in my wake, weaving through the asteroids with deft expertise. I lost count of the gang leaders after seven of them introduced themselves in quick succession. I head the charge, but I'm not arrogant enough to imagine I'm their leader. They're here under their own terms, pursuing their own agendas, and they just so happen to agree with my goals for the moment.

Ahead, I glimpse the station, rotating peacefully. Fairy hovers at my cheek, and I reach out to caress zir mind, dreading the moment ze leaves me again.

The vanguard ships start firing on the station, testing its shields. There's a gut-punch of loss the moment my beloved partner vanishes into the aether. I have to remind myself ze'll be waiting on the other side when I come out of this battle.

Assuming I *do* come out of it.

"Ze's gone then?" Joel, lounging in the copilot seat, must be able to read the loneliness on my face.

I'm not interested in discussing my dragon-partnership with Joel. It's going to take some time to feel comfortable letting my squishy feelings show around my erstwhile friend/current frenemy, even though Joel was brave enough to bare his soft underbelly to me.

"That just means we're in firing range," I say gruffly. "Get ready to man the guns."

Before we left Tortuga, Royal and his crew performed an inspection on my vessel. They were kinda jerks about it, laughing at its shabby upholstery and pathetic lack of weaponry. "Can't fly into battle in an unarmed ship," they said. And so, despite my citizen-of-a-pacifist-planet protests, they'd quickly welded a couple of shiny cannons to either wing.

"It ain't pretty," Royal said, "and you'll have to aim by movin' the ship, 'cause we don't have time to install a swivel. But it'll put holes in the enemy, good as any other gun."

I tell myself I'll only use the cannons to help overload Arrow Station's shields. That I won't fire to kill. But now that Fairy's gone—my ever-present conscience—I'm afraid I'll be unable to, well, stick to my guns. So to speak.

"Make sure to only fire when we're pointing at the station," I remind Joel, "and never if there's a ship in the way, got it?"

"I ain't stupid," Joel grumbles. "You fly right, and I'll shoot right."

We make a few gunning passes, but then I realize the pirate fleet is getting a little too close to frying the station's shields. We might actually blaze straight through everything and blow up the station before I have a chance to rescue my friends.

"I'm docking," I tell Joel. "We need to get Amy and Danya out."

"Better tell Royal to let up then, or they'll accidentally nail your tail."

I relay the message to the fleet. Royal's response: "Get in and out fast. We're about to light this place up."

I'm not sure I could stop them even if I wanted to. Praying it won't take too long to bust Amy and Danya out of whatever prison cell the Ediyas have them trapped in, I swoop in toward the docks.

DANYA

ARROW STATION

The first thing I notice when we rematerialize is that I'm still wet. I'm a bit disappointed that the slimy water teleported with me. Stars, I'd kill for a shower.

The second thing I notice is that it's dark. I blink fast, trying to adjust my eyes. "Where are we?" I whisper.

"The cargo hold on the small shuttle," Amy replies. "I didn't want to appear in the middle of the hangar in case Melanie beat us here."

She lets go of my hand and gropes around for the exit hatch. I hear the click as it releases, but she catches the edge of it before it can swing wide open. She sticks her face close to the opening, peering through. "Yup," she whispers. "Melanie's out there. And—ah, blazes, she caught Raoul. He's standing there with soldiers around him."

"Can you see Nox and Petra?"

"No..." She glances at me. "Can you hear what Nox is thinking right now?"

I concentrate, reaching down that familiar connection. "She and Petra are hiding in the other shuttle's cargo bay. They have some of the children with them. They were in the middle of smuggling the rest into the shuttle when General Bruna turned up. Nox says she heard Bruna calling for backup to fight whoever's attacking the station. There are more Greenjackets on the way."

This escape attempt is spiraling way out of control. Why did the Imperials have to choose *now* to attack? Why couldn't they have waited, say, three more hours?

Nox hears me thinking that and responds, ::*It's not the Imperials.*::

::*What? Who else could it be?*::

::*They don't know. Maybe pirates? Bruna and Ediya have no idea who the attackers are. They're both blaming each other. Pretty funny to watch.*::

I relay this information to Amy, but she just shrugs. "Doesn't matter who's attacking, so long as they keep those glitches busy enough for us to escape."

True. But first, we have to get Melanie and Bruna out of the way. And we have to do it fast or our chance will be gone.

"Any ideas?" Amy whispers.

I maybe have one. I don't know if it'll work, but...

I crouch down so that I can see through the slim opening. It helps to have my eyes on my target. All I can see is his back. A woman with an auburn ponytail is holding his arms. ::*Raoul?*:: I try tentatively. ::*Can you hear me?*::

This is just a hunch, but from what Amy told me of his abilities, I've been wondering if he, too, is telepathic. If *all* of the kids are.

I don't hear any response in my head, but I see Raoul startle and look behind him. *Gotcha.*

::*Raoul, my name is Danya, and I want to help you escape.*:: I send the mental message slowly and deliberately. ::*You can put people to sleep, can't you? I need you to do that right now. Target Melanie Ediya and General Bruna first. If you can, take out the soldiers too.*::

He's not used to sending thoughts, but I'm beginning to read some of them, disjointed and racing through his mind. ::*Can't—Ediyas immune— she'll know it's me—soldiers, too many, they'll attack—*::

::*It'll be all right,*:: I tell him. ::*Target Bruna and her soldiers then. We can handle Melanie.*:: I really hope that's true. ::*Do it now, Raoul!*::

"What are you up to?" Amy asks. "You've got that constipated look like you're talking to Nox in your head. What's she—"

Bruna and her soldiers drop before Amy finishes her sentence.

"Raoul? You sent him a mind-message? Oh, you're a genius." She presses a kiss to my temple, then shoves the exit hatch open and bounds out, yanking a gun I didn't know she had out of her pocket.

"Amethyst, don't you dare—" Melanie screeches, going for her own gun. But Amy's quicker. She fires off a blast that misses Melanie by centimeters, then ducks as her aunt returns fire. I hide in the belly of the shuttle as they trade blasts, wincing when I hear Amy curse.

Amy falls back, clutching a burn mark on her sleeve. I rush to help her. "It's just a graze," she bites out. "I haven't used this blasted blaster before. My aim's shit."

I cover her hand with mine, gently easing the gun out of her grip. "Give it to me," I whisper. "I was trained as a soldier."

"Danya, you don't have to," she says.

I don't know how much she's guessed. I never fully explained why I'm not a real Greenjacket. But she's touched my possessions and touched my thoughts. That must have been enough for her to piece together that I'm not a fan of violence.

"Yes," I tell her. "I do have to." Through our mental connection, I add, ::*I'm not fighting for some idealistic Cause. I'm protecting people I care about.*::

Her fingers loosen on the blaster. I settle my grip around it, swallowing back the nausea that always overtakes me when handling weapons.

A quick glance tells me Melanie's changed position. She's moving toward us, thinking she's injured Amy enough to subdue her.

I don't want to kill her. But I happen to know that the blaster model she's got in her hand is notorious for overheating. If I shoot it out of her hand, it might...

I center myself, bracing my arms against the opening of the hatch. I aim. And I take the shot.

She screams, her hand badly burned. The gun drops to the floor and begins making high-pitched warning beeps. She has just enough time to stagger back before it explodes, which probably saves her from full-body burns but knocks her flat on her back.

"Is she dead?" Amy whispers.

I shake my head, heart pounding, but feeling oddly satisfied with myself. My aim was never the reason I flunked out of soldier training. It was my inability to take a kill shot they derided me for. I always went for kneecaps or shoulders—injuries I'd seen people recover from. It takes a lot more precision to wound someone like that.

I'm just as good as Nox, but in my own way.

Raoul emerges from where he was cowering underneath one of the ships. The rest of the children are still under there. One of them is whimpering, and the sound cuts straight to my heart. "Get them aboard that shuttle, quick!" I yell to Raoul. "Amy—we gotta go pull Nox and Petra out of the cargo. One of them is going to have to fly this thing."

She nods. "We need to find somewhere safe to go—somewhere *remote,* where they won't think to look for us."

Just then, a new alarm starts going off. A huge red blinking light flashes above the airlock. *Pressurization in progress.*

"That's gotta be Bruna's backup!" Amy yells. "RUN!"

We pile into the larger shuttle. Nox and Petra have climbed up out of the cargo hold to take charge of the flight controls. Raoul and some of the older kids are busy strapping the younger ones into their safety harnesses. I watch them fumble and realize they've never been on a starship before.

Then the airlock finishes its pressurization cycle and opens up to admit a new ship. "Danya, come quick!" Amy yells, pointing out the viewport.

I've never been so ecstatic to see any ship in my life as I am to see this battle-scarred, sharp-nosed, silver-winged taxi ship.

"It's not Greenjackets!" I cheer. "It's Prince!"

Forgetting our haste, ignoring Nox's shouts of protest, I unbar the exit door and sprint toward Prince's ship.

CHAPTER TWENTY-FIVE

Prince

ARROW STATION

The wait for pressurization takes an unbearably long time. I jitter my leg, trying to breathe evenly. Am I about to drive straight into the middle of a fight? How many soldiers will there be? I've only got one blaster, plus these cannons I can't aim...

The doors whoosh open. There's a squad of Greenjackets waiting in the hangar, but they've chosen a really weird attack position: flat on the ground. One of them pushes into a sitting position, cradling an injured hand and looking furious. *That's Melanie Ediya!*

Then the door to one of the Greenjacket shuttles flies open and Danya tumbles out, beelining for my ship. Amy's hard on her heels, waving and shouting. I can't hear what they're saying, but just seeing them alive and well fills me up with something like parental pride. They didn't wait around for a rescue. Of course they didn't. They rescued *themselves.*

I don't even bother anchoring. I leave the ship powered on and tell Joel to mind the controls. I rush to disembark, throwing my arms open wide to receive both of them in a hug. Amy crashes into me. Danya's a bit more reserved; she stops just short of throwing herself into my arms, but she pats us both on the shoulder and grins like it's her birthday.

And then I feel another presence arriving to join our mushy reunion. "Fairy!" I cry. "How are you here?"

::There is no longer a repellent shield in effect.::

"Oh shit," Amy mutters. "The dragon shield is down?"

I guess Fairy broadcast the message to everyone. "Is that a problem?"

"Bruna called for backup a minute ago," Amy says. "She thought—we all thought—your attack was the Imperials. She called more Greenjackets to fight. I bet she ordered someone to power down the dragon shield so that her reinforcements can teleport here instead of navigating the asteroids."

Danya's eyes go wide. "Uh...then we need to get out of here *now*."

I'm all in favor. "Y'all know how to fly that shuttle, or do you want to ride with me?"

"We have to go with the shuttle," Amy explains. "Long story, but it's got some...precious cargo. We'll meet you back on Halcyon when this is all over."

I hug her again. Danya surprises me by darting in for a quick side hug. Then the two of them sprint back to their shuttle. I let them depart through the airlock first.

"I hope they teleport quick before the battle heats up," I comment to Joel as I strap back into the pilot seat of my own ship.

"If it comes down to it, I hope we do the same," Joel mutters. "I ain't interested in dyin' for the chance to shoot at some Greenjackets. Ain't no revenge worth my life."

When the red light clicks off, I guide the ship toward the airlock. But some instinct, or maybe Fairy's awareness bleeding into mine, makes me turn on my external cams before the airlock door shuts behind them.

Oberon Ediya comes sprinting into the dock. He crouches and braces his hands under Melanie's armpits, lifting her to her feet. Their lips move as they shout at each other, their faces twin masks of fury.

Right before the airlock door closes, cutting off my view, the sibling scientists begin running toward their fancy black starship, which, I note, is *definitely* armed.

Oh shit.

"Was that a 3650 Orca?" Joel strains against his safety harness to see the screen properly. "Gorgeous condition too. Looks like it had a bunch of fancy mods."

"Yeah," I say grimly. "Fancy mods like torpedo missiles and a couple of blast cannons. Their firepower is *galaxies* better than what I got. They'll give the pirates a run for their credits."

The airlock spits us out into asteroid-choked space. I have to immediately swerve and dodge; Greenjacket fighters, tiny two-seaters that are more gun than ship, are starting to teleport in.

As I maneuver my ship to dodge blasts and collisions left and right, I wonder what dose of calming mind-alts the fighter pilots had to patch to get a dragon to teleport them into a battle zone. I usually have to *beg* Fairy to take me to hot zones, and ze's been known to snatch me out prematurely if ze worries I'm in danger. The fighters must have two pilots: one to get super blissed and handle the dragon-'porting, the other to man the guns and make up for the other pilot's impaired reflexes once they get there.

When Joel curses and yells at me to aim better, I realize I've been unconsciously steering away from confrontations, making it impossible for Joel to shoot anything. Though once I'm conscious of doing it, I'm not very motivated to stop.

It doesn't seem fair to kill all these random soldiers who woke up today and got handed some shitty orders. This battle isn't even for the cause they signed up for. They won't bring down the Empire's tyranny getting shot at by trigger-happy pirates. They've been ordered here by their General to...help the Ediyas continue to experiment on little kids? I still can't figure out how *that's* helping anyone. All it's done is given a couple of my friends some weird powers and fucked up their lives in the process.

No, the Ediyas' experiments aren't worth anyone dying for. But I don't really want to kill the Ediyas either. At most they, like, deserve prison time...maybe.

Shit. Being a pacifist sure does complicate things.

That's when I notice the fat passenger shuttle drifting among the deadly, needle-nosed fighters and the hulked-out, cannon-toting pirate vessels. Amy and Danya's ship hasn't teleported yet—and the Ediyas' Orca has just cleared the airlock, jetting straight toward the shuttle.

Without thinking, I dive headfirst into the thick of the battle, hoping to cut them off. Joel lets out a wild cowboy yell and starts shooting. I cringe, watching the cannon blasts narrowly miss one of the pirates' vessels and blow a crater into an asteroid.

"Aim better!" Joel shouts.

"Shoot less!" I fire back. We're on an intercept course with the Ediyas' ship; if I get out in front of them, I can turn to face them, fire both cannons, and—

And probably hit their shields. Then immediately get smoked by their torpedoes. But maybe it'll give Amy and Danya enough time to teleport the shuttle somewhere far, far away.

That, I think, *is an outcome worth a little sacrifice.*

I'm so close—almost there—when the Ediyas' ship fires one of its torpedoes. *Too soon.* My confusion turns to horror when I remember I'm not their target—Amy and Danya's shuttle is.

All the ships fighting nearby seem to sense the torpedo's approach and disperse like a shoal of fish in the shadow of a shark. But not the shuttle. It's drifting aimlessly, like no one's at the helm. Like none of them know how to fly.

Blazes. Do any of them know how to fly? Why didn't I think to ask?

But I *did* ask. They just didn't answer.

Fuck.

Right before I intercept the Orca, the torpedo strikes the shuttle, ripping through its cargo space. A scream of horror tears out of my throat.

In the next second, all I can do is pray. No idea to whom. To the aether maybe, the life energy that surrounds us all. But I know, even as I desperately beg for salvation and aid, that help never magically shoots out of the sky like lightning. You fuck up, you pray, and then you dust your ass off and help yourself.

I'm still praying as I swing the ship around to face the Ediyas, and Joel tears into the Orca with both cannons.

AMY

INSIDE THE ESCAPE SHUTTLE

All the littles in the passenger bay are crying. Danya and I are doing our best to soothe them, but I don't blazin' know how to deal with kids. I wasn't even very good at *being* a kid.

What we need to do is teleport out of here, extremely pronto. But Nox, our pilot, seems to be having a slight difficulty. No dragons are coming when she calls.

"C'mon, just relax," I hear Petra snapping at her through the cracked-open flight deck door. Stars, what is Petra's damage? I've been around Nox for less than a day total, and even I can tell you she's not the type of person who calms down when being told to "relax." She's more the type who'll punch your lights out for it.

Sure enough, Nox's gritted-teeth response is a string of expletives telling Petra what to do with her shitty advice. And we're still here, still corporeal, still in the middle of a battle.

I'm tempted to offer to teleport us myself, but (a) I don't even know if I can teleport a whole ship yet, and (b) I'm not exactly calm either. If I was nine, I'd probably be crying too. I'm only holding it together because I got really good at smothering my emotions when university started going sideways for my former-gifted-kid ass.

We should have gone with Prince. I was a fool to think we could handle this on our own.

"If we're not going to 'port, for stars' sake, get us out of the battle zone!" Petra's yelling. "Our shields are gonna be dead soon!"

Nox loses what's left of her cool and screams, "I'm TRYING! Would you shut the f—"

The rest of her rant is drowned out. A sick-shuddering jolt goes through the shuttle, accompanied by the grinding screech of tearing metal. And then the whoosh as our air begins to seep out.

"We're losing pressure!" I yell. "Danya, where does this shuttle keep its masks?"

"Under the seat—"

We have seconds until we're airless. I release my safety belt and scramble under the seat. Thank stars, the breather mask is a collapsible bubble-helmet style, enough to cover eyes, ears, nose, and mouth. I jam it over my head and activate it, sighing with relief as it inflates with air.

Danya's got hers on too, as does Raoul. A couple of the older children are still digging for theirs. But the littler ones aren't doing anything. They're frozen in fear, already gasping as the air thins out.

I abandon my seat and dive for the nearest child, yanking their mask out and jamming it over their head as fast as I can. As soon as it begins to inflate, I'm on to the next. Rinse, repeat. My heart's pounding with fear that someone might suffocate before we can get helmets on all of them.

We make it, just barely. As Danya sticks a helmet on the last little boy, he breathes in deep and passes out.

Now I can't hear a word anyone says, but I can feel the deep cold seeping in through the breach in the hull and the shuddering motion as the shuttle spins out. I don't know if Nox and Petra got their helmets on in time; I can't see them through the flight deck door, and it certainly doesn't *feel* like anyone's flying this ship.

If we crash, we're going to want to be belted down.

I sprint back to my seat and just about make it before the grav-sim cuts out. I snag the safety belt and use it to reel myself in, strapping down. Danya and Raoul are up and moving, ensuring all the kids have their helmets on right, but the second that zero-grav lifts them off their feet, they begin clawing their way back to their seats to strap in.

Miri, the girl who sees auras, is in the seat to my left. She grabs my hand, tears streaking down her face, and I squeeze hers tight.

We might be about to die. I should just do it—try to teleport us. But I can't, because I'm too blazing scared.

Danya settles into the seat on my right, fastening her belt across her chest. I reach for her hand with my free one.

::*We'll be all right*,:: she says.

I think of that vision I had of her future: tanned and smiling, standing in a field, fingernails caked with dirt. She'll survive this. I have to make sure of it.

I close my eyes, grateful for the sound-dulling effect of the bubble helmet. I can pretend none of this is happening, that I'm far away from it all, alone and safe. I can ignore the symptoms of fear in my own body, the racing heart, sweaty palms, and dry mouth. I can go to that quiet place, and from there, figure out how to teleport a whole entire ship.

The way dragons do it—as a Devote once explained to me when I was a kid—is by expanding their semi-corporeal form to encompass the ship, then teleporting with the ship inside them. I obviously can't do that. (Even if I could, I wouldn't want to. What if I couldn't get the ship out of my stomach? What if I had to shit it out? Literally no one wants that to happen.)

But I've already teleported with passengers. Instinct told me to take their hand, the way dragons can tandem-'port groups of people if they're in physical contact with each other.

Well, I'm in contact with this ship right now. My butt is in the seat, my feet are pressing into the floor. My hands are gripping the hands of two passengers, one of whom is a telepath who can see what I'm thinking right now. Danya motions everyone else to reach across aisles and armrests and link hands.

It's like I'm outside my body now, my awareness racing through that chain of white-knuckled hands clutching each other. Down seats and through the floor to the gaping hole ripped in our cargo bay. Up into the flight deck, where two desperate pilots fight with the red-flashing controls to try to land safely on the asteroid that looms ahead of us, rather than crashing in an out-of-control spin and killing us all on impact.

I am the ship.

I yank us out of space and into the aether.

PART EIGHT

Year 3729, Week 51,

Daysix

CHAPTER TWENTY-SIX

Danya

TELEPORTING FEELS DIFFERENT THIS TIME.

I was just starting to get used to the rhythm of it: lose all sight, sound, and sense. Hold there for a missing heartbeat or two, all souped together in a big mush with my traveling companions' minds, trying not to "overhear" anything too personal when our thoughts accidentally overlap. Then the jolting thrust back into the physical world, the sudden awareness of bruises and aches that were easy to ignore before. The heaviness as gravity settles back in around me like a weighted blanket.

But this time, seconds pass, then a minute, then two—and I'm still floating in the between-space, unable to reconnect with my body.

At first, I'm thinking my perception of time must be skewed. We were in the middle of a terrifying space battle, fighting to survive, and also (in my case, at least) fighting not to be sick inside a bubble helmet. It'd only be natural for time to slow down, for every second to stretch out unbearably long...

Then I notice the confusion and fear building in the aether around me. It's all of the children, and Nox and Petra too. They've also noticed this isn't a normal transition. We're stuck in-between.

And Amy...

I can't feel Amy. Is she the one carrying us through? She's never done this before, has she? What if she messes it up somehow? What if we're trapped forever in the aether?

Isn't that what they say dying feels like?

Oh stars. Maybe we never teleported at all. Maybe we're just dead.

I'm still processing my feelings about *that* when, at last, we shudder back into reality. The stomach-swooping sensation of falling grips me for a moment before impact rattles my bones. Gravity is bearing down on us again. We've landed—crashed—but we're all alive. I think. Some of the little ones look like they've fainted.

I turn to Amy, ready to congratulate her for successfully saving our lives.

But Amy's chair is empty, the safety belt still buckled, gone slack without a body to fill out the space.

She's gone.

AMY

???

There's sand in my hair.

I open my eyes. It's night, but the planetary rings are reflecting an arch of light across the sky, illuminating the beach I've landed on. It's familiar and strange all at once. Familiar, because I know the curve of this coastline: I've been out for dozens of night dives on this very beach.

This is Phoenix Refuge.

But that's the strange part. There's no Phoenix Refuge.

The huts and gardens have been swallowed up by thick jungle that stops only at the water line. There's no floating garden anchored in the bay. It's as if humans have never set foot here at all.

Except they have. Because I'm not alone.

A woman is standing a few meters off, looking out across the water. She's brown-skinned like me, but I don't recognize her face. She has an aristocratic profile—strong nose and well-defined jaw. When she turns to look at me, her dark eyes pierce straight through my soul.

"Amethyst Ediya," she says. "We had high hopes for you."

I hunch my shoulders. I might as well be a worm groveling in the sand. "Sorry."

"And what do you apologize for?"

Startled, I look up into those intense eyes. She's smiling at me, motioning for me to stand.

"You exceeded all our expectations," she says. "The universe rejoices tonight."

"Um...you might need to explain a few things." I stagger to my feet, flexing my shoulders. I don't feel like I've been through a crash landing. In fact, I feel *great*. Not a scratch on me. The arm Melanie shot is healed, my sleeve whole and unsinged.

So where's the ship? Was I thrown out when we landed? The ship didn't land in the water, did it? I specifically pictured the beach when I 'ported, but I could have overshot...

"My name is Persia," the woman says. "I am...a watcher. A guide. Someone who whispers in the right ears, nudges the right ideas to the forefront of people's minds, all for the betterment of humanity."

"And you were watching *me?*"

Persia nods. "Since before you were born."

Something's ringing a bell with her name. *Persia.* A memory from my school days. Some history lesson. I was always shit at history...

"When your mother blended the dragon ancestors' DNA with her own child, we knew humanity was on the brink of change," Persia goes on. "However troubling your aunt and uncle's methods, the outcome of their research was of particular interest to those of us who observe. The pact we made with the dragons is closer than ever to fruition."

"Pact? You mean the one where dragons teleport us and we share our energy with them?"

"No, no," Persia laughs. "Dragons might never have shown themselves to humans, if they hadn't made an agreement with the watchers first."

Her form is beginning to change. It starts as a faint glow, an aura of white light that grows stronger and stronger. The beach wavers and disappears, leaving us floating in nowhere-space. If I had limbs anymore, I'd fall over backward at the sight of the being in front of me.

It reminds me of a dragon, with its semi-translucent form. It's roughly human in shape, but the bottom half is a trailing mantle of light. The arms are like outstretched wings. The head has no hair, no features, and yet it ripples in strange colors that suggest emotions. Its shine builds in intensity until it's so bright that I have to shade my eyes. But that doesn't help. It isn't the light that hurts, but the knowledge that this is something far beyond human comprehension.

And suddenly she clears her throat, and she's Persia again and the beach is back. But I know the truth of her now. Understanding has been inserted into my mind, the way dragons insert a thought or a feeling.

She once was the founder of Halcyon's first colony—that's where I remember hearing her name. But she has ascended to a higher form, just as dragons once did.

"Watchers," she calls them. But they had another name, long ago, in the Old Earth religions that still exist in pocket cults across the universe.

Angels.

And if what she's telling me is true, then they were the reason dragons chose to befriend humankind. They made some kind of deal —which was—

"The dragons agreed to help us shepherd humanity to enlightenment," Persia says, finishing my thought as if I've spoken it aloud. "The watchers knew it would take millennia, even perhaps millions of years. Humankind was in its adolescence when dragons arrived. It's early, even now. You are something of a surprise, as much as we *can* be surprised."

"So, wait, hang on." My brain hurts. "Humanity is capable of ascension already, right? Because *you*..."

Persia smiles. "Yes. Over the course of my life, I studied and learned and sought enlightenment, and in the end, I became what I am. I am certainly not the first. A handful of humans through the centuries— names you might know, and names long forgotten—have achieved this state. But it's vanishingly rare, and we don't have the capabilities that dragons do. Time manipulation and physical manifestation are beyond us. We hoped, over time, humankind might evolve and all might become as the dragons are. But despite the dragons' guidance, it remained impossible...until you."

I shake my head. "But I'm a gen-mod. I didn't evolve—I was created. Does that even count?"

"You are a product of human ingenuity. What is that if not a kind of evolution?" Persia's steady brown eyes crinkle in the corners as she surveys me. "You are not even one of a kind. Those children you set free from the Ediyas' research lab all have the same capabilities as you, hidden within their genes. Any one of them could learn to ascend over time. And in the meantime, they will pass those genetics on, until, generations from now, the capability to ascend will reach all but the most isolated pockets of humanity. By freeing those children, you have advanced human evolution by thousands of years. And that is why we rejoice to welcome you into our ranks."

"You—um—hold on. Am I ascending, like, *right now?*"

Persia's face falls a little. "You do not welcome this change?"

"I'm twenty years old!" I protest. "I'm a total mess. I thought I had way more time to figure things out before I turned into a bubble and floated away. There's still stuff I want to do with my life." I bite my lip. "Someone I want to kiss."

"You *did* kiss her."

"Well, I want to kiss her more. And court her. Take her out on some dates. Maybe someday...if things go well...have a bonding ceremony. Under some trees. In the rain. Make all our friends cry. You know, the sappy shit." I'm on a roll now. "And I want to quit university. I kinda already fucked off without telling them, so yeah, they probably kicked me out, but I wanna go back and properly *tell* them I quit." No more running away. I've decided I'm going to face things head-on now. After all, I've nearly been in a deadly starship crash. What else could scare me after that?

I keep going. "And then I think I want to take some time to try out new careers, and eventually find something that makes my brain sing. That's all stuff I need to do, to be who I want to be. And I can't do any of that if I'm an invisible watcher."

"No, you can't." Now Persia's eyes are somber. "I feared it may come to this, knowing how young you are. Most who ascend to higher consciousness do so when they're old and weary or after choosing to martyr themselves. You are an anomaly in so many ways, Amy. None before you have ascended without choosing it. So I will give you back that choice." She spreads out her hands. "If your heart's desire is to return to the physical world and live your life, you may do that. We will not stop you."

My shoulders slump in relief.

"But a few words of warning."

Ah. There's always a catch, isn't there?

"First of all, it may not be easy for you to return," says Persia. "It may take a whole life of study and meditation, like it did for me. Or it may take a truly selfless act of sacrifice, as it did for others. Your abilities may wane or take extreme effort to use."

"I'm fine with that," I say promptly.

"Secondly..." Persia hesitates, tilting her head to the side. "You expended a lot of energy teleporting the ship to safety. You were successful, by the way. That sacrifice of your energy is what brought you here. But it means that, unfortunately, your body may not survive the transition."

"You mean I—I *killed* myself?" Blazing shit on a stick, that's just my luck.

"Brought yourself to the brink," Persia corrects. "You may survive. You very well may not. Are you willing to take that risk?"

I understand the choice she's asking me to make. The certainty of eternal enlightenment, or the perilous *maybe* of a finite human life, which may already be over? I know she thinks it's a hard one, but honestly, I've never been more sure about a decision in my whole life.

"I want to go back," I say.

She nods, smiling sadly. "I hoped you would stay. It would have been enjoyable to have your...unique perspective among us. I sincerely hope we meet again someday, Amy." She leans close to kiss my forehead.

"And I hope that day is when I'm super old, surrounded by fat great-grandbabies."

That makes her laugh.

"To return to the physical realm, you must focus on something that anchors you there," she tells me. "Similar to how you anchored yourself with locations to teleport. Focus on what keeps you human, and your body may rematerialize."

"May?"

Persia shrugs. "You're the first of your kind, Amy Ediya. I don't know anything for certain anymore."

Then she disappears, and with her goes the beach—sand, sun, lapping waves, and all. It was only a projection then. Shame. For a minute, I thought I'd time-traveled.

Too bad I didn't think to try that. Now I won't be able to ever again...

Focus.

What anchors me to the world?

My body. Smooth skin over curves, sharp teeth and nails, bouncy-soft curls, sweat-smell and strange-tasting breath in the morning.

The things my body lets me sense. The heat of the sun, the flutter of fish brushing past me in water, the taste of salty noodles and cold lemonade. Music—the way it gets inside me, urges me to dance. The smell of rain after a long dry season, when the jungle soaks up every drop and bursts out with that sweet, earthy scent. *Petrichor,* Sister Liv once said, as we watched a storm lash the beach from our cozy shelter. *That's what that smell is called. Petrichor.*

And the way that kiss with Danya felt. Like lightning sizzling through me, making each nerve ending glow. I've had enough casual flings to know how different it feels when I kiss someone I *like*. To know that sex feels lightyears better when I trust that person with my heart as well as my body.

I know the heartache that's coming too—the way those crushes fizzled when the lovers got boring, or I got annoying, and we went our separate ways. Being embodied is *pain*, all different kinds of it. Missing Mum, breaking a toe, catching a cold, hearing a former lover call me a glitch behind my back. But those hurts, little and big, make the joys stand out in starker relief.

I choose that. I want it. The *ouch*es and the *oh-stars-yes*es and the *meh, whatever*s. Life. I want *life*.

And then one very big ouch hits me. I try to cry out, but my body is too tired to make noise. So I fade into black instead, my last thought more of a whimper than a bang.

Ah, fuck, I hope I'm not dead...

CHAPTER TWENTY-SEVEN

Danya

PHOENIX REFUGE

Chaos reigns all around me. The ship lists to one side, tilting my seat toward the sky. I'm still strapped in, hanging like an insect caught in a spiderweb, looking down at the rescuers breaking through the cargo hatch to get us out. They're all wearing gray-blue robes, which seems odd until I register where I've seen those robes before. The Refuge people were wearing them when we went to Amy's homeworld.

And of course, that's where Amy would take us. It was an emergency, and she wanted us safe. There aren't too many safe places left in the galaxy for a bunch of gen-mod kids with superpowers. It makes sense she'd drop us in a place she knows we'll be protected.

What doesn't make sense is why she disappeared on us.

The rescuers have started unbuckling the kids' safety belts and carrying them out one by one. They make me wait—suspended in a seat tilted until it's nearly on the ceiling—for close to last. Finally, one of them motions for me to take off my bubble helmet. Fumbling at the release mechanism, I lift the helmet off. Its tight suction on the skin of my neck is going to leave a red mark, but at least it did its job. I'm alive.

"Any injuries?" the gray-robed Devote yells up at me. "Can you undo your belt by yourself?"

I find the buckle and tug at it. When it clicks and retracts, I nearly fall and crush the rescuer below me. I grab the belt in the crook of my arm and dangle there for a moment, feeling utterly disoriented, like I'm going to have to relearn the laws of physics.

"Let go," the rescuer urges. "I've got you." And they do. When I fall, two sets of capable hands are there to catch me and set me on my feet.

That's when I think to look toward the flight deck. A pair of healers are in there, working furiously to resuscitate a prone body.

"Are they—is that—" My voice has gone all high-pitched, like the air is helium.

"One of the pilots wasn't belted in properly," the rescuer tells me. "She didn't do so well in the landing."

I swallow against sudden nausea. "My sister," I whisper. "I need—I need to know—"

They try to usher me out of the ship, but I break free and barge into the flight deck. I look down at the body—

It's Petra. Petra, bloody and broken-limbed, unconscious as the healers carefully lift her to a stretcher.

A sob rips out of my throat. Nox is huddled next to the pilot seat, knees up to her chest, wrapped in a shock blanket. She's pale and shaking, but she's awake. Intact, except for the splint on her wrist. They're probably going to have to re-treat that broken bone, after all she's put it through.

I run to her and throw my arms around her, hiding my tears in the shoulder of her uniform. She's stiff under my hands, unresponsive.

"Thank stars you're alive," I tell her, but she just stares into space.

WHEN THE RESCUERS GUIDE US OUT OF THE WRECKAGE, WE DISCOVER that it's the middle of the night. We're at Phoenix Refuge, as I suspected. The ship left a long, deep skid mark across the Refuge's sandy beach, before falling to its side and baring the huge hole in its cargo hold.

"Something must have pierced your shields and ripped right

through," one of the Devotes tells me. "You're all lucky to be alive. The children said you helped them get their bubble helmets on."

I nod, though I feel strange accepting the credit. Amy was the one who sprang into action, whose first instinct was to help; I simply followed her lead. But I don't know how to explain that Amy *was* with us and then disappeared in-transit...so I don't say anything.

The Devotes are already bundling the kids off to their dining pavilion, promising hot cocoa and snacks. Nox makes no move to go with them. Instead she plops down in the sand, staring out to sea. She's still in shock, and maybe I am too. I sit next to her, resting my head on her shoulder.

"I'm sorry, Dawn," says Nox after awhile.

I lift my head a bit, just enough to look at her profile. "Hmm?"

"I shouldn't have dragged you into this. I was selfish to make you go on that expedition in my place. You could've gotten killed. When they came back without you, telling everybody you were missing in action, I knew...I knew it wasn't true, but it could have been. Really easily." She bites her lip, a tear rolling down her cheek. I haven't seen Nox cry in *years*. "That's why I came to get Amy, when you were on Atlantis. I thought I could finish this myself, and you'd be free. Out of danger."

I don't answer right away, rolling potential responses around in my brain. Finally I say, "You don't get to make those kinds of choices for me."

"I know, I'm s—"

"I'm not talking about sending me out on the mission. Yeah, that one was your bad. But I'm glad you did it, because it showed me how much I was missing. My life was so tiny, shoved into the little boxes the Greenjackets made for us. Like, you fit in the soldier box. I didn't, so I went in the laborer box." I shake my head, half-laughing. "There's so much more than that, things they keep from us. They wanted me ignorant and hating myself, because it kept me obedient. I'll never regret leaving."

Nox has this tiny smile on her face, like she might be a little proud of me. That approval warms my insides, but I can't stop the flow of words as they pour out.

"But you don't get to swoop in and save me from danger like I'm a fair maiden in distress. When I went to Atlantis with Amy, I went because I *wanted* to. And all these things I've done, trying to rescue her, all that was my choice too." I sigh. "I *do* want to live free, far away from war and fighting and all that. You weren't wrong to want to give me a chance at that life. But I think...I had to *earn* it, to feel like I deserved it. And having my choices swept out from under me, yet again, just made me feel like I was being shoved in another box."

Nox sighs. Nods. "I know. I guess I'm sorry for that too."

She lifts her blanket so that it covers both of our shoulders, and we sit together in silence. I can feel her touching my mind—tentatively, exploringly, like I'm a stranger she's getting to know for the first time. And I guess I am. I'm becoming someone new, someone she doesn't quite know how to handle.

I think I like that.

There's a sound off to our right, a sort of *flump*. I crane my head to see if someone's coming, but I can't see any movement in the darkness. I nudge Nox. "Did you hear that?"

"Mm-hmm." She makes no move to investigate, but I'm jumpy enough that I can't let strange night sounds go unchallenged. I shrug off the warm shelter of the blanket and make my way across the sand.

Something dark is lying in the sandy trench dug by the ship's skidding crash. When I get close enough, I can tell it's a person. A body.

With curly hair.

Adrenaline zings through my already frazzled system. I'm at her side in seconds, turning her face-up. It's Amy, as I hoped and feared. She must have been thrown out in the crash...somehow...despite being belted in?

I press two fingers under her jaw. There's a pulse there, very faint. She's alive.

"Nox!" I scream. "Get a healer! Quick!"

THE NEXT FEW HOURS CRAWL BY IN A BLUR OF ANXIETY. AN emergency response team airlifts Petra to a nearby hospital; some of her injuries require surgery. But the healers say they can't find anything physically wrong with Amy. She's just...exhausted. Her heart struggles to beat, her lungs barely inflate.

"I can't imagine what would cause this," says one of the healers, as they place an oxygen mask over Amy's face to encourage her tired body to breathe.

They think she's going to live, but only if her body regains its energy fast. They inject fluids and nutrients into her bloodstream, keep the oxygen flowing, and closely monitor the weak flutter of her heart.

All there is to do is wait.

I'm going on hour three of crouching by her bedside, warming her cold hand between my sweaty palms, when Sister Liv comes in and taps my shoulder. I'm so out of it, I don't sense her approach. I jerk upright at the unexpected touch.

"That pilot with the maroon hair just landed," she murmurs. "He was asking for you and Amy. Should I let him in?"

"Prince? Yes!" I jump up, wincing as feeling rushes back in. My legs have fallen asleep from being curled under me for too long.

I've barely spoken when the hanging flap covering the doorway of the healers' hut is thrust aside. Dawn light spills through the opening, briefly illuminating everything in orange. Prince barges into the space, his spiky reddish hair slicked with sweat. There are huge dark circles under his eyes, but he's smiling, triumphant.

That smile drops off his face when he sees Amy lying unconscious on the low cot. "What happened?"

I wait until Sister Liv backs out of the hut before telling him. His expression is shocked, but I know he'll believe me. I haven't told anyone else about what happened; I let them think she was thrown out of the vessel when it crashed.

After Prince has a minute to wrap his head around it, he says, "I suppose it makes sense. Dragons take a little of our energy every time they teleport us. Stands to reason they'd do that because 'porting expends *their* energy. Amy doesn't have the ability to borrow energy from her passengers, so she used up too much of hers with no replacement."

"Can we try to give her some of our energy?"

Prince shrugs. "I dunno how, do you?"

"But what happens to her, if she used it all up?"

"Life energy isn't like pouring water from a bowl," Prince says. "It's like drawing from a spring. It replenishes itself eventually, as long as the person's still alive. It'll take time, but she'll build it back up."

I nod dubiously. It's hard to be so confident when Amy's barely hanging on by a thread. But Prince seems to know what he's talking about.

"What happened back at Arrow Station?" I ask. "The Ediyas...the General..."

"I shot down the Ediyas' ship, right after they blew a hole in yours." Prince exhales slowly. He looks down at his hands, picking at a thumbnail. "They crashed on some asteroid. Might be alive, might be dead. I didn't check."

"And the General?"

"Royal and his pirates blew Arrow Station to tiny smithereens." There's some grim satisfaction on Prince's face. "They took special care to light up the shuttle General Bruna tried to escape on. She's *definitely* dead."

So the Greenjackets are leaderless, just like Nox wanted. Except she's in no mood to hear it, not while Petra's dying in some strange planetside hospital. This doesn't feel like a victory.

I'm beginning to realize that war never does.

"Where'd your friend go? The mean one—Joel?"

"Oh, he wasn't interested in seeing Halcyon," Prince says. "I dropped him off with the pirates. They were headin' for a victory celebration on Tortuga, last I heard. I guess Joel's fully out of the Greenjackets now...I doubt they'll take kindly to hearing about his involvement with this whole mess."

"That depends on who takes charge after Bruna."

Prince doesn't seem very optimistic. "It'll be some bootlicker of the old General. That's always how these things go."

But I'm not ready to give up hope. Maybe it's for Nox's sake. I want her and Petra's little mini-rebellion to mean something, to *change* something. Otherwise, what was all this for?

"I hope you're wrong," is all I say aloud.

Prince nods, his eyes distant. "I hope so too."

PART NINE

Year 3730, Week 1,

Daytwo

CHAPTER TWENTY-EIGHT

Prince

GRANDMA & GRANDMA'S WAYSTATION CAFÉ

Two weeks later...

Grandma Rae brings my pie out herself, elbowing aside her waiterbots. "I heard what you and Joel X did, honey," she says, sliding the steaming pastry onto the table. "Grandma Toni and I wanted to tell you we're real glad. Pie's on the house today."

"Oh, Grandma, no need to—" I hold out my keycuff, offering to transfer payment, but Grandma Rae waves it away.

"I insist." The gray-haired old lady wipes her hands on her apron, then gives me a hearty pat on the back. "We always knew you kids was destined for greater things. Taking down that rotten General means we all sleep easier, knowing her terrorist attacks ain't going to blow up our home planets no more. Now dig in, or your pie's gonna go cold."

Feeling a tad guilty, I slice off the pie's triangle point. Today's flavor special is cherry, and its tart sweetness bursts bright on my tongue. "Grandma," I call. "Will you marry me?"

"Love to, but I can't," Grandma Rae calls back. "Toni says there's only room for two in our partnership."

"Guess I'll die alone then!" I say cheerfully.

"Hey, DeSanto."

I startle and begin coughing. "Blazin' shit, Joel, don't creep up on me like that."

Joel slides into the booth across from me. He's got a black eye and swollen knuckles, and he won't meet my eyes.

"Hey, man, you doin' all right?" I ask.

Joel scowls. "Ran into Heather. She hasn't got the memo there aren't any Greenjackets left to sell me to."

"You make it sound like the Greenjackets all died," I protest. "They're just…busy these days."

"Well, I don't fuckin' know. I've been a little busy myself, tryin' lay low after your pa turned me traitor."

I do feel bad about that—it was kind of my fault. I thought it would be fine to leave Joel at Tortuga Waystation with Royal while I went home and debriefed with the Halcyon Knights. But I clearly underestimated Royal's ambition.

High on their battle victory, Royal DeSanto got all the other pirate gangs blissed on expensive liquor and his private stash of mind-alts. Then, while they were sleeping it off, he and his gang squeezed the location of Sherwood Base out of Joel. They waltzed right up to the base, announced that they were there to fill the power vacuum that had recently opened up, and shot a bunch of Bruna's officers to prove they were serious. Captain Royal DeSanto promoted himself to General that night.

"That's actually why I invited you here," I say. "It's been a bit chaotic, this transition. Pa exed half the senior Greenjacket officers, and now he's short on reliable help. He asked me if you're still lookin' for a job."

It still feels absurd, thinking of my own pa as the new Greenjacket general. But I'm cautiously optimistic about the transition. Royal isn't interested in blowing things up to win political points. He's been working on restructuring the whole Greenjacket system, with the help of Nox Xiang and a slowly-recovering Petra Rochester. They're hoping to turn the Greenjackets back to their original concept: an outlaw organization that steals from rich Imperials and distributes aid to poor mining and farming colonies.

The Knights have been eyeing the new developments with great interest. More than one of them has suggested a partnership with the Greenjackets, if the new leadership puts its money where its mouth is.

"A job?" Joel spits the word scornfully, but I don't miss the treacherous shine of hope in his eyes. "Doin' what?"

"Oh, all sorts of stuff. They're going to need pilots to do aid runs so they can hand out supplies to the downtrodden." I grin. "And someone's gotta do the pirating part. Plundering Imperial ships and storehouses, making the Reds' profits hurt. The way I figure it, you're the kind of guy who could do either. Or both. You're...versatile."

Joel stares at me through slitted eyes a moment longer. Then he breaks into a slow grin. "Yeah, all right, I might be interested. Tell your old man I'll give it a shot—but on one condition."

"What's that?"

"I want my own ship. My own command. I don't want a boot on my neck no more."

I chuckle. "I can't promise anything, but there happen to be a lot of openings at the moment."

"Great." Joel's eyes fall to the still-warm pie at my elbow. "You plannin' to eat that?"

"Yes." I drag the slice back in front of me and dig in with a fork.

Joel orders his own slice, which Grandma Rae also provides on the house. Then he says cautiously, "What you been up to, DeSanto? You workin' with your pa now or what?"

"Oh no." I wave my fork haphazardly. "I'm only here to do him a favor. You were hard to track down, and he was busy." I shove in another bite while I consider how much I'm allowed to say outside of Chief Knight Jostlin's office.

I'm definitely not allowed to talk about the negotiations I've witnessed behind closed doors. As soon as Amy woke up, she started demanding that the Knights rework their treaty with the dragons. She wants us to convince them to bring their ancestors back home.

Hardly anyone knows what we found on Atlantis—Amy wants to

keep it that way—but she also insisted that it wasn't fair to keep the eels in exile forever. The dragons are...stubborn. But Amy's as hardheaded as they come. I think she'll convince them, in the end.

But I *can* tell Joel about my other assignment. "So I sorta got in deep trouble for that whole adventure. Amy and Danya both got kidnapped on my watch, and then I worked with pirates to start a Greenjacket coup...my boss wasn't all that happy. So they smacked me with boring paperwork as punishment." I lower my voice. "You know all those kids we rescued? We're trying to find them families."

"Are they all born from Greenjackets like that girl Danya?" The rumor mill has been busy, if Joel's heard that much.

I shrug. "Their donor records blew up with Arrow Station, so we don't really know. Right now, I'm working with the Devotes at Phoenix Refuge to match the kids with prospective adopters. It's a lot harder than you'd think. You don't just hand someone a kid. The Devotes do, like, a ton of personality tests and home inspections first. Then they ask the kid what their preferences are. Then they ask the dragons for advice..."

"Sounds like torture." Joel rolls his eyes. "You ever wanna turn pirate, I'll keep an opening available on my crew."

"Oh, believe me, Pa's already offered." I laugh. "Never say never, huh? But I'm happy with the Knights right now. Despite the punishment job, I think they're secretly glad how things turned out. I think they might finally let me graduate training and be a full Knight soon."

Joel clears his throat. "Well, uh, don't be a stranger, yeah? I'm...pretty happy with how this all shook out too." His blue eyes meet mine, holding five years of long-buried emotion. "I'm glad you're back."

My chest swells with warmth. "I am too." I didn't realize how much I've missed my old friend until I got him back. Things are still a little awkward between us, but now that our secrets are all out in the open, there's time to repair the trust we used to have.

Fairy grudgingly admits, ::*Maybe Joel isn't all that bad.*::

This might be the first time I've ever heard Fairy admit to changing zir mind.

AMY

Phoenix Refuge

A gentle wave laps over my bare toes. I wiggle my feet deeper into the soft sand, sighing at the cooler dampness underneath the sun-scorched top layer.

"Thinking about going swimming?"

I turn, shading my eyes to see Danya walking toward me. She's traded her Greenjacket uniform for a wrap skirt and bathing top that she borrowed from one of the Devotes. Her hair is a fluffy mess. Stars, I'd love to pounce her into the sand and kiss my way down that exposed skin...only I'd probably fall over before I could pounce. I'm still wobbling around everywhere like my limbs are made of noodles.

"I don't think I can swim yet," I say ruefully, "but I missed feeling the water on my feet."

"We'll work our way up to swimming then," she responds with a cheeky smile. "I'd love a long, slow walk along the beach, if you're up for it."

In response, I hold out my hand, and she slides her fingers into mine. We're a little unsure of each other yet, still in the shy courtship stage, but nearly dying has steeled my resolve. I'm not about to miss my chance with a cute girl because I was too awkward or too weak to make a move. And so far, every move I've made, she's countered with a bolder one.

I like that about her. A lot.

"Guess what?" she asks casually, swinging our hands back and forth.

"What?"

Danya's smile grows wider. "I heard back from the university this morning. They accepted me. Agriculture Technology, starting next quarter."

I throw my arm around her shoulders. "That's amazing! You're gonna be the most kickass farmer this planet has ever seen."

"I know! I can't wait!" She wriggles with excitement in my arms, bouncing on the balls of her feet. "What about you? Are you going back?"

I'm dreading the conversation I need to have with my academic advisor, but my mind is made up. "No. I think I want to try something else. I think..." I hesitate, because I haven't told anyone this, only thought about it while lying awake in the uncomfortable healer's cot. "I think I want to sign up for Knight training."

She raises her eyebrows. "Really? Isn't it dangerous, what they do?"

"Sometimes." I chew my lip. "I think that's actually why I wanna do it. I'm good at the academic stuff, but it doesn't get my pulse going, y'know? That whole adventure we just went on, having to dive for research and escape from tight spots...that was *perfect* for me."

"*Really?* That's weird," Danya says, wrinkling her nose.

I laugh and shove her lightly. She shoves me back, then grabs my arms when I threaten to fall over backward. We collide, chest to chest, her brown eyes sparkling into mine. I forget how to breathe properly.

"*You're* weird," I manage to tease back. "Playing with dirt and plants all day?"

"Shut up, you. Plants are sexy."

"Care to test that theory?" I take her hand again. "There's a spot over that way where the jungle hides a secret waterfall. Lots of plants. Lots of...privacy."

My pulse thrums in my ears, and I brace myself for her to say no. She's not ready. She needs more time.

But she gets this wicked little smirk on her face and tugs my hand. "How fast can we get there without you falling over?"

DANYA

THE CLEARING NEXT TO THE WATERFALL IS CARPETED IN SOFT MOSS and shaded under squat, wide-leafed trees. Giggling, Amy tumbles to the ground. She lands a little too hard, and I'm at her side in an instant. "Are you all right?"

"Fine," she says, and grabs the back of my head to pull me down for a kiss.

We've exchanged a few covert kisses since she woke from her days-long stay in the healer's hut. But nothing fiery, nothing that turns my knees to water the way this does. The knowledge that we're alone and secluded turns me on like a sunlamp—I'm sure I'm radiating. But I pull myself away with difficulty.

"Are you—is this—I know you're still not recovered." Words hard. Girl pretty.

She laughs. "I'm feeling better and better." Her fingers trail across the shocking expanse of bare collarbone I've got on display. I was afraid this outfit might be too revealing, but Halcyonites are much more laid-back about showing skin than Greenjackets are. No one even looked twice at me wearing an outfit that's basically underclothes. Apparently, this is commonly accepted as beachwear.

So far, it's just been Amy who's looked at me like she wants to rip it off.

She leans up for another kiss, but I stop her. "I, um...haven't...ever..."

That does make her pause. "We don't have to, if you're not ready."

"I want to," I say fervently. "But I...don't really know what to do?"

Amy's eyes are the molten color of the sun—and just as hard to look at when she smolders at me like this. "Just do what feels good," she says in a low, throaty murmur. "If anything feels wrong, tell me and we'll stop."

I nod. What feels good to me right now is the smooth, sweat-damp warmth of her skin, so I let my fingers wander. She's wearing the sleeveless wetsuit she uses for diving, skintight but covering everything from neck to ankle. I find its zipper at the back and work it down to her waist, peeling the high-necked suit away from the skin I want to touch.

She holds still as I explore the curves and ridges of her torso. I'm torn between shyness and desire, wanting more but afraid to ask too much.

"If you don't take off that cute little top soon, I'm going to have to rip it off with my teeth," she says, and ohhhh, I think I have a thing for sexy growling. The bathing top comes off, and her hands embark on the same journey mine have just been on. I kiss her again, sucking on her lower lip, and she moans into my mouth.

Somehow, the knot of my skirt comes undone too. Amy kicks off the rest of the diving suit, and I don't dare stop kissing her, because if I look at all the skin I'm touching, I think I might combust.

Her fingers go lower. I sigh against her cheek when she finds the part of me that's been burning for attention. I seek out her soft curls and damp warmth. I don't know what feels good to her, but I know what feels good to me. When I try it, she bites my neck and makes a joyous little squeak. I think that's a good sign.

It's not long before she's coming undone under my hands. She keeps up the gentle circling, but I'm only halfway there.

"It always takes...a long time," I gasp, embarrassed. "It's all right if I don't..."

"Mmm." Amy kisses my shoulder. Then my collarbone. Then between my breasts, and then she's moving down further. I'm missing her kisses on my mouth, but then her lips find somewhere else and I don't think I've ever moaned so loud in my life.

I was wrong. It doesn't take long at all.

AMY

We're still lying in the moss, sharing warmth and kisses, when the sky opens up and dumps a surprise rain shower over us. Shrieking and laughing, Danya scrambles to put her clothes back on, but I'm happy to let the cool drops wash over my naked body. Every sense is filled to bursting, awake, alive. Petrichor blooms up from the soil and all around me as plants drink in the rain.

When Danya leans down to clasp my hand, pulling me to my feet, I get one last fleeting flash—this one of *our* future. I'm dressed in dark blue, my hair in braids, new muscles filling out my arms. Danya meets me at the door to our home, fingernails still brown with earth, and presses an enthusiastic kiss to my lips. Behind her, a pair of toddlers play: twins born of our combined DNA. The next generation. The future of humanity.

I can't wait.

Thank you for reading! Did you enjoy? Please add your review because nothing helps an author more and encourages readers to take a chance on a book than a review.

And don't miss more of The Halcyon Universe with book three, THE INVISIBLE BRIGHT, available now. Turn the page for a sneak peek!

Also be sure to sign up for the City Owl Press newsletter to receive notice of all book releases!

SNEAK PEEK OF THE INVISIBLE BRIGHT

The reporter turns to face the cambot floating at his shoulder. It captures a wide shot of the scene: crashing waves on an idyllic tropical beach, a Refuge's thatched roof huts in the background. And in the foreground, twenty children between the ages of four and seventeen, arranged in rows, most of us wishing he'd get on with it so we can go eat lunch.

"I'm here with the Ediya Experiments for another interview," he announces. "These twenty children were conceived of stolen DNA, fertilized in test tubes, and birthed from incubators. Just four weeks ago they were rescued, thanks to young biology student Amy Ediya, niece to the mad scientists who were performing illegal tests on these poor innocent souls. Now, weeks after their miracle rescue, how are they feeling? How are the youngsters integrating into Halcyon society? And what's next for the Ediya Experiments?"

"If he calls us 'experiments' one more time, I'm going to kick him in the shins," my best friend Clara whispers behind her hand.

I hold in the giggle that's bubbling up in my throat. The cutesy nickname the newsies gave us is annoying, but if I ruin the shot, the reporter will only keep us here longer. Last week he made us redo a whole section of the interview because Harris kept loudly repeating a curse word he heard the reporter mutter under his breath.

"Let's start with the oldest." The cambot zooms in on Raoul's face. His expression looks a bit constipated underneath his pasted-on smile. "Raoul, at age seventeen, you're the big brother of the group. Do you think you'll be sad to say goodbye to the younger ones when they get adopted?"

We all look at Raoul as he opens his mouth to answer. The reporter is only repeating what we've told him in previous interviews. We consider each other siblings, and skinny, brown-haired Raoul has always been our protector. But he does get annoyed with us a lot. Sometimes he uses mind control to put us to sleep just so he can have some peace and quiet. It doesn't work on me very well, but that's fine—I'm not noisy.

From the conflicted churning of the energy aura around him, which displays his emotions as colors, I can tell that part of him is glad to shed the weight of his responsibilities. Lightning flashes of yellow tell me he's even a little excited.

But he can't say that to the newsies. So he mumbles something about how we'll all miss each other, which is true. He *will* miss us. There's dark gray sadness mixed in with the excitement in his aura.

I blink, focusing hard on Raoul's solemn face instead of the colorful energy radiating from him in a halo. I have to remember that the newsies can't see auras the way I see them. No one can—just me.

The reporter goes down the line, asking a variety of questions. Some are about our upcoming adoptions. Obviously, twenty kids can't go to the same home, so we've been split into singles and pairs, and we'll be scattered across a dozen different households. Losing each other is maybe the scariest thing that's happened to us so far, and that's counting the space battle during our rescue.

Some of his questions are about adapting to life here on Halcyon. That's been hard too. We were raised by nannybots and a skeleton crew of scientists who failed to teach us how to exist in a world we'd never seen. Every day is a new surprise, and often a new embarrassment. New rules stacking up on each other. Saray went outside in a thunderstorm and got scolded, but she didn't know what lightning *was*, let alone that it could have killed her. Table manners continue to elude the youngest kids; Ian keeps asking why spaghetti and pizza are made with the same sauce, but one requires utensils and one is for eating with hands. Not to mention the strange new array of flavors and textures that take getting used to after a lifetime of tasteless, nutrient-dense space station food.

When the reporter comes to me, he locks me in with an intense stare. I freeze. My siblings and I look human like everybody else, but sometimes our catlike golden, reflective eyes make people do a double take. It's the only outward mark of the genetic modifications that make us who we are—the reason why we were born at all.

"Miri. Our shy little sweetheart. I heard a rumor, and I wonder if you can tell me if it's true."

I stare at him, trying not to see the voracious spikes in his energy. Trying to notice only the stray beard hair on his chin that's a centimeter longer than the rest.

"I heard," he says, his voice hushed but plenty loud for the cambot at his shoulder to pick up, "that you kids have some kind of superpowers. I heard the Ediyas were trying to push human evolution farther than it's ever gone. Tell me, is it true?"

Fear washes through me. He's leaning too close, and I wasn't prepared to answer this question—I expected him to ask about adoption. *He did this on purpose,* I realize, watching the way his aura quests greedily outward like grasping fingers. *He thinks by surprising me, he can get me to tell secrets.*

My instinct is to shove him away. My energy butts up against his, and he rears back in surprise. I don't know what it feels like for him—maybe he thinks it's the intense glare on my "sweet" face that makes him recoil —but I can see the interplay of the aether between us. With the pure force of my will, I'm making him back down. If I poke at just the right spot in his aura, I can even make him apologize...

"Cut the cam!" a sharp voice interrupts, and the reporter turns away, his face scrunching in a flash of frustration.

Amy Ediya strides toward us across the beach. She's wearing nothing but a waterproof black underlayer, which covers her from shoulders to upper thighs but leaves her arms and legs bare. Her bouncy curls are soaking wet. Sand sticks to her legs as, with each furious step, she kicks it up. She looks like she's just crawled out of the ocean. Knowing her, she probably has.

"Do you mind?" the reporter snaps. "There's an interview in progress."

"Oh, I heard." Amy's expression is as dark as thunderstorm clouds. Her aura billows out from her body in a brilliant shifting rainbow. Her injury leached the life out of her, making her aura weak and colorless, but she's almost back to her full force-of-nature self.

She marches right up to stand between me and Clara, a hand on each of our shoulders. "I thought we agreed there were topics these children will not be asked about. They need to integrate into this society, and they can't do that if you're exposing them to constant scrutiny, or even putting them in danger, by revealing more than is necessary."

"It's a simple question," the reporter replies. "All she needs to say is *no*, and the rumors will die out."

"But a *no* isn't what you were fishing for, is it?" Amy glares him down, her golden eyes intense as twin suns. "I noticed you didn't ask the older kids. You asked one of the little ones. Why is that?"

The reporter waves his hand. "Fine, fine. If you'll back away from the shot, I'll retake the scene."

"No." Amy moves to stand in front of me, arms akimbo. "This interview is over, and it's your last. You'll wrap up this segment with some speech about how it's best to leave these kids alone to adjust to their new lives now. They don't want celebrity. They want to be normal. And you're going to let them, because as we all know, Halcyonite newsies are deeply committed to ethical journalism."

I don't really get what "ethical journalism" means, but that line makes the reporter's face go bright red. He clicks the remote in his hand, and the cambot's "eyes" shutter, its green lights blinking orange. He catches it as it sinks toward the ground, then tucks the skull-sized globe under his arm and storms away without another word.

As soon as Amy is sure that he's gone, she turns to face us. We're all grinning. It was fun watching her tell off the man who kept calling us "experiments."

But our smiles melt when we see how dead serious she looks.

"I need to tell you something really important right now," she says. "If you kids remember nothing else I've told you, remember this: *Don't ever tell anyone about your powers*."

"No one?" Clara pipes up. "Not even our adoptive parents?"

"Not until you're older," Amy amends. "When you're a grown-up, you'll learn how to tell if people can be trusted. But for now, don't tell anyone, ever. Got it?"

We all nod. Then Raoul says, "Would it be so bad if the newsies found out? They don't experiment on kids here. That's what you told us. You said we can be safe on this planet."

"On Halcyon, yes. There are laws to keep you safe, and the dragons will protect you." Amy lets out a breath. "But the newsies broadcast all over this galaxy. Lots of people on other worlds might want to capture and study you or use you and your powers to do bad things. Also...you should all know that my aunt and uncle didn't die when their station blew. They survived. They're going to prison, but that doesn't mean they're gone."

I gasp, and I'm not the only one. After four weeks living on a planet, learning about the outside world, I'm just beginning to understand how cruel the Ediyas were to keep us locked away. And how truly dangerous our powers might be.

Amy's been gently explaining to us that those special abilities are why we were born. Her aunt and uncle, Melanie and Oberon Ediya, were trying to make kids who had the same powers as the alien "dragons" who protect this planet: teleporting, invisibility, mind reading, maybe other things we don't know about.

It worked.

But it worked differently with each one of us. Raoul can put suggestions in people's minds, while Clara can read thoughts like a book. Talia has visions of the future. Saray tastes words like they're candy. Fatima can go invisible if she's frightened. None of us have figured out how to teleport yet, but Amy thinks we will someday.

When we first landed, it was hard to know which abilities we needed to keep secret and which were normal-people things that everyone could do. We scared a couple of Devotes by accidentally reading their thoughts or appearing out of thin air in front of them. But Amy's been coaching us, and I think we've done a pretty good job learning what to keep secret.

"Having these abilities...it doesn't make life easy," she tells us. "From the time I was little, I knew I had to hide my ability to see flashes of the past. People got scared when I did it, or they wanted to study me, or they told my mum I needed medication. I learned that it's better to never, ever tell anybody. Not unless you're *sure* how they're going to react."

She looks each one of us in the eye, one after the other. "You kids are more or less my family, so anytime you need to talk to someone...call me first. I promise I will always do what I can to protect you." She sighs. "But you have to understand that not everyone will be like that. So keep your powers secret. Understand?"

I nod.

Then I look around at the crowd of kids around me, each exuding watercolor rainbows of aether energy...and I blink twice, focusing my vision on the sharp outlines of the physical, tangible world. The colors recede, leaving only newly sunburnt noses and sandy feet.

I can be normal.

I *will* be normal.

Don't stop now. Keep reading with your copy of THE INVISIBLE BRIGHT.

And find more from Mindi Briar at www.mindibriar.com

Don't miss more of The Halcyon Universe with book three, THE INVISIBLE BRIGHT, available now, and find more from Mindi Briar at www.mindibriar.com

Miri harbors a secret, and if it comes to light, it may cost her everything.

As part of the *Ediya Experiments*, a group of children genetically modified with dragon DNA, Miri must hide her ability to see emotions in color. But that's not easy when she keeps accidentally altering people's feelings, often with disastrous results. When her latest mistake ends in her losing her job, she's desperate to find a way to control the powers she never wanted.

Leo's childhood crush on Miri ended in heartbreak for both of them. But when she shows up in his hometown, adrift and looking for answers, even wounded feelings can't keep his past love from rekindling. He doesn't understand why she insists on holding him at arm's length.

When the two of them witness a shocking crime in Leo's idyllic community, the investigation pushes them together, forcing them to admit feelings they thought long buried. But as they uncover secrets that cast an ugly light on their society, they find their lives unmoored.

Miri's powers are more dangerous than she knows, and if she can't get them under control, their future—and the planet—could go up in flames.

Please sign up for the City Owl Press newsletter for chances to win special subscriber-only contests and giveaways as well as receiving information on upcoming releases and special excerpts.

All reviews are **welcome** and **appreciated**. Please consider leaving one on your favorite social media and book buying sites.

Escape Your World. Get Lost in Ours! City Owl Press at www. cityowlpress.com.

ACKNOWLEDGMENTS

First and foremost, a million thank-yous to Lisa and the City Owl team—not only for doing great work getting this book out into the world, but also for being an amazing support system during the whole process. Thanks also to MiblArt, who've done it again with an utterly gorgeous cover!

Thank you so, so much to Skye and Tory for your excellent critiques of the full manuscript, and to Kelcey for the sensitivity read. Your insight is much appreciated! I also want to shout out Alex and Pam for your feedback on my first few chapters. Alex, you get an extra cookie for fielding sensitivity questions as well.

As always, I have to thank Heather and Julianne for being my first readers and always hyping me up. You guys get to share the prize for World's Best Sibling.

And of course I wouldn't have made it this far without Joe, who's always there to be a sounding board for sticky plot problems, and who keeps me going when the anxiety hits. All my love <3

Lastly, since I work in a library for my day job, I can't resist doing another recommendation list. I need very little provocation to yell about amazing books I've read, but I feel it's especially important to promote books by marginalized authors. So here's a list of sapphic books by authors of color that I've recently read and loved!

Adult:

- *How to Find a Princess* by Alyssa Cole
- *Escaping Exodus* by Nicky Drayden
- *Stormsong* by C.L. Polk
- *Ascension* by Jacqueline Koyanagi
- *The Jasmine Throne* by Tasha Suri

Young adult:

- *Girls of Paper and Fire* by Natasha Ngan
- *We Set the Dark On Fire* by Tehlor Kay Mejia
- *Cinderella is Dead* by Kalynn Bayron
- *Gearbreakers* by Zoe Hana Mikuta
- *You Should See Me in a Crown* by Leah Johnson
- *Hani and Ishu's Guide to Fake Dating* by Adiba Jaigirdar
- *Tell Me How You Really Feel* by Aminah Mae Safi

ABOUT THE AUTHOR

MINDI BRIAR'S favorite book as a child was "Commander Toad in Space," an early sign that she was destined to become a gigantic nerd. She lives in the Seattle area with her husband and three cats, two of whom are named after punctuation marks. She will be your friend if you offer tea, or if you want to talk about Star Wars.

www.mindibriar.com

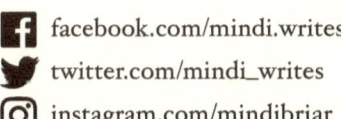

facebook.com/mindi.writes

twitter.com/mindi_writes

instagram.com/mindibriar

ABOUT THE PUBLISHER

City Owl Press is a cutting edge indie publishing company, bringing the world of romance and speculative fiction to discerning readers.

Escape Your World. Get Lost in Ours!

www.cityowlpress.com

facebook.com/CityOwlPress

twitter.com/cityowlpress

instagram.com/cityowlbooks

pinterest.com/cityowlpress

tiktok.com/@cityowlpress

www.ingramcontent.com/pod-product-compliance
Lightning Source LLC
Chambersburg PA
CBHW060603030726
47498CB00005B/1520